EMERGENCY

Books by W. C. Heinz

Emergency

Run to Daylight!
(with Vince Lombardi)

The Surgeon

The Fireside Book of Boxing
(EDITOR)

The Professional

W. C. Heinz

EMERGENCY

DOUBLEDAY & COMPANY, INC.
GARDEN CITY, NEW YORK
1974

Library of Congress Cataloging in Publication Data

Heinz, Wilfred Charles, 1915–
    Emergency.

        I. Title.
PZ4.H472Em [PS3558.E459] 813'.5'4
ISBN 0-385-06245-1
Library of Congress Catalog Card Number 72–89315

The author is deeply indebted to several hospitals and their personnel for their assistance in his acquisition of the technical knowledge and background basic to the writing of this book. It should be understood, however, that none of these institutions, their personnel or patients is represented here, and that all the characters, their names and the events are fictitious.

For E. and G.

I

THE ROOM

Beneath the surface of the ground, and under the central structure of a modern hospital complex in the United States of America, there is a room. Each year almost 45,000 persons—an average of more than one hundred and twenty a day—come to this room. They are ailing in body or in mind or in spirit, or in all three, some moderately, some inordinately, and so for some of them it becomes, among the many rooms in which they have lived their lives, a significant room, perhaps even the most significant of all rooms, the last of rooms, the final room.

This is the story, not of the room, but rather of those whose lives are markedly affected by it, those whose function it is to staff the room and those whose fate it is to come to the room. As this story evolves, they will speak for themselves, those whom chance has brought together in this room. They will speak of their own beginnings and of the planned and random happenings that led them here to one another and to this room. Only the past of this place and the history of this country, however, speak of the beginnings and the evolution of the room.

The room, like all doctrines and devices of man that, as they pass from generation to generation, are altered to meet his evolving needs, is a stepchild and it has had many fathers. The basic, red brick rectangle of the original hospital, which still stands as the center of the present medical complex, was erected in the years 1899 to 1901, and it was the creation of men who, although what they constructed with their minds and their hands still lives on to influence the lives of others, have themselves long been dead.

1

The story of that construction may be found in bits and pieces and in various places. It is there in the original architectural plans still in the files of the medical center's Director of Building and Planning, in the microfilm of old newspapers, in a few framed photographs on the wall of the medical library, and in the memory of a few men, old themselves now, who remember tales, mere anecdotes, they heard in their youth.

The rolled-iron "I" beams of the structural skeleton and from Pennsylvania, and the bricks with "Catskill" embossed on them and from the kilns to the south, came up the river on barges. From the weathered, wheel-splintered wooden wharves at the river's edge they were hauled in a painful procession by multi-horse teams, straining, frothing at the rub of sweat-stained leather, slowly up the slope from the valley floor.

High above the backs of the suffering, enduring animals, the florid-faced Irish teamsters sat and stood, lashing with whip and invective, and beside the wheels the short but big-boned Italians walked, armed with wooden V-blocks affixed to poles and to be wedged behind the wheels, between iron rims and cobblestones, at each stopping and resting. In this way, slowly up through the streets of the two- and three-story flat-roofed business section of the expanding city they moved, then slowly up past the white-clapboarded, gingerbreaded mansions, set back on sloping lawns and half hidden by aging, big-leafed, pod-weeping catalpas, slowly up to the edge of the green and brown dairyland plateau just beyond.

In the construction of the original hospital a number of men suffered minor injuries, one man lost an arm, crushed by a slipping beam, and one lost his life when a rope on a scaffold on which he was working gave way. He was an Italian mason, and at the moment he plunged to his death his wife and their two young sons were in the hold of a steamship between Genoa and New York, where they would land without a knowledge of the language, without friends and without funds.

At first the room was not a room as such, but a subterranean storage area, its expanse interrupted only by the support columns that sustained the four-story structure above. At that time the ill and the maimed were horse-drawn, too slowly and often

2

too late, to an examining suite and treatment rooms adjoining the hospital's main floor admitting office, but in the American Midwest a Michigan machinist, adapting other men's discoveries and modernizing other men's methods, was about to change the American way of life and the American way of death.

Before him there had been Eli Whitney, Massachusetts farm boy, maker of nails, producer of hatpins, fashioner of walking sticks, inventor of the cotton gin, unintentional abettor of slavery and catalyst of the War between the States, who had introduced interchangeable parts and assembly line production for the manufacture of muskets in 1789. More than a century later, however, it was Henry Ford, puritanical son of pioneer parents, intuitive technological genius, opponent of the bottle, Wall Street and the bugbear of International Jewry, advocate of the soybean, square dancing and the League of Nations, who was to reduce the assembly time of an automobile chassis from fourteen hours to an hour and a half, and bring the hospital close to the home.

Now man would be born in a place unfamiliar to his parents and die a lifetime later in surroundings strange to himself. Now the room itself would be born, swelling the first floor womb until, in 1951, child of necessity, it would come into being in the only easily accessible area available to it, in the support-columned, cavernous storage space, and underground.

"The fate of the architect," Goethe wrote, "is the strangest of all. How often he expends his whole soul, his whole heart and passion, to produce buildings into which he himself may never enter."

This man would never enter this room, nor would he expend his whole soul, his whole heart and passion, for the tedious task of designing it he would hand on to someone else. As the senior partner of a highly respected, chain-named architectural firm specializing in hospitals, clinics, laboratories and nursing homes, however, he would meet one day in the walnut-paneled private dining room in the C-wing, adjoining the original hospital, with the medical center's Director, its Chief of Medicine, its Chief of Surgery, the seven members of its Emergency Room Committee and its Director of Building and Planning.

"Of course it's a compromise, gentlemen," he would tell them, "but as someone has observed, every human benefit, every human virtue, every prudent act of man has been founded on compromise. Architecture *is* compromise. If it were not for that, any mechanical drawing teacher with a slide rule could do our job. It's the necessity to compromise that provokes creativity, and we welcome it. We have this sort of thing on our drawing boards all the time. We'll simply confront the problems as they arise, and continue to consult with you as we progress."

He was employing the first person plural in the corporate sense, for two decades ago he had made his own compromise. He would never, he had discovered, be another Wright, or Mies van der Rohe or Le Corbusier, and now he was sixty-one and it had been years since he had faced a drawing board and T-square or fingered a slide rule except for effect. He had put together, and continued to hold together an efficient and productive organization, however, and that, too, he reassured himself, is a contribution and a compliment to a man. Tall, slim, gray-haired, custom-clothed, his speech bespeaking his breeding and education, he might himself have been a Chief of Medicine, or Surgery, and so the medical men, who made the big decisions about how the big sums of money would be spent, saw themselves in him and trusted him. He provided a service, then, at meetings like this, at contract signings, cornerstone layings and ribbon cuttings.

"For example," he was saying, "and without going into specifics at this time, one of our basic problems is going to be two of the three existing support columns down the center of the room. Ideally, of course, we'd all prefer to see the nursing station centrally located with 360-degree visibility—visual access, in other words, to every booth. Now, we may be able to eliminate two of those columns if we can go up to the ground floor and put in a deep girder or steel truss. This would involve not only economics, but also the temporary disruption of your library and your medical records department, and it will be the first

4

decision to be made. Naturally, it can't be made until we come up with cost and time estimates."

That would be the last they would see of him, for with the signing of the contract the room would become the problem of the second junior partner. He would be in his late thirties, married and with two teen-age sons, his economic needs and his professional aspirations not yet fulfilled, the man who matured from the boy who, with scrap lumber and bent nails, built a tree house in the back yard and a succession of lean-tos and huts in vacant lots. His architectural instincts would be more structural than sculptural, and so his frustrations would be fewer and more moderate and, technically and temperamentally, he would be well equipped for such aggravating, meticulous, mechanical tasks as the designing of the room.

He would meet three times with the Emergency Room Committee and the Director of Building and Planning. With the two of the firm's draftsmen, the structural engineer, the electrical engineer and the mechanical engineer specializing in heating, air-conditioning and ventilation he would spend five days checking the original plans, now more than a half century old, and measuring the windowless subterranean storage area. During the next three weeks, high in an office building hundreds of miles from the site, sometimes sitting, sometimes standing at the drawing board in a corner of his private office, he would rough out the room.

Approach to be by descending exterior ramp, ramp and level, covered unloading area to allow for easy passage and temporary parking, but limited enough to discourage ambulance drivers, relatives, police and press from cluttering it with vehicles . . . Entrance to main emergency area to be by sliding hardwood door operated by tread plate . . . Support columns in main emergency area to remain, placing nursing station, approximately 15 feet by 20 feet, counter at front and writing shelves along north and south walls, immediately to left of entrance and in southwest corner . . . Booths to be separated by steel partitions, each booth approximately 8 feet by 10 feet, to accommodate portable examining stretcher, chair, stool, Mayo stand, intravenous pole, gooseneck lamp . . . Each booth to have

5

wall oxygen and wall suction, each to have single sliding curtain across the front . . . Minor operations room to be approximately 26 feet by 21 feet and free of partitions . . . Along east wall three open booths to be enclosed only by sliding curtains suspended from overhead tracks . . . Drug room to be entered through hardwood door with unbreakable glass panel . . . Room to be equipped with storage cabinets and refrigerator . . . Room door to be equipped with tumbler type locks, two keys for each lock, one of each to charge nurse, spares to administration office . . . Psychiatric room to be soundproofed, entrance to be through hardwood door, unbreakable window in south wall facing open area . . . Objective in room to arrive at informal living room effect.

Poison control room . . . holding room . . . fracture room . . . X-ray room . . . laboratory . . . staff toilets . . . public toilets . . . business office . . . waiting room. Out of all these components, and out of what he is himself, he would create no Temple of Athena, but he would affect the lives of hundreds of thousands he would never know. He would design the Emergency Room.

II

FRANK BAKER

For thirty-two years I have been walking to work up this same street, and it hasn't been much of a marriage. This is one of those neighborhoods that they built almost overnight about the time of World War I, all of the houses alike. There was a railroad tycoon named Bell who died, and a real estate developer bought his estate. Before he ripped down the mansion he auctioned off everything in it—chandeliers, plumbing fixtures, stairways, fireplaces—and then he put up three blocks of these houses, small, two-storied and clapboarded, all lined up six feet apart and ten feet from the sidewalk. If you live here and look across the street it must be like looking in a mirror.

When a neighborhood like this turns gray with age it's dismal. It's especially dismal at 7:40 in the morning in late February and nobody has shoveled a sidewalk since the first snowstorm in December. The cars parked along both sides of the street are wedged against the snowbanks and some of them haven't been moved in months and are still half buried. In front of one house there's a kid's sled with a broken slat. In front of another there's a Christmas tree where it was tossed on the day after New Year's, the tinsel hanging from it, and the garage where I beach The Whale is at the end of the block.

Roger was the one who named it The Great White Whale. Roger was all right. He was the best I ever had, but that's this business for you. Anybody who's all right starts his own service or he gets out. What you have left is the National Fraternal Order of Wandering Ambulance Bums. They all know each other from L.A. or Pittsburgh or Kansas City, and any time they happen to meet they sit around and talk about the five-alarm fires and six-car accidents and railroad crossing school bus wipeouts they worked. They're all Marty Conlins.

Mr. Marty Conlin is up there on that couch right now, and sound asleep. He knows that every morning at this same time I have to stand here fooling with this key in this lock and it may open on the tenth try or the twenty-fifth try, but do you think he'll ever get up two minutes early and come down and open this door? And he knows I'm not going to change this lock, and neither is Lustig.

This used to be the carriage house when all of this was the estate of that old railroad robber, and I suppose they never tore it down because it stands on a useless slope of ground where Bell Street meets Clinton Avenue. It is built against the slope with the carriage room, where I beach The Whale, on the first floor and the coachman's quarters, which is our office, on a kind of second-floor balcony in the back. Just to the left of the door on the first floor is the stairway leading up, and under the stairway is the toilet with an overhead zinc-lined wooden flush tank with pull chain that belongs in the Plumbing Hall of Fame in Flushing, Long Island, or Johnstown, Pennsylvania, or wherever it is.

In its glory days, with the carriage in here and the varnish and the leather and the brass all shining, this must have been something to see, but for as long as Lustig has owned it, it has been coming apart. The walls and ceiling of the carriage room are paneled with mahogany tongue-and-groove shiplap, but there was a leak in the roof and some of the ceiling boards swelled and buckled and a couple dropped out, and the walls haven't been cleaned down since the Harding administration.

About every five years Lustig tries to sell this thing to me. Twenty-five years ago I could have bought it for twenty-eight hundred dollars, and now he tells me he's got an offer of nine thousand five hundred for it. He says if I don't want to match that I had better find another place, but Lustig's talk doesn't bother me. If anybody has offered nine thousand five hundred for this he'll have to be let out of the State Mental Hospital before he can take possession.

When I finally get the door open there are the cats, and one of them wants to go out and the other two are doing a snake dance around my ankles and want to be fed. The whole place smells of cat leavings and cat food and kerosene for the heaters, and there stands The Whale. She's white, with red trim and Baker Ambulance and the telephone number in red on the front doors, and she was clean when I left her last night but she isn't now, because this is the age of specialization.

In the old days all anybody had to have was advanced first aid, but now you have to have at least one Medical Emergency Technician on a car. It's only a thirty-six hour course, three hours a week for twelve weeks at the Health Department, but once these ambulance bums take it they won't wash the car any more.

She's a beautiful piece, though, and she should be. The salesman tells you $14,500, but that's just the shell. The 135-amp alternator with built-in rectifier is close to $300 and naturally they don't allow you anything for the alternator that comes with the car. You've got your four red lights plus the 360-degree beacon ray and your two sirens, and inside you've got your tile flooring and reinforced ceiling with hooks to stack the collapsible stretchers. You've got your main cot with mattress, and how many levels do you want? You've got seven levels, with knee elevator and head elevator. You've got your Reeves litter and your orthopedic stretcher and your linen cabinets.

Then you've got your air conditioning, your intercom, your two-way radio-phone, your recording tachometer and your fire extinguisher. You've got your supplies, your oxygen supply with regulator, flow meter, outlets, masks, your portable oxygen cylinders, bag mask, aspirator with catheters, airways in three sizes, your hinged Keller-Blake half ring leg splint with stockinette, your padded boards, sand bags, bandages, sterile gauze pads, sanitary pads, umbilical tape, your scissors, basins, towels, blankets, pillows, bed linen. By the time you're done it comes to about $17,500, and at $30 a trip, which is the going rate inside this city when you get it, that is 584 trips before you are making your gas and oil and repairs.

I open another can of cat food, to get them away from my feet, and while I'm doing that the phone rings. I can pick it up on the wall phone down here, but I let him take it upstairs. It rings and it rings, so I know he's still in the sack. He knows I'm down here, too, but finally it stops and I can hear his voice, and at least I got him up.

I look inside The Whale and she's clean and in order, so I give him that. Every night of my life I remember what mileage she's got on her when I leave her, and now I open the recording tachometer where it's half hidden under the center of the dashboard and I check the tape. He's gone forty-two miles on two trips and I don't think he's stealing from me, because I don't see any way he possibly can.

After I take off my overcoat I decide not to wash her, so I get out of my overshoes. The streets will be running with slush and water again today, so she'd be dirty after the first trip anyway, and that's the way *he* thinks, too. The difference is, *I* have a right to think that way. *I* own her.

Upstairs we've got the cot where he sleeps and a couple of chairs and the desk and my files. We've got the kerosene heater. We've got a table with a radio on it and an electric burner where we make our coffee and the sink where he's shaving now.

"Good morning," I say.

"Yeah," he says.

He's twenty-six years old and he still doesn't know how to say good morning. He's combing his hair now, and it's a strange thing about his kind. They won't wash The Whale or pick up around here. They'll live in the middle of a mess, but they keep themselves immaculate, and about the hair I told him nothing over the ears at the sides or the collar in the back. I told him seventy percent of our trade is middle-aged or over, and they're suffering enough trauma already.

"Oh, no," I say, looking at the slip he left on the phone call he just took on a ten o'clock pickup at St. Vincent's to go to residence at 36 Conifer. "Not this one."

"What's the matter?" he says.

"Alice Wagner," I say. "Not at my age."

"What's the matter with her?" he says.

"What's the matter with her?" I say. "We picked her up last June. She's that chronic heart that goes 360 pounds to a second floor up an outside stairway with a tight right turn. You have to

10

turn her on her side, and you need an 8 to 1 pulley with a donkey engine."

"Yeah," he says. "I remember now."

He remembers now. Why, on a stairway if just an average patient gets an arm free the weight shift can throw you off.

"Never forget those addresses," I say. "They're 36 Conifer, 416 East Fifth, 210 North Jefferson. They're all 300 pounds or over."

"How about 62 Elm?"

"No," I say. "He's dead."

I pick up the phone and call Acme. I don't really think it's going to work, but it's worth the try.

"Hello, Tom," I say. "Frank Baker. How are you?"

"Good," he says. "You?"

"Good," I say, "but I'm jammed up. At ten o'clock can you make a pickup at St. Vincent's? It's room 231 and the name is Alice Wagner."

"Oh, no you don't," he says. "You should know better than that. Not Alice."

Everybody knows Alice Wagner. She's not only 360 pounds with that tough stair carry, but she's also too flexible and she's Medicare so you get only half rate.

"Well," I say after I hang up with Acme still abusing me. "You'd better try the Speed Boys."

The Speed Boys should be stunt driving at county fairs instead of running an ambulance service, but Conlin drinks beer and chases broads with them and he thinks they're great. They bummed on ambulances for a half-dozen years until about two years ago they went to the bank and got a loan and bought their own rig. They started out as Metropolitan Ambulance and then they changed it to Able Ambulance to get the alphabetical listing ahead of Acme in the Yellow Pages. We just wear dark blue zipper jackets and dark trousers but they dress like they're going to stand parade—light blue jackets with red trim and the name in red letters on the back, red piping down the trousers and peaked blue and red caps.

While Conlin is phoning the Speed Boys I look at his log for the night. He and Ansel picked up a pedestrian accident on

South Jefferson and a probable concussion, with cuts and abrasions, from a saloon on River Avenue, both of them to M.C. M.C. is what we call the Medical Center, and Ansel is Ansel Watkins and he lives just a couple of doors up Clinton. He works eight hours a day as a printer, and he rides shotgun for us when Conlin drives nights and weekends. He must sleep with his clothes on, but not all the time because the reason he has to moonlight is eight kids.

"It's okay," Conlin says when he hangs up the phone. "They'll take her because I don't think they recognized the name, but they won't like me for it."

"They need the money," I say. "They'd take a calving cow."

I make out the bills for the two they picked up last night, because nobody pays cash for anything any more. While I'm doing that the phone rings.

"Baker Ambulance," I say.

"Is this Baker Ambulance?" a woman's voice says.

"That's correct," I say.

"This is Mrs. Emma Holmquist," she says. "I have your bill here. Do you remember me?"

"Yes, ma'am," I say, because I have just looked her up in the desk file. "On November 18th we transported you from Washington and Central to the Medical Center. How are you feeling?"

"I'm not really well," she says. "I'm having trouble with my back and I've been extremely nervous since the accident."

"I'm sorry to hear that, Mrs. Holmquist," I say.

"I'm calling because I have your bill here," she says.

"That's the third bill we've sent you, Mrs. Holmquist," I say.

"I know," she says. "But my lawyer has instructed me not to pay any bills connected with the accident until we get a settlement from the taxicab company."

"Mrs. Holmquist," I say, "did you pay your hospital bill?"

"Well," she says, "I have Blue Cross and Blue Shield."

"And you paid the remainder?"

"Yes."

"And you paid your doctor?"

"That's right," she says, "but I'm under the advice of my lawyer not to pay any more bills."

"Mrs. Holmquist," I say, "in spite of what your lawyer may have told you, a receipted bill is as valid legal evidence of expenses incurred as an unpaid bill."

"Well, I'm sorry," she says, "but I'm under the advice of my lawyer and he said . . ."

"Mrs. Holmquist," I say, "I'm going to send you another bill at the first of the month. If it is not paid I'll turn it over to a collection agency."

This is some business. When they need you they need you more than they need anybody else in the world, but when it's all over and they're well again you're last in line. That doesn't go for the poor people in the Gut, though. You tell them it's thirty dollars and they go into the kitchen and get up on a chair and reach into a coffee tin or a teapot and they count out the thirty dollars and thank you. It's the ones who can afford it and with the lawyers who stand you up.

I remember this guy who went over an embankment out on the River Road and hit a tree head on. The cops were there, waiting for us, and as Roger and I were walking toward the car it blew.

"Get me out!" the guy was screaming. "Get me out!"

Roger yanked the door open and I took a look. The engine had come back into the car and was pinning one of his legs.

"Get me out!" he's screaming, and I said: "I'm gonna have to break your leg!"

"Break it! Break it!" he's hollering. "I don't care! Get me out!"

I stomped his leg four or five times and compounded it, and then Roger and I snaked him out and up the embankment. It burned half my hair and my eyelashes off, and six months later they serve me a summons here in the office. They claim I manhandled him, and the next thing I know I'm in some shyster's office for examination before trial. At an examination before trial all they let you answer is "yes" or "no."

"Did you break his leg?" the lawyer says.

"Yes," I say, "but . . ."

"No 'buts,'" the lawyer says. "Just 'yes' or 'no.'"

It's like my wife used to say, though, may she rest in peace. She used to say that no one had a gun at my back, and that's

13

the truth. On this merry-go-round we call making a living, though, most of us grab any old ring that comes along, and then if they let us we hang on for the rest of our lives.

I don't even remember any more who sent me to O. C. Tenner. Somebody said O. C. Tenner needed a high school kid to work after school and Saturdays and summers. O.C. owned a furniture store and ran a funeral parlor and ambulance service, and around the store I was his fetch.

"Franklin," he'd say, "fetch me that Boston rocker in the loft and put it in the corner of the window."

Or he'd say: "Franklin, tell Carlton to take the truck and you and he go down to the freight depot and fetch me that shipment that just came in from Grand Rapids."

Carlton was his son, and worked mostly in the funeral and ambulance departments, but he didn't really care for the business. Finally he ran away with somebody's wife, but I fetched O.C. everything—furniture, his lunch, a glass of water, his cigars, his hat and coat. After Carlton took off and I got out of high school and started to work for the old goat regularly, he kind of took a liking to me and I think he had in mind that some day I might do what Carlton was supposed to do and take over for him.

O.C. had the coffins displayed in a back room of the furniture store, and he had the embalming room behind that. He had the funeral parlor on the ground floor of the big white colonial that he and Mrs. O.C. lived in across the driveway from the store, but I gave that whole department a wide berth.

Not long ago I wheeled a DOA into the morgue at the Medical Center and an embalmer I know was there, working on this woman we'd brought in out of an auto accident the day before. He had the pump running on the floor pushing the formalin into the left carotid, and he was standing there trying to decide, I guess, what he'd do with the face.

"I don't understand this," I said. "I don't know how you can spend a lifetime doing this."

"I don't understand it, either," he said. "I don't know how you can spend a lifetime picking these people up."

O. C. Tenner himself sort of stumbled into the ambulance

business. In the early days of the automobile he and the other undertaker in town had the only rigs that could carry a patient horizontally, so the hearses served two purposes. O.C. said that one hand sort of washed the other because if the patient died you had the inside track for the funeral where the real money was. In fact, he claimed that his competitor used to pass up the living to take the dead, and I wouldn't have put it past O.C. himself.

It was the ambulance end of O.C.'s enterprises that interested me because I was a punk kid who couldn't afford a car and I thought that screaming around the streets to accidents and fires and drownings made me important. After I got out of school I worked full time for O.C., in the store and on the ambulance. When I turned twenty-one, and after O.C. damn near got us killed one day, he let me drive. Nine years later, when O.C. sold out, he sold the store to one guy, the funeral business to another and the rig to me. I never really had any free choice because I wasn't smart enough to realize that there have to be better ways of making a living than this.

"Baker Ambulance," I'm saying, answering the phone.

"Baker Ambulance?" the man's voice is saying. "Can you get to 313 Washington right away?"

"Right," I say. "That's 313 Washington. What's the problem?"

"A woman is sick. I think she's dyin'."

"What's the name?"

"Her name? Her name's Lowry."

"Is that a tenement?" I say. "What floor is it?"

"First floor," he says. "In the back."

"We'll be there in five or six minutes," I say.

While I'm putting on the blue zipper jacket Conlin is calling our answering service, telling them we'll be on the radio. Downstairs he opens the door and I start The Whale and move her out and he gets in. I turn on the beacon and the red lights, but it is only four blocks and almost no traffic so I hold her down and only touch the sirens at the intersections.

"Probably black," Conlin says.

"He sounded like it," I say, "but it can be a Rock."

15

A Rock is what we call an old-timer that you just can't move. I remember this neighborhood around Washington Avenue when it was all white, but it's black now except for a few whites who were born there and are the last of families that go back there seventy-five or maybe a hundred years.

When we get there it is in the middle of the block, one of those old, brick attached row houses that used to be private homes and now have I don't know how many apartments in them. There's no place to park so I leave her with the engine running in the middle of the street and I run up the steps to see whether we need the litter or if we can use the cot.

"In the back," this young Negro is saying. "It's down the hall to the left in the back."

He follows me down the hall and the door is open. The room is dark except for the gray light coming through the one window, and I can make out along the wall to the left old newspapers stacked from the floor almost to the ceiling. In the right hand far corner of the room there's a brass bed with this white woman lying in it. She may be seventy-five or she may be fifty-five, her gray hair stringy and her face sunken, and on the bare wood floor near the head of the bed is the bloody vomitus and some toilet paper.

"Ma'am?" I say. "What's the trouble?"

"What?" she says, raising herself on an elbow and squinting at me. "Who's that?"

"Baker Ambulance, ma'am."

"Ambulance?" she says. "I don't want no goddam ambulance. Who called an ambulance?"

"I did, Miss Lowry," the young Negro says. He's about in his mid-twenties, slim and in a clean shirt and neat slacks. "You're real sick."

"I don't want no goddam ambulance," she says.

"What's the trouble?" Conlin says, behind me.

"Bleeding ulcer," I say.

"Look, dear," Conlin says. "You need to go to the hospital."

Conlin dears them all, telephone operators, nurses, waitresses, patients who are old enough to be his great-grandmother. It's enough to make *me* sick.

"Hospital?" she says. "I'm not leavin'. I'm not goin' to any goddam hospital. I'm not sick."

"Look, ma'am," I say, "you're very sick, and . . ."

"I'm not very sick," she says, raising up again. "I know what to do for this. I can take care of myself. I always take care of myself. Get out! Get out of here, all of you!"

"All right, ma'am," I say.

"I'm sorry," the young Negro says, following us down the hall. "I didn't know what else to do."

"That's all right," I say. "You did the right thing."

"I didn't know," he says. "I've only lived here a couple of weeks and I heard her in there and I tried the door and it was open and I saw her and I thought she was dyin'."

"You did the right thing," I say.

"Thank you," he says. "I'm sorry."

"No problem," I say. "We get these more often than you think."

How often we get these dry runs I don't know. I just forget them because you can't get a signature and there's no place on Form 1040 or Schedules A, B or C for this kind of charity. The government just thinks I'm a rolling Rockefeller Foundation.

When we get out to The Whale there are two cars waiting behind her. I pull out, and as I do the red light on the radiophone comes on and Conlin picks it up.

"This is three-five-eight on nine, dear," he says. "You've got a little business for us? What's that, dear? Will you repeat? Wharton and East Fifth? Right-on, and thank you, dear.

"Pedestrian," he says, hanging up the phone. "Wharton and East Fifth."

I have lived in this town all my life, but the amateurs we elect to run it keep fouling it up. They keep making streets one-way and closing off others for their urban redevelopment, and I figure to go up two blocks, turn left and go down three to hit the new bypass north. I've already got the beacon turning and the four red lights and I switch on the electronic siren. The way the salesman explains it to you, it's only got a 90-degree angle of sound, but it's supposed to penetrate cars in front, and how would I know?

At the first intersection I turn on the electric motor driven siren, too. Its tolerance is almost nil, so in the winter it sometimes freezes up on you, but they say it has 360-degree penetration and that some people can hear one better than the other.

They're spreading out in front of us now, but even with both screamers going I still slow her at the intersections. Conlin thinks I have no guts, but he can get his thrills someplace else. All we can hear is The Whale, and if there's anything else coming with a siren on it, they're just like we are. All they can hear is themselves, like the time O. C. Tenner piled us up over here on East Second and Washington. O.C. had good vision in his left eye, but he couldn't see out of his right, and when I rode up front with him I was responsible for everything on my side. When I rode in back with a patient it used to scare the hell out of me, and sure enough, one noontime, on a rain slick but with good visibility and no need to jam it, O.C. took us into East Second and Washington with a fire department pumper coming from the right.

That pumper hit us up forward, which was lucky because instead of folding us it spun us. Some of the spectators said we turned around three times and some said four. I don't know how many times it was, but we had this woman pneumonia patient strapped down on the cot and I think it cured her. At least the way she was hollering when we stopped spinning she sounded a lot healthier than when we took her aboard. The pumper hit a parked car and the battalion chief slammed into the pumper. Three firemen and the battalion chief went to the hospital with assorted broken bones and concussions, and all O.C. and I got out of it was bruised ribs.

I turn her up the ramp now and head her north on the new bypass, three lanes in each direction. At this hour all of the working stiffs are coming into town and the traffic is light going our way, so I let her out to about 80. I don't know exactly how fast we're going, because I disconnected the speedometer to keep Conlin from trying for a new North American record. You don't need it anyway. You've got a license to speed, and the job you're on and conditions tell you what to do.

At Exit 3 I wheel her off and we're on East Fifth. We're only two blocks from Wharton, and I can see the prowl car at the right curb and the small crowd and I turn off the sirens and coast her in.

There are about thirty or forty people there, white and coloreds. One of the uniformed cops is directing traffic and the other is handling the onlookers, and on the street near the snowbank on the right there's a woman kneeling over the victim and a Negro man in work clothes standing there and looking at us as we pull up.

We yank the cot out of the back and lower it and wheel it up. The one cop and the Negro help the woman up and she's a Negro, too, crying, and the victim is a Negro girl, about eight or nine, with a pink blanket over her and lying on her back. I take off the blanket and she's a thin little thing. She's got on one of those fake leopard-skin coats and long red stockings and one white overshoe. She's bleeding from a corner of her mouth and from her nose and her left eye is swelling closed and she's unconscious.

"Get the ortho," I tell Conlin. That's the orthopedic stretcher, because I can see the right leg is broken, compounded, and there may be a broken back or neck and fractured ribs and maybe a fractured skull.

"She got a pulse?" I say to one of the cops, and now I find it.

"Yeah," he says. "She was still breathin' a couple of minutes ago."

"What happened?" Conlin says, while we're scissoring the ortho under her.

"Hit-and-run," somebody says, and I look up and it's George O'Donnell, a detective friend of mine. George is four years younger than I am, and we grew up in the same neighborhood and he's going for thirty-five years on the force now and he's one of the good cops.

"Call the M.C. for me, will you, George?" I say, as we're strapping her. "Tell them what we've got and we'll be there inside ten minutes."

"Sure, Frank," he says, while we're moving her onto the cot

and putting the blanket over her. "Can you take the mother?"

"Why certainly, dear," Conlin says to the woman. She's standing near the back of The Whale as we roll the cot up and lift it in. She's sobbing, and the Negro in the work clothes is standing with his arm around her.

"Are you the father?" I say to him, while Conlin is inside anchoring the cot.

"Yes, sir," he says.

"There's room for you, too, if you want to come," I say.

"Yes, sir," he says. "Thank you."

"You come around and get in front," I say to him, and Conlin leads the mother around and helps her into the second jump seat in the back.

On the way back I take it pretty easy, because I want to hold down the vibration and for all I know one good bump might end it for the kid. Even on the bypass where the traffic is giving me the outside lane I don't do more than about seventy, and when I take a quick glance at the father he's staring straight ahead and he's crying.

"We'll be there in a few minutes," I say to him, raising my voice over the sirens. "They'll take real good care of your daughter, sir."

He doesn't say anything. He's still staring straight ahead and crying, nodding his head now, and I don't try to say anything else. I'm too busy with the traffic now as we come off the bypass, and through the back window of the car ahead some real smart citizen gives me the finger before he pulls over. Besides, what am I supposed to say? Besides, I don't even know whether she's still alive.

When we're a hundred yards from the M.C. I cut the sirens, which is a rule they've got. I hear the father saying something now, but I can't tell what it is.

"Sir?" I say.

"She was just on her way to school," he's saying. "She was just gonna go to school."

"I know," I say. "We're here now, and they're ready to take good care of her."

I turn right at the emergency entrance and down the ramp and under the cover. There's a red rig ahead of us and it's Able. Naturally, the Speed Boys are parked right in front of the door, but there's still room for us behind them and I jump out and we unload.

"You folks follow us right in," I say to the parents and we wheel her through the two doors and swing right and down the short hall and hit the treadle and the door slides open and we're at the nursing station. There are a couple of people standing there at the corner, but they move out of the way.

"Verna," I say to Verna Palmer, the head nurse, "where do you want her?"

"Hi, Frank," she says. "Take her right into Minor Ops."

"These are the parents," I say.

We wheel her past the end booths across from the nursing station and into the room. It's empty and the nurse with the French name that I can never remember motions us into the middle area. We wheel our cot up next to theirs and raise it to the same level and Conlin grabs the blanket and I take off the straps and we start to slide her over on the ortho stretcher.

"Wait a minute," somebody says. "Don't touch that patient."

I look up, and it's a young intern I never saw before, dark-haired and with black-rimmed glasses. There's a resident I recognize standing behind him.

"Don't *touch* the patient?" I say. "Look, Doctor, who do you think put her on this stretcher?"

We move her onto their examining cot, and with the intern and resident helping us, we scissor the ortho stretcher out from under her. That tall, skinny kid orderly named Arnold, with the long hair and the steel-rimmed glasses, hands me our blanket and we get out of the way.

"You getting anything?" somebody says, and it's Tom Hunter. He was my doctor for years until he took over the E.R. here, and they've got the girl's coat open and her blouse open, and the resident has the stethoscope on her.

"Just barely," he says.

"Let's get the clothes off her," Tom says, "and let's get Neuro and Ortho down here on the quick."

Under the coat the girl is wearing a clean white blouse and a short red and green plaid skirt with shoulder straps. The intern is starting to try to pull the coat off her shoulders now, and this is the one, mind you, that tried to tell me not to touch her.

"No! No!" Tom says, moving in, and then he says to the second nurse: "Get a couple of pairs of scissors."

They cut the coat off her, Tom working on one side and the resident on the other. Then they cut off the blouse and the undershirt and the skirt and Tom has his stethoscope on her.

"Let's grab some blood," he says, "and don't just mark it 'stat.' Call the lab."

The orderly has picked up the pieces of clothing and stuffed them into a couple of those brown paper bags, and I walk away. I walk out looking for Conlin, and he's on the wall phone that's on that big square column that's always in the way. I wait for him to get off the phone, and then he's gabbing with the orderly.

"They got anything for us?" I say.

"I don't know," he says. "I didn't call them yet."

He gets back on the phone, but if he didn't call our service who was he calling? I wouldn't put it past him to be calling some babe, but I don't know, so I walk over to the nursing station where Verna Palmer is taking the history from the parents.

"Is she allergic to anything?" Verna is asking. "Penicillin?"

The mother is shaking her head and biting her lip to keep from crying. Over Verna's shoulder I take down what I need: the name is Anita Wade, the age is nine, the address is 211 East Fifth, the father's name is Thomas Wade. I make out my slip and explain it to the father, and he signs it without saying anything. I hate to do that, but I have to. In this business you're not a human being. You're a mechanical man, but I'm getting too old for this business. I can't take the kids any more.

III

ARNOLD HENKEN

This place is really weird. You know? I mean like this morning. I came on at 7, and here's this lady, like middle-aged, standing at the counter at the nursing station. There's this new intern there. The interns change every four weeks, and the residents every month. I asked Dr. Hunter about that, and he said that's to keep continuity, so the whole staff doesn't change like at the same time. It's kind of like a good idea.

So this lady is standing there and waiting and this intern is looking over some patient's chart and not paying any attention to her. He's a little guy, with black hair and black-rimmed glasses. His name is Stern, and he's a real nerd. He just graduated eight months ago, but already he's a great doctor. He complains about everything, and he calls me "Orderly."

I think about that. I mean I have this blue plastic name tag on with my name printed in white letters, but he still calls me "Orderly." Everybody else calls me Arnold, which is bad enough, you know? I mean my mother calls me Arnold, like mothers call their kid Harold or Peter or whatever it is, but even in school everybody called me Arnold. Then when I first got the job here and I was working upstairs the machine that makes the name tags was broken or something and people would ask me what my name was. I'd tell them Arnie, and they'd still call me Arnold. It's strange.

Anyway, this lady is standing there waiting and this intern named Stern is standing there and finally he looks up, and he says: "Madam?"

This lady says: "I fell downstairs yesterday morning, Doctor."

So he says: "You fell downstairs yesterday morning? And now you think you may have some broken bones, or ribs or what?"

I mean he's making it out like it's a crime.

"Oh, no," she says. "I don't have any broken bones."

"Well, what's your complaint, madam?" he says. "What brings you in here?"

"This," she says.

This woman has kind of dark hair. She takes her hand and grabs her hair in front and she lifts her scalp right up. I mean she has about a six-inch-long cut right across where her hair meets her forehead, and when she peels the whole thing back you can see back in there where it's been bleeding but it's all dried up now.

For a couple of seconds that Stern doesn't say anything. There's a nurse there named Anne Doucette, and she says: "Oh, my God!"

"Nurse," Stern says, "take this woman into Minor Ops."

Minor Ops is a room off to the right of the booths across from the nursing station, and that's where they take auto accidents and burns and things like that, and they do suturing —you know, sewing?—in there. Anne Doucette helps the woman out of her coat and has her lie down, and she's taking the personal history when Stern comes in.

"Madam," he says, "I don't understand this. You fell downstairs yesterday morning. Why didn't you come in then?"

"Well," the lady says, "it didn't bleed all that much or hurt too much and I had to go to work."

"So why didn't you come in after work?" Stern says.

"I didn't know it was like it is," she says. "I just thought I had a cut in the front and it healed. Then when I was getting ready to go to bed last night I started to comb my hair and it all lifted up and . . ."

"So why didn't you come in last night?" Stern says. He doesn't even let her finish what she's telling.

"Well," the lady says, "my husband was watching television in the living room. I went out there and I said: 'Honey, I think you'd better take me to the hospital.' He said: 'Why, what's wrong?' I took the comb and I lifted my scalp and he got sick to his stomach. So I couldn't come in till now, and I'm supposed to be at work at nine."

I got out of there before Stern could send me for something. I mean orderlies get $100 a week and nurses get like $170 a week and let Doucette get it. I mean I like Doucette and I don't mind working for anybody, except Stern. I go back to the nursing station and there's a kind of stout old man standing there. He's like sixty-five or something, but wearing a suit and a white shirt and a tie like somebody's grandfather.

"I think I broke my hand," he says, and he holds out his right hand and it's kind of red and puffy like.

"How did it happen?" Conley is saying. Conley is another nurse.

"Did you watch the fight last night?" he says.

"The what?" Conley says.

"The prize fight on television," this old man says.

"No," Conley says.

"Well, Jimmy Quarry was fighting," he says. I think that's the name he said, but I don't pay much attention to the jock scene. To me the whole jock scene is a real drag.

"Jimmy Quarry won," he says, or whatever the name is.

"Oh?" Conley says.

"And after the fight," this old man says, "I went to bed. In the middle of the night I dreamed I was fighting Jimmy Quarry and I must have punched the head of the bed, because I woke up and my hand was hurting and I couldn't sleep any more."

Conley tells me to take this old man into booth 1, and I help him out of his overcoat and tell him to sit down on the chair and that a doctor will be in to see him in a few minutes. When I go back to the nursing station there's a young woman and a young man there and the woman is screaming something at the man and Miss Palmer is trying to straighten it out. Miss Palmer is the head nurse, and this other intern named Wyman is there, too. I like Wyman. Wyman is all right, but I feel sorry for him because he has to work with Stern.

"You get away from me!" this young woman is hollering at the man. "Make him get away from me!"

This young woman is wearing dark blue slacks and she's like too fat for slacks, you know? She's wearing a light blue ski jacket and she has blond hair that's sort of hanging over her face and she looks like she's been crying and she's bigger than the man. I mean she's taller and she weighs more.

"Are you related to her?" Miss Palmer says to the man.

"Yes," he says. "I'm her husband."

"No, he's not!" this woman says. "He's not! He's not!"

"She took these," the man says and he hands over a pill bottle and Miss Palmer gives it to Wyman, and Wyman reads the label on it.

"Are you Mrs. Elaine Woods?" Wyman says to her.

"No, I'm not!" she says.

"She is," the man says. "We've been married for three years."

"How many of these did you take?" Wyman says to this young woman.

"Fifty or sixty," this young woman says.

"You shouldn't do that," Wyman says. "That's not the thing to do."

"Yes, it *is*," this woman says, and she starts to cry. "It *is* when nobody cares about you."

"I care about you," the man says, and he starts to put his arm around her. When he does she pushes it off.

"Get away from me!" she says. "Get away! I hate you!"

"Well, we'll get them out," Wyman says.

"Don't you put any tube in my stomach," this woman says.

"She's done this before?" Wyman says to the man, and I can tell he's thinking about maybe calling in whatever shrink has the duty.

"Once before," the man says. "She did it last year."

"I don't want any tube in my stomach," this woman says, and she starts to cry again.

"Mr. Woods, I think you'd better wait out in the waiting room," Miss Palmer says to the man, and then she says to me: "Arnold, let's help this lady down to booth 6."

Miss Palmer wants me there in case this woman tries to break away or punch her or something. I mean sometimes they really do. They punch you and kick you and everything. It's really weird, but this woman goes along with us until I pull the curtain closed on the booth and then she says she has to vomit. She does, too, before Miss Palmer can grab the pan, all over herself and the floor, and then she can't hold her bowels, either, and she does that right in her clothing.

What a mess, you know? The only good thing about it is that I don't have to clean her up. If it was her husband I'd have to do it, but Conley and another nurse named Whitaker have to put on O.R. gowns and caps and masks and gloves and make up a basin of soap solution, and they have to do it. All I have to do is take the clothing in a pillow case that they put in one of those big brown paper bags that go with the patient when the patient goes up to the O.R. or up to one of the floors or to the morgue. This time they tell me to take it down the tunnel to the laundry and tell them to do a quick wash and dry, and on the way back to tell Housekeeping to come and clean up the floor. The only trouble is that Housekeeping says they can't send anyone for an hour. They usually say that, so I have to clean up the floor.

Now when I get home after work my mother will ask me what I did today. She asks me that every night, and when I tell her about this she'll say: "Oh Arnold, I don't mean *that*. I don't like to hear about things like that." You know? I got an A in chemistry in school, so my mother thinks I should go to college and be a doctor, but the whole school scene is a drag, too.

This is weird here, sure, but at least it's not a drag and it's better than upstairs. Upstairs there were a lot of things I didn't like to do, like with male patients always giving bedpans and always giving enemas. Obtain bedpan. Warm bedpan by running warm water over it. Dry bedpan. Have patient flex knees. Place hand under patient's lower back. Lift up and place bedpan in position. To remove pan, blah, blah, blah. Cleanse region thoroughly. Empty pan in toilet. Cleanse pan. Wash hands. Chart on defecation sheet.

Down here they have four nurses and one in Minor Ops and Miss Palmer, and you very seldom have to give bedpans or enemas, and the enemas are even worse. Prepare solution in bag. Test temperature. Allow some solution to run through tube into bedpan. Insert lubricated rectal tube about 3 inches. Open clamp and raise bag about 12 to 18 inches above bed. Encourage patient to hold solution as long as possible. I mean, you know? That used to bug me the most, especially if it was a retention enema that they were supposed to hold for hours, and everything was directives. Like they had these directives for serving food trays. If patient is unable to feed himself, feed him. Tell patient what is on tray. Stand facing patient, and give small amounts of food according to patient's wishes. I thought about that. I used to think about it a lot. I used to think that sometime if there wasn't anybody else but the patient there I might try to serve the food facing *away* from the patient, and then there might be some *reason* for the directive.

One day I was thinking that and Miss Dimick called me in. Miss Dimick is director of Nursing Service 2, and I thought maybe she actually heard me thinking it, but she had a letter that the hospital got from some woman who said an orderly named Arnold Henken with hair almost down to his shoulders had served her father lunch. She wrote that the State Code for Hospitals, or something, says that people preparing and handling food have to have their hair cut short or tie it in back or wear a hairnet.

"Arnold," Miss Dimick said, "would you consider having your hair cut?"

"Well," I said, "I would consider it, but my mother would be opposed. She likes it the way it is."

"While you're serving food," she said, "would you consider wearing it tied in back?"

"I would consider that, too," I said, "but I don't think my father would like it."

"Would you ask him?" she said.

"I can't," I said. "He died when I was a baby."

"Oh, I'm sorry," she said, "but I don't quite understand this, because if your father is not living, how could he object?"

"It isn't *exactly* that my father would object, Miss Dimick," I said, "it's just that my mother always told me that my father wanted me to grow up to be a fine young man. I don't think that he'd think I'm a fine young man if I have my hair tied in back, but my mother can ask him."

"Your mother can ask him?" she said.

"Yes," I said. "Whenever there is a big problem in our house and my mother doesn't know what to do she asks my father at night. She says that sometimes he actually answers."

"Oh," she said. "Well, do you suppose you'd ask your mother then?"

"Yes, ma'am," I said.

Actually I didn't ask my mother, because I made this all up anyway. My father really died when I was a baby but my mother doesn't talk to him or anything like that, and about four days later Miss Dimick called me in again. She wanted to know what my mother said my father said.

"She said," I told Miss Dimick, "that my father said he was opposed to his son wearing his hair tied in back."

I'm not sure Miss Dimick was really buying all this, but she said she'd figured that was the way it would be, so she'd talked to Mrs. Donnelly, who is director of Nursing Service 1. She said that the Emergency Room is under Nursing Service 1, and that they very seldom serve food in the E.R. and that Mrs. Donnelly said she'd be very glad to take me.

So in my opinion it's a much better scene down here, and after I clean up the floor in booth 6, I check all the other booths that are empty to see if any stretchers have to be made up or anything. They don't have an orderly on from midnight until I come on at 7 o'clock, so that's what I'm supposed to do the first thing. Very often, though, I get too busy, but today there was only the stretcher in booth 10 that had to be made up new anyway.

That's another thing I like about down here. When I first got the job upstairs they taught us to make up the beds with square corners—you know, the sheets?—and after I learned that they put out a new directive. They said we had to make up the beds with mitered corners, and down here it doesn't matter. All you have to do is put on the bottom sheet and they don't care what kind of a corner you make. I usually make square corners, but sometimes when I get bored I make a mitered corner, and then you just fanfold the top sheet at the foot, you know?

So now I go to the linen supply closet and I get clean sheets, and when I put the one sheet on, it has St. Vincent's Hospital stamped on it. We get sheets here from hospitals from all around because when the ambulance guys leave a patient here they change the sheets on their stretchers. They take the clean ones from our linen closet and they leave the dirty ones from some other hospital, and I figured out once that if I was starting an ambulance service all I would need would be two clean sheets. Every time I delivered a patient I'd take the hospital's sheets and I'd never have to buy new sheets. I also figured out that it would be possible for a sheet to start out in a hospital in like California and end up here. I mean I never saw it, but it would be *possible*.

Every morning just before 8 o'clock, like this morning, Dr. Hunter comes in. Dr. Hunter is the head of the E.R., and he's a kind of a cool guy. He's like about fifty-seven years old so he's not *completely* with it, but when he comes in he always says good morning to everybody and he even says "Good morning, Arnold" to me. You know?

Dr. Hunter just took over this job a few months ago. He used to be a general doctor here in town, and then he gave that up. I don't know why he did, because when I asked him once he said: "Well, Arnold, the answer is kind of involved. Some day, if I have the time and you have the time and you're still interested, I might explain it."

I haven't asked him again, because I don't really care all that much. I mean I cared when I asked him, but I haven't cared since, and if I care again I might ask him again although I might not.

The first thing Dr. Hunter does when he comes in is look at the patients' charts in the chart rack at the nursing station. While he's doing that this woman comes in with these two small kids. This woman is kind of thin and sloppy-looking, and the kid she's carrying is in a kind of dirty pink snowsuit and he's about a year and a half old like and his face is all streaked because he's been crying. The other kid is in a kind of dirty blue snowsuit, and he's like a year older and he's pulling on this woman's hand and trying to sit down on the floor. He's sort of swinging around there on the end of this woman's arm.

"Yes?" Miss Palmer says to her.

"My baby has his finger stuck in a piece of a lamp," this woman says.

When she says that she lets the kid that's hanging on her go and he sits down on the floor. Then she takes the other kid's hand to show it and the kid starts to cry. He has this very pink swollen finger stuck through one of those round brass things that fits someplace in the top of a lamp.

"I tried soap and water," this woman says, "and then I took him to the Fire Department and they tried oil but it won't come off."

"Let's take him into a booth," Dr. Hunter says to Miss Palmer.

Miss Palmer takes them with the kid crying into booth 3, and Dr. Hunter checks another chart and then he and Wyman, the intern who's on with Stern, go over. Miss Palmer has the little kid's snowsuit off, and all he has on is a wet diaper and a dirty kind of T-shirt. He's sitting on the stretcher with Miss Palmer holding him, and the other kid is on the floor crawling around the wheels. The mother is just sitting there holding the snowsuit in her lap and looking tired.

"Well, what do you think, Doctor?" Dr. Hunter says to Wyman, while Wyman is examining the finger and the kid is screaming.

"We'd have to reduce the swelling before we could ever ease it off," Wyman says.

"That's right," Dr. Hunter says, and then he says to me: "Arnold, let's get an aluminum splint cutter."

I go out to the fracture room and get the cutter and bring it back, and in a couple of minutes, with the kid screaming and Miss Palmer and Wyman holding him, Dr. Hunter cuts the brass thing off. Then he hands it to the mother.

"I'm afraid you'll have to get a new one of these for your lamp," he says.

"Oh that's all right," she says, "the lamp was broken anyway."

So I have to change the sheets in booth 3, and when I finish that the two guys from Able Ambulance wheel in their stretcher with this old man on it. He's real pale and having trouble breathing, and when Dr. Hunter comes out from behind the nursing station to look at him, Stern comes walking up.

"What's this patient's problem?" Stern says to the ambulance guys, who are unstrapping the old man and taking the blanket off. Dr. Hunter is feeling for the old man's pulse.

"He tried to commit suicide," one of the ambulance guys says.

"How do you know he tried to commit suicide?" Stern says.

"Because the neighbor who called us told us," the ambulance guy says. "He found him on the floor with this cord around his neck."

He reaches under the foot of the mattress on the stretcher, and he pulls out this long electrical extension cord. He hands it to Stern.

"How do you know his neighbor didn't try to kill him?" Stern says. Now he's like a great district attorney, too, you know?

"Because the patient himself told us he tried to commit suicide," the ambulance guy says.

"Look, Doctor," Dr. Hunter says to Stern. "Shall we just get him into a booth?"

They wheel the old man into booth 3, where the little kid was, and after the Able Ambulance guys move him onto our stretcher and Dr. Hunter and Stern look him over and put their stethoscopes on him I help Conley undress him and get him into a hospital gown. I don't pay too much attention to him after that, because when I come out I hear somebody say that Baker Ambulance is coming in with a kid who was hit by a car and it looks kinda bad.

In a couple of minutes Baker Ambulance comes in, and you can tell from the way they roll the stretcher up to the nursing station that it's bad. When the ambulance guys just have some old person who only has like pneumonia or something they just sort of walk the stretcher up and they may like kid around with Miss Palmer or the clerk or some nurse for a minute, but when they have a bad one they come in like they're making one of those pit stops in one of those auto races, you know?

It's a little colored girl, and Miss Palmer tells them to take her right into Minor Ops. I follow them in, and Doucette tells them to put her in the middle space, and then just when they start to move her off their stretcher good old Stern comes in.

"Don't touch that patient!" he says.

There's a kind of an old guy, like sixty-two, named Baker who runs Baker Ambulance, and he takes a quick look at Stern and he says: "Look, Doctor, who do you think put her on this stretcher?" Then he goes right back to moving her with the other ambulance guy.

Stern doesn't say anything, because everybody gets too busy. There's a resident named Mosler who's listening to the girl's chest with his stethoscope, and Dr. Hunter comes in and he says: "Let's get her clothes off." He tells somebody to call Neurosurgery and Orthopedics to get them down here, and then he has to stop Stern from trying to *take* the clothes off. Doucette brings a couple of pairs of bandage scissors and they cut the clothes off. Even I would know enough to do that.

When they cut the clothes off they just throw them out onto the floor, and I have to pick them up and put them in one of those brown paper bags. Actually I put them in two bags—the clothes that are all cut up in one bag and the clothes that aren't all cut up in another bag. This girl has kinda nice new clothes, too, which is maybe why Stern thought he would try to take them off, although I don't really think he thought that at all.

So in the one bag I have the pieces of this sort of fake leopard coat and the pieces of this white blouse and the pieces of these red stockings and the pieces of underwear. Then in the other bag I have this red and green skirt that's only cut in one place and one shoe and one white rubber overshoe. I can't find the other shoe or overshoe, so I go out to leave these bags with the clothing at the nursing station, and I see the ambulance guy who works for Baker is talking on the phone. He's

33

talking on the phone that's on one of those big square pillars or columns or whatever they call them that hold up this whole building or something, so I go over to ask him about the other shoe and overshoe.

"Is this the city desk?" he's saying on the phone. "This is Marty Conlin and I got a hit-and-run for you. It may die."

I figure out that he's talking to the *News-Argus*. The *News-Argus* is one of the newspapers, and they give money for news tips, if they use them in the paper. I mean they give $2 for a very small story and $5 for a better one and $10 for a good one, and this Conlin is giving them the girl's name, which is Anita Wade, and her age and telling them she was on her way to school and giving the address.

"Yeah, she's black," he's saying, "but it's still a hit-and-run."

This Conlin is kind of a smooth guy who raps a lot with the nurses here. He's about twenty-five maybe, and he has his hair kind of sculptured and he may even use hair spray but I don't know. Finally he hangs up the phone.

"You want to use this phone or something, kid?" he says to me.

"No," I say, "I want to ask you about the girl's shoes. I can only find one shoe and one overshoe."

"That's all we picked up," he says. "The others must be at the scene."

So I take the brown paper bags over to the nursing station to explain them to Gloria Miller. Gloria Miller is the clerk, and at the nursing station this little girl's mother and father are there. They're kinda short, thin people, and the mother has been crying and Miss Palmer is getting the little girl's personal history from them. Then Baker, who runs the Baker Ambulance, comes over to copy something down from the chart Miss Palmer is filling in, so I explain about the clothes to Gloria Miller and she'll have to explain to this girl's parents why the clothes are all cut up. I'm glad I don't have to explain it to them —you know?—because I'm starting to feel sorry.

That's something I *really* don't like about this job—feeling sorry all the time—but it's still not as bad down here as it was upstairs. Down here the patients don't stay around long enough for you to really feel sorry for them like upstairs. Upstairs you have the same patients for weeks sometimes, and you pass them drinking water and bedpans and you feed them and you wash them and you rap with them some. Then you hear the doctors talking, and you find out that this patient or that patient isn't going to live. *He* doesn't know he's going to die soon, and his family doesn't know it yet, but *you* know it, and the next morning when you come in you open the blinds and you say: "Good morning, Mr. Schultz. It's a beautiful morning, and how are you today?"

I really disliked that—you know?—and then sometimes when the patient would die about five medical students and three interns and a couple of residents would come in, and the patient's family would be sitting outside thinking: "My, they have all those doctors in there and they're giving such good care." They wouldn't know the patient was dead, you see, and that the medical students and interns were just practicing putting one of those endotracheal tubes down the patient's throat. I thought about that a real lot. I thought that, well, the patient did get good care, and it doesn't hurt the patient now because he's dead, and it doesn't hurt the patient's family because they don't know. Besides, the medical students and the interns have to learn how to do it some time, but I still disliked it anyway.

So after I explain to Gloria Miller about the little girl's clothes I kind of hang around the door to Minor Ops in case they want anything but they don't. Carol Whitaker is in there helping Anne Doucette and there's Dr. Everett, who's the chief orthopedic resident, and Dr. Mabry, who's the chief neuro resident, and kind of a cool guy in spite of the fact that he's kind of a jock. I mean I think he played football like in high school or in college, and I heard him saying once that he should have gone into orthopedics and then he could have sort of a side job as the bone man with some college or professional football team, but I like him anyway.

When they don't need me around Minor Ops I go back to the nursing station because they're getting kind of busy. I mean we get a lot of people with head colds and stomach aches and boils and things. They don't have any doctors for these people any more, and they come into the E.R., and we get a lot of people who are on welfare and can't afford any doctors anyway.

I take some of these people now to whatever booths Miss Palmer or somebody tells me. Then the intern named Wyman tells me to take Mr. Kobak to X ray. Mr. Kobak is the old man who tried to commit suicide with the electric cord, and he's a kind of farmer like and he doesn't hear very well. You have to kind of shout at him, you know?

X ray is just across the hall, but they're getting ready to do somebody else in there so I tell them about Mr. Kobak and I push his stretcher against the wall and I kind of shout at him that I am going to leave him there for a few minutes. He just nods his head, and then this guy from the business office comes up with his clip board and his yellow forms. The business office has a branch right outside the E.R., and I don't know this guy's name except that Dr. Mabry always calls him "Hooks."

You have to see this guy. He's kind of short and he's bald and he has rimless glasses and he's very serious and he wears garters. The reason I know is one day he sat down in the nursing station and he pulled up his pants leg to show some doctor a bruise or something. I mean I saw a picture of some garters once in an old magazine like from the early 1940s that my mother had up in the attic, or otherwise I might have thought this guy had some kind of a growth. It was like seeing what they call living history. You know?

So one day Dr. Mabry was down here and this guy came walking up with his clip board and Dr. Mabry said: "Good morning, Hooks."

So this guy said: "Why do you call me Hooks?"

So Dr. Mabry said: "For Money Hooks. Before anybody here can get a needle into a patient to take a sample of his blood you're into his pockets for a sample of his dough."

So this guy said: "Let me tell you something, Doctor. If I didn't get the money, you wouldn't get paid. Nobody would get paid, and this whole place would come to a complete stop."

Dr. Mabry just laughed, but this guy "Hooks" was very serious and blinking his eyes like at Dr. Mabry. Now he comes up to me in the hall.

"Who's Kobak?" he says, looking at one of his yellow forms.

"He's right there," I say, pointing to the old man.

"Good," he says.

I don't tell him that Mr. Kobak can hardly hear. I figure I'll let him find that out for himself, and I don't think I want to stay around and listen to it, either.

Back at the nursing station there's this Negro woman with this little Negro boy. This little boy is about two years old and he looks all right now, but this Negro woman says he's been vomiting again. She says he's been vomiting every now and then for a couple of weeks, and sometimes he cries because his stomach seems to hurt. Dr. Hunter asks her a few questions about what she feeds the boy and stuff like that, and then he looks up on the blackboard to see what pediatric resident is on call, and it's Dr. Banks.

Dr. Banks is a female nerd. She's sort of short and thin and scrawny-looking and she has short blond hair and she wears thick-rimmed glasses and she's always in a hurry. I mean whenever she gets a call to come down here she walks like she's in a hurry and she never has time to say hello to anybody and she never smiles and all she does is give orders. Then when she has to wait awhile, like for the results of some kid's blood test or something, she sits around the nursing station reading some medical journal she's carrying around with her and letting everybody know how much she knows.

And the way she does it is what I would call like devious, you know? I mean some resident or even some attending in some other specialty like Neurology or Thoracic or Dermatology or something will get called to come down to look at some patient who has some very complicated problem, and after he makes his diagnosis he will be standing around in the nursing station explaining it to Dr. Hunter and the others. Dr. Banks will be sitting there reading one of her medical journals or something and seeming like she's not paying any attention. All of a sudden she will stand up and she'll say: "Oh, Doctor, I'm glad you're here, because there's a question you can answer for me." She'll ask the question, and the doctor will start to answer it, but before he can finish she'll be saying: "But isn't it true, Doctor, that . . . ?" Then she'll talk for five minutes, telling the doctor about *his* specialty, you know?

Whenever I think of Dr. Banks I think of Margaret Wittenauer, and I don't care to think about Margaret Wittenauer so I try not to. Margaret Wittenauer went to school with me, I mean *all the way* through school from the first grade through high school, which is another reason why to me the whole school scene was a real drag. Margaret Wittenauer knew everything, and she was always waving her hand in class, not to leave the room but to answer the question. I mean the teacher would say: "Can anybody tell me . . . ?" And by the time the teacher would say "tell" and before she even asked the question Margaret Wittenauer would be waving her hand to answer it. Margaret Wittenauer won everything. In our senior year in high school she won the English Award and the French Prize and the Chemistry Prize and she was valedictorian and the D.A.R. Girl of the Year and everything. Margaret Wittenauer got a scholarship to some college somewhere, and my mother thinks she's great. She's always telling me how Margaret Wittenauer is doing in whatever college it is she goes to, but I don't even listen because I don't want to hear anything any more about Margaret Wittenauer.

So now Miss Palmer tells me to take the Negro woman and the little boy who's been vomiting down to booth 9. He's a nice little kid who walks along holding his mother's hand and looking all around and not crying or anything, and then Arlene Woods comes in to get the kid's history and to undress him. Arlene Woods is the pediatric nurse in the E.R., and she really likes kids. She can even stand kids that scream all the time and kick and everything, and Arlene Woods is young and kind of good-looking and I don't know why she doesn't get married and have kids of her own, you know?

I hear them paging Dr. Banks on the speakers now, so I figure I don't want to be around booth 9. I go out to see if they've got Mr. Kobak in X ray yet, but he's still waiting, and Dr. Mabry and Dr. Everett and Dr. Hunter are looking at the X rays of

Anita Wade, the little girl that got hit by the car, so I know she's still alive. There's kind of an open booth there between X ray and the fracture room where they have this automatic developer that develops X rays in like ninety seconds, and they've got those lighted places on the wall where they put the X rays so the light shines through them. While I wasn't around Minor Ops they probably brought in the portable X ray, and now Dr. Everett is pointing out things like broken bones and the others are agreeing. Then they walk back into the nursing station and Dr. Everett gets on one phone and Dr. Mabry gets on another to call upstairs, so I listen to him because he's sort of like a character, you know?

"Is the man there?" he says when somebody answers. "Good. Then let me lay some words on him."

That's the way he talks, you know? He's still a pretty cool guy, though, and when somebody else upstairs, like maybe an attending or maybe even the chief of Neurosurgery, gets on the phone Dr. Mabry says: "Look, this is your lucky day, because you're not going to have to roll for the next O.R. Everett is scooping this little girl for Ortho. That's right, and he's on the phone now, telling them he wants to use his own dice."

This means that Dr. Everett wants to break into the operating room schedule, so that's how serious Anita Wade is. Then when he finishes on the phone, Dr. Everett asks me if I will wheel her into the fracture room. I go into Minor Ops, and they have one of those IV stands attached to the stretcher with the bottle on it and the tubing running to Anita Wade's arm. They have a tube in her nose, and I can see her one eye is all puffed up and swollen shut and I can't tell how many things are really wrong with her because they have a blanket over her.

Kay Conley is there with Anne Doucette, and Conley goes along to the fracture room. Conley goes ahead of the stretcher to kind of clear the way, because the E.R. is getting busy now and there are people standing around and kids like running around. After I leave Anita Wade in the fracture room I see them wheeling Mr. Kobak into X ray, so I wait till he comes out and then I wheel him back to booth 3. Then I walk along by the other booths to see if any stretchers need to be made up or anything, and when I get back by booth 9 Dr. Banks is coming out, walking fast and shaking her head. Next Arlene Woods comes out carrying the little Negro boy and talking to him. The little Negro boy has on one of those kids' hospital gowns with animals on them that they have here, and he's got one of those stuffed animals that the Women's Auxiliary makes. I think it's a plaid horse, but I'm not sure because the Women's Auxiliary has some really weird ideas about what different animals look like.

"What's the matter with Dr. Banks?" I say to Arlene Woods.

"Nothing," Arlene Woods says, "but Walter's mother says he's been eating paint."

"What color?" I say.

"Oh, Arnold," Arlene Woods says, "how do I know what color? He's been eating paint off the woodwork. I've got to weigh him, and then take him to X ray."

We have this scale here with a big dial like the kind you put a penny in and get your fortune, except ours you don't have to put anything in and naturally you don't get your fortune. Arlene Woods takes Walter's plaid horse, or whatever it is, and puts Walter on the scale, but Walter doesn't want to stand there, even a second. As soon as Arlene Woods puts him down and looks up at the dial to wait for the arrow to stop shaking Walter puts out his arms to her and almost falls off the scale. Arlene Woods tries that twice with Walter, and that's when I decided to do my hand noises.

I've been doing these hand noises like for ages. I mean I was like nine or ten years old when I saw this man do them on TV on the Ed Sullivan Show. He actually played music with just his hands. He played "America, the Beautiful" or something, and I thought it was real groovy, which is what we used to say then.

Anyway, I started practicing these hand noises but I couldn't even make a sound until one night I was sitting in the bathtub with my hands wet and all soapy and I made this noise. It wasn't much of a noise, but it was a noise, and I must have sat there for like an hour making this noise until my mother wanted to know what I was doing in there and told me to come out.

That was like what they always refer to as the breakthrough. After that I practiced without using any soap and then without using any water. Then with just my dry hands I practiced making *different* noises.

The reason you can do this—and I figured this out myself—is that when you press your hands together you form a kind of a vacuum, and then when you squeeze your hands in and out the air going in and out makes the noise. My best hand noise is probably the one that sounds like a mouse squeaking, although I have a very high clear noise that a soprano opera singer would call like C over High C or something, and then I have what I call my obnoxious noise, because when I make it my mother says: "Oh, Arnold, do you have to do that? Do you have to keep making that obnoxious noise?"

I used to make these hand noises a lot in school. I mean I could sit there with my hands under my desk and looking right at the teacher and she would never know who was making them. I don't really mean I made a *lot*, but like when Margaret Wittenauer would stand up to answer a question that hadn't even been asked yet and before she could say the first word I would just make a small hand noise.

Now I don't use my hand noises much any more, except like with kids like this Walter. Most kids like the mouse noise the best, so now when Arlene Woods puts Walter back on the scale again I get down by him and I make the mouse noise. When I do, Walter stops trying to get off the scale and he looks at me and Arlene Woods gets his weight. I don't know what his weight is, though, because Dr. Banks comes up.

"What are you, anyway?" she says to me. "A comedian?"

"No, ma'am," I say. You notice I didn't call her Doctor, and I probably could have thought of a lot of other things to say or not to say, but I didn't. I was just thinking that maybe it would be a good idea if Dr. Banks married Stern. Then I wouldn't have to feel sorry for anybody else who might marry them by accident or just sort of for something to do.

People like Dr. Banks and Stern depress me, so that for a

while after I'm around them I don't feel like doing *any* work, so I sort of cop out. I don't actually cop out by going to the john for fifteen minutes or by going back to the linen closet and taking all the sheets and pillow cases out and putting them back in again like I'm counting them or straightening up the closet or something. Instead, I just sort of flake off. The first thing I do is walk sort of rapidly down to Minor Ops, and I look in there like I'm looking for somebody or like I'm looking to see if there's anything for me to do. Then I walk more slowly along by the booths, as if I'm checking to see if anybody needs anything and I actually go into Mr. Kobak's booth.

"How are you, Mr. Kobak?" I say.

Of course he can't hear me. He's just lying there, looking up at the ceiling, and he doesn't even know I'm in the booth.

"Well," I say, "if there's anything you need, Mr. Kobak, just let us know."

When I come out of Mr. Kobak's booth I walk across to the booths on the other side and I make out like I'm checking on those. In one of them a very thin and pale old woman with an IV running into her is having a hard time breathing. In the next one Wyman, the intern, is examining some guy's armpit. In another booth one of the eye doctors is looking into some woman's eye, so I walk out into the hall and stop off at the X-ray booth.

At the X-ray booth Dr. Hunter and some resident from Thoracic and Stern are looking at the X rays of Mr. Kobak's collapsed lung. Then the resident puts up some different X rays of the old man's lungs, and he starts pointing out things.

"You see the lesion?" he's saying. "And look at it here, and all through here."

I'm looking, too, but I can't really see it. To me it all looks more or less the same, gray and black, because I never can see what the doctors see in X rays. I mean if Dr. Hunter is looking at some X ray and not in a hurry I sometimes ask him what it is. He explains it, pointing everything out, and I tell him that yes, yes, I can see it now, but I just tell him that because I'd be too embarrassed to tell him I really can't see it. Now I can tell, though, just from what the resident is saying, that Mr. Kobak

42

must have like cancer of the lung and that he doesn't have much chance.

"That's too bad," Dr. Hunter says. "What do you recommend?"

"I'll tell you what *I* recommend," Stern says. "I recommend we give him back the electric cord."

Dr. Hunter doesn't say anything. He just looks at the resident and the resident looks at him. I walk back into the E.R., and Jimmy Wilson is walking in. Jimmy Wilson is black and he's the O.R. orderly, and when I see him I feel better. Jimmy Wilson is sort of short and stocky and he looks like he's about twenty-five, but somebody said he's been an O.R. orderly for about twenty years so I don't know how old he is. Jimmy Wilson takes people who are going to have an operation from their rooms to the O.R., and he's always smiling and he even makes *those* people feel better.

"Hi, Jimmy," I say. "What's happening?"

"Hello, Arnold," he says. "How they goin' down here?"

"Good," I say. "How's everything upstairs?"

"Fine. Fine. Just fine," Jimmy says. "All the doctors are doing a great job."

Jimmy Wilson really loves doctors. Jimmy Wilson thinks all doctors are great. That is, Jimmy Wilson thinks all *surgeons* are great, but he probably likes other doctors, too.

"You got a Miss Wade here?" he says now. "Miss Anita Wade?"

So I take Jimmy Wilson out to the fracture room. Conley is still there with Anita Wade.

"Oh, my," Jimmy Wilson says. "She's just a little girl. What happened?"

"Hit-and-run," Conley says.

"Oh, my, that's too bad," Jimmy Wilson says, shaking his head, but then he says: "But she's gonna be all right. The doctors are gonna do a great job, and this little girl is gonna be all right."

Jimmy Wilson takes Anita Wade down the hall to the elevators, and I start to walk back into the E.R. but Dr. Hunter calls me. He's still by the X-ray booth, but he's all alone and I figure he wants to show me some other X ray that I won't understand anyway. Instead of that he has up an X ray of the little boy who was eating paint, and the boy is so small you can almost see his whole body in the one X ray.

"This boy has been eating paint," Dr. Hunter says to me.

"Is that so?" I say. It's always better to make the doctors think you haven't heard anything about what they're telling you.

"Lead poisoning," Dr. Hunter says, and then he points to something on the X ray. "See the lead lines?"

I can actually see it. I can actually see the lines across the bottom of this little boy's arm bones where they meet the wrists. I'm getting so that I can actually read X rays, and Dr. Hunter tells me he thinks this little boy will be all right.

IV

THOMAS R. HUNTER, M.D.

. . . and in the middle of it John Clarity called and asked me
when he could send his new assistant down to interview me for
The M.C. Bulletin. I tried to get out of it by protesting that
I haven't been running the room long enough to have anything
definitive to say about it, but Clarity said it would still be a
change from the usual mélange of bridal showers, bowling
scores, service award banquets and building plans with which
they customarily fill the paper. Those are Clarity's words, and
that's his description of his paper.

"Besides," he said, "she's only twenty-four years old and this
is only her second job, and so you can lie like hell about your
Army career and the quarter century you spent in private practice passing out aspirin."

Right after lunch, and precisely on time, she appeared at the
nursing station. Her name is Beryl Williams and she can't be
more than five feet tall or weigh more than 90 pounds. She's
intelligent and seems competent, but she has a problem in
that she doesn't care for hospitals.

"If you have the time," I suggested, "and if you'd really care
to see what my job is like, you might follow me around for half
a day. Then I could try to answer any questions you might
have."

"No thanks, Doctor," she said. "I'm not much for the blood
and gore. Actually I can take very little of the whole sickness
and suffering scene."

"Then you don't expect to find your work here particularly
enjoyable?"

"Oh, I'll get by," she said. "After all, I won't be writing any clinical papers, and Clarity understands. I need the job until my husband completes his thesis in geology, and then I'll be traveling with him and writing about South America or Africa or wherever he goes."

"Well, you're very honest about it."

"Why not, Doctor?" she said. "Honesty is the new thing, don't you know?"

I took her back to our holding room, which is the only place they could find to put a desk for me when I took on this task. There are two beds there that we use for patients when we have to keep our booths open and we're waiting for beds to be released upstairs. We also use the room for the coroner's cases, the DOAs that come in with cause of death unknown, and then it's a locked room, with only the priest permitted to enter, until the coroner arrives.

"According to your file in Personnel, Doctor," she said, "you're fifty-seven years of age."

"Correct."

"You were born here."

"Correct."

"You went to public schools here, then Hamilton College and then Georgetown for your medical training."

"Correct."

"You interned here, and then spent three years in the Army during World War II. Overseas?"

"Two-and-a-half years overseas. England, and then northern Europe, from France into Germany."

"Were you with a field hospital, or whatever they called them?"

"No. With an armored medical battalion of an armored division. I don't imagine you'll want much about that."

"I agree. Probably not."

Probably not. This child wasn't even born then, and her generation has the need to believe we imagined Hitler and that the six million Jews who died of disease and starvation in ghettos and slave labor camps and of suffocation in gas chambers must have been the products of propaganda. The unsuccessful abortion in Indochina has blackened all wars, and in the process it has denigrated the honor of all the good men who fought and died in them.

"And after the war," she said, "you went into your general practice here?"

"Not immediately. There wasn't any real need for another G.P. here right then. Mrs. Hunter and I were just married, and I heard about this appeal for a doctor in a small town up near the Canadian border."

"The town?"

"Arbor. A-r-b-o-r."

And we were flat out financially. All of the money I had saved from my Army pay had gone to pay off what I had borrowed to get through med school. All the equipment I owned was in my bag, but they had said that if I accepted the job I wouldn't need to worry about equipment or money, either.

"What sort of town was it, Doctor?"

"It was what I imagine it still is today—a farming community that spread out for miles around a crossroad in the middle of nowhere."

When we tried to look it up on the road map we couldn't find it, and I had to call them to ask for directions. We started out the next day, all our belongings in the station wagon, at noon and it was in the middle of winter, and it seemed as if we were driving forever. By late afternoon we had entered the wilderness, forty miles straight through a fir and pine forest to a town consisting of two stores and a half dozen houses and with a name I've forgotten. From there it was thirty miles to Porter, and now it was beginning to snow. From Porter it was another forty-five miles, and it was dark and snowing heavily when we finally slid into Arbor—the crossroads with one street light, the wooden ark that was the thirty-bed hospital, the four-room school, the general store with the gas pump, the red brick box that was the new post office, the old post office, the four houses and, rising high above it all and dominating it all, the Catholic church.

Of course I told little Beryl Williams none of this, and I seldom recall it any more myself. In this profession a man lives too many lives and too much. There is scant time to savor anything or suffer anything except the accumulated sadness, and when we arrived in that snowstorm that night they were waiting for us—the three selectmen and Father Giles Gosselin—in the former post office, which was to be our home and my office, furnishings and rent free.

They were French-Canadian-Americans, most of them, in and around that town, and for more than forty years they had had the same general practitioner and general surgeon, Dr. Adrian Flamand. As you entered the hospital you were confronted by the cross, on one side of it a picture of the Saviour and on the other a portrait of the same size and of the man I was replacing, a white-haired, imperious-looking Dr. Flamand. For all those years he and a succession of priests leading up to Father Gosselin had ruled the town and its environs, and since his death of a stroke some six months before our arrival the medical care had been solely in the hands of the nuns of the nursing order that ran the hospital under the close supervision of Father Gosselin.

It was Father Gosselin's wish that I open my office in the hospital, but it was my wish not to practice medicine under Pope Pius XII. Dr. Flamand, good Catholic that I'm sure he was, must have had the same wish, because he had had his own office in his own home, a half mile out into the countryside. He had left this house, and his medical and office equipment, to an aging maiden sister and she had donated the equipment to the town.

Attached to the rear of the old post office was a two-story box-like structure, dining room and kitchen on the first floor and an outside stairway leading up to the living room, bedroom, and bath on the second. All of the furniture, including that which we were to collect for my waiting room, was donated by the citizens, and when they came in you could see them brighten at the recognition of an old friend, a chair that used to belong to their late Uncle Jules or Aunt Angélique.

That's what we moved into that night, and the next morning at 8 o'clock I was seeing patients at the hospital and I had my office there for four or five days while the carpenter and some volunteers threw up some partitions in the post office and the electrician and a plumber made their improvements. The partitions were hardly soundproof, so when the conversation in the examining room was about to become indiscreet and I could imagine the ears in the waiting room tuning in, I'd put a record on the player. I'd drown them with a deluge of Beethoven's Fifth or Bach's organ Preludes and Fugues, Sonatas, Toccatas and Partitas.

"How long did you stay in Arbor?" Beryl Williams was asking now.

"Two years."

"Did you enjoy it there?"

"To a degree. I was young and eager then, and I didn't mind too much the eighteen and twenty-hour days and many sleepless nights because I was learning a lot of medicine by doing."

"I suppose that's why they call it practicing, Doctor."

"I suppose."

My very first week there I was making my rounds in the hospital at night with Sister Frances. Sister Frances was in her late middle age, an excellent nurse and an absolutely marvelous woman, and I don't think that I could have lasted two years there without her. On this night one of our patients was this ancient woman whose time was simply running out, and agonizingly. She was in intractable heart failure and desperately ill, and when we came to her I said: "I think this patient should have one half grain of morphine." Sister Frances wrote it down, and after we'd seen the other patients she said: "Thank you, Doctor, and we'll see you in the morning." The next morning the bed was empty, and I said: "Oh, this patient has succumbed?" Sister Frances said: "Why yes, Doctor." There was something about the way she said it, and then it dawned on me. I should have prescribed one eighth of a grain, and she must have known it. She'd been giving this dose for decades, and thus in my first week in that place, of all places, I had my introduction to euthanasia, if it was.

"Why did you leave Arbor?" Beryl Williams asked.

"Oh, for a variety of reasons, including, I suppose, greed. The people there were nice to us. They generally are to doctors, or used to be, especially in rural areas."

49

There was this highly excitable barber and handyman named Maurice. I can't recall his last name, but during our second week there he came in one night, carrying in his arms his unconscious nine-year-old son. The child had been hit on the head by a chunk of ice that had slid off a roof, and after we had carried the boy across to the hospital and I'd determined that it wasn't a depressed fracture, I gave him the same treatment he'd have received at Massachusetts General, the Mayo Clinic or in Outer Mongolia: wait and see.

We watched that boy for two weeks, and every evening after my office hours Maurice would come in with a bottle of scotch and the same question: "How's my boy doing, Doc?" Then, right at that time, our water pump failed. It was under our dining-room floor, and Maurice ripped up the floor boards, and for two nights there we ate in one corner while Maurice, like Poseidon emerging from the sea, stood chest-deep in the middle of the room, carrying on conversations with us while he fussed with the pump. When his boy recovered, and although I tried to explain that I had had very little to do with it, I had free haircuts and we had a friend forever.

I even learned to live with Father Gosselin and he with me, although it would be more accurate to say that we learned to accept each other. He was in his late fifties, stout, red-faced and a despot who ruled that town and countryside by fear of God and of himself. The year before we arrived he had been annoyed by something—I never learned what it was—so he started Lent two days early, and in Arbor it ran for forty-two days.

In Arbor and its environs the women were constantly pregnant, and that was my biggest problem. There were women there in their thirties who had whole chains of children and probably hadn't had three menstrual periods since their teens, and they all lived with the deadly fear that they were going to abort. If they went into the hospital hemorrhaging we had no blood bank but, worse, you were not allowed to do curettage to stop the bleeding because Father Gosselin ruled that you could not interfere with pregnancy until you had proved the fetus dead.

I would get those house calls where some girl would be bleeding badly, and she would beg me not to take her to the hospital. I remember many of those, and of course I remember the first one, when I had been there only a few days.

"Please, Doctor," this woman begged me. "Please, Doctor, don't take me to the hospital. I don't want to die."

"Why, that's ridiculous," I told her. "You're not going to die. I'm simply going to take you to the hospital and stop the bleeding."

I took her in, the poor thing sobbing all the way, while I, presuming that I was going to do a D. and C., kept trying to reassure her. I wrote out the orders for the Sisters to get her ready, and when nothing happened I found Sister Frances.

"I'm sorry, Doctor," she said. "I really am, but you'll have to see Father Gosselin."

I found him getting into his car outside the church, and for a half hour, sitting in that car, we argued theology, philosophy, birth control, abortions, the Inquisition and I don't remember what else. It ended with my booking the woman into the hospital in Porter, driving her the forty-five miles while Father Gosselin probably booked me into hell.

We didn't exactly make our peace, Father Gosselin and I, but at least we maintained a working truce. If I got to an urgent night case first I would do my business, and if he arrived first he would set up and perform his rites. In either event, the one would wait for the other and we would see each other home.

They had never heard, around there, of prenatal care, and almost all the deliveries were in the home. The home would be miles out into the country, and when I would get there at any hour of the day or night the patient would be on the bed with the family hovering around. There would be a roaring fire going in the fireplace, and so I would put aside the ether with which I had intended to put the patient out, and get out the chloroform, the tea strainer and ten layers of gauze.

I couldn't be at the patient's head and down where the action was at the same time, so I would give the patient's mother or husband my abbreviated course in anesthesia. There was that one occasion, too, where I had the patient's mother dripping the chloroform, because the husband was too nervous,

51

and the husband holding the kerosene lamp for me. Suddenly the husband fainted, dropping the lamp, of course, and there I was, holding the head in and stomping out the fire on the rug while the patient's mother ran for water.

"As nice as most of the people were to us," I told Beryl Williams, "there were just too many patients and the practice was just too much for us."

There were times there when I was almost practicing catastrophic medicine. There was the day when I got the call to go eighteen miles out into the country where a girl was hemorrhaging and probably aborting. I took the normal saline out with me, settled her onto the mattress in the back of the old Pontiac station wagon and set up the intravenous by suspending the bottle from the ceiling light. I was going to drive her to Porter, but on the way back I stopped at the office to see if there were any emergencies.

"Don't worry," I told the girl. "I won't be a minute."

It was summertime, and the place was jammed. They were sitting in the waiting room and on the porch, and on the stairway leading to our upper quarters there was a man gray with a heart attack. I got out some morphine and gave it, and with that my wife came down the stairs.

"Hurry!" she said. "Upstairs in our bed you've got Mr. Soandso in heart failure."

I renewed the morphine on Mr. Soandso and left his wife watching him, and as we came down those outside stairs there was this screeching of brakes and this horrendous crash at the crossroads. In minutes I was across the street in the hospital, suturing and running an emergency ward, and my wife was driving the poor girl in the back of the Pontiac to Porter where, happily, she survived.

It was too much for my wife, far from her friends and the culture in which she had been reared. She was a fine arts major in college, had no background even in biology, and one evening I came in from a call to conduct office hours, the place as crowded with patients as usual, and she was coming out of our dining room carrying a cup and saucer.

"The first one you ought to see," she said, "is an old lady sitting outside in a car. I've just made her a cup of tea."

I went out and found the woman, sitting there on the passenger's side of the front seat, her head on her chest. She was ice cold, had been dead probably a half hour, and there was my wife at my elbow.

"This lady is dead," I said.

"Why, she can't be," my wife said. "I just spoke with her. I just asked her if she wanted a cup of tea."

"And what did she say?"

"Nothing," she said. "She didn't say anything."

She had been carrying on a conversation with a dead woman, and then we had to go in and tell the old lady's son.

"You mentioned greed, Doctor?" Beryl Williams said.

"Yes, I guess Mrs. Hunter and I are guilty of a certain degree of it, being neither saints nor Schweitzers. You see, I'd had twenty years of schooling and then my training, and here we were in our thirties without a stick of furniture we could call our own, a couple of hundred dollars in the bank and an old station wagon. Often in Arbor we were paid nothing. Sometimes we were rewarded in produce—vegetables or meat or firewood or whatever—or in services, and when I heard that old Dr. Victor, who had been a general practitioner here for many years, was preparing to retire and was looking for someone to take over his practice, it was a chance for us to come home."

"And you left Arbor without a doctor?"

"No. Of course not. There was a young French-Canadian, a McGill graduate who had interned in the States, and he wanted to stay in this country. It was a good opportunity for him, and I'm sure he was good for Arbor. We came home and I went to work with Dr. Victor until he retired the next year and I assumed his practice."

"What motivated you to become a doctor?"

"Ego fulfillment, I suppose. Dr. Harrison A. Victor was our family doctor and delivered me and—interesting to me, at least, because I ultimately went to work with him—he was a boyhood hero of mine."

I might have said that Dr. Victor and anyone who played

53

major league baseball and had his picture on one of those baseball cards were my heroes. We collected those cards, hoarded them and traded them and gambled with them, flipping them out, trying to match either the face or the back of the card already flipped to the ground . . . Babe Ruth . . . Ty Cobb . . . Pie Traynor . . . Frank Frisch . . . Kiki Cuyler . . . Walter Johnson . . . spinning through the air.

They were almost mythical heroes, though, those major league ballplayers who played in distant cities, but Dr. Victor was of our town. He was the picture doctor, tall, slender, it seems to me gray-haired even then, his voice deep, his clothes immaculate. He wore a chesterfield and a gray Homburg, and for so long I feared him.

My first memory of him is when I must have been about four years old, my mother holding me on her lap by the window when his car drove up and he came in and, in that day before antibiotics, punctured my ear drum to reduce the pressure and drain the infection and avert mastoiditis. My second is of him holding the kitchen strainer over my face, while my father held my legs and my mother my arms on the kitchen table, and he did the adenoidectomy there to save them the money they did not have to hospitalize me. Then I remember him—possibly later that day or the next day—coming into the bedroom, and in my panic I would not let him near me until they let me hold the kitchen strainer.

Next I remember a winter afternoon, pulling my sled up the road that is now Alton Avenue and where we used to coast. I had picked up a piece of frozen snow from the bank at the side and I was sucking on it when his car came up behind me and he stopped and rolled down the window and said: "Thomas, if you're going to eat snow you're going to be ill, and your mother will be calling me to come and see you again."

A day or two later I was ill, probably with some respiratory ailment that had nothing to do with eating snow, and there he was, framed again in the bedroom doorway. Mixed with my fear of him must have been the belief that he knew everything and was everything.

"In those days," I told Beryl Williams, "all doctors, rightly

54

or wrongly, were held in high esteem. On the subject of medicine the lay world was largely unread and unknowing, and there were many doctors, as there are still a few today, who preferred to maintain a *mystique*. It made life much simpler never to be questioned. Up in Arbor, for example, if my predecessor, old Dr. Flamand, said a leg had to come off it came off. If there was any doubting, it wasn't expressed, and there was no request for a consultant because none was available. Even here, forty-five or fifty years ago, there was an aura of mystery and grandeur about a doctor. There certainly was, in my mind, about Dr. Victor. As I've said, he was a hero of mine, and for my own ego fulfillment I wanted to emulate him."

I wanted to emulate those major league ballplayers, too, until I found out that I am a physical coward. We played our pickup games on that field off Alton Avenue where that plastics manufacturing plant is now, and I had my dreams until we began to develop in our teens. Then the ball—always wrapped in black tape after the seams of the cover gave way—came up to the plate so fast and so hard that I stood, fearing it, in a getaway stance until that day I saw it coming and heard the crack of it fill my head and saw, I thought, white-yellow light and the world spinning and I came to on the ground.

"And as you shared his practice with Dr. Victor," Beryl Williams asked, "was he still a hero?"

"Oh, naturally I no longer looked upon him with the eyes of youth, but he remained an idol. He used his training, which wasn't as good as mine and nowhere near up to what they receive today, and he used his experience, which was vast, to the fullest, and he pushed himself hard. That's what you ask of a doctor, and he was a fine general practitioner."

"Ego fulfillment through hero emulation," Beryl Williams said. "If I may say so, that doesn't sound very noble."

"It isn't," I said.

"But surely, Doctor," she said, "you must have had some other, some deeper motivation."

"Such as what?" I said. I wanted to fend her off, because if we were going to get into philosophies of life I didn't want Beryl Williams to be my translator.

55

"I don't know what," she said, and now she was fending *me* off. "I simply think that ego fulfillment through hero emulation alone just wouldn't stand up under the stresses of a doctor's life."

"That may be so," I said, "but surely, in your article, you're not going to get into this kind of depth."

"Relax, Doctor," she said. "I'm just going to write a pleasant and I hope not too pedestrian piece about where you were born and grew up, your education, your professional background and what you do here every day."

"That will be fine," I said.

"For my own education, or edification, though," she said, "I'm interested in personal motivations."

"I suppose a writer would be," I said.

"There's a theory," she said, "that many, if not most, medical men are impelled to enter the profession because of the fascination of death. Do you subscribe?"

"When you use the word 'fascination,' " I said, "you mean fear."

"Well, yes."

"I'm aware of the theory," I said, "because we used to discuss it as medical students. Fear of death, of course, is perfectly natural, but one can't work very long in medicine without coming to accept death as a part of the cycle of life. One sees so much of it."

"That it becomes commonplace?" she said.

"No," I said. "I don't mean that at all. I mean only that many persons in other callings who don't deal with death regularly are able to postpone the recognition of it. Our society has been analyzed as a death-denying one. We're obsessed with youth and the attempt to retain it in appearance and activity. We resent the aging process because we are attempting to reject the reality of death. In our profession, of course, we deal with it almost daily and so we can't reject it."

"And so you can accept it?" she said. "I mean you, Dr. Thomas R. Hunter, personally?"

"I believe so," I said. "Of course, I haven't had to face that door yet."

What I told Beryl Williams is but a small part of it, and perhaps not the truth at all. I said that we who work in medicine come to accept death as part of the cycle of life. That is what we all say and it should be the truth, but I honestly do not know. I am not sure that any of us, until that moment, ever really knows, and I recall a conversation I had with a patient of mine who runs one of the ambulance services here. His name is Frank Baker and we were, as we still are, good friends and I was telling him that his X rays, which had just come back, revealed a tumor of the colon.

"Now don't be overly concerned, Frank," I said to him, "because it may very well be benign and easily operable."

"Tom," he said, "you people are really something."

"Something?" I said.

"That's right," he said. "You're always telling the patient not to worry, but you'd be worried yourself."

"Not until I knew there was real cause for worry," I said.

"C'mon, Tom," he said. "Don't try to kid me. Do you know who my most nervous customers are? You people. Doctors."

"If you say so," I said.

"If I *say* so?" he said. "I not only say so, but it's the truth. I've carried some of your people who were scared to hell."

But the doctor who is undergoing a massive heart attack knows, I was thinking, and the layman does not, but I said nothing. As it turned out, they took a malignant tumor out of Frank Baker, but they apparently got it all and that was more than five years ago and so he is certified as cancer cured. About the rest of us I do not know, because we who deal with death so often seldom speak of it among ourselves and never in relation to ourselves.

In fending off Beryl Williams I did not fend off myself. Although I used to debate and deny it in medical school, I know that behind first my fear of and then my adolescent idolization of Harrison Victor and my subsequent admiration of his profession lay that fear of death. We come into this life knowing only life, and although the realization that we will not live forever comes slowly it is implanted early.

It was implanted in me early at O. C. Tenner and Son. I

don't know whatever became of his son, but O. C. Tenner ran the funeral home that is now Barton and Davis in that big white mansion next to the furniture store on Schuyler Avenue. There was the thick carpeting and the carpeting on the stairs and the smell of flowers and the soft voices and there was my grandfather.

He was the first to go in my time, my father's father, and I could not have been more than six years old. He was a tall, erect man, with a full mustache and a deep voice and he would feign annoyance, clapping his hands to his ears and shaking his head at the noise I would make running through the house where we all lived. A week before, he had made for me, with his own hands, out of cardboard and strips of mirror he cut himself and chips of colored glass, my first and only kaleidoscope, and there he was now at O. C. Tenner's and I did not know why and they told me he was asleep.

They were to tell me, too, that my aunt was asleep, lying there unmoving at O. C. Tenner's and dead, I learned later, of a ruptured appendix and peritonitis. She was my father's youngest sister and a telephone operator and she, too, lived with us. Each day from work she would call the house and sometimes talk with me for whole minutes. Once a week, on payday I suppose, she would bring me something, a jar of candy, a bag of marbles, a coloring book. She bought me my first roller skates, and she was in her early twenties and they buried her in her wedding dress on what was to have been her wedding day.

They buried them all from O. C. Tenner's, my father's mother, my grandparents on my mother's side, an uncle who was my mother's brother. There were the rides in the fine black car of O. C. Tenner's that followed the hearse, and there was the cemetery and the minister's prayers and the lowering of them all into the ground and the first shovels of earth upon them. Then, for a week, there was the silence in the house, no music from the piano, no sounds of Amos 'n' Andy from the Atwater Kent that stood in a corner of the living room. The night after they buried my aunt I heard the rain start to fall on the roof and then against the window pane and then dripping on the window sill and I thought of my roller skates in the closet downstairs, and in my mind I saw the rain falling on my aunt and I cried, I guess, until I fell asleep.

"I'm curious about one other thing, Doctor," Beryl Williams was saying. "Are you a religious man?"

"Not in the formal sense," I said. "When one studies the functional efficiency of the human body in all its amazing complexity, however, and then gives some thought to this earth on which it lives and which in itself is but a minute part of the universe one has to believe in some unified, universal force. I suppose that makes me an eighteenth-century deist."

"Do you resent the formal religions?"

"I both resent and respect them," I said. "I resent any religion that imposes, or attempts to impose, doctrines that are contrary to what have come to be proven scientific facts. On the other hand, I respect very much what the formal religions mean to so many in times of stress and of tragedy. In fact, I have often actually envied those who, at such times, could find such support in their religious beliefs. As a doctor, and in spite of what I have said, I am grateful that they have that support. It's an aid to me in what I am trying to do for them."

"But as far as your own life is concerned," she said, "you're devoid of such support?"

"That's correct," I said, "and that may also be an answer to your question about motivation."

"In what way?"

"Oh," I said, "in the sense that we doctors are fortunate in having a philosophy of life built right into our profession. For example, I have had friends and I have had patients of my age who, being in other callings, were repeatedly troubled by doubt. Man is basically a noble being, and they doubted that what they were doing was making any contribution other than to themselves and their own families. This troubled and depressed them deeply."

"I can believe that," she said.

"Many mornings when they would get up," I said, "they would wonder what they were doing. A doctor doesn't have to be concerned with that. Each day, within your abilities, you are

59

going to aid others by easing pain, defeating disease and prolonging life. I was always aware of this, and thankful for it, as a general practitioner, and it would even apply now when I am not as closely involved with patients as I used to be."

"But after all your own years as a general practitioner," Beryl Williams said, "why did you give it up to take charge here?"

"You've already answered the question," I said. "It was all those years. It was all those years of broken sleep, and no weekends and no privacy."

I could have had my office outside the home, and after hours tell the answering service not to call me except in an emergency. That wasn't doctoring as I grew up to know it, however, and so my office was in my home, and when I would come in from calls for dinner before evening office hours there would be one or another of them there.

"Hi, Doc," he'd say. "I've got the boy here and he's runnin' a fever, but we know it's your dinnertime so we'll just wait and you enjoy your dinner."

Before I was halfway through dinner there'd be a half dozen more of them there, waiting. My wife would implore me to take my time and eat, please eat, but I couldn't with them all sitting out there.

Then there would be the imploring I, too, had to do. Twenty times a day I would be trying to convince them to follow my advice, or have the tests, or go into the hospital, or submit to the operation. Emotionally involved, I would be up and down, up and down, the adrenalin pouring out, stopping and starting again, and that is why we doctors get coronaries.

In the two years at Arbor and twenty-three here before I gave up the obstetrics I must have averaged fifty babies a year, and delivered over twelve hundred of them. I was delivering the children of children I'd delivered, and Dr. Victor in his forty-odd years delivered some grandchildren of his first deliveries. That sounded fine in the story they wrote about him in the *News-Argus* when he retired, and it was fine, I suppose, but after awhile the wonder of it disappears and it's work.

There was that woman south of here in Valley Farms who

was in her thirties and had been trying for years to get pregnant, and it had finally taken. She'd had inadequate prenatal care and was grossly overweight, and diabetes in the family led me to expect a large baby. On her last visit, which was about five weeks prior to delivery, the baby did seem large and, in fact, I thought we might have miscalculated the date. I couldn't feel the head in the pelvis, though, and the fetal heart was high on the right side, and now I was sure I was going to deliver a breech.

I had given the woman another appointment but she hadn't shown up, and then at about 10 o'clock at night I got the call that she had gone into labor. When I got down there I couldn't find the house at first and then recognized it by the usual sign: someone, the husband here, peering out between the curtains of a window, waiting for the doctor. He was an electrician, and their one-story white clapboard house was small but comfortably furnished, and he led me back to the bedroom.

The woman was very active, and when I still couldn't find the head in the pelvis I knew for certain it was a breech. After three and a half hours of labor the cervix had dilated about one and a half centimeters, the fetal heart was fine, the mother's condition was good but, considering the distance from my office and home, I decided I had better stay there.

I was there for almost three days. I called my office and canceled all appointments and house calls, suspending everything, and now all my world waited on this child, too. The woman kept on with the pains, dilating slowly, and after twenty-four hours the cervix was about two-thirds dilated, and she was exhausted.

"Oh, please don't let me lose my baby, Doctor," she was pleading. "Please don't let me lose my baby."

"You're not going to lose it," I kept assuring her. "The baby will be fine. It will just take a little more time."

To give her some rest I gave her 10 milligrams of morphine, and I got some sleep on the couch. Her mother had been summoned from somewhere to keep house and cook, but I ate very little and the husband ate almost nothing. He was one of those small, quiet men who very often marry larger women, and in periods of calm when we weren't napping and I wasn't on the phone to my office I played cards with him—gin rummy and hearts—to keep him from pacing the floor. I drew him out about his work, which didn't interest me, and about his background, which I forgot even as he recounted it, but I wanted to do something for him.

Finally I delivered the breech birth. It was a boy and they were delighted and I was, too. I was also physically and emotionally spent, and I left them with instructions and the assurance that I would call during the next day or two to see if they had made up their minds whether they wanted the child circumcised. The following day I had my office nurse try to call them, and the phone had been disconnected. Several days later I drove out of my way on house calls to stop by, but they had moved away. That house where, just days before, we had all gone through so much together, was empty. They had run out, not only on my bill and on me, but on all that we had shared there.

We are too paternal, we doctors, and when our patients slight us or turn against us it is as if we are being ignored or rejected by our own children. Some of us cannot help ourselves, however, and I remember that night I drove out through the blizzard to that child with pneumonia. She was a small, button-nosed, dark-eyed doll of a four-year-old girl and very ill. Her temperature was about 104 rectally, her pulse racing at something like 140, her respirations up to about 46. The mother was frantic, almost demented by the fear that she was going to lose her, and I feared we would, too. Of course they had the temperature in the house up to about 80, so I got them to turn the heat down and I got the bedroom window open and some of the covers off the child. I gave her 600,000 units of procaine penicillin in the buttocks and spent the night there sponge bathing her with rubbing alcohol and water and hovering over her while the parents prayed.

About dawn the child started to improve, and she came out of it. When I left, the parents were in tears, their relief and their gratitude was so great, but when I next saw them they were walking toward me down the sidewalk, the child between them, and they turned abruptly and crossed the street to avoid me because, I found out later, they had decided to go back to the doctor who had delivered the girl. Their rejection of me as a doctor did not hurt my professional pride, because only I can harm that, but their rejection of me as a man who had shared probably the most profound moment of their lives hurt my pride in all of us in the human race.

"Patients?" my wife would say. "I just don't understand them."

I would be out on house calls, by now working my twelfth or fourteenth hour, and someone would come to our door demanding to know why I hadn't been to his house yet, and then he would abuse me to my wife. Others would call on the phone and, berating my wife, reduce her to tears.

"But why?" my wife would say. "Why do they have to be like that?"

At such times, perhaps, it was that pride in the human race, more than anything else, that sustained me, and Beryl Williams and her generation would be appalled to know that I found it in that war. I found it, of course, in the acts of sacrifice that men made again and again for the men beside them, but most of all I found it in the horror of that slave labor camp we liberated in our drive to meet the Russians on the Elbe.

It was April, and between those towns east of the Ruhr the gently rolling farm land, rich brown and furrowed, ran as far as the eye could see. There was virtually no resistance to us then, and we raced across that countryside almost in glee until we came to that town with its V-weapon factory built a half mile into the hillside and its slave labor camp between the railroad yards, the Luftwaffe airfield and the SS barracks.

They had placed the camp there in the hope that, because of its proximity, we would not bomb the airfield and rail yards and barracks, but there was an enemy who had to be defeated before this war could be ended and so we bombed those objectives and in the process destroyed the camp, too. In that camp there were nine thousand political prisoners, in their zebra suits and fenced in like animals, and some who survived told us later how they ran in circles under that deluge of crashing explosives, of flame, of noise, of flying fragments of iron and concrete and of bodies and pieces of bodies, heads, arms, legs, torsos.

When we arrived there five days later there were twenty-seven hundred dead of the bombing and of starvation and thirst and dysentery and tuberculosis and pneumonia, and hundreds more were to die every day. As we walked through that rubble, the still living, who were little more than shrunken, yellowing cadavers of men, tried to raise themselves from among the dead and parts of the dead to salute us or just to touch our clothing, and soldiers who had been in it since the beaches and had seen much averted their eyes and some wept and others vomited.

We tried to assess what to do first, and as we made our determinations they were dying here and here and here, and then I saw that to which my mind has returned so often over the years when I have been oppressed by the selfishness and arrogance of men. There was a latrine area, without latrines, but a clearing of ground unmarred by bomb craters against a section of wire fence still standing, and I realized that these dying men crawled there, some inching their way like caterpillars on their stomachs. Then I watched, transfixed, for there was one who had relieved himself and had started back, trying to crawl, and had collapsed, and when I reached him and turned him over he was dead. I saw then, along that path of thirty yards or so winding among the craters and rubble, the bodies of a dozen or more others who, with their last strength and final breath, had crawled there and died alone rather than to urinate or defecate among their fellows, and I knew then and again that man is a noble creature.

For two days we buried them, we and every able-bodied male in the town, from boys still in their teens to the old burghers in their black overcoats and black hats. For two days we made them carry the shrunken, skeletal bodies and parts of bodies on improvised litters, on planks, on doors, on shutters, on window frames with blankets stretched over them and in boxes in a seemingly endless procession through the town and up the dusty, winding road to the hillside overlooking the town. We had made them dig there the common graves, sixty feet long, seven feet wide and four feet deep, and we made them lay them side by side there. Then we bulldozed them over, and I remember a small boy of about eight, suddenly appearing, suddenly jumping into one of the long graves, the bulldozer positioning, hovering just above him. Who he was or what he was doing there I don't know, but he had recognized his father among all those almost look-alikes, and we had to pull him off, sobbing and screaming. What became of him after that I don't know, and I don't know if today there is anything to mark that site on that hillside where we buried those thousands.

"So exactly what are your duties here in the E.R., Doctor?" Beryl Williams was asking.

"Well, they're in large part administrative," I said. "There's a lot of paper work, and it's my primary duty to keep things moving. We see forty-five thousand patients a year here, or an average of about a hundred and twenty-four a day, and during peak times I've got to be sure that there's a constant turnover in our booths and they're not backing up. If there's a log jam I've got to see what's causing it and get on the phone and get the medical or surgical or psychiatric people down here to clear it."

"And you don't treat any patients yourself?"

"Oh, yes. I'm sort of a playing coach, if you're familiar with sports."

"Not really."

"Well, my job is primarily supervisory, as I said, but there are times when we're very busy or when I can add something toward a diagnosis or treatment. Then I step in and play doctor again myself."

"And how do you get along with the younger doctors—the interns, for example?"

"I think that, for the most part, we get along well. I'm impressed by all that's been pounded into them and by the extent of their knowledge. As I think I indicated in speaking of old Dr. Victor, their training has been much better than what I received. I know I couldn't pass their exams, and as long as they know I know it I don't think we'll have any difficulty getting along."

There will be exceptions, of course, and this young Stern is going to be one of them. He's got a mind that may be brilliant, for all I know, but he's arrogant and, I'm afraid, insensitive.

"As a matter of fact," I told Beryl Williams, "I'm relearning a lot of medicine, thanks to the young and their training."

"Can you give me an example of that, Doctor?" she said.

"Yes. Yesterday—or it may have been the day before, because the days blend into one another here—we had a young male Negro, or black as I guess we're supposed to say now, with an ailment that I couldn't diagnose. One of the interns suggested that we run a test for sickle cell anemia. Sickle cell anemia occurs almost exclusively among blacks, and I hadn't had many blacks in my practice and I'd never seen it. Of course, I'd been reading up on it, but I wasn't that familiar with the test. He ran it, however, and he was right, and I learned something."

What I told Beryl Williams was accurate enough for a summation, but not all of it. After I had gone all over the patient and got what blood tests I thought were pertinent I came back to the nursing station, and Stern and Harvey Mosler, the surgical resident, were there and I went over it with them.

"That still leaves sickle cell anemia," Stern said. "Haven't you run the test?"

"I'm not that familiar with sickle cell anemia," I said, "or with the test."

"You're not familiar with it?" Stern said, as if I'd just said I can't recognize quinsy sore throat. "And you don't know the test?"

"That's what I said."

"I heard you, Doctor," Stern said, and when I looked at Mosler he was looking at me and shaking his head. "I just wanted to be sure."

We went back to that enlarged closet we call our lab, and it's a simple enough test. He made a solution of sodium metabisulfite and took a drop of that and a drop of the patient's blood. In twenty minutes we looked at it under the microscope, and could see the sickle-shaped cells.

66

"You see how simple it is, Doctor?" Stern said, walking away. "Any time."

Of course I was angered by his arrogance, and undoubtedly my ego was bruised, too. I have known his like before, though, and I have managed to live with them.

"Who was the intern, Doctor?" Beryl Williams wanted to know. "May I have his name?"

"Yes. His name is Stern. He's on today. He's rather short, dark hair, dark-rimmed glasses."

A couple of hours later Stern had a man in his thirties who was running a fever of 103. He'd done a work-up on him—eyes, ears, nose, throat, chest, abdomen, urine, and had prescribed aspirin, but he still had him down on his chart for FUO, or fever of unknown origin.

"And you've ruled out pneumonia, Doctor?" I said to him, after he'd signed the chart and I'd checked it.

"That's right," he said. "The lung fields were clear on auscultation and percussion."

"That's interesting," I said. "Let me take a look."

I went into the booth and put my stethoscope on the chest, front and back. I got clear sounding lung fields, and then I put the scope under the right armpit and I could hear the signs of congestion—the harsh breath sounds with crackles on inspiration—in a small area.

"On that fever patient," I said to Stern when I came out and found him, "I think if you put your scope on the right axilla you'll pick up some right upper lobe pneumonia."

He didn't say anything, but he went back into the booth. When he came out I was busy and we never mentioned it again, but when I looked at the chart later he had had the patient X-rayed, had crossed out FUO and written in right upper lobe pneumonia. He had given the patient 600,000 units of procaine penicillin and fortified the aspirin with penicillin orally. I suppose we were even for the day.

"If you're going to mention Dr. Stern," I told Beryl Williams, "there are others here who are equally worthy, and who are also helping to educate an aging practitioner."

There was that overdose of heroin that came in, that boy in

67

his late teens. Someone had found him on the floor of his room, completely out and barely breathing. His respirations were down to five a minute, and when we found the recent track in left forearm Mosler prescribed ten milligrams of Naline intravenously with a push, which means forcing it in rapidly, to start his respiratory center going again, and I hadn't known it as an antidote.

"We're kind of a team here," I told Beryl Williams, "and the hours are difficult, especially for the interns, and sometimes tempers get short. Whatever you write is up to you, but I wouldn't want anyone to feel left out, or be offended."

"That's fine with me, Doctor," she said. "I'd better not go into individuals, anyway, because I don't have the space. What I'd like to get, though, is some idea of what your typical day is like, beyond the playing coach thing. I mean, I'd like to get some sort of rundown on the kind of cases that come in here, avoiding the gruesome details."

"Well," I said, "about forty percent of our cases are emergencies, and the rest are walk-ins, many of whom would, in the old days, have gone to their family doctor. We get a lot of those on Monday mornings. They've been putting up with some minor ailment all weekend, and now the thought of having to go to work, too, sends them in here. They come here because their G.P., if they have one, isn't available. They know, too, that they can find a doctor here at any hour of the day or night."

"So what sort of cases," she wanted to know, "have you had already today?"

"Well, we had several children. We had a nine-year-old girl, a hit-and-run victim on her way to school."

"How is she?" Beryl Williams wanted to know.

"I don't know," I said. "She's up in the O.R. now, and I'll be calling Dr. Everett because I do want to find out."

It was two hours before they could get an O.R. for her, but as Bob Mabry said, she needed the time. He's a little too flip for a lot of people, I suppose, but he has impressed me more than any of the other residents here and what he actually said to Stern and Wyman was: "Relax. It's going to take this little lady a couple of hours to get ready for the prom, anyway."

What he meant was that, now that he and Cas Everett had assessed the damage and had an intravenous going, it was going to take that long to replace the blood loss and stabilize her before surgery. I don't know how much of it Stern and Wyman absorbed, but he gave them a fine lesson in the treatment of multiple trauma.

"Assessing multiple trauma," he told them, "is in many ways like working out a problem in mathematics. One and one make two. For example, when this girl came in here her blood pressure was 80 over 50 and her pulse was 130, and she was in shock. That's consistent with blood loss of a pint or more from the compound fracture of the femur and possible brain damage. As far as the compound fracture is concerned, pulses in the foot and the patient's ability to feel indicate that there is no arterial or major nerve damage at the site, and the estimable Dr. Everett cleaned the wound and put an antibiotic ointment on it.

"The simple fracture of the left tibia and the pelvic fracture are relatively incidental. The equally estimable Dr. Mosler inserted a Foley catheter into the bladder, and there was no trace of blood in the urine. The belly is soft, and when the patient vomited there was no blood in the vomitus. The patient is now wearing a nasogastric tube to keep her from aspirating any vomitus, and as there is still no evidence of blood there or in the urine we are not worried about the bladder, kidneys or stomach. In every ball game like this one, though, keep the spleen in the back of your mind for a later inning. Last year we had a young man here, victim of an auto accident. The day after he was released he was riding in a bus. It was rush hour and he was standing, holding onto a strap. The bus made a sudden stop, or hit a bump. It started the spleen going, and he bled to death on that bus.

"Now what about possible brain damage as cause of shock? I looked in the ears, and the absence of blood indicates there is probably no basal skull fracture. I checked out the pupils and the fact that they're equal and not widely dilated indicates that there is neither localized nor general intracranial pressure. The optic disks look like full moons, round and with their margins distinct, confirming this, and there's no sign of subconjunctival hemorrhage. Beyond that, there are no localized neurological signs. I got a knee jerk, weak but present, on the left and no Babinski. The X rays show nothing to contradict this, the patient is breathing well and showing signs of waking, and so when you add and subtract, the sum you come up with is: Ortho should and consequently will wait."

"While we're waiting for her blood to be cross-matched, though," Stern said, "why don't we give her some uncross-matched O-Negative?"

"Why bother?" Mabry said. "She's getting Plasmalyte 56 and half a gram of Keflin. Her blood pressure is now 90 over 60 and her pulse is 86, and they'll have her cross-matched in less than an hour."

"But why didn't Dr. Everett put a Thomas splint on the femur?" Stern said.

"You can ask him," Mabry said, "and he'll tell you she's not going to be transported anywhere but upstairs, so he stabilized it with sandbags. Remember, in this business the whole patient, not the particular injury, is the thing."

"Could be," Stern said. He had another patient's chart in his hands and he turned away and walked over and sat down at the counter to fill in the chart.

"You know something?" Mabry said to me. "I've seen this kid a couple of times now, and I think we ought to jack him up and drain his crankcase and do a ring job on his pistons. He's burning too much oil."

"Oh, I think he learned something," I said.

"The beginner's course?" Mabry said. "Trying to teach them multiple trauma, until they've seen enough of it, is like trying to teach them piano without a piano."

I believe Mabry became interested in medicine as a corpsman in Korea, and he got into it late. He told me once, when we were eating side by side in the staff cafeteria, that he is thirty-six years old, has two children and he owes $26,000 he borrowed in a half-dozen places to get through college and medical school.

One day he was down here at the nursing station, talking with several of us, and one of our interns was on the phone.

"Well," the intern said, when he hung up the phone, "I've got it."

"What?" Mabry said. "Neisserian infection?"

"No," the intern said. "My loan."

"Good," Mabry said. "Welcome to debtors' prison."

I was telling Beryl Williams now that, in addition to the girl hit by the car, we had had two other children that morning. One of them, a boy about a year old, a sheet metal worker with a pair of shears could have cured, but we get that sort of work here, too.

"He had his finger stuck in the brass ferrule of a lamp," I said, "and then we had another small boy who has lead poisoning from eating paint off the woodwork."

"How is he?" she wanted to know.

"I think he'll be all right," I said. "You'd have to see Dr. Emily Banks. She's the pediatric resident assigned here, and they've still got to make all the tests. On the patient's chart, though, she indicated that there didn't seem to be any evidences of severe brain or nerve damage. He's upstairs in the children's ward now, and they'll probably give him penicillamine, or something like that, with the expectation that the lead will be excreted in his urine."

"And the other cases?"

"We had a young woman who took an overdose of sleeping pills. She's all right, but this is the second time she's done it so she needs psychiatric help. We had another woman who fell downstairs and suffered a scalp wound. We had an old man who attempted to hang himself with an electric light cord, and there isn't much hope for him. He has one collapsed lung and the other is invaded by cancer. He's still here while we're waiting for a room upstairs. We had one mild heart attack—we get several of those a day, mild or severe—and we've had a number of people with respiratory ailments and other medical problems. Is that enough?"

"Plenty, Doctor," Beryl Williams said. "Tell me something, though. Do you really enjoy your work here?"

71

"I have up to now," I said. "I certainly enjoy the forty-hour week, and Mrs. Hunter and I enjoy uninterrupted dinners and unbroken sleep and evenings and weekends together for the first time in twenty-seven years."

"Oh, I forgot to ask, Doctor," Beryl Williams said. "Do you and Mrs. Hunter have children?"

"We lost an only child, a son, when he was seventeen. An auto accident."

"I'm sorry," she said. "Obviously I didn't know."

"That's all right," I said. "It was almost eight years ago."

It was almost eight years ago, and sometimes still it seems no more than eight days ago. It was July 8, and I was finishing up seeing patients in the office. There were two still to be seen when George O'Donnell, the detective who was a patient of mine, came in. He didn't look right, and as I stood in the doorway to my examining room, I motioned to him to indicate that if he wanted to see me right away I could take him then.

"It's all right, Doc," he said. "I'll wait."

I saw the remaining patients, and then I ushered him in.

"So?" I said. "How are you?"

"Not good, Doc," he said.

"Well," I said, "tell me about it, and we'll take a look."

"It's not me, Doc," he said. "It's your Tommy."

"My Tommy?" I said. "What's the matter with him?"

"Auto accident, Doc," he said. "He hit the Walnut Creek bridge, and he's gone."

"Gone?" I said. "What do you mean, gone? Where is he?"

"He's dead, Doc," George said. "He's in the M.C. morgue."

Dead? In the M.C. morgue? How could he be? Our Tommy? He had come in from caddying, and eaten early because he was going to pick up his girl. He was just upstairs showering while his mother and I ate. I was seeing my first patient when I glanced out the window and there he was in a clean white shirt, open at the neck, his sports jacket slung over his shoulder, walking toward that little Chevvy he'd fixed up. I had just seen him, it seemed only moments ago now, walking with that easy athlete's walk, right out there.

"I don't know what to say except I'm sorry, Doc," George

said. "You should also know it wasn't his fault. The two skid marks show that some maggot I'd like to get my hands on came around that curve too far to the left and Tommy was trying to avoid him when he hit the concrete guard rail. They're sure he went instantly, Doc. I'm awful sorry."

"I'm sorry that you had to tell me, George," I said. "I'm sorry for you, too."

"That's all right, Doc," he said. "Is there anything I can do to help around here?"

"No," I said. "I've got to go in and tell his mother now."

Tell his mother? Tell her that her son, with whom she had just spoken, is dead? Tell her that all the pains of birth, all the childhood sicknesses and hurts she nursed him through, all the lessons of life and living she had imparted to him were for this? Tell her that I wish that it were I instead of him? Tell her that I am ashamed that I am still alive, I who deceived him into believing that he, too, would have his chance at life?

I told my nurse and she broke down, and I called George O'Donnell back as he was getting into his car and asked him to see that she got home. Then I went in to find my wife, and I heard her on the phone in the hall, her voice free and laughing. I walked past her into the living room, and she finished talking and I heard her hang up the phone. Then she came into the living room, starting to tell me something—I don't know what —and when she saw me she stopped.

"What's wrong?" she said.

I didn't know how to tell her. I, who have had to tell so many, knowing each time that what I was about to tell them would change their lives and their worlds forever and hurt them as they had never been hurt before, now could not find the way to tell my own wife.

"It's Tommy," I said, going to her.

"What's the matter with him?" she said.

"He was forced off the road and hit the Walnut Creek bridge," I said, "and he's gone."

"Gone?" she said. "What do you mean, gone?"

"He's dead," I said.

We cried together then, and in the days and weeks that fol-

73

lowed I know she tried to shield me from her grief even as I tried to shield her from mine, for there are events and times that are beyond the help of tears because they are beyond understanding. The accidental death is outside the cycle of nature, and so outside any rationalist philosophy of life.

For a long while I was embittered, resentful in particular of those of our Tommy's age who appeared aimless and conscienceless in the thoughtless pursuit of their own pleasures and propagation. My wife lost herself in the intensification of her own work for others, causes and people, and in my own practice I worked harder than ever before, but not as well. I had too little patience for the hypochondriacs and malingerers whom I had always accepted as needing help, and at best I was little more than professional with most of the others until one evening after dinner my wife forced me out of it.

"Don't you see," she said, "what you're trying to do in your resentment and judgment of yourself and me and everyone who has survived Tommy? You, who have always refused to accept the concept of a God, are now trying to play God yourself. What makes you think that you qualify for the role and have the right to sit in such Supreme judgment?"

She was right, of course, and time has grown new tissue over the wound, but there is still the scar in me as there is in her. The week after Tommy's death I gave his golf clubs to his best friend, and I have never used mine or played the game since. There are good days, crystal clear spring mornings and soft summer evenings, but the best times are still for me often the worst times for I still live with my own guilt in living.

Then there are the reminders, as there were today when Frank Baker brought in the girl hit by the car and I had to speak with her parents. Their name is Wade, and they are quiet people, almost timid, and the father is the superintendent in the apartment house where they live. I told them all we knew at the time, summing up for them, as we always do, all of the fortunate factors and assuring them of the care she would receive.

"But she was on her way to school," the father said. "She was just going to school."

I know, I wanted to say. I know that she is innocent, even as our Tommy, with his high code of ethics and his empathy and concern for others, was innocent, and there is no explanation that we know for such injustice. A few minutes later George O'Donnell came in. He was picking up the girl's clothes to take them to the state laboratory in the hope that they may find traces of paint from the car that hit her.

"I don't give it much chance, Doc," he said, "and another maggot will get away. I'm tired of this business, Doc. I've been in it too long."

I am tired of my business, too, because I have been in it too long, and my business has been my life, especially since our Tommy's going. We die by bits and pieces, too much and too often with too many others, in this business, but out of our Tommy's going has come the conviction and trust that when my wife and I come to that door we shall pass through it more easily for our Tommy's going first. He took so much of us with him, for he was our son.

"As I look through my notes now," Beryl Williams was saying, "another thought comes to mind. I can understand how, after all your years in general practice, you eventually found the patient load too much. I can understand, too, how you and Mrs. Hunter enjoy the regular schedule and your free time. It would seem to me, though, that there would be times when you would miss it. I mean, that in your own practice you would most often be solely responsible for your patients, and so the reward when you succeeded in a difficult case would be much greater than here."

"Where I'm sort of a cog in a large machine?" I said. "Yes, that's true to some degree. A patient I see here I've probably never seen before and I'll probably never see again. If he goes upstairs I don't know what becomes of him unless I call and ask, and we're so busy here that I seldom call. In trying to answer you honestly, I suppose I must admit that I miss the respect that my patients used to have for me, but that respect was a burden, too. Actually, I welcome the lack of intimacy, the absence of personal involvement, because at my stage in life it makes my work much easier."

There was that lonely old man we had today, that Mr. Kobak, who had tried to hang himself. After we got his X rays we called Thoracic, and Ian Johnson came down and went over them with Stern and me. The old man had a left pneumothorax, meaning that there was an air leak, probably caused by a ruptured bleb, or blister, on the lung, and the air entering the pleural cavity had collapsed the lung. That was no problem, because Ian could drain that, but the pictures of the other lung showed a mass, upward from the right hilar area, or root of the lung, that, even before he got a sputum test or a biopsy, Ian said he would guarantee was cancer.

"You know what I would recommend," Stern said, in that way of his. "I'd recommend that we give him the electric cord back."

I went in to see the old man while we were holding him in a booth until they could get a bed for him upstairs. I would guess that he farmed once for a living, but he is hard of hearing and speaks, as he breathes, with difficulty, and so I did not go deeply into his background, even as I did not want to or have to.

"How long have you been having trouble breathing?" I asked him as he lay there on his back, staring up at the ceiling.

"Quite a while," he said, after I had repeated the question so that he could hear it.

"How long is that?"

"Three or four years."

"Have you ever been sick before?"

"No, not really," he said.

"Do you take any medicines?"

"Nope," he said. "I'm eighty years old."

"I know that," I said, "and I understand that you tried to take your life."

"What's that?" he said.

"I understand that you tried to commit suicide," I said.

"That's right," he said.

"Why?" I said.

"I've lived long enough," he said.

"Do you have any children?"

"Yep, two," he said.

76

"Then you've got someone to take care of you?"

"Well, once in a while," he said.

"Mr. Kobak," I said, "the reason you're short of breath is that you've got a collapsed lung. When you go upstairs, Dr. Johnson is going to put a tube in there, and drain it into a bottle."

"But I don't want him to," he said. "I don't want to stay in bed."

"It won't hurt," I said, "and you'll be able to breathe more easily again."

"But I don't care," he said. "Don't you understand? I just want to go home."

Ian Johnson, or someone else, would get his permission, or get it from one of his children, but I did not have to do it. I did not have to tell him, either, about the other lung, for he was not my patient and I was glad of that, that I do not know him any better than this, or know his family.

"And you don't miss the prestige?" Beryl Williams was asking. "We were talking earlier about your hero emulation and the ego fulfillment of a general practice."

"Not really," I said. "At least I haven't missed it up to now. One needs that at first, when one is young, but you come to realize that although some patients may almost worship you it doesn't change what you yourself really are."

While I was answering, I saw one of our orderlies, an angular, long-haired, rather unusual young man whom I haven't deciphered yet and named Arnold, standing in the doorway. Behind him were Frank Baker and his ambulance assistant, and on their rolling cot they had a body with a sheet drawn up over the face.

"I'm sorry," I said to Beryl Williams and I stood up, "but we're going to have to vacate this room. If there are any other questions we can talk for a few minutes more outside."

"That's all right, Doctor," she said, standing up, too, but checking her notes. "Let's see. I've asked you that, and I don't think there's anything more."

Frank Baker had nodded to me, and they had moved their cot in against the bed near the door. They were lifting the

77

body now from the cot to the bed, and Beryl Williams glanced over toward them and then back.

"Oh, I'm sorry," she said, lowering her voice almost to a whisper. "I certainly don't want to disturb any patients."

"That's all right," I said. "You haven't."

As we walked out, Father Tim Shea, the Catholic chaplain here, was coming toward the holding room, and we nodded as he passed. He must be in his late thirties now, and although he and his family were not patients of mine, I remember him as a wiry little sandy-haired kid growing up in the neighborhood.

"He's rather nice, isn't he," Beryl Williams said.

"Yes, he is," I said. "Everyone is very fond of him here."

"I'm just thinking that I might do an article about him sometime," she said, not associating his presence at the moment. "I might just ask Clarity about that."

After she left I had a 2 o'clock meeting in the Nursing Office about revising the Emergency Room rotation schedule for student nurses, but I wasn't there more than five minutes when Harvey Mosler, the medical resident, called me back.

"It's that Mr. Kobak," he said. "It looks like he's done it this time."

V

AGED AREA RESIDENT TAKES OWN LIFE AT COUNTY MED CENTER

BY JAY WHALEN

Anton Kobak, 80, of Market Road, Valley Farms, took his own life early this afternoon in the Emergency Room of the County Medical Center where he had been brought earlier in the day after an apparent first attempt at suicide in his own home had failed. The long-time area resident succeeded in his second attempt when, in a booth in the Emergency Room, as he was about to be treated for a respiratory disorder, he plunged a scalpel into his heart.

According to hospital authorities Kobak, a former dairy farmer, had been brought to the Center by ambulance shortly after 8 A.M. and after a neighbor had found him lying on the kitchen floor with an electrical extension cord around his neck. When the "News-Argus" reached the neighbor, John Williams, 62, also of Market Road, by telephone he gave the following account:

"I stopped by to see him because he hadn't been feeling well, and when I did I found him lying on the floor with the electric cord around his neck. He was conscious, and when I asked him what happened he said he had tried to hang himself from the light fixture in the ceiling but the cord slipped. He said he didn't want to live any more, so I called the ambulance."

At the Emergency Room, the hospital spokesman said, an examination of Kobak and X rays taken of his chest revealed that his left lung had collapsed as a result of pneumothorax—air entering the pleural cavity. The spokesman, John J. Clarity, public relations director of the Medical Center, said that a relatively minor operative procedure to drain the air from the pleural cavity and permit re-expansion of the lung had been planned. It was then, according to the police, that Kobak seized a scalpel from a surgical kit in the booth and plunged it several times into his chest.

"The patient reported he had experienced difficulty in breathing for some time," Clarity said, "and when questioned by Emergency Room personnel about his apparent previous attempt to take his own life had evidenced mental depression."

The investigation of the death was conducted by De-tective Sergeants George O'Donnell and Joseph Garrett. County Coroner James J. Marty signed the death certificate, attributing the cause to self-inflicted stab wounds of the heart.

Kobak, a widower for the past four years, was born in Erie, Pa., on January 27, 1893, and had been a resident of Valley Farms for more than fifty years. He had operated a dairy farm there until about ten years ago. He is survived by a son, Anton, Jr., and a daughter, Mrs. Harold Bryer, both of Alton, three grandchildren and one great-grandchild. Funeral arrangements have not yet been completed.

VI

GEORGE O'DONNELL

When I first took this job thirty-three years ago come May 22 I gave crime just about six more months in this city. I mean I was going to put on that blue suit with the shiny buttons and the shiny badge and the nippers and the billy and the service .38 Smith & Wesson with the twelve extra cartridges, and there wasn't any way that crime could survive in this town.

I was twenty-five years old at the time, and that's how bright I was. I was the Beautiful Dreamer. For three years I was on the list, but this was still the Depression and, compared to everybody else, cops and firemen were living good for a change, and nobody was taking his voluntary retirement. You had to wait for somebody to reach the mandatory age, die a natural or accidental death or get killed in the line of duty. So there I was, itching to get on and play cops and robbers, and finally I made it and the first assignment they gave me was crossing guard at the DeWitt Clinton elementary school on East Fifth.

For me that was the worst duty on the roster, because my heart was in my mouth every time those kids crossed the street, and I figured I wasn't going to catch many criminals there, either. I was thinking of that again since yesterday morning, because the first call I took was a hit-and-run over there on East Fifth where some maggot ran a light and hit a nine-year-old black girl on her way to school.

We'll never get him. I've got four witnesses, and two of them say the car was dark blue, one says it was black and the other thinks it was dark green. Nobody got any numbers, but two of them think it might have been a Plymouth or a Dodge and the one woman has no idea and the other guy thinks it might have been a Ford.

I went over to the Medical Center to pick up the kid's clothes and take them over to the State Lab, and Tom Hunter is there at the M.C. now. He was my doctor for years before he took the job in the Emergency Room, and he thinks the kid will live, but while I'm talking with Tom I'm remembering six or seven years ago when I had to walk into his office one summer evening and tell him his own kid was dead. Another maggot we never had a chance at forced that boy of Tom's off the road into the Walnut Creek bridge, and that's the trouble with this business. After awhile you take the good collars you've made for granted, but you never forget the ones that get away, and it's a terrible thing to have to tell a parent that his kid is in the M.C. morgue.

Yesterday I should have rented a white coat, because I no sooner got back from the lab than I was over at the Emergency Room again. They had this old man in there, a farmer named Kobak, and he'd tried to take his own life by hanging himself. Some neighbor of his found him on the floor in his kitchen, and when they got him into the Emergency Room they found he had a collapsed lung and probably cancer, too. They left him alone for a couple of minutes, which was the mistake, and he grabbed one of those scalpels and stabbed himself three times in the chest and penetrated his heart.

In the beginning, when I was a rookie, I used to romance every death, automobile victim, homicide, suicide, all of them. Not any more. Now a body is just a body, not a man who used to like to hunt or fish or a woman who wrote a poem, and if I didn't know them alive I don't want to know them dead. For that old farmer yesterday I said a silent prayer, that his soul may rest in peace, but I felt more for Tom Hunter.

It wasn't Tom's fault. When it happened he was up at a meeting, and if they want to give anybody the bag to carry they can give it to a young doctor, an intern named Stern. He was the one who left the old man alone with the surgical kit in the booth, but Tom wants to take the rap.

"We all knew he had tried to take his life," Tom was telling

Joe Garrett and me, "but I was the one who talked to him about it. I should have known that, given the chance, he might try it again."

"He was despondent?" Garrett said.

"Yes," Tom said. "He said he tried to hang himself because he felt he'd lived long enough. He had two grown children, but my feeling was that he didn't want to burden them, or that maybe they didn't want to be bothered by him. I should have seen to it that he was in either booth 1 or 2, where he could be observed from the nursing station, and I should have warned everybody not to leave him alone with access to anything he could use to harm himself."

The way Tom explains it, they've got a real problem in the E.R. The nursing station should be in the middle of the room, so that they can see into every booth. Instead, it's in one corner and there are three big columns in the middle of the room. Two of them cut off the view of four booths across the room and they can't see into any of the booths along the other wall, so I would say some architect should carry this bag, too.

So after we talked with Tom Hunter we sat down in the Poison Control Room, in the back of the E.R., with the nurse. Her name is Kathleen Conley and she's twenty-six years old and a little thing, and she was almost in tears.

"I don't think I did anything wrong," she said. "I really don't."

"So just relax," I told her. "No one is saying you did anything wrong."

"I think Dr. Stern thinks it's my fault," she said.

"Let's not worry about Dr. Stern," Garrett told her. "You just tell us what *you* know about it."

The way we got it from Tom Hunter and her, they were going to do this minor operation on the old man. A resident doctor was coming down from upstairs to put a tube in the old man's chest and drain the air out so that his lung could expand again.

"So Dr. Stern told me to prepare the patient," this nurse, Conley, told us.

"So what did you do?" Garrett said.

83

"I helped him out of his clothes," she said, "and into a gown. Then Dr. Stern came into the booth again and told me to get a closed thoracotomy kit."

"A closed what?" Garrett said, and I'm glad he asked. "And can you spell it?"

"I think that's right," she said, after she'd spelled it. "I'm so nervous."

"And this kit was closed?" Garrett said. "It had a cover that was closed?"

"Oh, no," she said. "The kit is really sterile instruments wrapped in sterile towels. The 'closed' goes with 'thoracotomy.' It means they weren't going to open the patient's whole chest. They were just going to make an incision in it."

"Oh," Garrett said.

The way we got it later, this kit contained a local anesthetic, a scalpel, scissors, clamps and an instrument they call a trocar. It's a plastic tube with a sharp pointed insert, and after they make an opening between the ribs they put that tube in there and shove the sharp pointed insert into the chest cavity. Then they pull the insert out and connect the tube to another tube, to drain the air into a bottle with water in it. In this business you learn everybody else's business.

"So then, after you brought this kit," Garrett said, "what did you do?"

"Well, Dr. Stern took the towel off and saw the kit was complete," she said, "and then he sent me for the underwater drainage bottle."

"And how long did it take you to get that?" I said.

"Well," she said, "I went down to Minor Ops, where we usually do these, but they didn't have a bottle there. Then I went to our main supply here and got one, and it must have been two or three minutes."

"And then what?" I said.

"And then I saw the patient," she said, shaking her head and her eyes filling up. "I saw the scalpel handle sticking out of his chest and the blood and . . ."

"That's all right," I said. "Just remember that the old man didn't want to live."

"I know," she said.

"And Dr. Stern wasn't in the booth when you came back with the bottle?" Garrett said.

"No, sir," she said. "He wasn't."

So we interrogated this Stern. He's a little guy, black hair, black-rimmed glasses, and one of those real smarts.

"As we understand it, Doctor," I said, "you were the last one to see the patient alive."

I'm trying to be diplomatic. I don't come right out and say that apparently he was the one who left the old man alone, but now listen to the music we got.

"I don't know that that's a fact," he says.

"All right," Garrett says, "if you weren't the last to see him alive, who was?"

"I'm not a detective," he says. "You are, but if you want to know something, it could have been any number of people. It could have been the nurse."

"We've already talked to Miss Conley," I say, "and she tells us you two were in the booth with the patient and you sent her for a bottle. When she came back with it, she says, she found the patient alone, with the scalpel in his chest."

"And if you want to dust it for fingerprints," he says, "I'll tell you now you'll find mine on it, because I was the one who extracted it from his chest."

"Doctor," I said, "how long have you been in this work?"

"What work?" he says. "Medicine?"

"No," I said. "Police work."

"What do you mean?" he says.

"Look, Doctor," Garrett says. "When you left the booth the patient was still alive, right?"

"That's right," he says.

"And there was no one else in the booth, right?"

"That's right."

"And I presume you left the booth for some emergency?" Garrett says.

"What difference does it make?" he says. "I don't see that it's any of your business why I left the booth."

85

"We're making it our business," I said, and I'd had enough of this. "Why did you leave the booth?"

"Well, if it really interests you, although I can't see why it would," he said, "I had another patient's chart to complete. The patient was ready to leave, and I had to sign the chart. I walked over to the nursing station, and I checked the chart and signed it."

"And then you came right back?" Garrett says.

"As I was walking back," he says, "I heard the nurse scream. When I got back there wasn't anything that anybody could do to save the old man."

"Thank you, Doctor," I said, standing up.

"If you want to know why this happened," he said, "it's because this room isn't designed right. The nursing station should be in the middle of the room where you can see into all booths."

"We understand that," I said, "and if we run into the architect we'll take it up with him."

"And, meanwhile," Garrett says, "you think it's a good idea to leave a patient, who has already tried to commit suicide, alone in a room with a scalpel on a tray within reach?"

"I'm not a psychiatrist," this Stern says, "and I'm not a male companion. I've got other things to do here than hold patients' hands and besides, if you want to know the truth, the old man didn't have long to live anyway."

"Thank you, Doctor," I said. "We understand how busy you are."

"You're welcome," he says, and he goes marching out.

"Tell me one thing," Garrett says to me. "Don't these guys have to take some kind of an oath or something before they let them become doctors?"

So today I called the lab and they've got nothing off that girl's clothing, and Garrett and I are catching up on the paper work they load you with these days. The phone rings and Garrett answers it, and I can tell from the way he takes that cigar with the inch of ash on it carefully out of his mouth and places it on the corner of the desk that he's getting some kind of banjo music that he doesn't enjoy. He's got some idea that the cigar

86

smokes better with the ash on it, and we'll go out on some burglary and he'll walk around the house with that cigar never out of his mouth and that ash on it, and the woman of the house will be following him with an ash tray.

"Look, madam," he says finally, "just tell your brother-in-law to go out and get a lock and put it on the door. What? How do I know where the nearest hardware store is? No, madam, the police department does not put locks on doors except forever."

I'm involved in a very interesting criminal investigation, too. We've got this Rules and Procedures manual. It's a loose-leaf with 283 pages in it already, and almost as many pages of amendments, and I'm adding the new ones that have been on the bulletin board for a month.

"Subject—Procedure for Obtaining Search Warrants when the Court is Closed."

"Subject—Envelopes for the Transportation of Fingerprint Reports of Criminal Identification."

"Subject—Safety Measures in Connection with Ice Rescues."

When the phone rings again I catch it, and it's Langer's. They think they've spotted a booster in their book department, and it's only two blocks away so we're over there inside five minutes.

Harry Webber meets us at the back door, and he was going to make the collar if we didn't get there in time. He had his twenty-five years in the department when he left to be security at Langer's, and he leads us through the stock room and out onto the first floor through children's clothing to where the book department is off in a corner next to stationery and office supplies.

The suspect is still there. He's in his twenties, clean-looking and wearing a raincoat and carrying a shoe box wrapped in white paper under his left arm. We stand off at a distance, and I'm watching over Webber's shoulder while Garrett goes around to the other side. I'm hoping Garrett doesn't get too close, because even though the cigar is out now he's still got it in his mouth and he doesn't look much like a book reader. While I'm watching I see the suspect with a book in his right hand start to look around sort of casually. I turn away, and when I turn back I see the hand with the book go under his other arm and come back empty.

That's enough, so I shake my head to Garrett. We just wait, then, for the suspect to leave and finally, after about ten minutes, he takes a paperback up to the counter and pays for it and puts the receipt for it in the book, and he ambles out the front door where Garrett stops him and flashes the potsy on him.

"May I see your purchases?" Garrett is saying to him when Webber and I come up.

"Why, sure," he says. "I bought this paperback. I paid for it, and the receipt's right in it."

"And this other purchase?" Garrett says.

"Oh," he says, and he's got the shoe box in his hands now, "these are shoes. I didn't buy them here. I got them over at Fine's. You can see their name on the wrapping."

Garrett takes the box, and Fine's name is printed all over the paper and it's all sealed with transparent tape. Then Garrett shakes the box and you can hear something moving in there, and he pushes one end of the box and it's flapped. Then he turns it up and shakes it and two books start to slide out.

"How many you got in there?" he says.

"Five or six," the young guy says. "I'm not sure."

"Let's take a ride," Garrett says. "Shall we?"

"Why not?" the young guy says.

We take him back and into the squad room, give him the spiel about his rights, and he still explains his whole operation. He's very nice about it. He says he's been doing it for about four months, and he just takes books that are on the best-seller list and ones that have just come out and got good reviews. His family lives downstate, and when he goes home about once a month he takes them down there and unloads them at a cut-rate book store.

"What do you get for them?" I ask him.

"Oh, 15 to 30 percent," he says, "depending on the book."

"You work?" Garrett says.

"Yeah," he says. "I'm a night clerk, or I was until now, at the Wayside Motor Inn."

"You on the stuff?" I say.

"Yeah," he says.

"What does it cost you a day?" Garrett says.

"A day I don't know," he says, "but about fifty-sixty a week."

"You ever fall before?" I say.

"Fall?" he says.

"Been arrested?" I say.

"No," he says.

So Garrett is typing him up, and I go over to the print board and ink the pad. Then I ask him to step over, and as he walks up I see him wipe his fingers on his pants.

"I thought you said you never fell before?" I say.

"That's right," he says.

"C'mon," I say. "I was beginning to like you. Now I watch you wiping the sweat off your fingers. You've been to bat before."

"It's just not my day, is it?" he says.

"How many times?" I say.

"Just once," he says. "They dropped me back home."

"Boosting books?" I say.

"No," he says. "Cameras."

This young guy is like a breath of fresh air. Today, with all the civil liberties gaff, you're lucky if they'll tell you their names without a court order. You're the enemy who's against freedom, where in the old days you were the hero who was protecting freedom.

When I was a kid Mike Finnegan had the beat in the neighborhood and I don't think he ever made a big collar in his life because there wasn't that much crime there, but everybody looked up to him, even after he hit you across the butt with the nightstick for playing stoop ball. We used to play at Old Lady Kurtz's, because she had the only cement steps on the block, and up would go the window and out would come her head, and she had a voice like the Third Street fire siren.

If Finnegan didn't get you that day he'd get you in the next day or two. If he caught you running you'd get the stick across the butt, and you'd always get the lecture and you'd always hope that he wouldn't take it to your house where your old man would lay his belt to you.

Years later, my first morning on the force, who's turning out the platoon but Mike Finnegan, and he's a sergeant now. I'm about to march out to catch criminals crossing the street at the DeWitt Clinton school when he stops me.

"Say," he says, "don't I know you from somewhere?"

"Probably," I say.

"Yeah," he says. "You're the O'Donnell kid who's always playing stoop ball at Mrs. Kurtz's."

"Not any more," I say.

Today a cop on the beat rousts some kids throwing rocks at a street light, and they're all lawyers. They're only in grammar school, but they know all about their rights. The cop doesn't tell their parents. *They* do, and the parents come in demanding to know who this cop thinks he is, talking to their children that way.

We're all Fascists. About a month ago Garrett and I have the night duty, and just before midnight we get a call that somebody's breaking into the Stereo Shop over on Fourth Avenue. The prowl car is there, covering front and back, and we go in the window they jimmied in the back and we can hear them upstairs. When we start up they hear us and take off to the roof. We chase them across two roofs, down a fire escape where one of them gets away, and we get the other in a blind alley.

We take this maggot back to the squad room and before he'll even give us his name he's got to call his lawyer. While we're waiting for his lawyer to show we stick him in the cage, and when the lawyer comes in he's a young long-hair and we get a lecture on democracy.

"What's this man doing in that cell?" he says.

"He's resting," I say.

"He hasn't even been booked yet, has he?" he says. "What right have you to incarcerate him? This isn't Nazi Germany. Don't you know that good men died to defeat Fascism in this world?"

"I know," Garrett says, "and while you were still in grade

90

school I was one of them who damn near died. You want to see my Purple Hearts if I can remember what I did with them?"

"In this country," the lawyer says, "we believe a man is innocent until he's proven guilty."

"I know," Garrett says. "It's just because we thought he was innocent when we found him and his partner in that loft that we chased him over two roofs and down a fire escape and into an alley. We just wanted to tell him that, but he wouldn't stop running."

So, like I say, this young guy we collared in Langer's is a pleasure. We book him with no trouble, give him his phone call and stick him in the cage with his paperback to read until we can get him arraigned in the court in the afternoon. Meanwhile, Garrett is still filling out the DD66, which is the long form of the DD45, on him, when we catch a homicide over on Washington. It's in one of those old brick row houses that used to be private homes when the neighborhood was white. Now it's black, with four or five families living in every one of them, and when we get over there it's like walking into a slaughterhouse.

The prowl car is there, and we go up the stairs between the spectators to where the victim is lying on her back on the kitchen floor. She's black, in her midthirties and she's wearing a black skirt and a white blouse that's out at the waist and her throat has been slashed and she's been stabbed numerous times in the chest and there's blood soaking her clothing on the floor and splashed on the walls.

"Good God!" Garrett says. "What went on here?"

"We got the perpetrator," one of the uniformed men says.

"Good," I say. "Let's see him."

"It's not a him," he says. "It's a her."

There's some rock music blasting from a white plastic radio standing on the windowsill, and Garrett turns that off and they bring in this black woman. She's sort of semi-stout, and wearing a pink housecoat with blood spattered all over it, and they've got her cuffed behind her back.

"And here's the weapon," the other uniformed man says. He hands Garrett a rolled-up sheet of newspaper, and Garrett opens it and inside there's a bloody long-bladed boning knife.

"Ma'am," I say to her, and she's standing there, looking down at the victim. "I don't believe I know your name."

"You an officer?" she says.

"That's right," I say. "Sergeant Garrett and I are detectives."

"My name's Annie," she says.

"Well, Annie," I say, "you know that you're entitled to legal counsel, to a lawyer."

"We explained that to her," one of the uniformed men says.

"I don't need no lawyer," she says.

"Then you understand," I say, "that you don't have to answer our questions at this time. You look to me, though, like an honest woman who always tells the truth."

"That's right," she says. "I'm an honest woman that always tells the truth. Everybody know me tell you that."

"Annie," Garrett says. "Is this your knife?"

"That's right," she says.

"And you brought this knife into this room?"

"No, sir," she says. "The knife stay in this room. This my kitchen, and the knife stay in that drawer there."

"Then this lady came to your kitchen?" Garrett says.

"That's right," she says. "She no good."

"And you took this knife out of the drawer there," Garrett says, "and you stabbed and cut this woman with it?"

"Yes, sir," she says.

"And you cut her under the chin there?" Garrett says.

"Yes, sir," she says. "Then I also stab her all over, but she kick me first."

"I'll tell you what we'll do," I say to the uniformed man. "Let's take the cuffs off in back and put them on in front."

"Sure thing," he says.

"This is a nice woman," I say, "and she's going to help us. Right?"

"That's right," she says.

"Are those all right now?" the uniformed man asks her.

"Yes, sir," she says, looking down at the cuffs. "You sure you got them locked?"

"Yes, ma'am," he says.

"I ain't goin' anywhere anyway," she says.

"Tell me something, Annie," I say. "When were you last arrested?"

"Is that her heart?" she says, looking down at the victim. "Is she movin'?"

"No," Garrett says. "That's just muscular reaction."

"Oh," she says.

"When were you arrested last?" I say.

"Let's see," she says, thinking. "It's hard to remember."

"How many times have you been arrested?" I say.

"Well," she says, "one time in Trenton, New Jersey. A fella hit me, I was livin' with. You see that scar here on my head?"

"So what happened?" Garrett says.

"So when he come at me and hit me I hit him."

"With what?" Garrett says.

"An ax," she says.

"You kill him?" Garrett says.

"No," she says.

"Look, Annie," I say, "are you legally married now, or are you common law?"

"Legally," she says. "I got my license in my bag."

"Where were you married?" Garrett says.

"You know what she say to me?" Annie says, looking down again at the victim. "She say: 'You don't have to accuse me no more. I tell you the truth. I got your man now.' All the time she say that, talkin' about how she get anything she want from my man and I get nothin' but beaten up. Then she call me names. Then she say to me: 'I don't need nothin' now. I got all your man can give me, and his money, too.'"

"Look," Garrett says to me, "let's get out of here and take this in."

"Annie," I say, "have you got a dress you can bring along with you? We have to have this one you're wearing checked out."

"You know somethin' else about her?" she says, still looking down. "She very quiet, but she sneaky with it all."

"Annie," Garrett says, "have you got another dress?"

93

"Sure I got another dress," she says, "but she got no right to talk to me that way."

At this juncture in the conversation I look over toward the door and there's a little black kid standing there. He's about seven or eight years old, and he's looking in and following the talk back and forth with his head and his eyes.

"Annie," I say, "is that your boy?"

"No, sir," she says, and then she nods toward the victim. "That's her boy. I feel sorry about that boy."

"That's right," the uniformed man says. "He's the victim's son."

"Does he realize what's happened?" Garrett says.

"I guess so," the uniformed man says. "He was crying when we got here."

"Does he have any family now?" Garrett says.

"I guess not," the uniformed man says. "We inquired about that, and they say there was just the two of them."

"Then we better take him in with us," Garrett says, "and call Child Welfare."

"It's too bad about that boy," Annie says. "I feel sorry about that boy."

"And you feel sorry about this woman, too?" Garrett says.

"Yeah," Annie says. "I believe I do. I didn't mean to kill that girl, but you know somethin'? She boastin' all the time. She all the time sayin': 'I got your man, and you ain't gonna do nothin' about it.' She got no right to say that."

So we took Annie with us, and the uniformed men brought in the kid. Garrett and the boss took Annie into the boss's office and got the stenographer, and Annie went over all of it again. When they pulled her record it turned out she'd been in the State Mental Hospital for eight months, but some shrink had stamped her walking papers and with it, the way it turned out, the victim's death warrant at the same time.

While Garrett and the boss were combing out Annie, though, the boy was sitting there in the squad room. He wasn't saying a word, just following with those big eyes whatever was going on, and I got to talking to him.

"Tell me something, son," I said to him. "Do you go to school every day?"

"Yes, sir," he said.

"And do you like school?" I said.

"Yes, sir," he said.

"And of the things you study in school," I said, "what do you like best?"

"In school," he said, "I like the poetry and I like the timetable."

"Well, that's fine," I said. "Poetry and the timetable."

"Yes, sir," he said.

"I remember poetry," I said, "but it's been so long since I went to school that I don't remember the timetable."

"Yes, sir," he said.

"Can you tell me what the timetable is?" I said.

"Yes, sir," he said. "Two time two is four, is the timetable."

"Oh, yes," I said. "I remember now."

The last I saw of Annie she was walking out with the matron, thanking us and reminding us that everybody who knows her will tell you that she always tells the truth. The last I saw of the boy he was walking out, holding the hand of the woman from Child Welfare.

They no sooner leave, though, than these two women come in. They're nicely dressed and obviously well-to-do, and they're standing at the railing and Garrett asks them if we can help them. The one of them says that she had her handbag picked, and her purse is gone with about $35 and her credit cards and her driver's license. Garrett asks them to come in, and they sit down at his desk across from mine.

"Now when did this happen, madam?" Garrett says.

"About two hours ago," the woman who was victimized says.

"Two hours ago?" Garrett says. "And you're just coming in now?"

"Well, we had these appointments at our hairdresser," the woman says, "and we were walking over there when it happened. She's a very good hairdresser, and it's very difficult to get appointments when you want them, so we thought we'd better take them while we had them because it probably

95

wouldn't make any difference. You probably wouldn't be able to catch the thief, anyway."

"You may be right, madam," Garrett says.

He gets out a new pad and he starts to take down the name and the home address. While he's doing this, who shapes up at the railing but Fat Bessie. We've been catching Fat Bessie's squeals on the phone for a couple of months now, ever since her father died, and this is the second time she's been in.

Fat Bessie's name is Bessie Myers, and she's in her forties and not very tall and she must weigh 200 pounds. Her father was a little guy that time passed by, and Garrett used to call him "The Village Blacksmith." He was only about five feet three, and he couldn't have weighed more than about 125 pounds, but Garrett used to call him that because progress ruined his business. He used to repair fountain pens. I mean the kind with the rubber tube in them, that you'd refill from an ink bottle. Then the ballpoints came in, but he kept coming around with his little old suitcase, a nice little guy, polite, taking off his hat when he spoke, asking us if we had a pen we wanted fixed.

They were on welfare, I guess, and Bessie's on it now. Her mother died when Bessie was a little kid, and she and her father lived together in an apartment over on Central Avenue where she lives alone now. Her father must have been dead about a month when Garrett and I had the night duty, and about 11 o'clock the phone rang and I picked it up and caught Bessie's first squeal.

It was Telstar that was bothering her at the time. It was going around up there, she said, and the FBI was sending these signals, these vibrations off it. They were directing them at her, and they were coming through her window and making her shake.

We've been getting these poor souls every now and then for as long as I can remember. During the war, when I still had the uniform beat over on North Jefferson, some guy who lived on the top floor of one of those tenements called in one night that somebody was trying to get in through the roof. They sent

Charley Feeney over to assist me, and the guy meets us downstairs in the hallway.

"They're up there now," he says. "I could hear them just before I came down."

So Feeney and I creep up the fire escape. It's pitch black and we're crawling around on the flat roof, service revolvers at the ready, and we're lucky we didn't wing each other. We're all over that roof, through the soot and the puddles, and when we can't find anybody we go down to the guy's apartment.

"I'm sorry," I say, "but whoever it was must have got away. We didn't see anybody."

"Oh, they're very difficult to see," the guy says.

"What do you mean, they're very difficult to see?" Feeney says.

"They're gremlins," the guy says. "Hear them? I can hear them up there now."

I thought Feeney was going to pass out right there. Gremlins were very popular at that time, and then, after the war, when the Russians got the first hardware into outer space, it was Sputnik. I was out of the blue suit by then, and in the middle of the night some guy would call in and say that the Russians were vibrating him. The way it went, they had developed this very special electronic device and they were bouncing the signals from it off the Sputnik. The signals were making him shake all over, and that was the way the Russians were going to conquer America by vibrating everybody from coast to coast.

You can't tell these people to go see a doctor, because they tell you they're not sick and sometimes they get very upset at the suggestion, so we started telling them that they should get one of those rolls of aluminum foil and tack a sheet of it over the window. We'd tell them that other people had had great success with that, because apparently the electronic signals couldn't get through the aluminum, and that would hold them for a while. Then if they called back a few days or a few weeks later, saying it wasn't working, we'd tell them maybe they should try another brand of aluminum foil.

I remember one guy who came in and said the aluminum foil was working fine on his window, but now the Russians were sending the signals through his door. He said he couldn't put the foil over his door, because he had to use the door, so he'd been chewing a lot of gum and putting the wads on the door. He said that worked for a while, but now he had more than five hundred wads on the door and it wasn't working any more.

"I think I should write the President," he said, and Eisenhower was in office at the time. "I think that he should know that the Russians are doing this all over the United States, and that he should do something about it."

"Yeah," Garrett said. "That's a good idea, because the President knew those Russians during the war, and he'll know better than anybody how to handle them."

"That's what I was thinking," the guy said. "In fact, I was going to suggest to him that maybe if he gave the Russians West Berlin they'd stop trying to take over our country this way."

"Yeah," Garrett said. "It sounds like a good swap to me."

Now that we've got our own satellites up there, and since the moon landings, they've stopped with the Russians. Now it's some race of outer-space people who own the moon, or it's A.T. & T. or, like with Fat Bessie, it's the FBI.

"Sir?" she's saying now at the railing. "May I come in?"

"Certainly," I say. "Please do."

She's wearing a black dress and a black coat and a small black hat. I get a chair for her and sit her down at my desk. She fills the chair all right, and she's kind of side-by-side with the two women who are giving Garrett the squeal about the pickpocket.

"Sir?" she says. "Are you the gentleman I talked with here two weeks ago about the vibrations that the FBI was sending at me off the Telstar?"

"No," I say, nodding over toward Garrett who's getting the one woman's name and address. "It was Detective Garrett."

"Oh, that's right," Bessie says. "He's a very nice man, isn't he?"

"Yes," I say, "he's a fine man."

"And he's very intelligent, isn't he," she says.

98

"Yes, he is," I say. "He's one of the most intelligent men I know."

"Then perhaps I ought to talk to him," she says, turning toward Garrett.

"No," I say. "He's very busy now. Perhaps I can help you."

"I don't know," she says. "You're probably very nice, too, but he seems to be an expert on electronic devices. Doesn't he know a great deal about these devices and signals and vibrations?"

"Yes," I say. "He does, but he's going to be busy for quite a while, so you'd better tell me. Then, if we need his help, we can get it later."

"Well," she says, "if you think so. Besides, if you work with him, you've probably learned a lot from him, too."

"That's right, ma'am," I say. "Now what seems to be your problem?"

"Well," she says, "when I was in here the last time and the FBI was vibrating me, this other gentleman told me that I should go and see the FBI."

"And did you do that?" I say.

"Yes, I did," she says, "and I talked with Mr. Bernard Briscoe. Do you know Mr. Bernard Briscoe of the FBI?"

"No, ma'am," I say.

"He's a very nice man," she says.

"I'm glad to hear that," I say. "And what did he tell you?"

"Well, I explained it all to him," she says. "I told him that the FBI vibrations from the Telstar were making me shake all over and that I couldn't sleep. I told him that the FBI probably had me mixed up with somebody else, some Russian spy. I told him that it must be a case of what they call mistaken identity, and I explained to him that I'm not a spy, and I asked him to have the FBI take the vibrations off."

"And did he do that?" I say.

"Yes," she says. "He said he wasn't familiar with any vibrations that the FBI put out from the Telstar, but he said he could see that I wasn't a Russian spy and that, if that's what they were doing, he would have them stop it."

"And did he?" I say.

"Oh, yes," she says. "Mr. Bernard Briscoe of the FBI is a very nice man."

"Well, that's just fine," I say. "Then you don't have the problem any more."

"Oh, yes I do," she says. "You see, they've started up again."

"The vibrations?" I say.

"That's right," she says. "Especially at night, when I'm trying to sleep, and very often during the day."

"Then why don't you go and speak to Mr. Briscoe again?" I say. "Perhaps somebody else has made a mistake there."

"Oh, no," she says, shaking her head. "It isn't the FBI this time."

"It isn't?" I say. "Who is it?"

"It's the white slavers," she says. "They're terrible people, what they do with women, and the white slavers are trying to do it with me."

At this point I notice that the woman whose friend had her poke picked isn't paying any more attention to Garrett or her friend. She's tuned in on Fat Bessie, and she's got this amazed look on her face.

"Sir?" Bessie is saying. "You've heard of the white slavers, haven't you?"

"Yes, I have," I say, "but they're not operating in this area. They haven't operated here for years."

"Oh, yes they have," she says. "And they're operating here right now. You see, you don't know, but I believe this other gentleman would know all about them."

"No," I say. "He's an expert on electronic devices, but I'm the one who knows about white slavers, and besides, he's still busy."

At the moment he's busy trying to get the attention of the woman who has the ear on Fat Bessie. Now the victim of the pick is also listening in, looking over with a strange look on her face, too.

"Madam?" Garrett is saying to the victim's friend. "Can you help us here a moment? Mrs. Wilson isn't sure of the time. Can you give us an idea of the time?"

"The time now?" the woman says to Garrett.

"No, madam," Garrett says. "The time when the pickpocket took Mrs. Wilson's purse."

This scene is beginning to grab me now, too. The two women are figuring that their hair appointments were at 10 o'clock, so it must have been about 9:50, and big Bessie is telling me that the people who are running the white-slavery ring are a man and wife named Washington. She says she can't seem to remember their first names, and I'm hoping that it doesn't suddenly come to her that the names are George and Martha.

"But do you really need the first names?" she's asking me. "I would think that, if you just arrested the people named Washington who are running the white slavery, and put them in jail, they would tell you their first names. Don't you think that they would tell you their first names?"

"Yes," I say, "I think they would, but . . ."

"Tell me something," she says suddenly, leaning over toward me and lowering her voice. "These other two ladies here. Are the Washingtons trying to get them into the white slavery, too?"

"No," I say. "They're here because one of them had her handbag picked."

"Are you sure?" she says, taking a side glance at the other two. "Maybe if you asked them, you'd find out that they're being vibrated, too."

"No," I say. "They're not."

"That's very strange," she says, "because, if they're not being vibrated, why are they talking to the gentleman who is an expert on electronic devices and vibrations?"

"Because he's also an expert on pickpockets," I say.

"Oh," she says, sitting back. "Then you're going to arrest them, the Washingtons?"

"Not right now," I say, "because I don't know enough about them."

"You see, that's the way they work," Garrett is saying. "In a crowd the one will bump you. When he does the second one will go into your handbag, and he hands the contents to a third one who disappears."

"What do you want to know about them?" Bessie is saying to me.

"Well, I'd like to know where they live," I say, "and what they look like and exactly how they work."

"They live across the street," Bessie says. "They live upstairs over Dino's Pizza, and they're colored."

"They're colored?" I say.

"That's right," she says, "because they're white slavers for a colored prince."

"A colored prince?" I say.

"That's right," she says. "An oil prince."

"An oil prince?" I say.

"That's right," she says. "The prince of an oil kingdom. You've heard of the oil kingdoms haven't you? The Arabs?"

"Yes, ma'am," I say.

"They're very wealthy, the oil princes are," she says, "and they pay enormous sums of money to the Washingtons and the other white slavers to vibrate white women and transport them to their countries where they have to surrender their bodies for the rest of their lives to these colored princes."

"And how do they transport them?" I say.

"By electronic devices," she says. "You see? You don't understand electronic devices like this other gentleman does. Do you?"

"Well," I say, "I think . . ."

"Sir?" Bessie is saying now, turning to Garrett. "Sir?"

"You won't see your thirty-five dollars again," Garrett is explaining to the victim of the pick, while the other woman is listening again to Bessie, "but if they're real pros they'll probably toss your purse, with the driver's license in it, in a mailbox and it'll be returned to you. You better cancel your credit cards, though, and apply for a new license."

"Sir?" Bessie is saying to Garrett. "Sir? Please help me, sir. I don't want to go into white slavery."

"It's all right, Joe," I say. "Miss Myers will wait until you're finished."

"So if we turn up anything," Garrett says, and he stands up

and the victim and her friend stand up, "I have your address, and we'll let you know."

The two women thank Garrett, and then, with their eyes half popping out of their heads, they both take another look at Fat Bessie sitting there and bulging out of that black dress, and they walk out. Garrett sits down, and he leans back and he looks over at Bessie and he takes a puff on that cigar.

"Well, now," he says, "what seems to be your problem?"

So she goes all over it again for Garrett, about the vibrations and the FBI and Mr. Bernard Briscoe and the Washingtons and the colored oil princes. Then she wants to know again if we're going to arrest the Washingtons.

"Well," Garrett says, "there's still one thing that's not clear in my mind. Exactly how are these people named Washington getting these vibrations through to you?"

"I thought you knew that," she says to Garrett. "The last time I was here you knew all about electronic devices and vibrations. Don't you know all about that?"

"Well," Garrett says, "the last time the vibrations were coming off the Telstar, and you felt that it was the FBI, but these people don't have a license to use the Telstar. They'd have to have a license."

"I know that," she says, "and that's why they use my television set instead."

"Your television set?" Garrett says.

"That's right," she says. "They send the vibrations into my television set, and when I'm watching television the vibrations come out and make me shake all over and don't you understand?"

"Sure," Garrett says, "but all you have to do then is pull the electric cord from the set out of the wall outlet and that'll disconnect them."

"Oh no it won't," she says, shaking her head. "I've done that, but they store up the vibrations. All day long, even when I'm not watching television, the Washingtons store up the vibrations in the television set, and then when I pull the cord out the vibrations still come out."

With that she starts to cry. She's sobbing and crying, and I give her my handkerchief, and now she's saying something about a gun.

"I'll get a gun," she's saying, still crying. "If nobody'll help me I'll buy a gun, and I'll protect myself with the gun."

Garrett and I are trying to comfort her, without too much success. Meanwhile I'm thinking that some maggot just might sell her a gun, and I give Garrett the word and I go into the boss's office and I call Tom Hunter at the Emergency Room at the M.C. and I tell him what we've got. He tells me to hang on while he calls the Psychiatric Department on another phone, and in a couple of minutes he comes back on and says somebody will be right over.

"It's going to be all right," I tell Bessie when I come back out, and Garrett has her pretty well quieted down now. "I've just talked with a man who's an authority on these vibrations from television sets, and he's sending somebody right over."

"He's not a doctor, is he?" she says. "I don't want a doctor."

"He's an expert on vibrations," I say, "especially the kind that are affecting you. He'll know exactly what to do."

That satisfies her, but we have to wait about a half hour. We get Bessie a cup of coffee, and she starts telling us about her father and what a fine man he was and the important job he had fixing fountain pens. We tell her that we remember her father and how he fixed our pens, and finally this young woman shapes up at the railing. She asks for me, and it turns out she's a psychiatric social worker. I fill her in, and then introduce her to Bessie, and she tells Bessie that she works for the man who can help her about the vibrations and off they go.

I don't know. In the old days, when I was young and new on the job, on my own time and with my own nickel I'd call up and find out what disposition they made of a case. What happened to that poor little boy? What about that poor woman? I wanted to find the end of everything, tie it all up in a neat little package, but not any more. The thing is to get the paper work cleaned up and go home.

VII

DAVID STILLMAN, M.D.

"That you, Squash?" Mabry said on the phone. It is his synonym for Shrink. "Meet you at the Wailing Wall in fifteen minutes?"

There is a four-wall handball court in the basement of the House Officers' Quarters, and every other Wednesday Mabry and I reserve it for an hour at 5:30. He almost always wins, and he needs to win and I need the exercise.

"Not tonight," I said. "How about a reprieve? I'm too fatigued."

"You're not fatigued," he said. "What you're suffering from is gluteal ischemia, preclinical to compression atrophy of the duff. You've been sitting on it all day, listening to those sad sacks tell you about their toilet training. You need to get the blood moving again. I'll see you there."

He hung up, and so I met him and we got in our hour. As it happened, it was one of those rare times when I just managed to beat him.

"Real good," he said. "Golda would be proud of you. How come you Chosen People don't make it big in sports, though?"

"Oh, I remember Sid Luckman," I said.

"When you were a boy," he said. "Long time ago. And Koufax and Mark Spitz. One in a hundred. Why?"

"We're not aggressive enough," I said. "Aggression is contrary to our cultural heritage."

"Not aggressive enough?" he said. "What about the Middle East? What about the Rothschilds? Who ran Hollywood? Show biz? What about Three-Ball Bieber, we used to call him, the loan shark down the block that my old man was in hock to half his life?"

"Let's say we're not physically aggressive," I said. "Israel is a historical anomaly. Generally we favor straining the mind rather than the muscles. Professional football players? They're laborers. Imagine grown men, married and the fathers of families, picking themselves up out of dirt and mud every Sunday. We prefer . . ."

"To sit in the owner's box and rake in the shekels," he said.

"When we can."

"You're all right, Squash," he said.

We've been doing this for several months now—the four-wall and then, after our showers, a quick dinner at Palumbo's. We enjoy each other; opposite poles that attract. For me he's a relief. He's like an open-faced sandwich.

"A lox and cream cheese on an open bagel," my father used to say of this kind. "So enjoy that you don't have to worry what's in him."

He's one of the spawn of the American overmortgaged lower middle class, in his midthirties and with a family but still in debt for his education. As a high school football player he could have had a college scholarship, but he went into the medical corps in Korea and met a surgeon and transferred enough of his adolescent admiration for professional athletes to want to emulate him. He grew up with Italians and Jews and Germans and the Irish and the blacks, and his way of attempting to exorcise prejudice is to keep the name-calling jocular and in the open.

"Giuseppe," he'll say to Joe Palumbo, "I think your lasagne has killed more Sicilianos than the Mafia. What else have you got tonight?"

Palumbo's is one of those caverns down three steps from the street level. His business is mostly beer and bar sandwiches for the medical students and the house staff, but we go there because Joe will serve us quickly and we can sit in the back booth near the kitchen where it's quiet and talk.

"Bad day," Mabry will say, as he did tonight. "Ortho called me in at 6:45 this morning to take another look at a hit-and-run kid I saw in the E.R. the other day. May lose her. Fat embolism, probably from fractures of the femur and tibia, hitting the lungs, and we're sweatin' out the brain. They've moved her into Powell Samuels's Space Control."

What Mabry calls Powell Samuels's Space Control is a two-room accident trauma unit associated with a digital computer. The multiple physiological changes taking place in a patient in shock are recorded by a bank of monitoring devices and fed into the computer which prints out the analysis in less than a minute. When they were setting it up about five years ago they called us in for guidance because some of their engineering and data processing personnel couldn't take the day after day subjection to the severely injured. They were finding the daily imminence of death frightening and depressing, and by simply giving them the opportunity to sit down and talk about it, by assuring them that doctors and medical personnel know these fears, too, but are shielded by their training and experience, we were able to reduce their anxieties.

"Post that," he said, "I spent six hours on my feet taking a meningioma off a spinal cord. You want to know why you beat me tonight? That's why."

"I apologize," I said.

"Don't apologize," he said. "Just level with me. What the hell did you do today?"

"Made rounds at eight," I said. "Got in an hour of paper work. Had an E.R. Committee meeting at ten."

"The old guy who took his life?"

"Right."

"Bad show."

"Everybody's fault," I said, "including mine. Every month we have that meeting with the new interns rotating into the room, and I haven't made it clear enough that the depressed patient, as placid as he may appear and especially one who has already attempted to take his own life, must be watched without interruption."

"Who really blew it?"

"I did. Hunter did, and an intern named Stern left the patient alone with the exposed closed thoracotomy kit."

"Know the lad," Mabry said. "Like to wave him off the track for a pit stop. How many patients you see today?"

"Oh, a half dozen."

"What's the problem of that obese broad you were walking through the E.R. this afternoon?"

"She's being vibrated."

"What do you mean, vibrated?"

"She's being vibrated electronically through her television set by a young black couple in her neighborhood. They're white slavers, and they're preparing to abduct her into the harem of a black prince of one of the oil kingdoms of Africa."

"Good luck to all of them," he said. "What did you do for her?"

"I got her confidence."

"How?" he said. "I'm interested, because I still don't know what the hell you really do."

"Well, she's been down to Police Headquarters for help, and finally told somebody there that she might get a gun to protect herself. They called the E.R. and a psychiatric social worker brought her in. We were short-handed this afternoon, so I went down. She didn't want to see a doctor, who might confirm her fears that she's mentally ill, but I convinced her that I've known other people who felt they were being vibrated and that I'd been able to help them."

"She buy that?"

"Not right away, but after some prepping."

"Such as?"

"Oh, you empathize. You don't abruptly destroy her delusions. You don't take away her fairyland and leave her with nothing. You say that it must be very disturbing to have the sensation of being vibrated, that we all know how trying and tiring it is not to be able to get a good night's sleep. Then you start to explore, in a leisurely conversational manner, her background and life style."

"So where did that get you today?" he said.

"When this woman was a child her mother died, and she'd been living with her father until he died a few months ago. She's a lonely middle-aged female who's physically unattractive and so engages in this sexual fantasy about being abducted into a harem. You still interested?"

"I asked for it," he said. "Go ahead."

"All right. These people suffering from paranoid delusions take their clues from the outside real world and invest them with their inner unreal world."

"What the hell does that mean?" he said.

"For example," I said, "some month or more ago this woman believed she was being vibrated through Telstar by the FBI who thought she was a Russian spy."

"You had to listen to that, too?" he said.

"That's right. Now, Telstar is real, the FBI is real and Russia is real. In her paranoid mind the unreality of being arrested by the FBI and executed as a Russian agent by the American Government became real when she used the three real props to support her fear."

"What did you do about that?" he said.

"I didn't have to do anything. For some reason she no longer found that particular fantasy believable or intriguing. She has replaced it with this new one. One of the new props she has adopted from the real world is her television set, through which she believes this black couple named Washington are vibrating her. It's also real, or true, that signals do come through television sets in a way which very few of us understand. Now, many blacks, as personified by the Washingtons, have moved into her neighborhood and the white fear of miscegenation is real. The Arab oil countries and their rich potentates and harems are also real, so taking those props and being, as I said, lonely and sexually deprived, she has erected this fantasy world in which the Washingtons will force her to submit to a lifetime in an Arab harem."

"So you listen to this broad and then you get to understand her and then you feel sorry for her and then . . ."

"Wait a minute," I said. "I do come to understand her and I am sensitive to her emotional agonies, but I don't take over her woes, if that's what you mean by feeling sorry for her. When she starts to cry I don't get down and wallow in tears with her. If I do that nothing happens."

"Sorry, Squash," he said. "So what do you do?"

"Well, I'm primarily concerned about her mention of obtaining a gun. Was it a passing remark or a real threat? Is there a real danger that, if I don't keep her in, she may harm herself or society."

"You mean society or herself," he said.

"No, I don't," I said. "My first responsibility is to the patient, and only my second responsibility is to society, even though I am a member of society myself."

"Look," he said, "if she goes out and gets a gun and kills herself that's her own bag. Bad, but not as bad as if she kills some poor innocent sob who had nothing to do with her bag. You've got to put him first."

"Wrong," I said, and even in our own specialty we debate this. "We're doctors, not society's keepers. A hold-up man kills a cop. In the exchange of gunfire he receives a bullet in his brain. He's brought into the O.R. alive, and you may be absolutely convinced that society will be better off if he doesn't survive. As his doctor, however, you must do everything you can do to keep him alive."

"Different," he said. "Society already has this guy bottled up. It doesn't even know that your broad is running around loose and might get a gun and wing some sob."

"Not so different," I said. "If your hold-up man is young enough he may get a parole after twenty years. Before he does, a parole board, advised by a psychiatrist, will have to decide that he is no longer a menace. Today I had a similar decision to make. My decision, however, was partially influenced by the fact that, so far as we know, this woman had never actually menaced society and so I was more free than the prison psychiatrist to decide whether hospitalization, a form of incarceration, would benefit or tend to interfere with the therapy of this patient. Primarily, it's the province of judges and juries, not doctors, to decide what's best for society."

"Words. Words," he said. "So you turned her loose, or have you got her up in your zoo?"

"I decided the gun was fantasy, too."

"How did you decide that?" he said. "I'd like a little assurance that I don't have to go home from here in an armored car."

"Well, I got her talking about what her life had been like

with her father. He apparently had been a very gentle man, and it had been a placid existence, devoid of any violence. I asked her if she had any fear that her apartment might be robbed, and she said she has a double lock and a chain lock on the door. I asked her if she ever had the fear that the locks might not be enough, that someone might still force his way in, and that she might need a gun. 'Oh, no,' she said. 'I wouldn't even know how to use a gun.' "

"And you bought that? That convinced you?"

"Not just that. Our whole conversation. Decisions like this we make on what today you call that gut feeling. I just do not feel that she's going to do it."

"So on your gut feeling you just turned her loose?"

"No. I put her on medication. Thorazine."

"She'll take it?"

"I believe so. I had to convince her. At first she was opposed. I told her that I knew a lot of people who were bothered—disturbed—like she is, and that they took these pills and the disturbances ceased. Then she said: 'But how do I know that the Washingtons didn't give you these pills to give to me?' I assured her that I don't even know the Washingtons, and that's when you may have seen us. I walked her up to the pharmacy, and after I showed her all the rows of pills that others take she agreed."

"You hope," he said.

"I believe. When I weigh the harm that might be done to her if I hospitalize her, especially against her will, which would have been the case, and I weigh the absence of any evidence of violence in her past or in her nature, I believe."

"But you don't know."

"We never know, but in this case I almost know. Many times we're less secure, and we sweat it out, day after day and night after night. Did we do the right thing to let the patient go? Will he stay on his medication? You see, there's that other ethical and disturbing factor. When we hospitalize a patient against his will we are depriving him of his civil rights."

"Oh, hell," he said. "We do the same thing all the time in a life-or-death decision. The patient is comatose. No family around. I crack his skull without permission. I'm depriving him of his civil rights."

"Not quite the same," I said. "You know he'll die if you don't operate. We're not that certain that it's life-or-death when we commit."

"How many patients," he said, "did you say you saw today?"

"Six, I think."

"I still don't know how you do it," he said. "Sit there and go through that kind of stuff you went through with that fat broad, patient after patient, hour after hour. Like they say, after awhile who's listening?"

"I am. I have to. It's not just what the patient says, but how he says it. We don't go by a hematocrit, or an EEG like you. I have to go by my own feelings, and the intonation may tell me something."

"Back to your civil rights," he said. "You put anybody away today?"

"Yes," I said. "A young man who walked into the E.R. a few minutes later."

"He go quietly?"

"Voluntarily. His civil rights were not involved."

"Tell me about this kook," he said.

Joe Palumbo had brought us our salad and the veal scalloppine, so while we ate I summarized it for him. When the opportunity arises in a compatible situation I accept it, for although we in psychiatry are less the stepchildren than we used to be, we are still under suspicion within the profession and outside of it. Within the profession they still suspect that we may have been poor physicians or that we're more than a little imbalanced ourselves. Outside the profession there is, I suppose, the latent fear that maybe we can read minds.

"Here comes the shrink," somebody will announce when I walk into, say, a cocktail party. "Everybody line up for the couch."

There will be another counterphobic joke or two, and the room will split out. The men will go for another drink, and the women will come over to talk. There is a myth that masculinity connotes strength, and so the male is less willing to bare his life, the fears he is constraining, especially to another man. Beyond that, if the woman is not the family provider she can take the time for treatment without endangering the finances, and if all you have to do is dust you ruminate.

Even among the patients who accept us there remains that latent suspicion. The long-time patient of the medical or surgical doctor will exercise his curiosity about him, his family, his life, but they seldom explore us. It is as if they are afraid that they will find that we are, indeed, the modern witch doctors, and so we are isolated. When I find a Bob Mabry, who couches his curiosity in cynicism but is genuinely curious nevertheless, I find it therapeutic.

"A classic case," I told him, "of psychotic dissociation."

"What's the English translation?" he said. "I'm not up on my Swahili."

The young man is somewhere in his early thirties, but exactly how old he is we're not sure. He had walked into the Emergency Room of his own volition, complaining of pains in his back, sometimes in his chest, of headaches and of occasional difficulty breathing. An intern had checked him over without finding anything. Tom Hunter looked at him and talked with him and then talked to me.

"I don't think he's a simple hypochondriac," he said. "He's a little vague at times, gives occasional evidence of extreme nervousness, and I think he may be psychosomatic."

I took the patient's chart, and I took him down to our room at the rear of the E.R. where we have attempted to create an informal and relaxing setting. There is a sofa there, two armchairs, a rug on the floor, a coffee table, an end table with lamp, Currier & Ives prints on the wall.

"Are you employed?" I asked him, after we had been seated.

He's well built, with the appearance of having been a neighborhood athlete, if not a scholastic one. He was cleanly shaved, wearing a dark blue quilted jacket over a clean blue work shirt, dark slacks and black loafers.

"I work in a garage," he said, "but some days I can't work, because of the pains."

"These pains," I said, looking at his chart, "they're in your back?"

"They start in my back and in my side," he said.

"They're sharp pains? It feels like a knife is sticking you?"

"No," he said. "It's more like a numbness. It's in my back and side, and then they move to my chest and it's hard to breathe. Then it's like spasms that go to the right side of my head, and sometimes everything seems kind of blurry."

"And can you remember when these pains started?"

"I think so," he said. "I mean they sort of came on gradually, starting like about four years ago."

"And I imagine you have been to doctors about these pains?"

"Sure," he said. "Three or four doctors. They can't find anything wrong with my back, and they can't find anything wrong with my chest and they can't find anything wrong with my head."

"How's your weight?"

"About 170. It doesn't change, even when I can't eat much."

"So your appetite is affected, too?" I said.

"Sometimes," he said. "Sometimes I don't eat all day, just coffee. Maybe for two-three days I don't eat much, but my weight doesn't change."

"And these pains come and go?"

"That's right," he said, "and when they do I can't walk and I can't breathe and I can't work."

Organic pain, of course, is not commonly migratory. It is psychoneurotic pain that wanders. In the rest of us conflict and anxiety may fight their way out in a tension headache. The psychoneurotic or psychotic turns his troubles to various parts of his body, and now he was becoming openly disturbed.

"I don't know what to do," he was saying. "Sometimes I can't sleep and I can't work, and it scares me."

"I'm sure it does," I said, "but we're going to find out the causes. I see here that you're thirty-two years of age?"

"That's what I think," he said, "but I'm not sure."

"You don't know when you were born?" I said, and now, as is so often the case, a simple question was going to prove to be a key.

"Not for sure," he said. "I think I may have been born about a thousand years ago, just before the year 1000. I think I was in Norway at the time."

I felt myself freeze, and then in that first millisecond I fell back on those automatic reflexes that are born of training. Do not change facial expression. Do not register surprise, dismay, approval nor disbelief. Do nothing, in other words, to interrupt whatever might be the magic of this moment in which one human being offers a very, very inside piece of himself to another. I was face to face with psychotic thinking.

"Do you have any idea," I asked him, "what makes you unsure about your age, about when you were born?"

"Things I read, and things I see and things I hear," he said. "Ever since I was about twelve I've been unsure. Let me ask you something. Can you be two people?"

"In what way?"

"Some people I know can be two people. One girl I know, a friend of my sister, can do it. She can change herself into a cat."

"You've seen her do it?" I said.

"Right," he said. "Absolutely. One day she changed herself into a cat, and jumped right up into my arms."

"Where was this?"

"Harwood Lake," he said. "You know Harwood Lake? One day last summer I went out there to go swimming. I didn't swim, though, because of my back, but this girl I know was there, this friend of my sister, and she just changed herself into a cat and jumped right into my arms."

"And you don't understand how she was able to do that?"

"Right," he said. "It's certain forces. Certain forces do this to certain people, and they do it to me."

"And you feel that you're sort of at the mercy of these forces?"

"Right. You know atoms? You're familiar with them?"

"Yes, I understand something about atoms."

"Take this magazine here," he said, picking up one of the magazines from the coffee table. "It's made of atoms, right?

Now, if you put this magazine in water and leave it long enough it will dissolve. The atoms will change. Right?"

"It will change," I said.

"It's the same with fire," he said. "I mean, when you burn something the atoms change, or they're supposed to, but my atoms don't change because they've been the same for a thousand years. Do you understand that?"

"No," I said. "Frankly, I don't."

"Let's say you put a piece of wood on a fire," he said. "The wood will burn and become ashes because the atoms change. I can put my hand in a fire, though, or I can walk right through a fire, but I don't burn because my atoms don't change."

"And you've done this?" I said.

"Absolutely," he said. "Many times. I don't do it any more, though, because I don't have to. I've already done it."

"And you feel that these atoms that don't change have something to do with people being two people?"

"Exactly," he said. "I may look like I'm maybe thirty-two years old, but that's just the way I dress and the way I seem. It's not the way I really am, because actually my atoms are the same as they were when I was born in the year 940, and when I married this girl."

"The girl who jumped up into your arms?"

"Right. The same one. You see, that's the whole thing. She and I were married—at least I think we were—in 968 or 969, I'm not sure. We were in Norway at the time. We were with Leif Ericson. You've heard of him?"

"The explorer? Yes."

"The same one," he said, nodding. "We were married—at least I think we were—just before we got on the ship with him and discovered America."

"You and this girl," I said, "you came over here with Leif Ericson?"

"Right," he said. "That's how we got here. You see, Columbus gets all the credit for discovering America, but we did it, years before him. You've heard of that, haven't you?"

"Yes," I said. "Some historians hold to that belief."

"Of course," he said. "We actually discovered America, but they keep giving Columbus the credit."

"And you were saying that, ever since you've been about twelve, you've had trouble knowing who you are?"

"Right," he said. "I keep going from lies to the truth, and after awhile I don't know what the truth is any more."

It is what we call fragmented reality testing. He does not know what is real and what is fantasy.

"And this girl," I said, "does she believe that you and she were married?"

"Sure," he said. "She knows. She knows as well as I do."

"Do you ever talk to this girl?"

"Only through séances."

"Do you date her?"

"No," he said, "I've never been out with her, but she knows all right. She knows everything I do. In fact, she knows everything I'm goin' to do before I do it. You see, the atoms —or whatever it is—keep me from getting to her or her to me. They keep a lot of people from getting to me. Like the people who are going to kill me whenever they get the chance. I can hear their voices when they try to sneak up behind me."

It is the typical auditory hallucination, more common than the visual or the olfactory. Almost always these voices seem to be coming from behind, and often the patient who does not confess to them will reveal himself by repeatedly turning his head.

"Now if these people want to talk to me," he was saying, "why don't they walk right up instead of trying to sneak up from behind? Maybe it's the atoms. Sometimes people I know try to come to my house, but they can't get near me. The atoms, you see, are like a glass shield, like a man from Saturn has, around me."

He is projecting, employing the common defense mechanism whereby one blames one's own difficulties not on one's own weaknesses but on the imagined evils inherent in objects or things, such as atoms or his Saturn shield, or other persons. He is young and virile, but in all probability he is sexually and socially frustrated. He takes the real fact of his isolation and, needing an explanation he can accept, has this delusion about the atomic shield.

"You understand that, don't you?" he was saying. "You understand what I'm saying about this shield?"

"I'll be honest with you," I said. "I follow what you're saying, but I don't really understand."

"I knew it," he said, "but there are people who understand."

"There are," I said. "Who are they?"

"People who know me," he said. "You know the Leightons? Jerry and Will Leighton that live over in Connorsville?"

"No. I don't."

"You've heard of Jeremiah, in the Bible?"

"The book of the Old Testament? Yes."

"Well, Jerry is Jeremiah, and Will is Wilbur Wright."

"Jerry Leighton is Jeremiah from the Bible?" I said. "And Will Leighton is Wilbur Wright?"

"And invented the airplane," he said, nodding. "You understand how that could be?"

"No," I said, "I don't, but I have the feeling that if you and I got to know each other better we'd find a lot of things to talk about that we both understand."

"You see?" he said. "You don't want to understand, because it would burden you, and you don't want to be burdened."

"Let me correct you," I said, because we were at the point now where I had to begin to apply the reins to his psychotic thinking. "There are a lot of things that I don't understand, but they don't burden me."

"It's terrible," he was saying now, and he was beginning to become emotional. "It's like a huge weight that these people are pushing down on me so I can't breathe."

"And these people are plotting against you?"

"Definitely," he said, "and you know something else? I saw people on TV last night who are plotting to kill the governor. I don't know their names, but I know their faces."

"Well," I said, "we've got to simplify your life, so that all these things, these thoughts, aren't coming in to confuse you and make it so difficult for you."

"It isn't all that difficult," he said, starting to withdraw. "Only sometimes it is."

"There are a couple of things we can do," I said. "We can bring you into the hospital."

"I know," he said. "That's why I came in here."

"But we don't want to run up a lot of bills."

"Don't worry about that," he said. "I've got enough money to pay for everything."

"You've got money?"

"In the bank. I'm sure I've got enough."

"You're sure?"

"Right. I own some oil wells."

"You own some oil wells?" I said.

"Of course," he said. "I own three oil wells. They're in Oklahoma."

"Would you be willing," I asked him, "to go to the State Hospital?"

"Oh, no," he said, shaking his head. "I've been there."

"You have?"

"I think so," he said. "I think I was there when I gave them the money to set it up. You know? And then they turned on me."

"How did they turn on you?"

"They turn people into animals there."

"I don't believe that," I said.

"I do," he said. "Either they turn people into animals or they turn animals into people. All the people who are there could have been animals, you know. I'm not sure."

His delusions of grandeur—his discovery of America, the ownership of three oil wells and his gift of money to set up the State Hospital—is classic for the paranoid schizophrenic. That role as benefactor evidences respect for the hospital, while his disparagements of the institution, revolving around people and animals, exemplifies his ambivalence.

His problem could, of course, have been the result of physical injury to the brain, or it could have had its seat in organic structural brain changes. I checked him out for cognition—he recognized objects, even the prints on the wall as Currier &

Ives—and for memory and orientation. He knew the day of the week and the date and what he had for breakfast. He sequentially named the Presidents from Franklin Roosevelt to Nixon. I put him through the Serial 7s—subtracting 7s from 100—and he ran them all the way, with hesitation but without error.

"So from that," Mabry said, "you decide there's nothing physiologically wrong with his squash, except he's just a nut."

"I left him for a few minutes," I said. "I saw Tom Hunter outside the room, so I went out to fill him in. While I was talking with Hunter I was observing the patient through that window we have there. I saw him look around the room, then pick up one magazine, look at the cover, then pick up another and then put that one down. Then I watched him arranging the magazines, trying to remember which one had been where. Here again he's classic."

"How?" Mabry said.

"Somebody vague may be checking on him," I said. "His defense against this anxiety is to have an orderly world, and avoid suspicion. He compulsively goes to great efforts to accomplish this, but these unconscious mechanisms are quite common, in lesser degrees, in most of us. A kid, going to school or coming home, will hit every telephone pole on the way. You're a sports enthusiast. Your baseball outfielder, coming in from his position and running out there again, will be sure to step on second base. These good luck gimmicks, if you want to call them that, employed by the kid and the ballplayer, are in reality compulsive defenses to ward off the worry that something bad might occur. Now, if you get in there and break up these defenses you may be unnecessarily increasing the anxiety."

"So you've got him up in your zoo?"

"For ten days or two weeks. He's on one of the phenothiazenes, and he'll be on medication the rest of his life but he'll be able to work and otherwise function. At least, that's the prognosis. That's what we believe."

"But you never know."

"Seldom, but how many absolutes, how many certainties, are there in life?"

"Oh, come on," he said. "I know I cured that guy today. That's for certain. Six hours, but a real big win."

"And that's good," I said. "That's fine, and you deserve to be self-congratulatory, because you surgeons always need to win, and right away. You can't wait for gratification, and that makes a good surgeon and we need you."

"My third year in med school," he said, "they carted us up to the State Hospital. Awful. There was one guy there who'd quicklimed his wife and daughter. He was lying on his back on the floor, pawing the air with his hands and feet and barking like a dog, and he kept it up the whole time we were there. That place scared the hell out of me. How can you be around that kind of thing?"

"The mysteries of the mind are frightening, because we're not certain that something like that may not happen to us. But how can you use a scalpel? I was extremely uncomfortable, even afraid, when I had to."

"You're kidding."

"No, I'm not. Sticking a knife into a living person is an unnatural act."

"You're still kidding."

"I assure you I am not," I said. "When you operate on a patient that patient is draped, with only the operative area exposed. This is aseptic technique, but it has a secondary virtue. It allows you to exclude from your mind the reality that this is a human being into whom you are going to stick that knife. You don't say to yourself: 'Now this is a man. He has a wife and two children.' You are able to close your mind to that, and it becomes a mechanical, technical problem. Otherwise, you couldn't do it."

"You know something, Squash?" Mabry said. "You would not only make a lousy surgeon, but you're already a lousy handball player."

"I agree," I said.

"Oh, hell," he said. "Listen. I almost forgot. How's our

runt friend, Nick Braff? You still pounding the positive think-ing into his squash?"

"I'm still seeing him one night a week," I said. "I think we're making progress."

It has been almost two months now since an intern called me from the E.R. sometime after 2 o'clock one morning. When I got down there they were starting to repair the damage the patient had done to his left wrist. He is a small man—five feet two—but with muscular arms and full shoulders, and even after I glanced at his name on the chart and because I don't read the sports pages, I failed to recognize him as a well-known jockey.

He had made a sincere attempt to take his life. There were, first of all, the hesitation marks—the three superficial razor scratches across the wrist, and then the deeper cut. He had made the same mistake that many of them make, however, be-cause when he had bent his wrist back to make the cut the radial artery had withdrawn behind the edge of the radius and all he had severed were some small veins. How long he had sat waiting to die I don't know, but when the blood had begun to coagulate and the bleeding to stop he had wrapped the wrist in a handkerchief and he had walked into the E.R.

"Have you talked with him?" I asked the intern after he had put eight stitches in the wrist and bandaged it. "Do you know what this is about?"

"Hell, no," the intern said. "He cut himself. I sewed him up."

I introduced myself to the patient then, and I took him down to that room we have there. He had been drinking, it turned out, when he had made his attempt, but that had worn off and now after he had sat down he lighted a cigarette and he was looking at the floor.

"So you tried to kill yourself," I said, because it is better to confront it immediately. "Why?"

"What's the use of talking about it?" he said, and then he looked at his bandaged wrist. "I couldn't even do a good job of this."

"Well," I said, "you've probably done a good job on many occasions in your life. Isn't that right?"

"What's the use of talking about it?" he said again.

"What do you do for a living?" I said. "They haven't filled it in here on your chart."

"Not much right now," he said.

"What did you used to do?" I said.

"I'm a jockey," he said.

"Oh," I said. "I probably should have known that, but I don't follow sports closely."

"You're wise," he said. "You're smart."

"And if you're not riding now," I said, "what do you do?"

"I gallop horses in the morning," he said. "For walk-around money."

"And why is it that you're not riding in races now?"

"I just can't make it any more," he said.

"And why is that?" I said.

It began to come out then, and the rest of it has come out in our meetings one night a week, on a night when I am on call. We sit in one of the rooms in the Electro Convulsive Therapy unit across the hall from the E.R., and talk for an hour or more, depending on how busy I am.

He was the only child of an alcoholic father and an overworked mother and, typically, because of his small stature, he was the one who, when they were choosing up for neighborhood games, was always chosen last, or left out. He left home when he was fifteen and got a job around the stables at the race track, and two years later he was riding in races.

"It made me big, Doc," he said one night. "Hell, when you weigh only 106 pounds and they put you up on an animal that weighs 1,200 pounds you're as big as anybody."

He is a victim, I realized, of man's adoration of physical stature, of a culture that in our own time has celebrated the skeletal growth of the average American male between two world wars. It was a good life for him as a jockey, however perhaps too good. He won many races, some of them the most important in this country, and many years he earned more than $100,000. He married a woman five inches taller than himself, which is understandably not uncommon among jockeys, but after three years, that marriage ended in divorce. Then, one

123

day in a race, riding into a turn, he fell. Two other horses stepped on him and he was in a coma for days, hospitalized for two months with a fractured skull, several broken bones and a punctured lung. For a while after he was released, he suffered from double vision and dizzy spells, and when he tried to ride again he could not summon up the courage. That was his problem, as it still is, when he came in that first night after slashing his wrists.

"So what did you tell him?" Bob Mabry asked me when we talked once at Palumbo's about that first night. "That he's not a nut? That his squash isn't Swiss-cheesy? That, hell, a lot of people give the thought of suicide a riffle and even try it, so he's not so abnormal."

"No," I said. "Never that."

"What do you mean?" Mabry said.

"That's neighborhood psychotherapy," I said. "Jones has a problem, so one day over the back fence he tells Brown. Brown says: 'Oh, hell, you're not alone.' Then he gives Jones his own problem, which may even be similar. That helps Brown, makes him feel good, but it harms Jones, may even destroy him. It diminishes Jones's problem that, for Jones's good, shouldn't be diminished but, with all its possible serious implications, should be recognized and acknowledged for what it is."

"So what did you do?" Mabry said.

"As I said," I told him, "I confronted it as best I could on a first meeting."

"And you don't think he'll try it again?"

"I don't think so," I said, "otherwise I wouldn't have released him. First of all, after his attempt, he walked in himself. Secondly, after a few minutes we managed a fairly frank, free-flowing conversation, and he agreed to come back and see me in three nights. I was reasonably secure."

The danger, of course, had been that when he had brightened during our conversation it might have been because, unknown to me, he had now definitely decided to do away with himself by some more efficient method. I took that chance.

Pt. is significantly depressed, I wrote on his chart. *Is not suicidal at present time. Will see as outpatient.*

I wondered and worried about it, but three nights later he walked in. As I told Bob Mabry now, it's been almost two months, and I believe him to be much improved.

"He still off the booze?" Mabry said.

"He tells me he is," I said, "and I believe him."

"You think he'll ever ride again?" Mabry said.

"I don't know," I said. "If he doesn't I don't know what else he can possibly do that, in his own mind, will restore his stature."

It was then that Joe Palumbo came over to the table to tell Mabry that there was a call. We had finished eating, so we settled up the bill, and Mabry went to the phone.

VIII

NICHOLAS BRAFF

"Look, Nick," Whitey says. "Do me a favor, will ya? Why don't you wrap it up and go home?"

"Do you a favor?" I said. "I don't owe you anything, Whitey. I did you many a favor."

"All right," he says. "Then do yourself a favor, but knock it off and go home."

"Do myself a favor?" I said. "I don't even owe myself a favor. I don't owe anybody."

"Look," he says, "you're talkin' in circles. You have a couple more and you'll be walkin' in circles. Just go home."

"It's early," I said.

"I know," he says, "but you been here since three o'clock. For four hours you been soakin' it up."

"*Almost* four hours," I said. "I know what time it is. I learned to tell time."

Ain't that a laugh? *I learned to tell time*. That's ridiculous. Everything's ridiculous. Why, them reporters used to write that Nick Braff has a clock in his head. Like Arcaro, is what they wrote. Clock in his head. Why, when McGeady was breaking me in, and we were staying at them six-dollar-a-night-for-two motels with no rugs on the floor around them half-milers, he'd sit there every damn night with that stop watch in his hand. He'd start yakkin'—bitchin' about some racing secretary or the price of feed or the world in general—and then he'd punch that watch and keep talkin' and then he'd punch it again and say: "How much?"

How much? Hell, while he was yakkin' with that watch going, he'd ask me a question, to be sure I was really listening to him and not just clockin' in my head, and then he'd say: "How much?"

"It ain't hard," he'd say, while I was learning. "People who don't know think you're some kind of a smart genius if you can come within 2/5ths of a second, but it's 2/5ths either side of the second, and that's 4/5ths and damn near a whole second."

Then in the mornings it was something, too. We'd go out there together, me on one of his animals and old McGeady sittin' on that old stable pony and spittin' tobacco juice, and if he told me to work a mile in 1:41 he didn't want me coming down in :42. If I did you could be sure he'd be right alongside me, bouncing along on that pony while I'd be bringing his animal back, yakkin' at me, and all of a sudden—splat!—there'd be a hit from that tobacco juice right on the toe of my boot.

"And clean your goddam boot, too!" he'd say.

It was a funny thing about that tobacco chewin', because he was the neatest man I ever knew. Even with that he was neat, because he could hit a dime at five paces, and in them third-rate motel rooms he was always sittin' around with one of them paper cups they have in them dispensers on the wall. When I first came around him, and the way I grew up, I was a slob, but the boots had to be polished every night and the jodhpurs and all the clothing, including underwear, clean and the tack rubbed down until it used to shine. We stabled in some awful dumps on those half-milers, but the way we took care of those animals and those stalls you'd have thought we were Greentree or Calumet.

"McGreedy," they used to call him, but hell, he wasn't greedy. He was just the best at training cheap claimin' horses and schoolin' a jock I ever come across, but he fought with everybody—trainers, racing secretaries, stewards, patrol judges, owners—always trying to get the best for anything he dropped into a race.

"You gotta remember this," he used to tell me. "There are no Cadillacs in my stable, so I gotta fight for anything I can get and you gotta save everything you can save on any horse I ever run."

Then he'd watch me. Damn, how he'd watch me, from the

time he'd boost me up until the time I'd get back. Them other jocks would be laughing and kidding going to the gate, but I would be one serious citizen. McGeady had better not see me laughing on one of his, and I never rode a race for him that he didn't tell me everything I did—whether I took a long enough hold coming out of the gate, and whether I pulled him up too short or sawed on his mouth or whatever, and especially if I went around a bunch when he thought there was room to come through on the rail.

"Damn, I've told you this a hundred times!" he'd scream. "I can't run a horse that much the best, and you gotta save ground. You can't take the married man's route on one of mine. Goin' wide is for those blue-blood stables with all the silverware in their trophy rooms and those fashionable jocks with all their money in stocks and bonds. I'm just a poor, hungry old man and you're just a poor hungry little man, and you'll be that all your life if you don't use your brain and if you don't show some guts."

Hell, that Whitey's got some nerve, asking me to do him a favor. I did him a favor, and I don't mean tonight. Many a favor. Like the time the guy who owned the building raised the rent and Whitey says he couldn't afford it, it would put him out of business, and I told him he should buy the dump. Whitey says he thought of that but the bank won't loan him enough so I loaned him $10,000 for three years before he paid it back, no interest.

Many a favor. Like the night after I won that goddam Special on that Windborne I picked up the tab for one hell of a blast there. I coulda had it anywhere. I coulda had it in any fashionable joint I wanted, any one of them, but I brought it there for Whitey, and them free-loaders must have come from a hundred miles around. What the hell did I care? The only one I cared about in the whole goddam joint besides Whitey was old McGeady, because after he sold my contract for that $5,000 he knew he'd never get another boy like me and I knew I'd never know another citizen like him.

Why, I won that goddam Special because of him and all he taught me about rating an animal and saving ground and time, and he was lucky he had a clubhouse pass. Them other jocks they knew I had a hell of a come-from-behind animal under me, but they knew as well as I did that he had only one run in him so they sent that P. J. Petrie out to pull my cork. That was a joke because I knew P.J.'s animal couldn't go the distance and he'd come back to me, and then them other three they thought they'd slow that damn pace down to where they'd all have plenty left comin' home. That was a joke, too, because like I told Whitey I learned to tell time, and after we like walked that first half mile in :50 I turned that sob loose. They thought they had me locked in there pretty good, but when I set that animal to running Bobby North was lookin' over his shoulder and he hollered: "Here he comes!" and that beast just made his own hole inside Bobby's animal and that rail and win by six.

"You did all right," McGeady said to me that night at Whitey's, "but tell that owner of yours to stop talkin' about that horse bein' another Citation."

"What's that mean?" I said.

"You know damn well what it means," he said, and he was right. "You finished tryin' to make it look like you still had some horse, but he was empty. In another eighth of a mile you'da had to get off him and walked, so don't try to sell me that."

So right up there over the cash register Whitey's still got that picture of me on that animal in the winner's circle with the owner's wife at the head holding the bridle, and ain't that ridiculous? I mean my picture is on the goddam wall and he don't want me in the goddam joint, but Mister Whitey is gonna be surprised. He's gonna be oh-plenty surprised when I do it and he hears about it or reads about it or however he finds out, and then he'll be a sorry sob. There'll be a lot of sorry sobs, and that Doc Stillman is gonna be one of them but he ain't a bad guy. He's a kind of a stranger, but a gentleman, and I told him a lot, most all of it, but how could I ever tell him I hit that little colored girl?

"Her condition remains critical," they say, every day I call the goddam hospital since that first night I bought the paper to see if she died or where she was.

"But is she gonna live or die?" I say.

"I'm sorry, sir," they say, "but that's all we're permitted to release on the condition of the patient. Are you a member of the family?"

"No," I say, "but I'm a friend of the family."

"Would you care to leave your name?" they said the last time. "So that the family will know of your concern?"

"No, thank you," I said, and I hung up because I know damn well they told the cops this same guy calls every day, and the cops put them up to it to see what I'd say. Maybe they thought I'd say that this is Nick Braff, and I told that Stillman I'm off the sauce but I got loaded again that night, and when I woke up I figured I could still get to the track in time to go out with the last set and I hit that little girl when the light changed because the great Braff with the great seat and great hands and the clock in his head was afraid he'd lose his goddam job workin' horses mornings.

No, sir, that ain't the way it's gonna go. It ain't gonna go that way at all, because I ain't gonna go see that Stillman tomorrow night or any other night because if I saw him again I might tell him, the way he just sits there, a real nice quiet-type fella, asking a question now and then and nodding and just smokin' that pipe and listening. The first thing you know you're tellin' him things you ain't thought of for years, that you didn't even think you remembered any more, and it's for sure that if I told him this thing he'd get me to tell the cops or he'd tell the cops himself and what good would that do? It wouldn't make that little girl any better, and all it would do is get me ruled off and maybe sent to the can. What good would that do?

Hell, if I had the money I've thrown away I'd a told the cops. I coulda paid for everything, the hospital and all of it, and then they mighta only yanked my license and set me down for a year, if I just still had the money I tossed off, most of it, like McGeady said would happen, on that broad.

"Well," he said, after he sold my contract for that five gees and we were sayin' goodbye where he was stabled there, with him sittin' in that same old canvas chair, "I wish you luck, because you're gonna need it."

"Oh, I'll do all right," I said. "I'll win my share."

"I know you will," he said, "because you can ride, but I'm not talking about that. I'm talking about what's gonna happen to you when you begin making that dough, because you've been wantin' to spit the bit now for a year. You gotta remember that when you start wearing them silk pajamas it makes it tough gettin' up mornings. After a year you'll stop working horses mornings and start living it up late and that won't hurt your weight, because you're small boned, and the nervous type that don't put it on too much, but it will affect your whole thinking.

"Then you'll marry some broad," he said, "and she'll do the rest for you. She'll stand a hand or two higher than you, and she'll find ways to spend that money that you never even knew existed. 'Now don't take any chances,' she'll tell you every day when you leave the house. 'Don't get hurt.' So while she's out spreading that dough around you'll be going wide on the turns taking that married man's route to protect that money factory. Hell, I've seen it happen dozens of times."

It happened, too, and that was the start of it, and I'm glad McGeady wasn't around to see it. That's a hell of a way to think, though, because I ain't glad at all, because after I come out of that hospital he woulda got me outa that fall the way he got me out of the first one and just by whippin' my tail until I did it.

The first thing I remember when I come to after that first one was seeing them white-painted walls in that little first-aid room that they had there. I'm lying on that cot, and there's that nurse there and the goddam veterinarian and some doctor they called out of the clubhouse and there's McGeady.

"What the hell am I doin' here?" I said. "I'm ridin' in the seventh."

"Lie down," McGeady says. "You already rode in the seventh, if that's what you call riding."

I was some rodeo cowboy up to then, and as McGeady said later if I'd a had another mount that day I'd probably got right up on the sob and rode him like nothing happened. The next day I didn't give it a thought, going to the gate on that first one and comin' out, and I was fine until we come to that first turn and then I could see that animal stumblin' like the other one and me trying to hang on and going down and the whole goddam cavalry troop runnin' over me.

That was a hell of a four or five days. I tried, but I'd break a sweat just going to the gate, and I just couldn't put them up there runnin' and bust them in there.

"You're a coward!" McGeady would scream at me when I'd come back out of the money on something he knew should have won it or got a piece of it. "Ain't that awful? Why, those other jocks tell me you're out there hollering for room when you could put a whole set in that hole sideways. I've got stable fees and entry fees and feed bills piling up here, and I'm being ruined by a yellow little coward I gave almost three years of my life to. Ain't that awful?"

Then he gave me the silent treatment. He wouldn't say a goddam thing to me, sitting around that motel room, me watching the TV but not even knowing what I was looking at, and him going over the *Form*. In the mornings he'd just tell me how he wanted the animals worked but nothing else, until the day he finally made me do it.

"All right," he said that morning, "this is it. I'm running that Trapper in the sixth, and he's gotta win it for me to get out of town. If he don't, you and I are done. I've still got almost two years on your contract, and I'll set you down. You won't ride again, and if you don't ride how in the hell are you ever going to make a decent living? You won't, and you'll have to go home and live off your Old Lady just like your Old Man."

That did it. I wasn't going back to that sick mess, and the truth was I was more scared of McGeady if I didn't bring that Trapper Jay home on top than I was of getting killed. That Trapper Jay was a big five-year-old brute that they'd gelded and the best McGeady had, and on that turn for home I saw that opening and I just set my teeth and hit that sob, and I just put him in there and he just spread horses and made his own hole and we win by almost two.

"You see?" McGeady said, when I come back feeling like the whole world was finally off my shoulders. "That whole thing was just a bad dream, but you're over it now."

So they buried McGeady like three years ago and I paid for the plot and the stone, which wasn't a hell of a lot to do, and it wasn't a hell of a lot of funeral either. There were three of those gyp horsemen who'd known him for like forty years and a couple of grooms and that boy he was breakin' in at the end. We all went out from the funeral parlor in two cars. That's all it took, two cars followin' the hearse, and it was so goddam pathetic that when it was all over I just stood there by that grave in the sunshine in that cemetery and I was crying like a kid.

"Bums!" the Old Man screamed when I first told him I was bustin' out to try to be a jock, and when I think of him calling people like McGeady a bum I could laugh. "You wanna be a bum? They're all bums hang around the track."

That was a laugh, all right. That was ridiculous, like everything's ridiculous, because if they ever ran a World Handicap for bums, the Old Man would have to be top weighted, he's so goddam many lengths ahead of the field. Bums he called them, him sittin' around in his undershirt and, when he couldn't get the money from the Old Lady for the hard stuff, soppin' up the beer, always talkin' about how he could get this job or that job but the one guy was a thief or the other was a miserable sob or the pay wasn't right, and the Old Lady taking in laundry and cleaning offices at night until, after I took off, she eventually just give out and died from being tired, I think, from just working herself to death.

"Be a jockey?" he screamed that day. "Who give you that idea? I'll split his head."

He might have, too, if he was oiled enough. Like I told that Stillman, when he was really drunk he wanted to fight everybody and when there wasn't anybody around he'd fight me. Fight, hell, it wasn't any kind of a fight, just him chasin' me around that kitchen and finally pinning me in the corner behind that goddam table, and then turnin' the table over on me and beatin' the hell out of me because I come in late or give

133

him some lip or flunked some goddam subject in school, but probably because he was ashamed of me I was so goddam small.

"Be a jockey?" he screamed at me that day. "You can't no more be a jockey than I can be President Eisenhower! Who give you that idea? Tell me!"

"Nobody," I said. "I figured it out for myself."

That was a goddam lie, but I never told him the truth half the time anyway. Like as not, if I'd a told him it was that Al Barone, hanging around Goldman's down at the corner and making book, he'd agone down there oiled up and split his head like he said.

"Hey, jock!" Barone used to say to me. "Hey, Arcaro! How come you're here when it says in the *Form* that you're ridin' in that stake at Belmont today?"

Or sometimes it would be Santa Anita, or Hialeah or Saratoga, and then I got to reading about Arcaro and all them Derbies and all them stakes he won and all the money he made. Then I got to thinking and romancing the whole idea, and finally I got up the courage and I asked that Barone one day how the hell you get to be a jock.

"You know somethin'?" he said. "You just might make one. You meet me here tomorrow morning at eight o'clock, and I'll take you out to the track."

That might have been the greatest morning in my whole goddam life because it was in the spring and it was a clear morning and the leaves were all just out and we went down to the rail to wait for that Donovan, that Barone knew, to come back with his last set. I just stood there bug-eyed, watching those horses come by with the boys hunched over them and everything otherwise so quiet that you could hear the sound of their hoofs as they came down the stretch and then getting louder and then the boys clucking to them and then talking to them as they went by.

Then that Donovan saw Barone, and he come over to the rail on his stable pony and reached down and shook hands with Barone and then with me. Then we followed him, walking behind the pony following the set back to the stable where the grooms were just starting to sponge them off by the time we got there, and them horses just gleaming there in the sun.

"He says he ain't got nothing right now," Barone said when he come walking back from talking with Donovan, and I thought I was gonna be sick to my stomach I wanted it so much. "He says he's got three exercise boys, and he ain't got time this meeting to start teaching you."

"Tell him I'll do anything," I said. "Tell him I'll do anything around here he wants me to do, and I'll work the cheapest of anybody just to stay."

"You tell him yourself," Barone said, and he took me over to Donovan, and I don't remember all I said but he musta finally felt sorry for me because he finally said if I really meant that I'd do anything around there he'd take me on for the rest of the meeting. Then Barone drove me home and I was away up there, except that I had to tell the Old Man, and I waited until we finished eating there in the kitchen that night.

"You're gonna what?" he said, jumping up. "You're gonna quit school to be a race-track bum? You are like hell! Why, I'll split your goddam head!"

"Let the boy go," the Old Lady said.

She was standing there at the sink, starting to do the dishes, and the Old Man couldn't believe his ears. I don't think the Old Lady had ever stood up to him before in her whole life, and he just stood there with the funniest surprised look on his face like somebody had just yanked him up and choked him right down two steps out of the gate.

"I said let the boy go," she said. "There's nothing for him around here."

"I'm goin' out," the Old Man said, and he went into the bedroom and grabbed up his shirt and he was still tuckin' the tails in when he went out the door. When he came in I heard him because I couldn't get to sleep that night. I heard him bangin' around the kitchen, probably looking in the refrigerator to see if there was any beer left, but I didn't give a damn any more because I was goin' with the horses and already I was seeing myself a great jock.

Then that morning I was up at 5 o'clock, and you couldn't

even get a bus until 6:15. The Old Lady made me breakfast, which I could hardly eat I was so goddam excited, and every morning for the three weeks left in the meeting I took that bus and I didn't come home again until night.

That Donovan worked my tail off, too, which was all right with me. He had me muckin' out stalls and wrestlin' those hay bales that weighed damn near as much as me and walkin' hots, which made me feel real important, and with the first money he paid me I got me some boots and new Levis and a cap, and those exercise boys were real nice and finally put me up on the stable pony one day and let me ride it around under the shed.

I rode that pony every chance I got, sittin' there on it and just making believe I was up on a real one. Then the afternoons were great, hanging around the jocks' quarters with them exercise boys between races, and then out on that balcony they have for them there on the clubhouse turn with the jocks who didn't have anything in that race out there in that sunlight in their clean, bright silks for the next race watching the pack come into the turn and go out of it and talkin' about this rider or that horse and my ears perked for everything.

"I'm sorry," that Donovan said to me when the last week of the meeting opened, "but at the end of the week I'm shipping out like everybody else and I haven't got room for you."

"But I'll work for nothin'," I said, "just for my keep."

"I know, and you're a hard-working kid," he said, and then he said: "Do you know old McGeady?"

"I know who he is," I said, "but I never met him."

"Well, he's losing his boy," he said. "Of course, you won't be able to work horses for him yet, but he's hard up and he can teach you. I'll talk to him."

So the next day he told me he'd seen McGeady, and I went over there. I was scared as hell, because if McGeady didn't take me I didn't know how I was ever gonna make it, and there he was, sittin' by his barn in that canvas chair and chewin' that tobacco.

"Well," he said, "I don't know. Donovan tells me you've never been up on anything but the pony, and I don't know."

"But I'll do anything," I said.

"I know," he said. "Donovan tells me you're a good doer. How old are you and what's your weight?"

"I'm seventeen," I said, lyin' by about six months, "and I weigh 102."

"You mean going on seventeen, or seventeen?" he said.

"Goin' on seventeen," I said.

"You see?" he said. "You were lying. I've got no use for liars around me. My life is hard enough without having my help lying to me."

"I'll never lie to you again Mister McGeady," I said, and I meant it. "I'm sorry, but I'll be seventeen in less than six months."

"You got small hands and feet," he said. "You know what that means?"

"No, sir," I said.

"It means you're lucky," he said. "You're luckier than most of them."

"How's that?" I said, because I didn't know what the hell he was talkin' about, and it was about time I found out I was lucky about something.

"You'll never grow too big for it," he said. "A lot of kids like you come around wanting to be jocks, and I can tell from the size of their hands and feet that by the time I spent a couple of years of my life making them finished riders they'd grow too big for it. You're just born lucky."

Born lucky? All my life I'd been too goddam small compared to them other kids to play in their goddam ball games, and all my life they were beatin' up on me on the street or in the alleys if they could catch me, and now I had it on all them sobs because I was born lucky.

"Then you're gonna take me?" I said, because I figured that's what he meant.

"There you go," he said. "I don't like people around me who jump to conclusions, and you're one of those people. Right?"

"Right," I said. "I mean, no sir."

"I wouldn't be able to pay you anything," he said, "just your keep. Then if I made a rider out of you you'd get your fee and

137

the piece of the purse, but I don't know that I can make a rider out of you anyway."

"I don't care," I said. "I'll work for nothin'."

"I'm shipping out like everybody else Sunday morning," he said. "I don't know what time they'll move us, so be here by seven and don't bring any wardrobe trunk because we travel light."

Some wardrobe trunk. All I had was that old zipper bag with an extra pair of jeans and another T-shirt and underwear and socks that the Old Lady washed for me and a pair of old sneakers for when I wasn't wearing the boots. That night I didn't tell the Old Man, and he was still sleeping the next morning when the Old Lady got up to make my breakfast and cry a little when I left to make that 6:15 bus to the track.

At the track McGeady was all set to go, waiting for the railroad people to tell him when to load his two and the pony. He was sitting there in his canvas chair again in front of the barn where he was stabled, and when I walked up to him I had this cigarette in my mouth and he just reached up and snatched that cigarette out and threw it on the ground and hit it with a spray of that tobacco juice.

"That's awful," he said. "There have been more stable fires blamed on defective wiring that were started by help that smoked, and I just can't follow you around all day with a wad of tobacco in my cheek, because I've got other things to do. Why didn't you tell me you smoke?"

"I don't," I said. "I mean I won't any more."

"Not around me you won't," he said.

We were three days in that horse car goin' south, with the horsemen bitching every time we got sidetracked or hung up in some freight yard, but with me living every minute of it. The railroad allowed you one man to take care of three horses and that was McGeady, so I was stowing away along with a half dozen others in that car who shouldn't have been there, either. Whenever we'd feel that train slowin' down night or day we'd be in them holes between the bales of hay, and it was amazing how everybody lived like that, keeping the car clean and keeping themselves clean, washing and shaving in a pail of water, and feeding the animals three times a day and the rest of the time just sleeping or lookin' out the open door or just talkin'.

McGeady wasn't a big talker, but when he talked everybody else listened. Mostly he just talked to me, though, and he sure had me captured, telling me about some of the great races he'd seen, and especially about the best jocks he'd seen and what each one could do, like how McCreary was the best at rating a horse without taking a big hold and about Guerin's rhythm, and how Woodhouse could kick and push at the same time as a horse takes off and how Georgie Woolfe had been a picture hand-ridin' a horse and how Atkinson handled the whip and how Shoe was the best of the new ones and how Arcaro was the best all around. Then, when we got down there and the meeting started and when he didn't have one of his entered, he'd have me over at the gate with him, watchin' how they broke 'em out, or at the wire, watchin' how they finished on 'em.

In the mornings, after that Billy Noel had worked his two or three for him and we'd sponged them down and rubbed them with the body brace and walked them, he'd have me in that barn, sittin' on a bale of hay with the reins tied to a bucket for pressure like a horse's head and practicin' with that whip. He'd have me whackin' that bale and practicin' at switchin' hands with my hands full of the reins already but without puttin' the whip in your mouth, and practicin' how to twirl the whip because them starters won't let you go in the gate with the whip up.

"It's a matter of pride," he said. "Most of those fashionable riders can't switch without passing it through their mouths and most of them can't twirl a whip up and so they have to use rubber bands, but you'll do it. You'll do it because with the stock I can afford there's nothing I can do to make them into quality horses but maybe I can make you into a quality rider."

The first time he put me on one of his, just to ride it around under the shed, and he pulled up them stirrups from the way I'd been ridin' long on that pony, I thought I had no perch and I'd fall off. Then the first time he let me work one and it run off, with me yankin' at it and sawin' on its mouth until I was exhausted, I damn near did fall off.

"That's awful!" he screamed at me after it had run itself out and he come gallopin' up on that pony. "That first day you came around why didn't you tell me that you don't have any brains in your head? You weigh 102 pounds and that animal weighs 1,200, and you think you're going to tire it out? When one of them runs off with you let it run. Now I've spent all that time on you, and you don't even have brains enough to know that!"

It was a long time before he put me in that first race and I was proud as hell gettin' into them silks and scared as hell, too. I can't even think of the name of that animal any more, like Fly Leaf or Flying Leaf, and I ain't gonna think of it tonight. He knew it didn't have much chance and I didn't improve its chances any either, because I was all over that animal, and when I come back my silks were hangin' out at the waist and I'd lost the whip and I thought he'd give me holy hell for sure.

"Well," he said, "you had to get wet sometime, and you did. That wasn't too bad. It could have been worse. You'll learn."

That really surprised me. That's all he said, and I thought I never would learn. I rode eighteen goddam races, most of them on his and some of them on friends of his, and I got a few of them up into the money and I must have got beat a half dozen noses before I brought that thing called Spearchucker in. Hell, he had that race won on the turn for home, but I was so goddam hungry to win one that I rode him down that stretch like it was the goddam Derby and won by six when I coulda just hand rode him easy and won by two.

"Congratulations," he said when I come back to the winner's circle, listening to that applause and livin' it, "but you just gave my horse away. Now if I run him back for this price they'll bet him off the board and there'll be fourteen claims in the box for him. I just wish you hadn't done that."

Hell, there's a lot I wish I hadn't done, and there's many a time I've wished he was still around. I probably wouldn'ta seen him much any more and maybe I wouldn'ta seen him at all, but maybe it woulda been different if I'd a just known he was around.

Like with that broad, and she's gonna be goddam surprised, too. Hell, I'd never even met her yet and he didn't even know she was alive but he sure as hell called that marriage like he'd studied all her past performances in the *Form*. I don't know what the hell she did all day, but there was no way I was gonna let her run loose alone at night, and I'd get to that track so goddam hung over just in time to climb aboard that first animal that I wouldn't sober up until the sixth race, and like he said I'd be out there protectin' that money factory and that's the way the whole goddam thing happened.

"You just can't play it cozy!" he'd holler at me over and over after that first spill and before he got me out of it. "When they've got you in a blind switch you just can't be back there three feet. You've got to be six inches from the heels of that horse ahead so that when you see that hole open either side you're in there. If you're back there three feet that hole will close before you can get into it, and your animal will hit those heels and I'll have to bury you. I haven't got the money for that."

And it happened just the way he said it would, with me tryin' to play it cozy like he said and layin' back there too far, and I wouldn't even know what the hell happened if I didn't go look at the film patrol movie when I couldn't put it together afterwards. I could remember goin' to the track that day and riding the first two races, and then there's that whole goddam piece right out of my whole goddam life that I still can't remember at all. I still can't remember gettin' up on that horse, and I still can't remember ridin' that thing except what I saw in that movie where it's like I'm watchin' someone else even though I know it's me when that animal stumbles and I'm tryin' to hang on and I go down and all them other animals come over me and play soccer with me down that backstretch.

Maybe I shouldn't have watched that movie, but that Stillman says he doesn't think it made any difference, and all I was trying to do was piece together that part of my life that I can't remember at all, from coming back to the jocks' room after ridin' that second race and then wakin' up in the hospital after them five days. That's what they told me later, that I was out five goddam days, and that scared the hell out of me, because that's like bein' dead five days if you can't remember anything or that you were even alive, until I come to all wired and pulleyed up and could hardly make out anything at first, and then I saw them two nurses that was that one nurse and sometime later that I don't know when the hell it was I saw two of my Old Man and that was enough so that I didn't give a damn if I died right there.

Race-track bums. That's what he called them, and then when I started to make it good he'd be around the stable mornings at least once every goddam week and sometimes twice a week. There he'd be when I'd come back with the last set, waitin' for me, all cleaned up and shaved and even wearin' a goddam tie and smilin' to everybody and bein' so goddam nice that everybody thought he was a helluva guy, and I'd peel him a fifty or a C-note from whatever I was carrying for walk around money.

That was ridiculous. The whole goddam thing's ridiculous, because if I just had the money he bummed off me all them goddam years I coulda just sent it to them people of that little girl. No name. Just to that Mr. and Mrs. Wade that I never even saw or wouldn't ever want to see, instead of him drinkin' it up and hauntin' me all my goddam life.

Like I told that Stillman. Like I told him about those goddam nightmares I had when I come out of the hospital and started gettin' up on those goddam things again so chicken-scared that I was shakin' all over and there was no way I was gonna bust those sobs in there the way McGeady finally made me do it that first time. Like I told him about that one where I'm walking down the sidewalk like at noontime in this whole crowd or sometimes I'm trying to get to the jocks' quarters at like Aqueduct and I'm like six inches tall and all I see is all these big shoes and I'm gonna get walked on when I wake up shakin' all over and breakin' a sweat. That one's bad enough, I told him, but the other one is worse when I'm like six inches tall again and it's the Old Man chasin' me around the kitchen and through the rest of the flat with the goddam whip, and while he's runnin' after me he's got the goddam whip in his mouth. The first time I had that one, and right in the middle of being scared as hell, I had to laugh. I had to laugh that he wasn't even up on an animal and the miserable sob still couldn't pass a whip hand-to-hand without passin' it through his mouth, and I was even sayin' to myself that I bet he couldn't even twirl it comin' out of a gate without a rubber band around his finger when he gets me in that corner of the kitchen in that goddam nightmare and he takes that whip out of his mouth and I wake up screamin' and sweatin' and sometimes I even have to get up and puke.

Dreamin' is natural, that Stillman said, but I told him not like the dreams I got, and he said that's the way I'm just naturally tryin' to relieve my tension or some goddam thing. Like that time I told him about this other dream I get sometimes where I'm like ten or eleven years old and I'm in this goddam bathtub and my mother is washing me and calling me Nicky and, hell, I don't ever remember her washing me, except maybe she did when I was very small, and she never called me Nicky but always Nicholas, and this goddam dream always makes me cry. So he says that's because now I'm having this feeling of helplessness, or something, and that I'm like embarrassed and like ashamed of needing somebody or something.

So the last couple of times I seen him I told him I was gettin' better and that I was cuttin' down on the booze, and I wasn't lyin' to him, either. I figured I was maybe gettin' better but, hell, I knew I was never gonna get better with me just gallopin' horses mornings, me just a goddam exercise boy after what I was and what I coulda been, and them trainers that used to run after me duckin' me now whenever they see me comin' because they're scared as I am to put me up on one, bein' scared that I'll get killed and maybe rack up their animal and maybe kill somebody else, too.

So, instead, I killed that poor little girl or maybe I didn't kill her and I don't know and I'll never know. I know one thing, though, and that's that the Old Man and that broad and

Whitey and that Stillman and a lot of other people are gonna be goddam surprised, and that Schwartzman, too.

"What do you want a hand gun for?" he says to me.

"I'm gonna hold up the Valley National Bank," I said.

"I'm serious," he said. "What do you want it for?"

"For my own protection," I said. "What the hell do you care?"

"I don't know about you," he said. "Are you feelin' all right?"

All of a sudden he's Mister Nice, but he sold me the goddam thing. Thirty bucks he took for a piece of junk with a goddam plastic handle and cheap shiny barrel and after all the money he made on me from the stuff I took to him like them cuff links. Four hundred bucks he give me for them things that that stupid broad paid sixteen hundred for, except I had to pay the bill when it come with the others, and there I am with a pair of sixteen-hundred-buck cuff links with my initials on them in diamonds and I don't even own a shirt with them kind of cuffs. It's ridiculous. Everything's ridiculous.

"Those things cost sixteen hundred," I told that Schwartzman.

"You got took," he said.

"I didn't get took," I said. "They come from a high-class place."

"High-class places got a license to steal," he said. "I ain't. Besides, where am I gonna find somebody else with the initials N.B.? Four hundred bucks."

Some citizen he is, so I had to give him thirty bucks for this piece of junk, but I made him throw the cartridges in, too. Then I put them in right there, and scared the hell out of him.

"How do I know this thing will fire?" I said, cockin' it.

"Don't shoot it in here!" he says. "Put that thing away, please!"

So he's gonna be a surprised sob, too, or maybe he won't be but I don't give a damn. When I took the goddam piece of junk out in the park that night it fired all right and it will fire again and it ain't gonna be like the first time with that goddam razor blade when I tried to cozy it like hangin' back there three feet instead of six inches from their heels, and this time I'm gonna bust that sob right in there just like spreadin' horses.

IX

ROBERT F. MABRY, M.D.

I think my feet hit that treadle plate at the E.R. door in a dead heat with the front wheels of the ambulance stretcher. You could call it a photo finish, except that at the time I don't have any idea who the passenger is. All I know is that I'm finishing dinner with Squash Stillman at Palumbo's, kicking around complexes, or whatever, when they give me a blast on the blower with a gunshot wound of the head that's starting on the way in.

"Oh, come on," I say. "I've been playing doctor all day. Now I'm going home and play exhausted husband and father. Get Pete or Freeman."

The Regular Academics like Peterson and Freeman are the sons of the Regular Army types. These two R.A.s have been up in an O.R. for two hours playing now-you-watch-me, redoing an ulnar nerve anastomosis, one of those Swiss watch jobs you do squinting through a microscope, so I thrill Stillman with a Daytona Five ride back to the factory and drop him in the parking lot.

"If this patient just happened to try to part his own cortex," I tell Stillman getting out of the car, because I don't know if it's a suicide try or a holdup victim or an accidental shooting, "and I happen to get him to your couch, you may want to monitor this. No extra credits. Just experience."

"Thank you, but no," he says. "I'm too depleted, and you can tell me about it tomorrow. May good fortune attend your endeavors."

So I sprint in, take the stairs down, meet the patient at the door and we wheel him into Minor Ops. While the ambulance people are transferring him from their stretcher and I'm finding his pulse so that I know that we've still got a live one, he moans just once and I see he's an adult but short and small boned.

"Anybody know what happened?" I say, and I find the entry wound, blackened and oozing a little and about the size of your little fingertip, in his right temple.

"Shot himself," one of the ambulance characters says. "That's what the cops say. They found a .22 handgun lyin' there, and his landlady heard the shot or heard him fall or something."

"Do we have a name?" one of the nurses says, starting the chart while we're starting to strip his shirt and undershirt off, and then she says: "He looks familiar, like he's been in here before."

"I don't know if he's been in here before, dear," the same ambulance dude says, "but his name is Nick Braff. He's Nick Braff, the jockey. You got a celebrity."

I don't believe this. It's ridiculous, like my whole life. I'm one of fifty kids taking the exam, and the next day this major calls me in and he says: "Of all those who took that test, Mabry, you have the highest aptitude to be a good medic. Do you want to be one?" If I say no, and if I get out of Korea alive, I'm running a number 7 bed-laster in a shoe factory like the Old Man. I've never even thought of being a doctor, but I say yes, and so forty minutes ago, while Squash Stillman and I are sitting in Palumbo's kicking around Nick Braff's bag in life, Nick Braff is putting a .22 to his head and I've never even met this poor little runt before and here we are.

"C'mon, c'mon," I'm saying to that nurse named Madeline something who's got the cuff on him. "What are you getting? And let's get his shoes and pants off, too, somebody."

"His blood pressure," this Madeline something says, "is 145 over 90."

His pressure is up but his pulse is only about 100, so I'm thinking, that this could be from mobilizing his adrenalin. Also, he's more stuporous than comatose and his respirations are regular, so it figures, and I hope I'm right, that his brain stem isn't about to flake out from pressure from a big clot somewhere up there in his attic.

"Has he had any seizures?" I say, because convulsions could mean serious damage to the cerebral cortex, the old gray matter —about six square feet of it, it says in the textbooks—that's the clearinghouse for the bodily responses, language, foresight, abstract thought and all that. Half of that textbook stuff was abstract thought to me, because there I was, thirty-one years old and starting against all those young brights from Harvard and Yale and Stanford, and actually flunking anatomy and neuroanatomy, when I knew that, if we'd ever get done with those printed pages and get with some patients, I could give those R.A.s points.

"Seizures?" somebody says, and it's that intern Stern, who makes it with me as definitely one of those brights. "Not since he's been here."

"Look, Doctor," I say. "I know that. I'm asking the ambulance people. Where are they?"

"One of them's on the phone," somebody else says. "I don't know where the other one went."

I'm still looking for the exit wound, but there isn't any. It didn't come out either of his eyeballs, so the damn thing is still in there somewhere, but I figure that that's not too unusual for a .22 short, anyway, and I try to rouse him.

"Nick? Nick Braff?" I shout at him, but I get no response. "Can you hear me, Nick?"

I'm shouting at Nick Braff, and this is what I mean about my life. Four years ago I'm still in med school and, what with the Old Man laid up in the hospital again with that bullous emphysema and no insurance and no dough and the loans I had to take out to keep me in there, I'm $8,000 in debt. Nick Braff—and this is what I mean—is riding a horse named Wind Song or Wind something in that Special that was the biggest thing in years. The sports pages are full of it, so I decide to make book. I'm holding about $400 that I hustle in two days, when I figure I might as well go the whole way so I take it down to that horse parlor behind the poolroom on Merchant Street and I lay it all on Nick Braff, whatever his horse's name was. If he doesn't come in I'm gone, because there's no way I'm going to be able to pay off, but it's a Saturday and it's on TV and I'm down in that student lounge with all those eager souls who bet with me thinking that, if they win, they're going to get paid. When that thing started it looked like I was as good as gone, because some other horse is away out there and Nick Braff on his Wind something is shut off back there somewhere when all of a sudden he comes busting out, and he wins going away with me out of my chair riding right up there with him all the way. That night, after I collect and pay off my own winners, I'm still more than $500 to the good to lay against the Old Man's latest bills just before one of those big blebs in his lungs burst and took him.

"Nick?" I'm saying now, shouting at him again. "Nick Braff? Can you hear me?"

I shake him a little, still calling his name, but I still don't really rouse him. All I get is a moan.

"He had no seizures," the other nurse says. "The ambulance men say that he did some moaning, but that's all. No vomiting, either."

"So let's get that IV going," I say to Harvey Mosler, the surgical resident, "but we won't sock it to him too fast, because his brain, swelling the way it is, won't like the extra fluids."

"You want the portable X ray, or are we going to wheel him in there?" Stern says.

"Neither," I say. "We don't need to know right away exactly where that damn thing is. We need to know what he's doing."

I still haven't roused him, so now I bend over his chest and lean down hard on him with my knuckle digging into his sternum. When I do he lets out another moan and grimaces on the left side of his face, and he brings his left hand up to push my hand away.

"Hold his left arm down," I tell Stern.

I lean down on him again, and I notice that this time he also grimaces a little on the right, not as much as on the left, and he moves his right shoulder slightly. His right mouth droops a little, but the muscles around his right eye winced, so it's not a brain stem facial paralysis. I'm reasoning now that the trouble is above the tentorium, the membrane that keeps the back burners of the brain from weighing down on the brain stem,

148

and if I'm right and it's all upstairs we'll have a little better shot at it.

"So let's get that Foley into him," I say to Mosler. "You got it?"

"Right," he says, and when he puts it up in there we get the expected reaction. There's that moan, and the left hand goes down to try to push it away.

In a couple of minutes we get 250 cc.'s and it's clear, so we know that his kidneys and his bladder are okay, but meanwhile I've reached under his head and bent his neck forward and around. It's not stiff—no obvious guarding of the muscles —so I know there's not a lot of blood in the spinal fluid at the moment.

Now I start to really frisk him, from the top down. There's some swelling and redness around his right eye and blood underneath from the entry wound. I hold his lids open and flash the light into his eyes, and his pupils are round, about equal in size, and they react to the light. The eyes wander about the room a little and seem to move together, so we've got some good signs.

"Ophthalmoscope?" I say. "Nurse? Somebody? Let's go on the snap count here."

When somebody hands me one I look into the back of first his right eye and then his left for fresh hemorrhaging and any sign of swelling of the optic nerve head that would indicate threatening pressure inside the skull. It's absent, but when I bend over him to look that closely I catch alcohol on his breath.

"The veins are a little full on the right side," I say, "but no papilledema. Let me have an otoscope."

I want to look in his ears for blood behind the drums, but they're full of wax and it's not worth cleaning them out now. There's no Battle sign, anyway—blood under the skin over the mastoid bone—although it may show up later to suggest a fracture at the base of the skull.

"Let me have a pin," I say. "Anybody got a pin?"

I stick him, not hard enough to break the skin but hard enough for him to feel it, on both sides of the face, on the fore-

149

head and over both cheekbones. He winces a little, and I go to several places on his arms and hands, his thighs and his feet. He's not quite as responsive on the right as on the left but not totally numb, either.

I'd like to get him, now, to squeeze my finger, but I can't rouse him enough to get the idea through to him. I tell Stern to pick up the left arm and raise it and I raise the right.

"Nick?" I'm shouting. "Nick? Can you hear me? We're holding your arms up. When we let go, I want you to hold them right where they are. Do you hear me, Nick?"

"Uhnn," he says, just groaning again.

I don't know if I'm getting through but, when I signal Stern and we let the arms go and the right one comes down, he holds the left one up there for a couple of seconds. Then, when I try to get a response from his legs, the left one moves a little better than the right, but I can't really test him.

"Let me borrow somebody's tomahawk," I say.

With the reflex hammer I tap each tendon in order, and the reflexes seem a little jumpy on the right side. Then, with the handle of the hammer I start just above the heel of his right foot, and I scrape up toward the little toe and across the base of the toes. Babinski . . . 1896 . . . or some such date that all those textbook brights would remember, even if they had no idea why the reaction is what it is. The normal response above six months of age is for the toes to curl downward, but now his big toe goes up and the others fan a little. His left foot is normal, though, so it has to mean trouble along the path between the cerebral cortex on the left side and the beginning of the nerves to the right leg.

"I get a positive Babinski on the right only," I say. "How's his pressure now?"

"It's 150 over 70, Doctor," the nurse says.

I'm taking his pulse again, and it's slowed from about 100 to 70. The slowing, along with the change in his blood pressure from 145 over 90, worries me now, because it's a strong indicator of increasing pressure upstairs. Right in the middle of this, though, and while I'm taking his pulse, I notice the scars from the first time he tried to take the same trip, but with the razor blade. I've forgotten all about Squash Stillman, and tomorrow I'll have to tell him that he struck out, but I can't carry that bag now.

"Let's give him 20 milligrams of Decadron and pronto," I say, because it's a real potent cortisone preparation to help reduce the brain swelling.

"But that's 5 cc.'s of Decadron," this Stern says, and now he's a walking conversion table. "Isn't that a lot?"

"Look, Doctor," I say. "I know it's a lot, but he needs it. He's starting to fall apart, so I want a syringe full, and I'll slip it into the IV tubing."

"Yes, sir," he says.

"And somebody check to see if those X-ray gals are ready to go," I say, figuring I'll want first just anterior-posterior and stereolaterals of the skull, and then possibly an arteriogram. "Somebody else get the lab on the ball because he needs a CBC, blood volume, and a couple of units of blood ready."

"I've already called them," Stern says.

"X ray is ready," somebody else says.

"Good," I say, "so let's wheel him over and see what kind of trash he's got in there. Meanwhile somebody check with the O.R. about a room."

We follow him out through that usual E.R. scene, with babies squalling and kids running around while their mothers and their sires are making their beefs at the desk. Since Tom Hunter has come on here during the day there's order, but on a busy night it's still like a barnyard.

We wait for the films in that alcove next to X-ray, where they have the instant developer and the viewing boxes on the wall, and it's really ridiculous, my life. I'm eighteen years old and I can get a football scholarship, but I'm going to be a real hero, instead. We were all going to be real heroes, more than half that graduating class, and I'm going to be a tail gunner, or something, until that major tells me I've got all that aptitude to be a medic and I'm at Fort Sam for twelve weeks, all of us learning first aid and how to be scrub nurses and crawling on our bellies with the live ammo over our heads. All you see is movies, and never a live patient, and you practice giving shots

151

to an orange until the last day when they line you up, sixty guys in two rows. That captain walks down the line with the syringes, and he says: "Now you men on this side give those men over there a shot, and then you men over here give these other men a shot." A half dozen guys pass out and a half dozen others jump away and try to refuse it, but everybody graduates, and here I am with Nick Braff.

"All right, Doctor," I say to Stern. "We've got a right side point of entry, but we've got the right sided weakness implicating the left side of the brain. Where do you think we're going to get the ball?"

"Well," he says, and he runs it right back at me, "for a small missile such as a .22 calibre, it would have to penetrate directly through the brain and strike an area on the left side where the motor pathways converge, but without injuring those on the right. This would probably have to be down at the base of the brain near the mesencephalon, where the left peduncle passes ventrally into the brain stem. This would give the right paralysis and the right Babinski sign."

He's a bright, all right, and knows the anatomy.

"You mean," I say, "that it missed the right peduncle, which is exactly next door, and the basilar artery, which is right under it, and the oculomotor complex just above it?"

"It would be possible, wouldn't it?" he says.

"Like a 1000 to 1 shot," I say. "Anyway, he doesn't demonstrate any signs of brain stem difficulty. His pupils are okay, he moves his eyes together and he's not deeply comatose. The blood pressure and pulse changes tell us that he has some increased pressure, and we're going to have to do something about that, but my bet is that he aimed the gun too far forward, and that the bullet entered the skull obliquely, just above the sphenoid wing. It hit the inside of the frontal bone and ran around the inside of the skull like a steel ball in a pinball machine. It probably did minimal damage to the right side of the brain, although there must be bone fragments, skin and hair blasted inside. By the time it got around to the left side the velocity had diminished, and the bullet had fragmented. Then it probably injured the left frontal cortex in the motor area, which would give us our findings, the right arm and leg weakness and the Babinski."

The X rays are out now, and I snap them up onto the view boxes. There it is, all laid out for us.

"You see the point of entry on the right side?" I say. "Not a very large hole, but look at the bone fragments just inside. All the pieces of lead are on the left, and there's that one large one away back there."

"Correct," Stern says, as if he's giving *me* marks.

"You know how to get a 3-D look at those lead fragments?" I say.

"No," he says, "I don't."

I place the two stereolaterals right next to each other. I tell him to stand back and cross his eyes, so that the two images will come together.

"This is amazing!" he says. "It looks like you could reach right in and pluck it right out. You know?"

I'll have to go in on the right side, I'm thinking, walking into X ray, and clean out the debris and damaged brain tissue. What worries me, though, is what may be happening on the left. The bullet fragments are probably sterile, and because it's better to wait a few days if we can, they don't need to come out right now. If he's building up a blood clot on the left, though, we may have to open that side, too, and go after that right away, and then I wouldn't bet on Nick Braff in *this* Special.

"How's he doing?" I ask this Madeline something.

"There's no change in his vital signs," she says. "He awakens a little when we move him, but he doesn't move his right side too well."

Now I'm figuring that I'd better grab an arteriogram. Into the blood vessels on the left I'll shoot some of that dye that shows up on X rays, and if a clot is displacing them from their normal positions we'll see it.

"I think I'd better 'gram him," I say.

"You don't want us to call the neuroradiologist, Doctor?" one of the X-ray dolls says.

"Hell, no!" I say. "He'll monkey around with a catheter in the aorta, and take seven hundred pretty pictures while the patient flakes out on us. Just get me an arteriogram set, and I'll do a quick direct carotid stick."

I put on sterile gloves and paint his neck with antiseptic. Then, for anesthetic, I inject a little Xylocaine into the skin on the left side.

"Hold his left arm down," I tell Stern, "because I don't want him blocking this field goal try."

With my left fingers I feel the common carotid artery in his neck just to the left of his windpipe. With my right hand I jab the needle downward and, as it enters the artery, blood spurts back.

"Right through the goal posts," I say. "Now I want two films per second for the first four seconds, and then one per second for four more."

I tell them what projections I want, and I get Stern to help me into the lead apron. Then I fill the syringes, and I'm ready.

"Shoot!" I say.

The injection is painful, and when I go in, my Nick Braff moves a little.

"Look," I say to the doll who's holding his head. "You've got to hold his gourd still. It won't burn your hands off."

Those X rays come out of that processor like a loose roll of toilet paper, and I slap them up to look at them. The large arteries with the dye in them show up bright against the gray of the skull, and as I look along the row of films, the arteries fade into the smaller arterioles and then the capillaries, and finally, at the end of the line, the veins stand out as the dye appears again as it starts to leave the skull.

"Very good," I say. "No displacement worth worrying about, so right now no clot. The circulation looks a little slow, so you can bet the brain's tight from swelling."

"How are you going to handle that?" Stern says.

"That's always the problem," I say, "and in the old days it was responsible for a lot of postoperative death. We'll give him more Decadron, and start the Mannitol as soon as we get to the O.R. That should dampen down the swelling so, with luck, we can get him safely opened and closed."

They wheel him back to Minor Ops now, and when we get

there I find out I can have O.R. 4 immediately. I call upstairs then to check if Peterson and Freeman are still playing tick tack toe with that ulnar, and it turns out that they're closing. I tell the nurse to pass the word to them that I'll need one of them to scrub with me on this one, and when I come off the phone there are a couple of detectives who want to talk to me.

"What do you think, Doc?" one of them says. "You think he'll make it?"

"He's got a chance," I say. "There are a lot of lead fragments, pieces of bone, hair and skin strewn around in there, but his vital signs are pretty stable at the moment. Of course, we can't really assess it until we get in."

"You find any signs of a struggle on his body?" the other one says. "Bruises, or anything like that?"

"No," I say. "Nothing like that."

"Then you figure he tried the Dutch act?" he says. "Suicide?"

"That would be my opinion," I say, "because he tried it before, and he's been under psychiatric counseling. He didn't leave a note?"

"Nothing," the same one says, "but if you can fill us in on the other attempt you can save us a lot of trouble."

I tell them about the first try with the razor blade, and I give them Stillman's name. They give me their names and their phone number.

"So we'll appreciate it," one of them says, "if you'll give us a call on his condition when you're through operating."

"It'll be late," I say.

"No matter. We're on all night," the other one says and off they go.

"So let's shave his head," I tell this Madeline after they leave, "and clean up the entry wound. Put a dressing on it, and we'll do the final prep upstairs."

"You want me to save his hair?" she says.

"Yes," I say and she knows without me telling her that it goes along in a plastic bag with the chart in case I lose and the mortician wins.

Lose? Hell, I'm not gonna lose. At least, that's the way I think and that's the way I've always thought. *Gimme the damn ball,*

155

I used to think, *and I'll take it in*. Or if I was out there with the bases loaded and half those kids afraid they might have to handle a bad bounce I used to actually pray: *Hit it to me. God, please, let him hit it to me. Just let him hit it to me this once, God, if you don't ever do anything for me again*.

I don't understand it, because the Old Man was never that way. For thirty years or more he just fought a draw every day with that number 7 bed-laster, the toughest machine in the shop, sewing around those heels and toes while it kicked hell out of him, and he never complained because he never thought he could win and, hell, he couldn't. In the summers, when I'd take his lunch pail to him, I saw how hard he had to work and I knew how we lived with hand-me-down clothes and three of us in a bed. One Christmas I got a pair of shoelaces and a comb and some hard candy, and Helen was living upstairs from us and having the first of her five kids then in the same kind of life and I said the hell with it, I can win.

"You mean you want to be a doctor?" the Old Man said when I came off the war and I told him, and you would have thought I'd said I wanted to be the president of the Rogers and Carney Shoe Company, which was the biggest thing in his world. "You can never be a doctor."

"The hell I can't," I said. "I can be a good doctor."

For some reason, once that Osterman got me bugged on it and even when I was under that textbook trauma, I knew I could do it. I knew that once I got with those patients I'd be better than those brights, and in gross anatomy it started. There were thirty tables and four guys to a cadaver, and I'd blow my lunch hour and get there early and do my table and then somebody else's, because I could see it all exposed there and not just read about it. That second year, after I'd flunked those two textbooks and I had to hit them day and night when I wasn't slinging hamburgers in the White Tower, I'd have the three other guys doing the dissecting and I'd sit there with my nose in the book and one day I actually fell asleep with my face on the cadaver's belly.

Hell, when those brights were like ten years old and in the fifth grade and playing cops-and-robbers after school, I was up in Hokkaido, ninety miles from the Russians across that Sōya Strait. I'm the doctor, Osterman tells me. I'm nineteen years old and I'm the doctor for eighty guys at that radar site, checking the whores for VD and swabbing throats and handing out pills and calling Osterman when I'd get in trouble. Then that afternoon he called me and he said: "Listen, Mabry, you've been doing a good job playing doctor up there so I've got a real one for you now. Headquarters of Air-Sea Rescue in Tokyo just called me and told me we've got a jet shot down up there and they know where it is. They said: 'We see you've got a medic in the area, so send him.' Now they're sending a copter up, and it'll be there in a few minutes and you'll have to jump out of it. You haven't ever jumped, have you?"

So I said: "Out of a plane, with a parachute? No, sir." So he said: "Well, you don't have to do it, but they'll teach you and you can save that pilot and you want to be a doctor, don't you?" So I said: "Yes, sir."

Always I have to be a hero, running with the damn football or making that stop and throw at short, but what do I know? There's a blinding snow falling outside, but by 4:30 when the copter arrives it lets up except that now it's getting toward dusk. This major climbs out and he says: "Are you the medic?" I say: "Yes, but I don't know how to jump." He says: "That's all right. I'll teach you in the copter. Get in."

So we take off, and this major comes back and puts the chute on me. He says: "Don't worry. It's easy. We're going to hook you up, and all you have to do is go out the door and the chute will open. I'll go with you." And I believe. I have faith. I'm that stupid.

Finally we spot it down there in the snow, and it's an F-86, with its nose under water in this frozen rice paddy, and the tail end is starting to burn. While we're circling and looking down, and this is ridiculous like my life, the cockpit of the thing flies open and this guy comes flying up toward us and his chute opens. Then the next thing I know the major is hollering at me and I'm airborne on this chute and I'm landing in three feet of snow.

We get over to the pilot and he's out flat and complaining of a pain in his back. He says: "Doc, it was a choice of drowning or burning to death so, hell, I just pushed the button. Do something for my back, will you?" So I give him a shot of 100 milligrams of Demerol, and when we're ready to move him I look up and here's another copter coming down and landing and I'm wondering what the hell I was doing jumping, but that's the R.A.s for you. We get him into the copter and get him back, and it turns out this was the third time he's been shot down, and he has a wife and four kids in Alabama and all he's worried about is that his back will keep him from flying again.

That night they had that party and got me drunk, telling me how great I'd be in Air-Sea Rescue, so I transfer and in fourteen months I jump a half dozen more times while I still don't know a damn thing about jumping. I'm all over Korea, picking up these guys and putting the IV to them and stopping the bleeding. While those brights are like 11 now and still playing cops-and-robbers I'm living with Australians and those Turks that were great big brutes that smelled like goats and used to go out at night and cut the ears and the scrota sacs off the North Koreans and bring them back, and I'm like standing off and looking at myself and wondering what the hell I'm doing there and thinking it's ridiculous.

When I go upstairs to scrub, now, it turns out that I draw Peterson. While we're standing there side by side at those two sinks and I'm trying to work out my game plan, he's telling me how they found a sharp kink and a swollen area in that nerve, a neuroma bound down by scar tissue, and how, under the microscope, he delicately dissected it free, cut out the scar, hooked up the nerve again and made a nice new bed of fatty tissue for it so it won't scar down again. He thinks it's a brand new play, and he wants to write it up for the *Journal*.

"We took all kinds of photographs," he's saying, "and I'll do some diagrams, because you know how you've got to document everything very carefully."

Oh yes, I'm thinking, I know, because I remember the night when you guys were so busy writing sage notes on that kid's chart and documenting everything so carefully that you forgot to really look at the patient. It turned out later that the kid had been horsing around, coming home from school, or some place, and he'd hit his head on a curb. He had a headache, but he ate a good meal, vomited and then passed out. Instead of procrastinating on paper, you guys should have scooped him upstairs, because he'd ruptured his middle meningeal artery, the old Artery of Sudden Death, and by the time I looked at him and we drilled his skull it was too late, and I was just damn glad that I wasn't the one who had to walk out of there and tell his parents.

Of course, I'm only half listening to him now, because I'm thinking that I'd better turn a large skin flap and a good-sized bone flap completely surrounding the point of entry, and then we can clean up the bone from either side. I can put two burr holes just at the margin of the temporalis muscle, and make a large cut around between them with the air drill. Then, with the muscle as a hinge, the whole flap of bone can be folded down, and the first time I ever saw holes go in the skull was the night that Osterman and I scooped that pilot who'd crashed and had that cervical spine fracture and Osterman wanted to put him in traction.

That Osterman is celebrated now and I always knew he would be, but then all he had was two years of general surgery and we didn't have the tools for it and they didn't have any at the supply house, which was like Central Supply. We probably should have air-lifted the patient out, as the head R.A., the Surgeon General for the whole Far East, said later, but when that Osterman saw one he really thought he could hit out of the park there wasn't anyone who was going to drag him away from the plate.

"Let's go over to the hobby shop," he says to me, "and see what they've got there."

All they've got there is one of those ordinary hardware store hand drills, so Osterman takes that and a 1/8ths bit. Then he gets some pieces of wood and crosses them and puts some stainless screws in the ends to make skull tongs to fit into the burr holes, and he hands me the drill and the bit.

"Here," he says. "Sterilize this."

You couldn't really sterilize it, because the grease ran all over the damn thing, but he takes it and he's drilling away at this pilot's skull when the sergeant comes in. He's a real R.A., too, so he says: "Hey, wait a minute, you people. You haven't signed a requisition for that drill." It's ridiculous, but we put that pilot in traction and he lived to fly again another day and Osterman got his tail chewed for being too aggressive.

So I go in with Peterson, now, to crack Nick Braff's skull. Squash Stillman has that theory he was selling me at Palumbo's that we can go in there and perform because once the patient is draped we forget he's a human being, and he may be right except that just once while I'm opening it's like it used to be in the war when I'd sort of stand off and look at myself as a character in a scene. Here I am, I thought, just that once, son of number 7 bed-laster, who used to read about this hot-shot jockey and made that big, for me, killing on him in that Special, and now I'm peeling *his* potato and I'm going to crack it. I don't know.

I begin that long, curved skin incision just above the right eyebrow. With Peterson pressing his fingers along the margins to compress the blood vessels until I can get them clamped, I curve the cut up over the forehead and then down to just in front of the ear. As I turn the skin flap down over the cheek, we get old, dark blood, and I can see that the entry wound needs cleaning up, but I can do that later.

"You got the Mannitol going?" I say to Charley Brooks, who's one of the good young gas passers.

"He's had about 200 cc.'s now, and it's going fast," Charley says. "How much more do you want in?"

"Another 150 cc.'s or so," I say. "Then let it drip slowly until we get open."

As I look over at Charley Brooks I notice somebody at my left shoulder. I turn, and it's Stern.

"You A.W.O.L.?" I say, and I start clamping.

"The rush has let up down there," he says, "and I'm number two tonight anyway. All right?"

"It's fine with me," I say, and I can't knock the quest for knowledge. "Do you know why we're using 20 percent Mannitol?"

"It's a concentrated type of sugar solution," he says, "and it acts osmotically to draw excess fluids from the circulation to the kidneys."

"And thereby wrings out the edema fluid in the swelling brain," I say. "That's why we wanted that Foley in him, because without it his bladder would be up to his chin."

I put in the two burr holes, about an inch apart and down low in the temple on a line between the ear and the eyebrow and under the temporalis muscle I've just cut. With that nitrogen-powered drill I start at the one hole and I cut a wide arc in the bone paralleling the incision I made in the skin, a big loop up over the eyebrow and then down just forward of the ear and terminating at the other hole. Then Peterson and I lift the edge of the bone flap, and I reach under with a curved elevator, carefully to avoid doing any further damage to the dura which is underneath and no more than half a millimeter thick. When the bone breaks between the two burr holes it goes with a snap, and I turn the flap of bone, hinged on the temporalis muscle, down over the turned skin that is lying over the cheekbone.

"It looks like he missed the middle jeeper," I say, and I mean the middle meningeal artery which lies on the surface of the dura.

"So he's lucky so far," Peterson says, and I'm thinking that that's more than you could say the night you missed it in the kid.

The rent the bullet made in the dura is larger than the entry wound in the skin, and it's jagged, full of blood and small, whitish scraps of destroyed brain tissue. The dura itself, instead of being a normal gray-white, is deep blue-purple from the blood underneath and, with the brain beneath the dura swollen and tight, I don't dare open the dura because if I do the brain will ooze out like toothpaste, and it will be so-long Nick Braff.

"Brooksie?" I say. "Can you hyperventilate him a while?"

Charley Brooks forces the air in and out of the lungs, and in a few minutes, as the pressure in the skull goes down, I can feel the dura become softer. Then, when I make my incision in the dura, I get my first look at the brain, and I don't like what I see.

"There's more damage than I expected," I say, "but at least it's mostly up in the frontal lobe."

"So, if he ever wakes up," Peterson says, "it shouldn't bother him too much. It could be kind of like a half lobotomy, and then he'd be happy as hell."

I ignore him, because I'm tracing the route of the bullet now. The path of direct injury is black with old blood, clotted and jellylike, and even well away from it the small surface vessels are bruised and dilated from the blast effect so that almost anywhere I touch, new bleeding, clean and red, seems to well up.

"Put a pattie right there, will you, Pete?" I say.

I want to start retracting the brain now, always gently Bobby boy, and you do it using those small squares of wet pressed cotton with the string sewn on them so we won't forget them when we close. You use them as buffers, between the flat, narrow retractor and the brain tissue, because where normal brain gives way easily and smoothly and retains its integrity, injured brain breaks and begins to ooze blood, and you know that those nerve cells will never recover and that any damage you do will be forever.

"Suction, Pete, and right on the pattie," I say, because if he applies it to the brain, no matter how gently, it will make it bleed.

"And let's adjust the light," I say, but the overhead lamp isn't enough. I've got to use my headlight, which gives a beautiful beam that points right along my line of vision, but the helmet-frame also gives me a headache. Then I ask for my loupes, my telescopic glasses, and now I can see.

"Cautery forceps," I say, because as I start to move the damaged tissue, there are those bleeders that are oozing. I put the tips across one stretched surface artery, and I press the pedal with my left foot. There's the faint spark and the small sizzle-sound, and where I've touched the pink artery a gray-white band shows.

"You can get at it better from your side," I say to Peterson, "so will you cut it?"

"Small Metz," he says, and she's got it in his hand already. The bleeders we don't get with the cautery we cover with gelfoam, which will help coagulate the blood, and gently, always gently, I retract the frontal lobe. Now I can see that the superior saggital sinus, the big vein running front to back along the midline, is intact. How my Nick Braff missed it I don't know, but he did, and now, retracting very carefully so that the veins entering the sinus won't be torn, I can see partly over to the other side. There's no obvious bleeding over there—nothing fresh, anyway—so I elevate the frontal lobe off the orbit, the skull cavity that holds the eyeball. The bone there is okay, so the bullet must have struck the inside of the frontal bone just high enough so that it didn't pierce the orbits or the sinuses, and at a glancing angle that bounced it across the frontal lobes to the other side. All I've got to do now, is clean up the dead tissue and get out.

"Irrigation!" Peterson is saying now. "C'mon, nurse! C'mon!"

She hands him that big bulb of saline, and while he's carefully washing away the worst of the clotted blood I'm teasing out the bone splinters and pieces of skin and hair that the slug carried in with it. Finally, after about forty-five minutes that seem like ten to me, and with the possible sources of infection out, nothing bleeding, and the brain fairly soft, I figure I've done all the lint-picking that's necessary. Old Mom Nature has her hand in here, too, if we just give her a chance.

"So let's get out of here," I say. "I want 4-0 silk for the dura."

"And the other side?" Peterson says.

Oh, no. I'm thinking that at this hour this R.A. is not going to bug me about right side weakness and going after those fragments on the left.

"Got the wires for the bone flap?" I say to the scrub nurse. "And Brooksie, how's he doing?"

"Pretty good," Charley Brooks says. "His pressure's down a bit, but his pulse is regular at 76. He doesn't need much anesthesia now, but do you want more Decadron?"

"Yes, about another 10 milligrams," I say, "and you're keeping his fluids down?"

"Look, Bob," Peterson says, and he's not going to let go. "Your X rays show several bullet fragments in the left side, and you say he has weakness of the right arm and leg. When you add that up, don't you figure to explore the left hemisphere also?"

"And why not look at his left ball, too?" I say, and then I cool out, because maybe Stern will learn something from all this although Peterson won't. "First of all, we know from our arteriogram that there's no obvious blood clot on the left side. The blood vessels are intact, and not shifted from normal. Right?"

"So you mean," he says, "that you'll leave those contaminated lead fragments rattle around in there as a source of infection until he sneezes them out through his ears, or something?"

"C'mon, Pete," I say. "We grabbed the hairy debris and skin out of this side because they would have infected. We know that bullets, as they leave a muzzle of a gun, however, are sterile, and usually don't get contaminated as they go through the skin and deeper tissue. Our immediate bag is to get him over the acute phase of this, and as long as the fragments are not causing bleeding, we're safe in leaving them in there for a few days. Right now I need a few 2-0 silks for the galea, and then wire for the skin."

"And if he wakes up," Peterson says, "and he can't talk because of one of those fragments in his speech area that you've decided to just let sit there, what are you going to say to his lawyer?"

"For chrissake, Pete," I say, because I've had it since 7 o'clock this morning, "it's a calculated risk, no matter what we do. If we flip him over and go through all this on the other side we'll have another two hours of anesthesia, plus the general trauma of more surgery, plus the good chance of further local injury to a particularly vital part of his brain. I think his left cerebral cortex is mostly bruised and banged up, and we can't do anything about that now. After the swelling has gone down in a few days, and if we have to, and we may not, we can look in there and clean up the dead tissue and get out the available bullet fragments."

"And not all of them?" he says.

"There's at least one deep one," I say, "and under any circumstances we might do more damage than good getting down to it. He can just walk around with it like a filling in a tooth."

"And if he goes bad," he says, "while you're waiting in the wings for your cue?"

"If he goes really bad," I say, "we'll just have to go in there and take our chances at that time."

"Well," he says, "it's your ball game."

"Right," I say, "so let's have a dressing."

I wrap the head in several rolls of Kling gauze, just snug enough so it won't fall off when he moves. I pull his lids open and look at his pupils. They're equal, and with the last readings I get from Charley Brooks I know we haven't done any more damage to him, and I figure that by the time I make rounds tomorrow he should talk a little and respond to commands and begin to move the right side. In two or three days there may be a temporary worsening, mostly due to the brain swelling, but that's rarely fatal these days, and, hell, I'm not going to lose, anyway.

"Thank you, Doctor," this Stern is saying to me. "I really appreciate the chance I had to observe you."

"You're welcome," I say. "My pleasure."

I write a short note in the chart, and a page full of orders for Intensive Care. I find that phone number the two sleuths gave me, and when the one named O'Donnell, or something, answers I tell him the subject is living. Then, on the way down from the O.R., I stop off at Powell Samuels's Space Control to check the chart on that little black girl who was hit by some goon who ran a red light and got away with it. She's the same as she was when they called me in at 7 in the morning, so if it's fat emboli in the blood stream at least they haven't hit the brain yet but I don't know. It's after midnight now, and in that little lounge down the hall the kid's parents are sitting and the nurse tells me that, because they can't sleep, anyway, they're there all day and all night, going home just long enough to cook their meals. I don't know, because here's Nick Braff, who doesn't want to live any more and I've probably pulled him out so that he can wake up again to his misery, and here's a kid who hasn't had her chance to live yet, and there's not much any of us can do about it but wait.

"Oh, come on now," Edie will say when I come home some night a sore loser again. "When will you learn that you can't win them all?"

Then I'll get the song about Johnny beating up on the neighbor's kid again or Marcy's coming down with another cold, but you can't win them all? What do you learn when you learn that? To lose? When that Osterman hooked me on skull-cracking I knew you go in there with negative findings that would turn the chest cutters and the belly boys and the rest of them off. I knew we get more strike-outs than home runs and that a toe twitch is supposed to be a triumph, but you still have to go up to that plate swinging for the fence and believing because it's the only chance they've got. Today I spent six hours plucking that meningioma off the spinal cord of that telephone lineman but he'll climb his poles again, and I didn't work four years driving that cab eight hours a day and them pump gas weekends just to get to college and then get twenty-six gees in debt to the A.M.A., the Health Professionals' Loan, the State Loan, the City Education Fund, the First Bank and the rest of them to get through med school and all that textbook trauma to lose.

"A doctor?" the Old Man said. "You can't be a doctor."

It's ridiculous, coming from what I came from, but I made it and I'm a damn good doctor, and when I shake this residency in June and start to unload those loans I know something else. The kids will never get pocket combs and shoelaces and hard candy for Christmas.

X

ARNOLD HENKEN

Any day now it could happen. I mean like I half expect that almost any day now my mother will come walking in here, smiling and nodding to everybody she doesn't even know and telling them that she's my mother and that she's heard all about them from me and then asking them how I'm doing.

I don't really think it's going to happen, but it's like a nightmare because she used to do that all the time when I was in grammar school. All of a sudden the classroom door would open and there would be my mother, smiling and nodding to the teacher.

"Oh, hello, Mrs. Henken," the teacher would say. "Do come in, please. Class? We all know Mrs. Henken, Arnold's mother. And we're happy to have her visit our class. Mrs. Henken, won't you please come in and join us? There's a seat right there at the back of the room, and we'd love to have you."

So my mother would come walking in, smiling and nodding to everybody. She'd take a seat at the back of the room, and without even turning around, which I would never do, I could just see her settling down back there and still smiling and waiting for me to get called on. If the teacher was a real human being with sympathy, like Miss Taylor, she'd just have me read a page in our book, or maybe a poem, but if she was real sick like Mrs. Bauman, and liked to persecute people, she'd call on me for something that she knew I didn't know.

"Oh, I'm sorry, Arnold," Bauman would say. "Is there anyone who would like to help Arnold with the question? Margaret?"

So Margaret Wittenauer would answer the question, and that

used to really gross me out. I mean in the first place Bauman wasn't sorry at all, and in the second place Margaret Wittenhauer wasn't trying to help anybody but Margaret Wittenauer. That's how phony it was, and when I got to high school I told my mother the second day I was there that they had a rule that parents could only visit on Parents' Day. Of course, I made up the rule, but they really did have a Parents' Day.

"Is that so?" my mother said when I told her about the rule. "Why would they have such a rule?"

"I don't know," I said, "but they said it's what they call progressive education."

"Oh," she said. "Well, they probably know more about it than I do."

"Probably," I said.

The great thing about that was that it worked. In fact, it was one of the greatest things that ever worked in my whole life, but now I can see from the questions she asks me every night that my mother might just have the idea that she might just come smiling and nodding in here some day.

"And they're all very friendly?" she'll say for about the twentieth or thirtieth time. "Dr. Hunter and Miss Palmer and all of them, they're all very friendly?"

"I guess so," I told her when she asked again last night. "They're all sort of very friendly, but with a couple of exceptions."

"Oh?" she said. "There are exceptions? Who are the exceptions?"

So I told her about Stern and Banks. Of course, I referred to them as Dr. Stern and Dr. Banks, so she'd know they're doctors. Then I didn't tell her about Banks asking me if I was a comedian when I was making my hand noises for the little kid with lead poisoning because I didn't want her to know that I'm still making my hand noises, which I don't do very often any more, anyway. I just told her the way they just call me "Orderly" and the way they're not friendly with anybody, and I reminded her that it was Stern who left that old Mr. Kobak alone when he killed himself with the scalpel.

"I know, Arnold," she said. "I know exactly how you feel about that poor old man, but you have to grant Dr. Stern one mistake. We all make mistakes, and I'm sure he'll never do it again. You will grant Dr. Stern that one mistake, won't you? I'm sure, too, that when you get to know Dr. Stern and Dr. Banks better you'll like them both. There's goodness in everyone, Arnold, and when you seek it out you'll find it in them, too."

The way my mother talks about me granting Stern his one mistake and me getting to know Stern and Banks better to seek out their goodness you'd think I was a doctor. The only time Stern and Banks ever talk to me is when they want me to get them something, but that's the way my mother is. She really thinks everybody in this world is equal—she really does—so I wouldn't ever tell her that today two people actually called me "Doctor."

The first one was a little old white-haired lady who came in this morning. She was wearing this kind of old gray coat and an old gray hat and carrying a black pocketbook, and she just walked in and walked over to booth 7 and took the stool there and moved it to the front of the booth and sat down. Booth 7 is where they usually take the real emergency heart attacks and strokes, and after awhile I went over to this little old lady and asked her if I could help her.

"No thank you, Doctor," she said, which really surprised me —you know?—and then she said: "I'm just waiting to hear from the *other* doctor."

So I was busy then for a while. I had to help Arlene Woods get a little screaming kid into a Papoose Board, which is a kind of a frame that you strap them in when they won't hold still. Dr. Hunter wanted to look at this kid's left arm, which was sort of burned and blistered from I don't know what, and then I had to take a blood sample to the lab. This blood sample was marked "Stat," which meant that they wanted it tested right away, so I figured I might as well wait for it. I mean I didn't have to, because they would phone it back to the E.R., but it only takes like about eight minutes, anyway, with this automatic analyzer they've got. This automatic analyzer has a lot of long thin tubes twisting around and that you can watch the blood go through, and it kind of reminds me of a pinball machine. In eight minutes it does twelve different blood tests— you know?—and marks them all on this sort of a graph paper, so I watched that and asked Eileen O'Brien, who's the technician who usually runs the machine, how it works.

"I don't know, Arnold," she said. "The last time you were in here I explained to you how this works."

"I know," I said, "but some of it has sort of slipped my mind. You see, I've been thinking that being a lab technician is very fascinating work that I might like to go into, and so I'd like to learn all I can if you have the time."

"Oh," she said, and then she explained it again.

Actually, I don't think being a lab technician is all that fascinating. I just said that to make Eileen O'Brien feel important because, in fact, I think it could be kind of a drag, always like looking through some microscope or studying some test tube or something and never knowing anything about anybody except about their blood or their urine.

For example, while I was in the lab waiting for the automatic analyzer to test the blood sample and Eileen O'Brien was explaining it to me again, they had this workman brought into the E.R. and one of his legs had been cut off by some machinery. As soon as I got back to the E.R. they sent me back to the lab again with this workman's blood samples, and while I was walking back there the second time I was thinking that, if I had been in the E.R. when this workman came in, I would have some kind of an idea of what kind of a person he is and now all I'll know about him is whether he's like an A-positive or an O-negative and what things like his calcium and sugar are if I want to know that which I really don't.

"Oh, it's you again," Eileen O'Brien said when I came in this time with the workman's blood samples. "Now, you don't want me to explain how the automatic analyzer works, or do you?"

"Oh, no, thank you," I told her. "I understand it very clearly now, and it's very interesting."

"Good," she said.

Anyway, when I finally got back to the E.R. the second time

and I walked by booth 7, there was this little old lady who called me "doctor" still sitting there and still waiting, so I went over and I told Miss Palmer. Miss Verna Palmer is the head nurse, as I probably said, and she explained it.

"Oh, that's old Mrs. Greiner," she said. "She's harmless. About a year ago her husband died of a heart attack here one night in booth 7. She was here with him and every once in a while she comes in, usually at night, they tell me. She seems to be waiting for her husband. I don't know, because we don't ask her. If we need the booth we just tell her, and she gets up and goes home."

The second patient who called me "Doctor" was this man—what they call a kind of a derelict—that two detectives brought in because somebody had beaten him up and he was drunk. They never call anybody drunk around here, though, because like on the patient's chart they write A.O.B. instead. One day I asked Dr. Hunter about that, and he explained that A.O.B. means Alcohol on Breath.

"You see, Arnold," he said, "in legal medicine drunkenness, or being under the influence of alcohol, is defined according to the amount of alcohol in the blood or in exhaled air. For our purposes, there's usually no need to make those tests. The patient's breath smells strongly of alcohol, but if, for example, a severe diabetic or an epileptic, behaving in a drunken manner, with some evidence of alcohol on his breath, was brought in here and the examining doctor wrote "drunk" or "intoxicated" on his chart, the hospital could be in real trouble. If it ever got out, we could be charged with negligence and maybe even malpractice."

"Especially if he was the President of the United States," I said.

"The President of the United States?" Dr. Hunter said.

"That's right," I said. "I'm just imagining that if like the President of the United States was here like making a speech before election, and he was a diabetic or an epileptic and after his speech he was in a hotel and acting like he was drunk and they brought him in here. Then I'm imagining that like if some doctor wrote 'drunk' on his chart, and some newspaper writer or television commentator let it out, the hospital would really be in trouble. Isn't that right?"

"I don't know, Arnold," Dr. Hunter said. "I guess that's right, but you have a wild imagination."

That's what my mother always says, that I have a wild imagination, but I don't think that it's all that wild. I mean like I remember reading once in history, which was usually really very boring and which I didn't really like, that General Grant used to drink a lot when he was just a general, so he probably drank a lot when he became President of the United States, too. Now, if you had a President like General Grant, and he was also a diabetic or an epileptic and he came in here, some doctor, probably Stern, might write "drunk" on his chart, and I don't see what's so wild about that.

Anyway, this second patient that called me "Doctor" and who looked like what they call a sort of a derelict, and my mother always calls a poor unfortunate, was really drunk. I mean he really had A.O.B. He could hardly walk and he could hardly talk straight, and he had a lot of cuts and what they call contusions, like bruises, on his face. One eye was all puffed up and almost closed and his nose was bleeding, and when they got him to lie down in booth 5 the detectives were trying to find out from him who beat him up and why they did it.

"Did you recognize them, Charley?" the one detective asked him. "You ever see them before?"

This detective is kind of stocky and middle-aged, and he had on this dark brown fedora with like a small brim and he had a cigar in his mouth. It wasn't lighted any more, because they don't allow smoking in the E.R., except in the nursing station, but he kept it in his mouth, anyway, sometimes even while he was talking.

"Look, Charley," he said. "Don't go to sleep on us. Did you ever see the two guys before? Charley?"

"Who?" this patient named Charley said. "See who?"

"The two guys," the detective said. "The two guys who beat you up. Did you recognize them? Did you ever see them before?"

"No," this patient said. "I never saw 'em before."

"What did they look like?" this detective said. "Can you describe them? Were they white or colored?"

"White or colored?" this patient said. "I believe they were colored."

"You *saw* them?" this detective said. "And you *believe* they were colored?"

"Definitely," this patient said.

"Look, Charley," the other detective, not the one with the cigar, said. "Where did this happen? Where were you drinking?"

"Drinking?" this Charley said. "I haven't had a drink in two years. Can I have a drink now?"

"No," the detective with the cigar said. "Charley, why would they want to beat you up? Do you know why they beat you up?"

"They wanted my money," this Charley said. "They took my money."

"They took your money?" the same detective said. "How much did they take?"

"Seven or eight hundred dollars," this patient said.

"Seven or eight hundred dollars?" the other detective said. "Where did you get seven or eight hundred dollars?"

"From my sister in Seattle, Washington," this patient said. "She's a very wealthy woman, and she sends me money."

"So how much money did they take?"

"What?" the patient said.

"So how much money did they take?" the detective said. "And don't go to sleep on us, Charley."

"A thousand dollars."

"A thousand dollars?" the detective said. "A minute ago you said seven or eight hundred dollars."

"Maybe about five hundred," the patient said. "I'm tired."

So I left then because it was getting to be sort of a drag, this whole conversation, and because Miss Palmer wanted me to take some gall-bladder woman, with an IV going in her left arm, up to D3. This woman wasn't like severely ill, because when I went into booth 8 to get her and smiled and said hello like you're supposed to do, she smiled and said hello back to me, but I thought of taking her down to the main bank of elevators

173

and pushing the button on elevator 1 three times anyway. That's what we do when we have a Must Special. A Must Special is a patient who is really very severely ill or very severely injured, and that you have to get up to Intensive Care or Coronary Care or the O.R. right away. You run them down to elevator 1, and then you push the button on elevator 1 three times, and the elevator operator, who is usually Frankie Perez, lets the passengers out and comes right down and takes you up like express to whatever floor you're going.

That's kind of cool, so while I was pushing the cot with this woman on it out into the hall I thought of doing it. I mean I considered it. I considered that D3 is not where you ever take a patient who is a Must Special, but I also considered that, when I told Frankie Perez the floor, I could hold my finger up to my mouth behind the patient's back, like for him not to say anything, and maybe he would think that the patient was really severely ill. After that, though, I considered that maybe this gall-bladder woman would smile and say hello to Frankie, too, and then he'd get suspicious, so I considered against it and I didn't do it.

So after I took this gall-bladder woman up to a semiprivate on D3 I had to bring the cot back and change the sheets, and then we were pretty busy and I forgot all about this A.O.B. in booth 5 for like a half hour until he started hollering, because there were people all over the place, patients waiting by the nursing station and patients in the other booths and kids whose mothers had no place to leave them and who were just hanging around whatever booth their mothers or brothers or sisters were in.

"Help! Help!" this A.O.B. started hollering. "Oh please, God! Please help me, God! Don't let me die, God! I don't want to die, God! Please don't let me die, God!"

When this patient started hollering like that you could hear him all over the room, and what made it weird was that it was like a scene I saw in a movie once about a time machine. Right in the middle of the day once, this time machine that this really far out guy had made blew a cathode-ray tube or something and it stopped, and when it stopped everything stopped. I mean in this city in this movie all the traffic stopped. People who were walking on the sidewalks or crossing the street stopped, some of them with one foot still in the air. People who were talking stopped talking, right in the middle of a word and with their mouths open, and that's what it was like when this A.O.B. patient started hollering about dying. Everything stopped. I mean the doctors and the nurses didn't stop, because they knew he wasn't dying, but the people all over the E.R. stopped and even the kids hacking around the booths stopped, everybody looking over at booth 5 with their mouths open like the time machine broke down.

What happened then was Miss Palmer went tearing over to booth 5, and I went over, too, in case she needed help in restraining this patient. Miss Palmer is a very polite, nice-appearing sort of middle-aged woman who just looks like she might need help, but when she gets mad she doesn't.

"Now, you just stop that!" she said. "You may think you're sick now, but if I hear one more cry out of you I'll give you something that will really make you sick. Do you understand that?"

That really cooled it, because this patient just stopped. He stopped right in the middle of whatever he was going to holler next, with his mouth wide open and staring at Miss Palmer like the time machine broke down again. Then he looked over at me, and I remember now that that's why I'm telling this.

"Oh, Doctor," he said to me. "Please help me, Doctor. Please?"

So I wouldn't ever tell my mother that two patients actually called me "Doctor" today because, even considering the patients, that would get her going again about how I should further my education. That time machine, though, makes me think of Anita Wade, the little girl who got hit by the car. My mother always asks about her so I'll tell her about Anita Wade, although it's kind of sad. I mean it may be even sadder than just *kind* of sad, because now they have Anita Wade up in what they call the Trauma Unit, and they think that maybe she's going to die.

That Trauma Unit is *really* away out, which is why I think

of it when I think of that time machine that that Dr. Voltz invented in that movie. Actually he wasn't a doctor, but some kind of a crazy European scientist or something, and he just called himself Dr. Voltz. It wasn't actually that great a movie, either, and Dr. Powell Samuels, who thought up this Trauma Unit here is actually a doctor here and he's not crazy. He's like a real brain—you know?—and he worked this whole thing out with some engineers from the university and with some people who have this monster computer, and it took them like months and months to do it.

It's like two rooms—you know?—with the patient in the bed in the one room and all this equipment around with knobs and dials on it and monitor screens on the wall with like blips and lines on them. Then in the next room there's more equipment with more knobs and dials and a teletype machine and a tape recorder and another monitor, and all this is connected to the patient, and then there's this telephone connected to this monster computer that's some place miles away. I forget where Dr. Vincent Ranier told me it is, but it's like forty or fifty miles from where the patient is here, and it's doing all the figuring out for this patient. You know?

Dr. Vincent Ranier is the resident who is in charge of the patient in this Trauma Unit, and then there's this sort of young, like twenty-five-year-old, graduate engineer who's in charge of the equipment, and then they have special nurses that understand all this, too. I sort of understand it myself, you know? I mean I understand it when Dr. Ranier explains it to me, and then later when I think about it I'm not sure, but then there's a lot that I do understand in kind of a general way, like after you've been studying for some exam in school and then you get this general question that you're supposed to write at least a whole page about. You don't understand the whole thing—I mean, not completely—but you know enough so that if you write it a certain way to kind of avoid what you don't know you can give the impression that you do know. Sometimes it works and sometimes it doesn't, but when it does then you're like pretty satisfied with how much you must know.

Anyway, about two days ago some surgical resident that I don't know was down in the E.R. Even though I didn't know who he was you can always tell the surgical residents and the interns that are in surgery because they like to walk around the hospital in their green operating room suits that look like pajamas and with their surgical masks hanging under their chins like they just came from saving somebody's life with some very difficult surgical procedure or something. I mean it's like when I was still in grammar school and my mother thought it was a good idea for me to join the Boy Scouts and I thought it was kind of a good idea, too. We would have our troop meetings like 7:30 on Friday evenings, so on Friday I would put on my uniform when I got up in the morning and I would wear it to school and all day. Then, after a while, I would just put it on to go to the meeting, and at the end, before I dropped out after like two years because I just couldn't get gung-ho about walking for miles and sleeping out all night on pine branches, I wouldn't put it on at all but I would go to the meeting with maybe just the shirt and wearing like corduroys.

So this surgical resident was talking in the E.R. to Dr. Hunter and Miss Palmer, and I heard him mention to them that they had moved Anita Wade from I.C.U., which is the Intensive Care Unit, to this Trauma Unit. So, when I got a chance, I went up there that day and I went up yesterday and I went up again today.

The way Dr. Ranier explained it to me, Anita Wade was doing all right for like about thirty-six hours or so after they operated on her for the broken bones in her legs. Then all of a sudden she started to get worse, and I asked Dr. Ranier why.

"Do you know what fat emboli are?" he asked me.

"No, sir," I said, "but I would like to know about them."

"They're globules of fat," he said. "They come from the marrow where her bones are fractured and they travel through the blood stream, and in this case they're affecting her lungs and maybe even her brain."

"And that's why she's unconscious now?" I said.

"That's right," he said, "and when they interfere with the

177

functioning of the lungs they retard the oxygenation of the blood, and that's why we have her on the respirator."

"And what does the computer do?" I said.

"Well," he said, "that's quite complicated. What it does is give us immediately the answers to four or five things that we want to measure at the same time, and that tells us what's happening to the patient."

"But what would these things be?" I said, because I was really interested.

That was like two days ago when I asked Dr. Ranier this. He wasn't doing anything else, anyway. His whole job is just running the Trauma Unit for a year, and he was just sitting in the room with the teletype and some of the other machines, and he was like waiting to make some tests again or something, so he took me into the next room where Anita Wade is and explained the whole thing.

Of course Anita Wade was unconscious and didn't even know we were there. They have her left leg in a cast, with this traction apparatus like holding it up, and her right leg in a cast, too, and an IV in her left arm and a catheter tube in her bladder. There's this tube in her nose and another catheter in her right arm and one in her neck, and that's how they make all these tests that the computer, wherever it is, figures out.

The way Dr. Ranier explained it, they want to measure like the output of the heart and how much air Anita Wade breathes in and how much air stays in her lungs after she breathes out and how much oxygen there is in the blood going to her lungs and how much in the blood leaving her lungs and how elastic her lungs are. If they had to do this all themselves, he said, they'd never get it done.

"It might take forty or forty-five minutes to compute the lung volume," he said, "and we might want that eight or ten times a day. It might take twenty minutes to compute the output of the heart and we might want that ten times a day, too. The patient would be dead before we got the answers, but the computer can do one of these computations in a tenth of a minute."

So after Dr. Ranier explained how the computer tells them

what's happening to the patient I didn't ask him what they do about it to help the patient because I knew that would be too complicated. Besides, Anita Wade's parents were standing in the doorway looking in, and that made me feel sort of bad, like ashamed or embarrassed or something, because I wasn't actually doing anything for Anita Wade.

When we came out I sort of smiled and nodded to them, and Anita Wade's father smiled at me, and then Dr. Ranier talked with them for a couple of minutes. After that he came into the other room and he said that they're there all the time, even at night. He said they told him that they can't sleep, so they just go home to eat and then they come back. They take naps sitting in the lounge down the hall, and then they come and just stand in the room, looking at Anita Wade who's just lying there, with all the tubes in her and the casts on her broken legs, and doesn't even know they're there.

I asked Dr. Ranier then if the computer was really helping Anita Wade and how long she might be there, and he said he didn't know the answer to either question. He said the computer was certainly supplying them with the information they wanted, but whether they could continue to use that information to help Anita Wade he wasn't sure. He said they would probably know in twenty-four or forty-eight hours, and then I asked him what they would do if it turned out that the information they got from the computer wasn't helping.

"Let's not think about that now," he said.

My lunch hour, which is really only a half hour, was over then, anyway, so I didn't ask him anything else. Then yesterday, when I went up there, Dr. Ranier and Miss Varga, who is one of the nurses in the Trauma Unit, were busy making some test for the computer. They were putting some kind of green dye solution in the tube in Anita Wade's neck, and they could tell by watching on a kind of orange screen on one of the monitors how long it took to go through her heart and her body. Dr. Ranier was calling out some information on the intercom for the engineer in the other room to give to the computer, but when I went in there the engineer was hanging up the phone because, he said, the chief computer programmer, or whatever they call him, wherever that computer is, was out to lunch.

"So what do you do now?" I said.

"We wait," he said. "We've got it all on tape, and I'll play it into the phone when he gets back."

"And the patient will be all right?" I said.

"Oh, sure," he said. "She hasn't changed for better or worse."

I didn't hang around there any more then, but when I went back today I could tell from this kind of a conference that was going on by Anita Wade that Anita Wade wasn't getting better. Dr. Samuels, who thought up this Trauma Unit, was there with Dr. Mabry, the chief neuro resident who's a pretty cool guy, and with Dr. Ranier, and Dr. Samuels was doing the talking and the other two were listening and nodding.

Miss Varga was sitting at a desk in the other room, and she sort of knows me because she's a good friend of Miss Palmer. Every afternoon at 3:30 she comes down to meet Miss Palmer so they can drive home together in Miss Palmer's car, so I asked her how Anita Wade was doing.

"Not good," she said. "They're starting to talk about her as a possible donor."

I sort of didn't know what to say, you know? I mean I just sort of figured that Anita Wade was going to get better and that she was going to live, and now they were thinking that they could maybe give her kidneys to somebody and her eyes to somebody else and maybe even the aorta which they might put in somebody else's heart and I don't know what else.

So I didn't say anything. I just walked out, and then I had to go by Anita Wade's parents again. They were just standing in the hall, probably waiting for the doctors to get finished with their conference, and of course they didn't know what the doctors were talking about but I did, and I didn't even want to look at them, but I did. I looked at them and smiled and nodded, and Anita Wade's father smiled and nodded back like he always does and that made me feel even worse.

When I got back to the E.R. I felt bad all afternoon, and it was sort of good that we were very busy. We had patients in the hall and everywhere, and the first thing I had to do was make up booth 7, because they'd had a heart attack patient in there while I was upstairs, and then we had a severe asthmatic and a woman alcoholic and a girl college student who took a drug overdose and I forget what else. Finally, about 3:30 I decided to sort of hang around the nursing station, to wait for Miss Varga to come down and meet Miss Palmer to drive home in Miss Palmer's car. Then I could ask her what the doctors had decided about Anita Wade, but the only trouble was that good old Stern was there.

"You know something?" he was saying, and he had this ball-point pen in his hand. "How long have I been here in the E.R.? A week? Ten days? With all the writing on all the damn charts you have to do here I'm on my second ball-point already. How do they ever expect us to practice medicine while we're prac-ticing penmanship? Will somebody answer that? It's prepos-terous."

Actually, his penmanship is preposterous, too, because when Mrs. Cutler, who's been a nurse for like forty years, comes on at 3:30 to take over for Miss Palmer and she has to check all the charts to see who's in what booths and what's wrong with them, she's always complaining that she can't read Stern's. She's al-ways saying that she wishes somebody would teach people like Stern how to write.

"Why, children in the third grade used to write better than this," she's always saying, like half talking to herself. "I don't know what's happening to the world."

She's always saying that she doesn't know what's happening to the world, too, when we get a lot of welfare patients com-plaining at the nursing station that they have to wait too long or when somebody starts tearing down some old houses she remembers so that they can build a ramp to some new highway, or something. She just sort of remarks it to herself, though, while she's shaking her head, and she doesn't make speeches about things like Stern.

"And I'll tell you something else," Stern was saying now. "You don't see my name up there. My charts are up to date, and they're not going to hold up my pittance."

What he was talking about was this blackboard they have up

on the wall in the nursing station. They have the names of the doctors on it who are on call for the E.R., and then once a month, like now, they have the names of the interns and the residents whose charts aren't completed, and if their charts aren't completed they don't get their checks that pay day until they finish their charts.

"You'd think we were children," Stern was saying. "We can't have our candy unless we're good boys and girls."

I was wishing that Dr. Hunter would walk into the nursing station then, because he was the one who started this about the charts and getting paid, but instead Dr. Mabry walked over from Minor Ops. That was all right, though, because it got Stern to forget about the charts. He started asking Dr. Mabry about this rather famous jockey who shot himself in the head and got in the newspapers and on the radio today and that Dr. Mabry operated on. I think Stern must have watched the operation, or something, from what he was saying and asking Dr. Mabry.

"There's still some clumsiness on the right side," Dr. Mabry was saying, "the right arm and leg, but that should improve."

"And he's talking?" Stern said.

"When he wants to," Dr. Mabry said.

"You did a beautiful job, Doctor," Stern said. "You really did."

I mean that would be like me telling Mrs. Donnelly, who's director of Nursing Service 1, which includes the E.R., that I think she's doing a beautiful job. Who would ever do something like that except Margaret Wittenauer and Banks and Stern?

Right then, though, I saw Miss Varga come in looking for Miss Palmer. I walked over to her, and I asked her what the doctors had decided to do about Anita Wade, and she told me.

"They've decided to give her until tomorrow morning," she said. "Let's hope."

"But what I don't understand," I said, "is why if she's still alive tomorrow morning they don't just keep her in the Trauma Unit."

"There comes a time," she said, "when, if you're just keeping the patient alive by mechanical means, it's pointless. Also, when you're no longer able to help the patient and you're just using the patient for testing it becomes unethical. You understand why that would be, don't you?"

"I guess so," I said.

"Who are you talking about?" somebody said, and it was good old Stern again.

"Anita Wade," Miss Varga said.

"Who's she?" Stern said.

"The little Negro girl who was hit by the car," Miss Varga said.

"She's still alive?" Stern said. "I thought she expired a couple of days ago."

"No," Miss Varga said, and she walked away. I walked away, too, because I get very depressed by that Stern.

XI

BOBBY CARLTON

This is some town. I don't understand it, but it takes forever to get a doctor. It's like there's a football away up in the stomach and chest, and somebody keeps pumping it up harder and harder. Take two Alka-Seltzer. You'll like it, so you take four, and when it doesn't stop you're still lying here alone in this nowhere town, wherever it is, because you can't get a doctor.

What's with this Bick? Justin Bick, manager. Some name and some manager, all the time running around like the ship is sinking. Women and children first. He's got a hundred and fifty room motel, with dinner club, and he can't get a doctor. I wanted to ask him what business is he in, motel or mausoleum?

Some laugh, so instead of laughing, Bick, get me a doctor, and let him tell me it's my way of life. Bad hours. Bad food. Drink too much. Smoke too much. Too much nervous tension. Give it up. And go into what, Doc, the shingle and siding business? I know. I know. I'm too young a man to be hurting myself like this. How old am I? Older than it says. Until you make it, you've got to be a bright *young* comic, Doc, so I'm not thirty-one like it says, but I'm thirty-four. And my name isn't Carlton, like it says, it's Ehrenberg. I picked Carlton out of the phonebook and this isn't my nose, either. I picked it off a photograph, and it cost me a grand, make that closer to eleven hundred for everything.

"So you can't be funny with your own name?"

"You see, Mom, you don't understand."

"I understand, but maybe you should explain it to Myron Cohen."

"Mom! That's a good line, and I didn't know you ever heard of Myron Cohen."

"I hear."

And then the other time: "So you can't be funny with your own nose?"

"Mom, please try . . ."

"So I try, but who told you that you can't be funny with your own nose? Jimmy Durante?"

"Mom, you're great. You should be on stage."

"On stage I am. Right here."

Some stage. A butcher's chopping block in the kitchen where she worked day and night punching out leather novelties for Sussman and twice a week carting them in a brown paper shopping bag down the stairs and up the street to the subway. Two hours later she'd come back, and I'd be watching for her from the window and then run down and carry the groceries up the stairs and then watch her sit down at the kitchen table and count out what was left and put some in the sugar bowl for the rent and some in the tea pot for an emergency, like my clothes.

Some clothes. When we first came over here I wore those short pants and I had this little cap with ear flaps that you can turn down in winter. All I knew to say was: "How you do do?" Some linguist, and when she'd send me down to the street to get some fresh air the kids would start on me. One of them would grab my cap and holler "Saluggi! Saluggi!" and then they'd start throwing the cap back and forth with me chasing it. Some clothes, because after that there was this woman who gave me a suit that had belonged to a grown man, but Rebekkah Ehrenberg cut it down so it fit.

That was the least of it, Doc, because by then she'd lost a whole family—mother, father, two brothers—to the ovens, and a husband to starvation and whatever else it was when they buried him with all those others. How we hid out all those years, until they took him just before the Allies landed, I don't know, and how she found him again I don't know either, because I was too young, and afterwards I was afraid to ask.

I can remember us on the roads, though, and we must have walked halfway across Germany. I remember just parts of it, everybody walking along the sides of the roads, some heading one way and some heading the other, and being afraid of the black Senegalese, or whatever they were with the red fezzes, and day after day the American tanks and trucks passing us for hours and at night sleeping in the hay in the barns with the others. How she knew he wasn't at Buchenwald or Belsen or Dachau or wherever but at Nordhausen I don't know either, but she found him. He was lying there on the concrete floor with the others, looking like the others, all of them in their zebra suits, all of them with their boney faces and yellow skin and wet eyes, but he looked like my father, too, and the next day he was dead.

Come on, Bick, come on. Let's get somebody. Let's do something. You're my buddy. You're my pal. They liked me in your room, didn't they? Your Tahitian Room or Polynesian Room or whatever it is. I've played so many of these South Sea rooms that I should wear a sarong and get a new light brown skin. You see, Doc, this isn't my real skin, either, and listen, Bick, forget what the guy wrote in the paper. What makes him a critic? The material is dated? So's his newspaper, at the top of every page. That's a take-off on an old gag, Bick, that I used to do on the amateur nights. It's the impression of Bette Davis knocking the movies when she says: "Everybody and everything in Hollywood is typed. Why, when I made the movie, *The Letter*, even the letter was typed."

They liked me, Bick, and it wasn't my fault opening night that your air conditioning wasn't working and also they couldn't hear me in the back of your room. When I walked out there with that spot on me I couldn't see a thing through the haze, and that's when I told them that your maitre d'—what's his name, Joe Fragetta?—just lost his job to Smokey the Bear.

"Seriously," I told them, "you're all part of a test being conducted here by the American Cancer Society, and the winners get a free trip to Marlboro Country. That's Willow Lawn Cemetery."

What's dated about that, Bick? That's timely. Sure, I stole the line from Jimmy Breslin, but before I went on I asked Joe Fragetta for the name of the cemetery in this town, and that was mine.

"And you, sir," I said to one of them I could see up front,

"I don't know what you're smoking, but if it's what I think it is, in about ten minutes you'll be flying over Mexico City."

And then do you know what else I was doing, Bick? I was using the laugh time to try to straighten out the cord to the mike, after the way that singer left it. If I didn't know you people booked her for a singer, and if I hadn't heard her screaming something about her heart in San Francisco just before I went on, I'd have thought she was an acrobatic dancer and had had the mike cord around her waist for a lifeline. There was a knot every foot, and what's with your M.C.? Didn't anybody ever tell him he's supposed to clear the cord for the next act?

Some M.C., Bick. You better check out this guy. What's he doing afternoons, driving a bus? I mean you know what time he called rehearsal? Nine o'clock in the morning! In the morning, Bick. So tell me what he's doing afternoons if he's not driving a bus? Dressing up in drag and playing Avon Calling? So I close in Springfield with the 11 o'clock show and it's not all that far but the first thing out for here, bus or plane, is 9:30. Then I rent a car, and I hate to drive and I usually get lost so I left at 6 A.M.—get that—and I'm here by 8 o'clock, looking for this place, when I see it.

It was awful, Mom. I'm waiting for this light to change, and I'm just about to start up when here comes this car from my left. It's running the light, and the next thing I know I hear the tires make a short grab and then I see this body flip off to the right and the car goes on.

You wouldn't know one car from another, Mom, but it was a dark green Ford, and I don't know why but in that second I even saw part of the license plate. It was 3N36. I saw that much, and then in the paper that night I saw this little story that it was a child, a girl, that got hit and she's critical in the hospital.

I know, Mom. I think about it. I want to do it. I want to call the police and tell them, but Mom, you have to understand. It's tough in the business, and I'm lucky I'm even making a living. So I call them and three months from now, or whenever it

187

is, I'm a thousand miles from here and I get a subpoena and I blow a whole booking.

I know. I know. First I thought that somebody else must have seen it. Then I thought that I'd just call and give it to them without giving my name, and then I thought that if I'm going to do it I might as well do it right, and I'm still thinking about it. I'm thinking now, in fact, that if this Bick will just get me a doctor and before I leave this town, I'll call, Mom, and if nobody else saw it I'll tell them. That's what I'll do, Mom.

Anyway, Bick, you've got some M.C. There I was with that mike cord all twisted into figure 8s, so while I was clearing it I told them the one Jeremy Vernon did about the guy and his wife who smoked the cigarettes with the premiums on the packs. One day his neighbor dropped in and started admiring the new lamp and the new TV and the new reclining chair, and the guy said: "Yeah, Wilma and I got these for smoking these cigarettes." So the neighbor said: "Great, but by the way, where is Wilma?" And the guy said: "Wilma? Oh, she died last month trying for this coffee table."

They liked me, Bick, so don't go with that critic. That critic is one of those guys who figures that if he doesn't knock you he loses the franchise. Ask Joe Fragetta. Always ask the maitre d'. The critic sees one show and the maitre d' sees every show, so if you ever get to be a club comic, Bick, always be nice to the maitre d'. Anyway, ask him, Bick, but first get me a doctor.

Is there anything I'm alergic to, Doc? Yeah, I'm allergic to doctors who don't make house calls. Just suppose your plumber stopped making calls. "Your toilet is stopped up, Mrs. Brown? No, I'm sorry. Mr. O'Brien doesn't make calls any more, but if you bring it in at three o'clock this afternoon he'll look at it."

You don't think that's funny, Doc? Well I don't think it's funny lying here with this indigestion, or whatever it is, and Bick can't get a doctor in this whole town, whatever the name of it is. I know the name, and if you give me an hour I'll think of it, because every morning of my life now when I wake up—make that every afternoon, Doc—it takes me I don't know how long to figure out where I am and the name of the town.

Let's see now, Doc. I know I'm not in Utica, because in Utica I had to take second billing to the stripper—they always tell you it's the broad who brings them in—and after the club closed that first night at 3 she said: "Stick around, Bobby, please, because I'm scared to be alone with these thugs." They were thugs all right, the three of them that owned the place, and every night they'd sit at one table with her and I'd sit at another by myself. They'd pour one drink after another, but she must have been spilling them down her front instead of down her throat, because at 5 o'clock, when they'd finally give up again, she'd be as sober as when we came on and they'd be half crocked and I'd be so soaked that I couldn't do any good and I'd still be hung over when I'd walk on again the next night.

And I'm not in Allentown, either, or was it Harrisburg? It doesn't matter, because the joint isn't there any more. The Luau Lounge, and I think some Hawaiians paddled over in their war canoes and burned it down. Some lounge. It was like a bowling alley with bamboo walls and plastic palm trees, and it had fish nets hanging from the ceiling with starfish in them. Some owner, too. If he didn't like the singer he'd turn off the mike. Also he had this hydraulic stage, which he didn't tell you about, and my opening night was my closing night because I was doing fine, considering there weren't any people in the place, and he pushed the button right in the middle of my Jackie Gleason impression. All of a sudden, here's the stage going down under me, you know? You may fire when ready . . . As our ship sinks slowly in the west . . . The boy stood on the burning deck.

And then I'm not in Hartford because that's where they had this Colony Room. It was a nice respectable room, but the first night before I went on I saw these cards on the tables, propped up between the sugar bowl and the salt and pepper shakers.

Welcome
to
The Colony Room
Featuring
Roast Prime Ribs of Beef
And
Bobby Carlton

So the next day I called my agent, and I screamed. I hollered: "I thought I was supposed to get star billing here?" He said: "That's right. That's right. It's in the contract. What's happening?" So I said: "What's happening? I'm the supporting act to a dead steer!"

He thought I was serious—that's how good I laid it on him—but I kind of liked the owner of that Colony Room and he gave me an education. He was so fat that he sat on two bar stools at the same time. Actually he did, and after my second night he called me over to where he was sitting on these two stools and he said: "You've got a lot of talent, son, but let me give you a little advice. If you want to be successful in this business you have to develop at least one routine that's original and your own." So I said: "Such as?" He said: "Well, we had a comic in here last month who does this bit about an Italian immigrant in a phone booth." So I said: "But that's Danny Thomas's." Then he said: "Well, we had another who did a routine about moving to the suburbs." I said: "But that's Alan King's." So he said: "Who cares? Everybody steals. Just do it well."

So then I know I'm not in Boston, Doc, because in Boston everybody really steals. It's a city of thieves. I mean that, because when you work a room in Boston the local comedians sit there with paper and pencil to take down your stuff. They actually do, and if they're not writing you're worried. That's the truth. Instead of hiring a lawyer and threatening to sue them you end up knocking yourself out actually trying to get them to steal your stuff and give you your confidence back.

It's ridiculous, this business, Mom, but you never know, and tomorrow could be the day. It's absurd, Mom, and I could never explain it to you. You meet people, and they say: "But how did you get to *be* a comedian?" It's like you're an alcoholic, the way they ask it. I can tell it from the way you look at me, too, and shrug, Mom, but you had your grief and I never gave you mine.

You remember when you used to send me out to the park to get some fresh air? You had that thing about fresh air, and maybe I'm running away from fresh air, because they don't have any in the rooms I work like this one here. Maybe that's why

I'm having this trouble breathing now, I never get enough fresh air.

"So get some fresh air," you'd say, "and with the others play the games."

With the others play the games, Mom? Where we came from I didn't know their games. Baseball? Football? What did I know? And all of a sudden somebody would holler: "Pile on!" They'd all jump on me, Mom, and I'd be at the bottom of the pile. I couldn't move. I couldn't see. I couldn't breathe, and I was afraid I was going to die.

"The dirt," you'd say, shaking your head, when I came in. "Why always on the clothes the dirt?"

"It's the games," I'd say. "It's the games we play."

"If it's the games," you'd say, "that's good. So the games enjoy."

The games enjoy? Mom, I used to lie in bed at night, before you'd finish with the *Lederschneiden* and come in, and I'd think: *Why do they always pick on me? What's wrong with me?* Lots of nights I'd cry myself to sleep, but why tell you, Mom? What could you do?

It was the radio that did it, though. It was that old console you bought secondhand, and that stood in the corner. It had that green eye that blinked when we tuned it in, and on Saturday afternoons you used to sit there and listen to Milton Cross and the Metropolitan Opera. It was the only time you took off all week, Mom, on Saturday afternoons, and that did it, because the first imitation I did was of Milton Cross introducing the opera, and you laughed. "Good afternoon, opera lovers, from the Metropolitan Opera House in New York. This is Milton Cross, and our opera this afternoon is *Il Trovatore*, by Giuseppe Verdi . . . and now for the first act. As the curtain rises we see . . ." You laughed, and then I started to do Fred Allen and Jack Benny and Henry Morgan, and then the kids started to laugh. They stopped piling on, Mom, and they started to laugh.

"Hey! Do Allen's Alley! Do Mrs. Nussbaum! Do Titus Moody! Hey! Listen to this kid do Allen's Alley! C'mon, do Mrs. O'Rourke."

Mrs. O'Rourke was the sixth-grade teacher. She was probably fifty years old but she seemed like a hundred, and she had a voice like Lionel Barrymore.

"Boy! Stop that talking! Why were you talking, boy? He asked you a question? I'm the only one who asks questions in this room so, boy, stay after school."

Then in high school I'd campaign for any kid running for office so I could do my Danny Kaye impressions I took from records, like "Minnie the Moocher" and the fifty Russian composers he did in *Lady in the Dark*. Then one day I did that gag I took from a Willie Howard record, and I was so naïve I didn't understand it but the other kids did.

"There was an old woman who lived in a shoe, and she had so many children she didn't know what to do—obviously."

That one got me sent to the principal, and I was afraid he was going to make you come to school, Mom, or maybe even expel me. The kids liked me, though, and they liked me in the Army when I did that routine I made up about the sergeant talking to the recruits.

"Now, men, you're gonna have to learn this and it's complicated, so listen carefully. I'm gonna tell you about the infantry company. An infantry company consists of four platoons. They are called as follows: the first platoon, the second platoon . . ."

They liked it. All the routines I did in the Army they liked, and so I thought that when I got out, the whole world would like me and I'd be a star overnight.

"Look, dear, this is Bobby Carlton, and I'm trying to get Mr. Bick."

"I'm sorry, Mr. Carlton, but Mr. Bick isn't in his office."

"But where is he? This is important."

"I don't know, sir, but he's somewhere on the premises. He should be back shortly."

"Look, I'm sick. I'm ill, and he's supposed to be trying to get me a doctor."

"I know, Mr. Carlton. He's been trying, but he hasn't had any luck yet. I'm sure he'll keep trying."

"Tell him I called, will you? Will you tell him to come in here, or call me, as soon as he gets back?"

"Yes, sir, and I hope you'll be feeling better."

It could be your food, Bick, but I don't know because I had this same pain last week in Springfield, but not so bad, and I didn't eat too much last night, anyway. When I came off at 10 I had another drink and I ate the shrimp cocktail but not much of the steak and I passed up those wood chips your chef calls French fries. Then, when this started, I went back to the kitchen and your chef gave me two Alka-Seltzer—he should— and I came back here and I lay down. After that I felt better, and I did your second show for you, Bick, and they liked me and now you can't get me a doctor?

So what am I supposed to do, Bick, threaten to scream to my agent? So he'll say it's not in the contract, the doctor? So, what's he going to do? Send me up a doctor from New York? So maybe he knows a doctor in New York knows a doctor here. That's crazy, but he gets 10 percent of the gelt, so let him get 10 percent of the grief.

"Hello? Hello? Listen. This is Bobby Carlton, and let me talk to Mort Singer."

"I'm sorry, Mr. Carlton, but Mr. Singer is out."

"He's out? Where is he?"

"He was called out to a conference, sir. He can't be reached right now. When he comes in shall I have him call you back?"

"No. Never mind."

"Is there any message, sir?"

"Yes. Tell him I called to wish him a happy Washington's Birthday, and I'm sorry I'm a little late."

"I'll tell him, Mr. Carlton. Thank you."

Agents. If I had a good agent I wouldn't be playing rooms like this in towns like this where you can't get a doctor, but they've got you trapped. I'd be in Miami, or Vegas, where you can get a doctor, but the little agents knock you to the big agents so they can keep you small and hang onto you for these starvation jobs in all these Bridgeports. You want a cheap comic? Good. I got Bobby Carlton. So what can you do? You can just hang in there because you never know what night somebody is going to be out there and catch your stuff and the next day you'll have it made. That's what they say, anyway.

Some agents I've had. Vultures. The first one was that one I found in the classified ads in *Show Business*. It said: "Looking for all kinds of entertainers, singers, comedians, dancers for TV and top night clubs." It was in the old Roseland Building, down a hall, around two corners, an office the size of a coat closet with no window, a pay phone, and the walls covered with these photos of acts, getting yellow with age, and stuck up there with adhesive tape and thumb tacks. They said things like, "Thanks for giving me my start. Tarza and her Snake." "Thanks for my first break. Dolores Delight and her Doves." He was bald, and his teeth were yellow like the pictures, and he had this frumpy bleached-blond secretary who was his wife.

"You see those pictures? You see what they wrote? I made them stars, all of them. Sure, we'll get you some shows, but we'll have to try you out first. We've got this talent contest at eight o'clock tonight."

What do I know? I'm twenty years old, and they laughed at me in the Army, and it's one of those joints in Brooklyn where you have to take three subways and walk ten blocks. It's not a talent contest, it's an amateur night, and there are nineteen other acts waiting and I'm the only one who's there alone. Everybody else has brought his claque—relatives, friends and neighbors—so the owner makes his profit off everybody sitting there and eating and drinking for two hours until the show goes on at 10 o'clock.

I did Danny Kaye and stuck out my jaw like Barry Fitzgerald and, with the heavy brogue, did the: "Ah, well now . . ." I did Jerry Lewis screaming, "Hey, Dean!" I did Bette Davis and I did Cagney, with the elbows locked and the fingers spread, and I did Gary Cooper's "Howdy, ma'am . . ."

For more than two hours it went on, and at the end they paraded us across the stage and the M.C. held an envelope over our heads and what was left of the crowd applauded. There was five dollars in the first-prize envelope, three in the second and two in the third, and the last three people would always win because by the end of the show they were the only ones anybody remembered. That first night I was in the middle of the pack and I won nothing, but the next place put me third from the end and I won third. Then they moved me up to next to last and I won second, but I could never win first because all these joints were owned by Italians and they always saved the last spot for an Italian guy who wore a tux from his wedding jobs and sang *Sorrento*.

"So you're a comedian? Who told you that you're funny, your mother?"

Agents. What did I know? I'd be up and out by 9 o'clock and most of them didn't come in until 1, because they only had one or two clubs to book for the weekend and they could do it with one or two phone calls. Now he's on long distance? What's he doing on long distance when his farthest club is in Queens?

"So what's your opening line?"

"Well, I walk out and I say: 'Thank you.'"

"What are you thanking them for?"

"For the applause."

"What if they don't applaud?"

"Well, I'm polite."

"Polite? In this business who cares about polite?"

"So I say: 'Is there anybody out there? I thought I heard breathing.'"

"You got a car?"

"No."

"No good. I need somebody to drive the stripper."

"You've got nothing else?"

"I'm workin' on something for you. See me next week."

So next week it would be the same. Always they were working on something for you, and Marty Abrams went into the Army for two years and when he came back the agent didn't even look up.

"Nothing," he said, "but I've been workin' on something for you. See me next week."

Agents. There was that one who kept his hat on all the time and he had this hearing aid. I figured he must have had the batteries under the hat, and you couldn't tell if he was listening to you or if he was tuned into WNEW.

"Nothing," he said, "and it's the bad time of the year now.

Everybody's closing for the summer, and I don't handle the mountains. Go see Sol Spiegel."

Sol Spiegel, the Crown Prince of the Catskills. He had that opening at the Serene Lake Lodge, $75 a week and room and board, but they wanted a social director.

"You have to conduct games," he said. "You know how to conduct games?"

"Sure," I said. "Of course I know how to conduct games."

What did I know about games, Mom? The only games I knew were "Saluggi!" and "Pile On!" Some games, but I knew Marty Abrams, and he was booked to work his second summer at a place in Fallsburgh and he knew all the games. In an hour, while I bought him lunch at the Stage Delicatessen and took notes, he explained shuffleboard and badminton and calisthenics and balloon races and "Simon Says" and how you conduct "What's My Line?" and "You Bet Your Life."

Serene Lake Lodge. It wasn't a lake, it was a pond, and it wasn't serene because it was full of turtles and frogs. I got off the bus at noontime, and they picked me up in a station wagon and took me to my room which was one of the dressing rooms off the stage in the casino. There was this filthy sink and Kleenex with make-up on it all over the place and a naked light bulb in the ceiling and dust and dirt everywhere, so I got a pail and a mop, even before I had any lunch, and I was starting to clean it up when the extension phone rang and it was the owner.

"Hey, M.C.? What are you doing? What did I hire you for? Get some activity going! Start a game of 'Simon Says'!"

They were old people, Mom, middle-aged and older. They wanted to sit in the sun and relax. They didn't want to play games. They wanted to be left alone, and then in the casino they had it set up for dancing and everybody was a half mile away. They told me that the big show was Saturday nights, so for two nights I saved my best stuff, and then on Saturday morning they told me that for Saturday nights they always bring a comic up from New York.

"Hello, M.C.? Hold on. There's a long distance for you."

"Hello, Bobby? Sol Spiegel. Listen . . ."

"I'm listening."

"They've changed their minds up there. They want to do something different, so . . ."

"But I didn't have a chance. They never told me that on Saturday nights . . ."

"I know. Listen . . ."

"I saved my best material, because . . ."

"I know. Listen. Come back to the city, and I'll get something else for you."

So the next place the owner had that Ivy League son who had a name like Keith or Kevin and called his father "Daahd." He wore riding breeches and riding boots and a turtleneck, and he walked around slapping his boots with a riding crop and saying: "Don't touch the dog, he's vicious! Don't go near the horse, he kicks!" He thought he was the new Ziegfeld, and every night he ruined the show with some schlock idea. At the end of the second week they cut me from $55 to $35, and when they wanted to cut it to $25 I told them I'd take the money I had coming and the round-trip transportation.

"The round trip transportation!" the old man hollered, and you would have thought I was charging him round trip air fare from Krakow instead of bus fare from New York. "Round trip I pay nobody! One way!"

"I'm sorry, Daahd," the son said. "I've already called Sol Spiegel, and Sol Spiegel says you have to pay him."

"Sol Spiegel says?" the old man was screaming. "Sol Spiegel says? So from Sol Spiegel's pocket I'll take it out! From Sol Spiegel's pocket I'll take the round-trip out!"

So while he was screaming about Sol Spiegel's pocket I grabbed the money and left, and the next place was where the owners had those twins, about six or seven years old, who walked around tossing lighted matches and chanting: "Our father owns this hotel! Our father owns this hotel!" The casino was an old barn, and they had me rooming there with three bus boys. Every morning at 6:30 the alarm clock would go off, and they'd have a parade across the stage and then down off the stage and across the floor to the men's room.

The owner liked me, though, starting with that first night

when I did my Johnnie Ray impression, or I would have zapped those twins before I did. He played clarinet in the band with the three high school kids with complexion problems, and when I did Johnnie Ray singing "Cry" and came to the line: "So tear your clothes off and go on and cry," I tore off my shirt. He was impressed, like everybody else in the joint, that I ripped up a good shirt, but this was an act I could do only once.

In the morning I'd lead calisthenics, and then I'd set up the shuffleboard tournament and the croquet tournament and the bridge tournament and conduct "Simon Says." In the afternoon I'd give mambo lessons, and every night at 8 o'clock in the casino I had an hour show. I'd put on Groucho Marx make-up and wave the prop cigar and do that walk and line up the contestants for "You Bet Your Life" and "What's My Line?" I'd get the men dressed in baby clothes and fill the baby bottles with Coke or ginger ale and they'd sit on the women's laps, and the first one to finish a bottle would win. On the weekends, when the acts would come up, I'd M.C. the show, and they'd give you such corny intros to use that you'd be afraid the audience would think they were your own lines. They'd want you to carry the props around, and go into the act. The magicians wanted you to take off their capes, and they'd saw you in half if you let them. While the dance act was on they wanted you to sit in the dressing room where they had the poodle locked up because when he got lonesome he'd cry, and you never had a name any more because you were the M.C.

"Hey, M.C., where's the croquet set?" . . . "Hey, M.C., the badminton net fell down!" . . . "Hey, M.C., somebody threw the shuffleboard disks into the deep end of the pool!" . . . "Hey, M.C., what do we do now?"

I knew who threw the shuffleboard disks into the deep end of the pool and I knew what to do now, but I wanted to keep the job. Then one night we were supposed to have a balloon dance, and I spent two hours blowing up the balloons until I was almost sick from it. I had a whole dressing room full of them, and when I went out to get some string and came back it sounded like the sound effects I do for that routine about the Japanese machine gunner in the cave who still hasn't heard the war is over. When I opened the door and saw busted balloons all over the floor and those kids still sticking pins in the rest of them I grabbed the two of them and I really let them have it.

"Our father owns this hotel!" they were screaming. "Our father owns this hotel!"

"Yeah," I said, "and he's a lousy clarinet player, too."

"We're gonna tell him what you said!" they were hollering. "We're gonna tell him what you said!"

"Good," I said, "and then I'm gonna break both your legs, so don't come running to me."

So they ran, instead, to the kitchen where their mother was working on the books. In five minutes I had my two weeks' notice, and that's how I didn't last through Labor Day, Mom, although I never told you.

I never really told you, Mom, about the Catskills or the agents or these towns, because I don't want to kill your dreams and, anyway, there's always tomorrow. I remember, Mom, how you studied for that citizenship exam and how I used to rehearse you, and then we went to that municipal court, or whatever it was. The Grossmans went with us, for sponsors, and also Mrs. Klein, the wife of the dry cleaner, and there was that woman judge. You answered all the tough ones, Mom, like how many Senators and Representatives and the Bill of Rights and I forget what else, until she asked you the easiest one of all. She asked you how many states there are in the Union, and you didn't say anything. You just stood there, and there wasn't a sound in the room, with everybody looking at you and waiting, and then you must have seen the flag up there next to the judge, because all of a sudden you started to sob: "Red, white and blue! Red, white and blue! Red, white and blue!" And I looked at the judge, and she got up and came down and she threw her arms around you and there were tears in her eyes as she hugged you and she said: "God bless you, Rebekkah Ehrenberg, you're an American citizen. God bless you forever." And everybody in the room was crying, Mom, everybody.

C'mon, Bick, c'mon. I'm waiting, Bick, and while I'm waiting

I'm getting scared, because it's getting worse. It's like "Pile On!" all over again, Bick, with everybody on top of me and on my chest and I can't breathe, and I don't know anybody in this town. Don't you understand, Bick? They're all strangers to me, like last night before the first show when I looked out and the room was packed and I said to Joe Fragetta: "What is it? Who are they?"

"I don't know, Bobby," he said, "but it's gonna be tough."

"But who are they?" I said.

"Everybody," he said. "We got a 'Sweet Sixteen' party over here, and another one over here and one more over there. Then over there we got these women from some bowling league and we got a couple of wedding anniversaries, and in the back we got a dozen detectives."

"A dozen detectives?" I said. "What are you pushing here besides the booze and the food?"

"Nothing," he said. "It's some kind of retirement, or something, for one of them. It's gonna be tough."

Tough? Tough is the word for your steak, but this is going to be murder. Bowling stories I've got, but half of them I have to knock out because of the "Sweet Sixteens." I can't tell the one about the detective and the pimp, either, and then Fragetta brings one of them over and introduces him.

"You're the comedian?" this sherlock says. "Listen, we're giving the boss, the lieutenant, a retirement party after thirty years, so will you say something funny about that?"

"Like what?" I say.

"I don't know," he says. "You're the comedian."

"So what else does he do?" I say.

"Who?" he says, and now I see he's half loaded.

"Your lieutenant," I say. "What else does he like to do besides catch criminals and put them in jail?"

"Well," he says, "he likes to fish."

Great. At least he didn't tell me that the guy just divorced his wife of thirty years and married a young chick, and I should say something funny about *that*. Great, but then it turned out that one of them—maybe this same guy because I couldn't see them back there through the haze—bailed me out. It was when

I was just starting to get them moving, but not too good with that mixed mob, Bick, that I heard him. I couldn't tell what he was saying, so I tried to ignore him, but he kept it up.

"I'm sorry, sir," I said, finally, "but I work alone."

Then he said something else. I couldn't hear that, either, but now everybody in front was turning around and looking, so I laid it on him.

"Look, sir," I said, and I gave it just the right pause. "Maybe I'll get arrested for this, but do I come where *you* work and leave *my* fingerprints all over the place?"

That got them, the detectives and everybody else, and from then on they liked me, Bick. It's an old line, Bick—"Do I come where you work and steal your shovel?"—but you see how I changed it and made it mine? It's like when we used to sit around the Stage Delicatessen at 3 in the morning, and one guy would be back from the mountains and one guy would be back from a club in Brooklyn and somebody else from the Bronx. With the chicken soup with noodles and the corned beef sandwiches and pickles we'd tell how we had this heckler and how we buried him with this line or that one, and everybody knew that most of the time the truth was that we never thought of the lines until we were on the way home.

That one was the truth, though, Bick, and you can ask Joe Fragetta. Ask him about the second show, too, because after I had this indigestion and lay down I still didn't feel too good, and then when I looked at the house I felt even worse. Half the people who were there for the first show, including the cops, were still there for the second one, and that's the kind of a town this is. I couldn't repeat. You know what that means, Bick, when you can't repeat? You have to come up with a whole different act, so you know what I did?

"Thank you. Thank you. You're very kind, and we're all good friends now, so I'll tell you what I'm going to do. I'm gonna . . . excuse me, sir? . . . You, sir? . . . Are you in show business? You're not? Then how come you've got your foot up on my stage? . . . What's that, sir? . . . I can't hear what you're saying, but you're a good laugher, and I wonder if you'd like to go on the road? . . . You wouldn't? . . . Okay, so I'll tell you what I'm gonna do. I'm gonna do like the singers do. I'm gonna take this microphone off here and stroll down among you, and you name your favorite jokes and I'll tell them to you . . . And then we'll have a community sing . . . Everybody follow the bouncing ball, and you, sir, would you like to be the bouncing ball? . . . And you don't think I can sing? That's where you're wrong, because I'll have you know I recorded for Decca . . . That's Maxine Decca, and she lives in the Bronx . . . Oh, you liked that, sir? Well, tell me something. How long have you and your wife been married? This lovely lady is your wife, isn't she? Twenty-seven years? You *do* have a sense of humor, sir, so maybe *you'd* like to go on the road . . . And this foursome over here . . . Charming . . . You know what a foursome is, don't you? Two guys take out two girls, and if they're uncooperative they force 'em . . . And what was I saying? I forget, but I have another idea. We'll all join hands, and this gentleman on the end will stick his finger in the wall socket . . ."

For thirty-two minutes I kept it up, Bick. I know I'm supposed to give you forty minutes, but I'm not supposed to have repeat audiences, and they liked it. You think that's easy? I'll tell you how easy it is, because when I came off I was soaking wet, sweating like I'm sweating now, Bick, and maybe that started it.

I don't know what started it, Bick, but it's worse now. It's worse in my chest, the way it's thumping so I can hear it in my ears, and I can even feel it in my arm, and I'm scared, Bick. I don't know what it is, but I could be having a heart attack. I need a doctor, Bick, or get me an ambulance, because I don't want to die. I don't want to die in this town, or anywhere, because I'm too young to die.

"Hello? Listen. This is Bobby Carlton again. Get me Mr. Bick."

"Mr. Bick is on the other phone, Mr. Carlton."

"Get him off the phone. Please. Tell him never mind the doctor. Tell him to get me an ambulance."

"Here's Mr. Bick now, Mr. Carlton."

"Bick? Listen. Never mind the doctor. Get me an ambulance. I think I'm having a heart attack. Just get me an ambulance."

I'm too young to die. You know that, Mom. I'm only thirty-four. That's too young to die, and I never asked you how old he was, and all I remember is that this next day there was like a parade through the streets of the town, and they were carrying him and the rest of them. Then I remember a hillside in the sunshine and there were long wide trenches in the ground and what must have been bulldozers there. After that they were putting them into these trenches, one next to another in their zebra suits, and when the bulldozers started to push the dirt back into the trenches I don't remember jumping in. I just remember that I was lying on top of him, holding him and crying that he was my father, and then there were two soldiers, brown pants and brown leather boots, and then they were pulling me off him and lifting me out.

XII

FRANK BAKER

If he's not looking in the mirror and combing his hair he's on the telephone cooing to some broad. When he gets bored with that he goes around the corner and comes back with another container of coffee and another one of those jelly doughnuts that looks like an orangutan's iridescent tail light. I don't think he eats a square meal a week, and I'm the one who has to go around picking up the containers where he put them down when he finished them or when the coffee got cold, on the floor, on the desk, on our files, on the table, on the top of the space heater.

I just get tired of having it out with him all the time, the way I'm tired of the whole thing. Roger was the one, but Roger was smarter than I am and he grew up and got out of it, and if he keeps hawking that insurance the way he's been doing he can sit back some day and just let the renewals come in. If this one had any brains or any money or could get any credit I'd sell him the whole service—The Whale, Lustig's rat pack, the cats, the coffee containers, everything—and I'd take off for Florida. I'd get a small place there, and every morning I'd walk down to the pier and sit there in the sun and drop my line over and catch my next meal, but what's the use of even thinking about it?

"You got a slip on this Braff?" I say, looking at his trip log for the night before, while he's reading my newspaper.

"No," he says, "but it's on the log, and it's here in the paper. It's on page one, and you didn't see it?"

How would I see it? The moment I come in and put the paper down to take off my coat he either picks it up to look at it or he puts his coffee container down on it to leave a ring on it.

"What's it doing on page one?" I say.

"It's Nick Braff, the famous jockey," he says, "and he shot himself. It says right here: 'Braff was taken to the Medical Center Emergency Room by Baker Ambulance. According to ambulance driver Martin Conlin, Braff was unconscious throughout most of the trip, occasionally evidencing pain but never sufficiently conscious to give any explanation for his act.'"

"Where did they get that?" I say.

"I called them," he says. "They pay you for these news tips. It's on page one, so I'll get a sawbuck for it."

Now he's a news reporter, too, as well as a Medical Emergency Technician, a lover and a coffee taster. AP Conlin.

"You think the reason he did it," he says, and this fits Mr. Marty Conlin, too, "was because he was fixin' races?"

"Is he alive?" I say.

"It says here they operated on him, and he's in Intensive Care and his condition is critical. It's good advertising. Right?"

"For what?" I say. "Fircarms?"

"No," he says. "For us. Baker Ambulance."

Of course. The next time somebody shoots himself he'll leave a note saying he wants Baker Ambulance. I'll be wealthy and fishing off that dock in Florida before I know it.

I look at our schedule, and all we've got is a transfer, after 10 and before noon, from St. Vincent's to Valley View Nursing Home. I'm figuring that after he gets done studying his name in the paper I'll do the crossword puzzle, when the phone rings.

"Is this the ambulance?" this woman's voice says, all excited and before I can say anything.

"Yes, ma'am," I say.

"Get down here quick!" she says. "We've got a man with his leg caught in the machinery! Can you get down here quick?"

"Right away, ma'am," I say, "but who is this and where are you?"

"Gorham's Grain and Feed!" she says. "Do you know where we are, because . . ."

"I know where it is," I say, "and don't worry, ma'am because we're on our way right now."

We bounce down the stairs and Conlin swings the door up, but before I start The Whale I check the cats. Two of them are at the food I just put out for them, and when I don't see the gray and white one I look under The Whale. It's not there so I get in and start her up, but that's why I get rid of the kittens. They're liable to be around the wheels, or like that time I stepped on the starter and I heard the scream. I didn't know what it was, but when we got back I looked under the hood and she must have crawled up in there to keep warm and got caught in the fan.

I wheel out now, and Conlin jumps in and I turn on the beacon and the four red lights. I turn her left and switch on both sirens, and halfway down this block that I have to live with every day there's this character who has finally shoveled his car out of the snow and slop. He's got it double parked now while he and his wife are moving one of those metal porch gliders out into the space so nobody will park there while he's gone. I ease her by that, and then I have to go around that Christmas tree with the tinsel still on it that's been flopping around here ever since the holidays and that's out in the street now. This is some world.

Conlin is on the radio-phone giving the broad that "dear" business and telling her where we're going, and when I get onto Washington and start down the hill toward the river, I see this prowl car with its beacon turning coming in on my side from East Third. We can't hear each other, but they see us, and as they swing around in front of us they give the big follow signal and we open up. I've got eyes all over my head now, and when I glance at Conlin I can see he's loving it.

You should, if you're going to stay in this business, and I used to. When I started with old O. C. Tenner and we'd roll on one of these foot-to-the-floor jobs like a head-on or a four-car pile up I used to almost shake all over wondering what I was going to see. You still wonder, but I've just seen too many brains on too many dashboards and smelled too much of that mix of anti-freeze and oil and gasoline and gore.

At the bottom of Washington we wheel left onto Water Street and it's just ahead of us on the right. It's the old four-story concrete and wooden ark that's been there for as long as I can remember between the dock and the railroad siding. We pull across the tracks, and there are a half dozen guys in heavy work clothes and one woman in a green coat with a fur collar out there by this loading platform, waiting for us.

"Oh, thank God you've come!" this woman says, as I get out. "I thought . . ."

"Where is he?" I say.

"Upstairs," one of the guys says. "Follow me."

I get up on the loading platform and I follow him, and it's a narrow wooden stairway with a right turn. I jump back out and I tell Conlin to bring the litter, and then I follow up the three flights of the stairs with one of the cops after me, and there he is. There's this workman, maybe in his forties, down on this metal-covered deck where there's an opening. He's on his back, with a coat under his head and a couple of his buddies kneeling over him, and his right leg is off below the knee with a bloody towel over the stump.

"You're going to be all right," I say to him, and when I lift the towel just enough to take a look at the bleeding, I can see there's grain matted in there with the drying blood.

"The hell I am," he says, through his teeth, and he's pale and a little shocky.

"Can somebody get a piece of rope, like clothesline, at least two feet long?" I say, and I'm thinking I'm stupid. I should have brought a tourniquet up, but I'm slipping.

I'm making a compress out of my handkerchief now, folding it up because I want to block off that femoral artery there in the thigh. Actually he's lucky, because whatever it was that he caught his leg in, it crushed it and compressed the vessels, where if it had cut it off clean he probably would have bled to death. What I want to do now is just be sure it doesn't start pumping on the way in.

"How did this happen?" the cop is saying now while I'm working with the bandage scissors cutting the bloody pants leg and the underwear up the length of the thigh.

207

"Some goddam fool left the cover off the hole," one of the other workman says, "and Pete stepped in it and got caught by the screw."

"I pulled it right off," this Pete is saying, his face twisted and tears in his eyes. "I took a hold and pulled as hard as I could, because if I didn't I was goin' right down the hole, and it just come right off."

"You're going to be all right," I say, and if I ever wrote a book about the ambulance business that would be the title of it. "I just want to put a tourniquet on, and we'll have you in to the hospital in minutes."

"Somebody call my wife," he's saying now, through his teeth. "Charley? Is Charley here?"

"Sure, Pete," Charley is saying, and he's the one who hands me the rope. "I'll call her as soon as you leave, and I'll tell her you're gonna be all right."

"Thanks, Charley," he's saying. "Thanks a lot."

I've got the wad of my handkerchief in place. Then I put the rope around and I make sure I've got enough pressure on to block off the artery and not just the vein. When I finish with that we slide him onto the litter, and while Conlin is blanketing him and strapping him, I ask this Charley about the lower leg.

"It's over here still in the screw," he says.

He leads me over and down in this shaft there's this big screw that moves the grain, I guess. Where the leg is wedged down in there I can just see the top of it.

"As soon as I heard him scream," this Charley says, "I figured it was this, and I shut it off. It's a goddam shame."

"Can you back this thing up," I ask him, "and get it out?"

"You *want* it?" he says. "What do you want it for?"

"It's the law," I tell him. "It's got to go into the hospital, too."

"I can back it off a little, but I ain't takin' that thing out," he says. "I almost threw up twice already."

I look for the cop. He's over by a window, questioning the other workman and writing in his notebook.

"Look," I say to him. "We've got to get this man out of here as soon as we can, but we've got to take the leg, too. While we're getting him downstairs, this other man here is going to ease off on that machinery. When he does, will you just reach down and pull it out? Somebody here will find something to wrap it in."

"It's got to be something clean?" this Charley says.

"No," I say. "Anything will do."

"How about a grain sack?" this Charley says.

"Good," I say.

"Look," the cop says now. "How about me helping carry him, while one of you guys gets the leg?"

I understand him, and I can remember that boiling hot afternoon years ago when O.C. and I had that farmer in that hay baler out there just beyond where that West Shopping Center is now. It was hotter than Hades, and he was so mangled that we practically had to blotter him up, and there was this cop there, and he said: "But how are we gonna get him out?" So old O.C. said: "I'll tell you how we're going to get him out. We'll run him through, because nothing's going to hurt him now. Right, Franklin?" Being O.C.'s fetch, I was the one who had to crawl in there and cut the baling wires and cut his clothing loose, and then we hand turned it because the belt was off. When he flopped out of there onto the rubber sheet we had on the tailgate where the bales are supposed to land, that cop just turned green and lost his lunch.

"No good," I say to this one now. "It's a very tricky carry down this narrow stairway with tight turns and we're trained for it. We haven't got time to argue. Right?"

"I guess so," he says.

We make the carry and get him outside, where there's a pretty good audience now. George O'Donnell calls them moths, when he's on the scene and telling the uniformed cops to get the moths back, but I call them ghouls, and while we're loading now the woman in the green coat comes up.

"Is he all right?" she says.

"He's doing fine," I say, and what else does she think I'm going to tell her with the patient listening. "He's going to be all right."

"I don't know what Mr. Gorham's going to say," she says. "He's away, you know."

"Yes, ma'am," I say, while we're anchoring the cot with the litter on it.

"This business has been in his family for years," she says, "and nothing like this ever happened before, and when he hears about it I just don't know what he's going to say."

"Yes, ma'am," I say.

With that the cop comes up with the grain sack, with some twine around the top. I thank him and hand it in to Conlin and close the back doors.

"You want us to take you all the way?" the other cop says.

"You don't have to," I say.

"Why not?" he says. "We can stand a little ride."

"And on the way in," I say, "tell your dispatcher to let the M.C. know what we've got coming, will you?"

I don't know these two, but with Conlin, the Voice of Baker Ambulance, in the back, I don't want one hand on the wheel and one on the phone because there are more than a few cowboys in prowl cars. They tell me they get bored just cruising around, and as it turns out these two take us in a lot faster than we need to go because I know I've got a patient who's not going to die. He hasn't even really felt the big pain yet, and I remember that Italian railroad worker O.C. and I had years ago and who lost his left leg under a train and he didn't even realize it until he tried to get up to walk and fell on his face. After he got out of the hospital he bought a plot in Willow Lawn Cemetery, and he had O.C. bury the leg. I didn't go out for the ceremony, but O.C. said the guy was there with his wife and his grown son, and that was years ago and I guess he's joined the leg by now.

When we get to the M.C. they're waiting for us, and we whip him right into Minor Ops and off our stretcher. When I don't see Conlin around I figure he's getting us the clean sheets and pillow case, but when I go out to look for him I find him on that wall phone that's on that big square column.

"Were you calling our service," I say, when he hangs up, "or are you playing newshawk again?"

"What's wrong with that?" he says. "The guy says if they use it it's a couple of bucks."

"You bring in the grain sack?" I say.

"No," he says. "I forgot."

"I'll call the service," I say.

They have nothing for us, and when I get off the phone Conlin is coming in with the sack. I follow him back into Minor Ops, where there's this student nurse standing there observing on the edge of the group working on the patient, and Conlin hands her the sack.

"Here, dear," he says. "Here's a present for you."

"For me?" she says, taking it, and looking at it. "What is it?"

"It's his leg," Conlin says.

"Oh, my God!" she says. "What am I supposed to do with it?"

I step in, then, before Conlin can tell her to have it mounted, I tell her to put it over in a corner, and when Verna Palmer is free to tell her it's there.

"Thank you," she says. "I really didn't know."

We've got some time to kill before that transfer from St. Vincent's, so I stop at Al Mooney's, where he gives me two cents off a gallon, and I tell him to fill it up and let me have the bills for the month. We go across the street to the diner, and I have a cup of tea and some toast while I'm checking the bills and Conlin has another one of those jelly delights and more coffee.

This transfer is a thin old woman, in her eighties, who may have hardening of the arteries of the brain because she's senile. She's one of the happy ones, though, and while we're moving her out she starts jabbering at Conlin.

"Why," she says to him, "I know you."

"You do, dear?" he says.

"Why, of course," she says. "Don't you remember me?"

"Sure I do, dear," he says.

"You remember," she says. "You remember when there were no automobiles, don't you?"

"That's right, dear," Conlin says. "I remember. There were nothing but horses."

"Oh, no," she says. "There were bicycles, too. Don't you remember the bicycles?"

"Why, of course, dear," Conlin says.

"I knew you'd remember," she says. "Do you want to know something?"

"What's that, dear?" he says.

"My sister wants to know why I go out with you," she says, "but I tell her that you're no worse than the others."

"That's right, dear," he says. "Your sister's got me all wrong."

On the way over to the Valley View, with Conlin in the back with her, I could turn on the intercom but I don't want to have to listen to that. After we unload her and go back to the barn, I no sooner get The Whale backed in and get up to the office than we get a call from the Wayside Motor Inn. They say they've got somebody out there with what sounds to me like a cardiac arrest, and ten minutes ago we were a half mile from there, but that will happen almost as many times as not.

On the way out Franklin Avenue to the Wayside I'm remembering that I haven't had a call there since about a year ago when we picked up that Mr. Big who slipped on the ice at the foot of one of those outside stairways and broke a leg. He must have been running a conference or something, because along with that thin nervous character who manages the Wayside, there were a half dozen young flunkies around him, all in dark suits and white shirts and agreeing with everything he said, while he was lying there on a sofa in the lobby and giving orders.

"Now you don't have to set any speed records," he said to me while we were loading him. "I've been through a lot in my life and I can stand a little pain. Understand?"

"Yes, sir," I said.

When we got him into a booth in the E.R. he had to wait, so I figured that as long as he's from out of town I might as well slip the tab to him right then. I made it out in a nice round number, and while I was doing it a couple of his flunkies walked in.

"What's this?" he said, when I handed it to him. "Fifty dollars for a ten-minute ride? What do you think I am?"

"Well, sir," I said, "I think you're an important businessman, and I think you've been greatly inconvenienced. I also think you're going to sue the motel, so I figured you were entitled to the $50 Special, which you got. Am I right, sir?"

"I guess you're right," he said, eying me, and then he turned to one of the flunkies and he said: "Write out a check for this gentleman and hang onto this bill. I wish we had a few like him working for us."

It's the Robin Hood system for redistributing the wealth, and if the M.D.s can do it I can do it, too. There's a good 10 to 12 percent who never pay, and some of them just can't afford it, so I figure what you can get off the rich you're giving to the poor.

Out at the Wayside, now, this same thin nervous manager is waiting for us outside the lobby entrance. He motions us ahead and he runs in front of us down about four or five units where he waves us to a stop and we bounce out.

"I don't know what's wrong with him," he says, "and I can't get a doctor. Nobody can get a doctor any more, but he's in pain and he's having trouble breathing. You think it's a heart attack?"

He wants a diagnosis through the door, but he's probably right. When we get into the room, which is on the ground level, there's this young guy, maybe in his early thirties, in bed, pajamas on, pale and sweating a little and grimacing and having trouble breathing and moaning with each breath.

"I don't know what it is," he's saying between breaths. "It's like a heavy weight on my chest, and the pain is in my left arm, too, and I can't breathe. I thought it was heartburn. I thought it was something I ate, because I'm belching a lot, but it doesn't help."

You're belching a lot, I'm thinking, because of all that air you swallow trying to breathe. It has nothing to do with anything you ate.

"It's a little better," he says, "when I don't lie flat. I can breathe a little better then."

"You're going to be all right," I say, and there I go again.

"We'll have you on your way and into the hospital in minutes. Just try to relax."

We go out for the cot, and while Conlin is shoving it out to me, this manager is right there yakking at me.

"You think it's a heart attack?" he's saying. "I don't know what I'm going to do, because he's our feature act. You know?"

"He's what?" I say, and we've got the cot out, now.

"Our act," he says. "Bobby Carlton, our comedian in the Tahitian Room. We booked him for the week and he just opened two nights ago. What am I supposed to do now?"

Tell them some funny stories yourself, I'm thinking, but I ignore him. We get the patient onto the cot and semi-recline him and blanket him, and I ask him where his wallet is. He motions under the pillow on the bed and I get it and put it in the breast pocket of his pajamas, and then we load him. While Conlin is anchoring the cot I'm getting out one of the D cylinders of oxygen and I rig it.

"Now this is going to help you breathe," I tell the patient, and I ease the nasal cannula up in there. "Just relax, because we're on our way. Mr. Conlin is going to stay right with you."

"You're doing fine, pal," Conlin says, and if they're not dears they're all pals of his.

I close the back and the manager is still at my elbow. Before I get behind the wheel I take my pad and I write the telephone number of the hot line to the E.R.

"Look," I tell the manager, handing it to him. "Call this number. It's the Emergency Room at the Medical Center. Just tell them who you are and that Baker Ambulance is coming in with an acute cardiac."

"Call who?" he says.

"Never mind," I say, getting in.

"I don't understand," he's saying. "I've been up for two nights. My night clerk got arrested for shoplifting. Can you imagine that, shoplifting? He's got a good job here and he's shoplifting, and I don't get any sleep now . . ."

When I get out on Franklin Avenue I one-hand her long enough to call the service and tell them to let the M.C. know what we've got coming. Then I open her up, except that as we come to Temple Emanu-El I see the hearse at the curb and some people on the sidewalk and I cut the sirens and slow her just a little for old Mrs. Strauss, may she rest in peace.

How many times I had her in back here for a passenger I don't know, but since the emphysema got worse it must have been four or five times this past year alone. Usually he'd ride along in back with her—two nice old people who'd thank you for everything you did—and yesterday afternoon when we got out there Doc Levias was there and you could tell she was really bad. I think the old man intended to ride along again, but while Conlin and I were loading her I heard her take this one more breath and let out this one last moan and I took a look and I knew.

"Doc?" I said to Levias, and he was standing on the sidewalk with the old man. "You want to check something here?"

He got in then, and she was gone, all right. He told me to take her in and he'd be in himself in a few minutes, and as we were pulling away I happened to look in one of the rear-view mirrors. There was the old man, who didn't know yet, holding his wife's purse in one hand and waving goodbye to her with the other as we started down the street.

I don't know. She's well out of it now, and the old man would be, too, but when you know them for years you feel something. Most of them, like the one I've got in back now, you've never seen before and you'll never see again, but The Whale is the fifth rig I've had since I bought out O.C. thirty-two years ago, and how many have died in the back of those rigs and how many were born there I don't know but I've had both happen within an hour. All I know is that they go out of this world a lot easier than they come in, with the mother moaning and groaning, and then all of a sudden there it is and they're hungry and they want to eat and some of them want to name the baby after you instead of the husband. There it is, so all you have to do is make sure the airway is clear, and you clamp off the cord and you don't have to sever it, being this close to the hospital. Then you wrap the baby in the cotton ether blanket and put it up on the mother and I've even wrapped aluminum foil over the blanket to hold in the heat and reduce the shock. At the hospital they want the placenta, too, so they know it's all there, and it's a mess no matter how you try to handle it.

So now I'm a block from the M.C. and I've got to cut both sirens because some M.D.s formed an Anti-Siren Committee. It was getting so, they said, that patients on the front side and especially in the wing over the E.R. entrance weren't getting any sleep at all. I'll buy that, but now you have to slow it down almost to a crawl, because you can have the beacon turning and all the lights blinking like it's Christmas Eve and they still don't see you. Here's one right now, in fact, crossing the street from the left, and if I don't slow almost to a stop I run over him. When he finally sees me he jumps back, scared, and I've seen him somewhere before. Then it comes to me that he's that Mr. White, or Wade, that colored fella whose daughter was that hit-and-run victim we picked up at Wharton and East Fifth, and I've just closed my mind to her but she must still be alive.

Close your mind to them all. That's the only way you're going to stay sane in this business or, better still, be like Conlin and don't have a mind. Right now we're rushing this comedian in and Verna Palmer is motioning us to booth 7, and they're ready for him and I know what Conlin's thinking. He's thinking he wants to get to the phone, and he wishes this poor guy, whatever his name is, was Jack Benny or maybe Bob Hope or Jimmy Durante.

XIII

VERNA L. PALMER, R.N.

I don't know what's come over me. I mean, I don't usually get talkative like this. No, it isn't only that you take a pledge, but it's just that you respect everyone's privacy. Oh, when Mother was still alive I used to tell her a lot, more at the beginning than later, and it wasn't just that she was failing at the end, but after a while it gets to be the same sort of thing over and over. After all, I'll be down there ten years next month. Well, thank you very much, but it's the truth.

Anyway, the last year or so I've had the feeling every now and then that everything, like time, is standing still. It's sort of an eerie sensation, you know, as if you've lived this same day before, maybe last month, or last year, or maybe five years ago. What it is, I suppose, is the same parade of patients, sixty to eighty a day on my shift, with the same ailments and the same injuries. The names are different and the faces are different, but most of the time you don't register the names or faces, really, and then the weather never changes. The what? No, I mean that there aren't any windows down there and so, until you come up to the cafeteria for lunch or come up for air at 3:30, you don't know if the sun is shining or it's raining or snowing or what. One day is just like another and so every once in a while I'll sort of stand back and look at that same stream of patients and get this feeling that I've lived this exact day before and my life is standing still and what am I doing with it?

I was mentioning this to Inez Varga on the way home this afternoon. She doesn't have the same problem at all, because up in the Trauma Unit you get to know the patient and the family as people and you can look out the window and see the weather changing. Right now, though, they've got this little Negro girl up there who's breaking everyone's heart. She's a hit-and-run victim and we had her through the E.R. and everyone thought she was going to be all right, and now they just don't know. I wouldn't want that, either, of course, but as Inez and I were talking on the way home we came to the conclusion that one of the reasons it was such a hectic day in the E.R., and this whole thing mounted up on me, was that this is another one of those times when no one's dying and no one's getting cured and time is really standing still.

That happens in a hospital. It really does. I'm serious. Inez was saying, because she gets a chance to read every directive and every bulletin and I don't, that the daily average at the M.C. of beds made available is seventy. Sixty-seven patients are discharged and three die, but every now and then there'll be a period when patients aren't dying and patients aren't being cured. You're right. It's sort of a *Death Takes a Holiday*. It can go on for days, and no one can explain it except that some zany will always say it has something to do with the moon. Oh, there may be a death after a day or two, and a few patients discharged, but generally speaking the beds upstairs just aren't being vacated and the back-up starts. The directive goes out to admit absolute emergencies only and so, like today, we've got people in the Holding Room and in the hallway and tying up the booths, waiting for someone on the floors to get well or die. Then you've got their relatives complaining all day at the desk, as if it's *your* fault, and then early this afternoon, right after lunch, we had another one of those scenes in booth 7.

Booth 7? That's the booth where we put our real nonsurgical emergencies, like strokes and heart attacks. We've been putting them in there for as long as I know, and it never occurred to me to wonder why we don't put them in booth 1, which is right across from the nursing station and nearest to the door, until the other day. I mentioned it to Dr. Hunter, and we figured out that it's because of these big square pillars that some numbhead of an architect, or whatever he was, put down the middle of the floor. They're always in the way when you're trying to swing a stretcher around, and they cut off the visibility into some of the booths from the nursing station, but anyway, the reason we use booth 7 for these acute cases is that one of the pillars is in front of the booth and so we use it as a stacking station for our crash cart and resuscitation equipment.

Anyway, just after lunch Frank Baker, of Baker Ambulance, and that boob of an assistant of his who thinks he's the new Cary Grant, brought in this acute M.I. Myocardial infarction. That's a heart attack where a part of the heart muscle dies when an artery becomes blocked and the blood supply is cut off. Right. Exactly, and we'd had the call telling us what Frank Baker had coming in, so we held booth 7 open and I got old Mrs. Greiner to go home again. She's that old lady I think I told you about whose husband died one night in 7, and every now and then she comes back and sits there and waits for him. You remember? She's harmless, but it's pathetic when you think of it.

Now I've seen a lot of these scenes in booth 7, and I have no idea why this one got to me today. When they brought the patient in they had him semi-reclining, and they were feeding him the portable oxygen and, of course, he was in a bad way.

"I can't breathe! I can't breathe!" he was gasping after we got him into the booth and onto our examining stretcher and while we were transferring him from their oxygen to ours. "Please! Help!"

How old? I think it said thirty-one on his driver's license. I know it's young. Do for a living? That's interesting because I was realizing later, maybe for the first time, some of the thoughts you have even in the middle of a real emergency. Here we are, a half dozen of us in that 8-by-10 booth, with the examining stretcher, the intravenous stand, the crash cart, the cardiac monitor, the EKG, and I don't know what else. We're bumping into one another and reaching over one another. It's life or death, and somebody—it was Harvey Mosler, the surgical resident—said: "Maybe he threw a massive embolus." That's a clot. Then Bob Mabry, who's the senior neurosurgical resident, but just happened to be there, said: "I'm betting the heart. Is he cyanotic?" So I looked at his finger nails, and they were blue, and I also noticed that they were manicured. Right

then, and it's ridiculous, of course, but because of the mani-
cure I'm wondering right in the midst of all this excitement
what he does for a living, and Mabry says: "This guy has had
rhinoplasty." That's a nose bob, and somebody else said: "Who
is he?" Well, Gloria Miller—she's our clerk—had his wallet,
because she was starting his chart, and she said: "His name is
Bobby Carlton, and Frank Baker says he's a comedian." Then
Harvey Mosler said: "Hey, I know him! I mean, I saw him the
other night out at the Wayside. He's very funny." I mean, right
while I'm trying to get a blood pressure, but it's so weak that I
don't think I can get it and Dr. Hunter is telling me to blow
the pressure cuff up to 140 and he'll try to get it by palpation
of the radial artery in the wrist, I'm wondering if he was
ever on TV and maybe I saw him.

So we've got the patient stripped—he was in pajamas—and
they've got an intravenous going of Dextrose 5% and water,
and Carol Whitaker is running that. Dr. Hunter is putting a
Foley catheter up into the bladder, Harvey Mosler is running
the monitor and Bob Mabry is up at the head saying that the
neck veins are distended and the patient is bubbling as he
breathes in.

"And where the hell are the girls from the Garden Club?"
he's saying. "Let's get them down here!"

It's what he calls the girls from Anesthesia. They wear these
flowered cloth caps that they sew themselves, so I tell him
they've been called, and with that one of them—Betsy, whose
last name I don't know—comes in and she gets an endotracheal
tube down into the patient's throat to assist the breathing and
get more oxygen to him, and Harvey Mosler at the monitor is
saying that the patient is going into ventricular fibrillation. He's
having rapid, irregular contractions of the ventricles.

"So let me have the paddles!" he says. "Let's go!"

We wheel the defibrillator in and Dr. Milton Stern, who's
one of our new interns and don't get me started on him, plugs
it in. I hand Harvey Mosler the electrode paste, and he smears
it on the paddles and he tells Stern to set the charge at 400
joules.

"But that's all the way," Stern says.

"Goddammit!" Mosler says. "I know that! Just do what I say!"

The joules? No, it's pronounced the same, but it's j-o-u-l-e-s, and it has something to do with the voltage. You see, what you want to do is shock the patient's heart to stop this fast, irregular action which is more like quivering than beating. You want to restore a normal rhythm, and you have these two circular, stainless steel paddles with the electrode paste on them so the patient won't be burned, and they're placed on either side of the chest.

"All right!" Mosler says. "Everybody off!"

What he means is that when he pushes that button on one of the paddle handles, if you happen to be touching the patient, you could end up against the wall. That's how powerful it is, really. I mean, when he pushes that button the patient jumps and the arms and legs go out and then he just collapses back. It's what they call a total body muscular twitch, but it's more of a total spasm or jerk or convulsion.

"Good," Mosler was saying now, watching the monitor screen. "He's gone into a normal rhythm."

Now the blood pressure was up a little to about 90 over 65 and the pulse was a little better, down to 120 from 140. Dr. Hunter had 150 cc.'s of urine, which was pretty dark because the patient was probably dehydrated, and we sent a couple of ounces of that to the lab, along with some blood that Stern, or rather Bob Mabry, drew because they wanted to find out the arterial blood gases and a complete blood count and the potassium and the blood sugar. That was a scene, too.

"And don't forget to heparinize the syringe," Stern was telling Carol Whitaker.

"Yes, Doctor," she said, "but I've got it here in two dilutions, one to 1,000 and one to 10,000."

"I don't give a damn!" Stern screamed at her, and Carol's been a nurse far longer than he's been a doctor. "I'm going to have enough trouble trying to find the artery."

"Look, Ace," Bob Mabry said, and he came down and moved Stern out of the way. "Let me try to pin the tail on the donkey."

That's what it's like, too, because you want to draw the blood from the femoral artery in the groin, but when you insert the needle you just might hit the vein instead. If you do you'll get blue venous blood, of course, and then you won't be sure where you are. You won't know whether it's blue because you're in the vein, or whether you're in the artery but it's blue because the patient isn't getting enough oxygen, and then he's really in bad shape. Anyway, Bob Mabry hit it the first time—bluish but with red streaks—and Mosler was calling for ouabain, which is digitalis and a heart stimulant, and telling Carol to get some Lasix and Lidocaine and bicarb ready, and meanwhile they were hooking up the EKG, to get an electrocardiogram, and Mosler started reading off the tape.

Well, what it actually does is record the electrical activity of the heart. There are different waves, like P and Q and R and others that are caused by the heart's contractions, and the EKG strip, where the needle marks on the graph paper, tells you how the different chambers are reacting to the electrical activity, and from that they can get an idea of where the damage is.

I know. I don't understand it completely myself. I mean I wouldn't be able to read the graph, but Mosler was reading it out loud, like: "He has a deep Q. He's got a depressed ST. There's a deep inverted T here. He's extending over the lateral wall. This guy's got an inferior lateral M.I. What's his B.P.?"

"It's starting to go down," I said. "It's 80 over 65 now."

"Any urine?"

"Not yet," Dr. Hunter said.

So then they started some Lidocaine, which depresses the irritability of the heart muscle. They add it right to the intravenous, and then they started some Levophed, to try to get his pressure up a bit, and Gloria Miller came in to ask if they wanted her to call CCU—the coronary care unit, you know, to alert them that we'd be sending the patient up—and now Mosler blew *his* top.

"Christ no!" he hollered at her, and he's usually very calm. "I don't know if we're even going to get this guy out of here!"

"The blood pressure's not going up," I told him. "Do you want to increase the drip?"

"And he's in bigeminy now," Bob Mabry said, and that

222

means that the heart beat is uneven, one beat right after the other and then a pause.

"Goddammit," Mosler said. "Let's get another IV going, and give him another bolus of Lidocaine. And where the hell is the lab work?"

So Stern started another intravenous in the other arm, and I went and called the lab. All they had were the blood gases, and when I came back with them the patient was fibrillating again.

"So let's zap him again," Mabry was saying.

"And get some bicarb going," Mosler was saying. "I want an ampule in him every five minutes, and give him two right now!"

Then they put the paddles on him again, and they shocked him again.

"It didn't work," Mabry said. "He's still fibrillating."

"You'll have to ventilate him better," Mosler said to Betsy whatever-her-name-is, "and let's start to massage him!"

"I'll do it," Bob Mabry said.

I moved the stool over for Mabry and he got up on it. What you do is place the ball of your right hand on the lower part of the chest and put the left hand on the right and you push down and release in rhythm while you count: "A thousand and one. A thousand and two. A thousand and three." You're compressing the heart and forcing the blood out, and you go up to a thousand and five and start over again.

"Good," Mosler was saying. "I'm getting a pretty good pulse. Keep hyperventilating him, and let's shock him again."

When Mosler put the paddles on him this time and pushed the button there was a reaction, but not much. I mean the patient jerked and the limbs went up, but just barely.

"He's still fibrillating," Mabry said.

"Then we don't hit him again," Mosler said, "until we ventilate him better and correct the acidosis. Are we getting much resistance to the ventilation?"

"Yes," Betsy said. "He's pretty stiff, so let me see if I can suction out some of this gunk."

"And take the massage, will you?" Mosler said to Stern. "And let's get more bicarb into him. Also, let me have another hundred milligrams of Lidocaine."

"He's stopped breathing!" Betsy said. "His pupils are going up!"

"Is the cuff inflated on the tube?" Mosler said. "Did you give the bicarb?"

"Yes," I said.

"Then let's shock him again, and see what happens," Mosler said. "We'll hit him twice."

"There's a pattern," Mabry said, after Mosler shocked him, "but it's not good. The complexes are very wide."

"His pupils are getting wider," Betsy was saying. "There's no spontaneous respiration."

"Keep the massage going," Mosler was saying. "Give him more bicarb. Stop the Lidocaine drip, and let's have a small ampule with Isuprel with an intracardiac needle."

"I'll do it," Bob Mabry said.

Isuprel stimulates muscular irritability and it's injected right into the heart, so I mounted the needle—it's about six inches long—and passed it to Mabry. He was on the patient's left side, and you put it in between the ribs and it's pretty tricky because all hearts aren't the same size and they don't all lie in exactly the same position and you want to miss the coronary arteries and get into one of the ventricles.

"Damn it, I'm not in!" he said, and then he pulled it back about three inches and went in again, and when he pulled the plunger this time there was blood mixing with the Isuprel, and he injected it.

"It's in," he said.

"But he's fibrillating again," Stern said.

"So let's shock him right now," Mosler said. "Off, everybody!"

When he hit the button there was very little reaction. It was even more flaccid than before.

"Nothing," Bob Mabry said. "He's in ventricular standstill."

"His pupils are fixed," Betsy said. "No respiration."

"What's his pressure?" Mosler said.

"I can't get it here," I said.

"How long have we been at this?" Mosler said. "Anybody know?"

"Yes," I said, because we always time these. "Twenty-seven minutes."

"I guess that's the ball game," Mosler said. "Agreed?"

"So let's zap him once more," this Stern said, and he picked up the paddles. "Okay? Everybody off?"

"No!" somebody behind me said, and it was Dr. Hunter and he just pushed by me and he reached down and yanked the defibrillator plug out of the wall. "That's enough."

Stern just sort of shrugged then and walked out, but Dr. Hunter was right, of course. You see, you can keep a patient biologically alive as long as you can keep up the massage and as long as you can keep pushing the oxygen into his lungs, but actually he's physiologically dead. Dr. Hunter was talking about that later. That's right, but, anyway, Gloria Miller had called for Father Shea, which we do when the patient is a Catholic or when we don't know his religion and it looks like he may expire. When Stern walked out Father Shea walked in, so we left and I told Gloria to tag the body and tell the dieners in the morgue to come for it right away. As I said, they haven't been too busy for the last couple of days and I couldn't find our orderly, that Arnold, who was probably goofing off somewhere, and with the patients filling the waiting room we needed that booth.

That's it, you see. That's what I've been realizing lately, that we're running a sort of assembly line. The main thing now was get the booth cleaned up and ready. Bob Mabry was off in Minor Ops checking some workman who'd fallen off a building and landed on his shoulders and head. Mosler was filling out this comedian's chart. Stern was playing doctor now in another booth. Dr. Hunter was probably going from booth to booth and trying to speed up the traffic flow, and now it was up to me to try to find out who the survivors were and notify them or have one of the chaplains do it if we could establish a religion.

Of course I have to. All the time. Even when the family is present in the waiting room a lot of the doctors aren't up to it and will ask me, or one of the girls, to tell them. Then, when you get someone from out of town, like today, it's up to me to get on the phone, and sometimes, while I'm holding that phone

225

and I can hear it ringing, I'm hoping that no one picks it up. It's like Dr. Hunter said once. He said that what you're going to tell them is going to change their life forever.

Well, I'll tell you what I did. In the first place, the patient had had a gold watch on, and a ring with a star sapphire, and then Gloria and I had to count the money in his wallet. Two of us always do it, and then we both sign the form that goes with the money and the valuables up to the safe. I remember once we had a drunk who was hit by a car and died in Minor Ops. From his clothes you wouldn't have thought he had a penny to his name, but he had wads of money in all of his pockets, and it was all in ones and fives, with a few tens. Gloria and I counted over fifteen hundred dollars. There were bills all over the desk, and we had to count it twice and it took us forever. Bob Mabry said he was probably a numbers runner, or a bookie. I don't know.

Anyway, today this comedian had a couple of hundred dollars in his wallet along with a couple of credit cards and his driver's license. The address on the driver's license was in New York City, but I hesitated to call that because you don't know who you're going to be talking to. If he's married, and his wife answers, you hate to give her the news like that, or maybe he's got an elderly parent who has high blood pressure and could be killed by the shock. What we usually do is call the police in the town or the city, and ask them to send a patrolman to the address, and then if they need help they can get it.

Today Frank Baker had told Gloria that this comedian was appearing at the Wayside Motor Inn, and Harvey Mosler had seen him there, so I called there and talked with the manager. I think his name is Bink, or something like that, and he seemed a little hypertensive, or something.

"Doctors!" he was saying after I told him. "You can't get a doctor any more! That's why he died! I tried three doctors, and every one of them was out of his office, too busy to come. I have to work night and day now, and why can't we get doctors to do that or get more doctors? I don't know what I'm going to do now with only half a show for tonight, and I don't know what the world's coming to, either."

He sounded like Mrs. Cutler, who relieves me at 3:30. She's always saying that she doesn't know what the world is coming to, and then this Bink said he didn't know anything about this Bobby Carlton's residence or family anyway. He said I could call some theatrical agent named Singer—Mort Singer—in New York and he gave me the number and I called there.

"Mort Singer Enterprises," this female's voice said.

"May I speak to Mr. Singer, please?" I said.

"May I ask who's calling?" she said.

It's all right to ask that, of course, but it's the *way* they do it. Real superior—you know?—and with one of those New York voices that grate on your nerves, so I told her who I am.

"I'm sorry," she said, "but Mr. Singer is in conference and can't be disturbed. May I ask the nature of your call?"

"Is Mr. Singer acquainted with a Mr. Bobby Carlton?" I said.

"That's correct," she said. "Mr. Carlton is one of our clients."

"I'm trying to reach Mr. Singer," I said, "because Mr. Carlton suffered a heart attack this afternoon and has just passed away in our Emergency Room."

"He just passed *what?*" she said.

"He just passed away," I said. "He has just died."

"He's just died?" she screamed. "Oh, my God! How could he? I just talked with him on the phone an hour or two ago. How could he?"

"Excuse me, miss," I said, "but may I please speak with Mr. Singer?"

With that the phone clunked down on the desk, or on something, and I could hear voices in the distance. I could hear this secretary screaming, "Dead!" And then this man's voice came on.

"Mort Singer here. Who is this?"

So I told him.

"Are you sure?" he said.

"I'm sure," I said. "He was brought here about thirty-five minutes ago by ambulance from the Wayside Motor Inn, and . . ."

"That's right," he said. "I booked him in there."

227

"And he had a very severe heart attack. The doctors here did everything they could for him, but he expired about six minutes ago."

"Shocked," he said. "I'm really shocked."

"What I'm calling about, Mr. Singer," I said, "is to ask if Mr. Carlton had a family, and how they might be informed."

"He's got a mother he lives with when he's in New York," he said, and then he said to somebody: "Get me Bobby's address and phone number."

"You see, Mr. Singer," I said, "the problem is how best to tell the mother. We don't want to do this by telephone, because someone should be with her, and I'm wondering if you . . ."

"Well, I'll tell you," he said. "I don't know the mother. All I know is that she's not so young any more and she's had some illness, because I know Bobby had some stiff medical bills, and I can't handle it myself because in less than two hours I'm making a plane to Los Angeles. I have to be out there for a meeting at nine o'clock tomorrow morning. You understand."

"Yes," I said. "I understand."

He gave me the address, which was the same one as on the driver's license, and what it came down to was me calling the police and asking them to inform the mother. It took some time finding the right precinct, and meanwhile Mosler was still sitting there filling out the chart, and going over it with Stern.

"The ball game was lost when we started," he was saying. "This guy was in cardiogenic shock, and he probably infarcted his whole left ventricle. There's one thing we might have tried, and that's rotating tourniquets over the thighs, to decrease the flow to the heart at least a small amount. You see, he wasn't perfusing his kidneys too well, and that Lasix is a very rapid acting diuretic, and they might have helped . . ."

"And let me say this," Dr. Hunter said, walking over. "When he's not perfusing his kidneys because of markedly decreased cardiac output it's a good bet that he's also not perfusing his brain. I'll give you an example. About two or three years ago, right in this room and probably right in booth 7, they got one of my patients, who was like this one, started again with shocking and massage and hyperventilating him. When they got him up to CCU they did a brain wave, and it wasn't totally flat.

228

There were low amplitude spikes, and by then he was breathing on his own and his heart was going on its own. That meant that legally they were not justified in removing all tubes, but he was like a decorticated animal. There was no evidence of cerebration, and his only response was massive reflex action with limbs extended and rigid. After a week they had a gastric tube in him for feeding, so they transferred him to a nursing home where he lay like that for six more weeks and wiped out the poor family financially as well as emotionally."

"I understand," Mosler was saying. "I agree with you. Aggressiveness is called for, but only up to a point."

"What they'd saved," Dr. Hunter was saying, and looking right at Stern, "was a vegetable. What I'm saying is that this is not a vegetable farm we're running down here, and that's why I pulled the plug."

What Stern said, if anything, I don't know because the desk sergeant at the police precinct in New York was on the phone now. I'd like to have heard anything that followed because Dr. Hunter is really terrific, now that he's been here long enough to take hold, and I've been thinking of going to him and telling him that if this Stern doesn't stop talking down his nose at my girls and ordering them around like they're domestic help I'm going to be having requests for transfers. He was the one, you know, who had Kay Conley in tears when he left that old man alone in booth 3 and the old man stabbed himself to death with a scalpel and Stern tried to blame it on Kay. I wouldn't want to go through that again.

So when I got off the phone from talking with the police sergeant in New York, and he told me he'd send a patrolman around to notify this Bobby Carlton's mother, John Clarity, who's our public relations director, was calling to find out about it. He said the *News-Argus* had called him about a half hour before, and I don't know how they find out about it so soon. We'll have a stabbing or a shooting or three or four out of a multiple car accident, and we'll no sooner get them into the booths or Minor Ops when the paper will be on the phone. They want to print it sometimes even before the family is informed.

I don't know. I just wanted to be a nurse and care for people and help them get well and now, as I said, it has just seemed to me lately, and especially with the backup today, that I'm working in some sort of a factory with an assembly line. When? Oh, for as long as I can remember. I think I must have been about five years old. Mother used to say, when someone would ask her about it, that it probably started while World War II was on and there were pictures in the papers and magazines about nurses. I don't think that was it at all, though, because I think it grew out of my deathly fear of sickness and of doctors.

Oh, definitely. You have no idea. I can still remember my tonsillectomy, when I was five, and Mother standing in the doorway of the room and waving goodbye to me when they wheeled me down the hall to the elevator and to the O.R. right upstairs in the M.C. That's right, and after that I had this terrible fear of Dr. Victor, who was our family physician then, before he retired a few years later and Dr. Hunter replaced him. He was really very nice, tall and distinguished, but I was afraid to have him even touch me because, I guess, I was afraid he was going to take me back to the hospital and up to the O.R. and have them put me to sleep again.

Anyway, he had this nurse, Mrs. Waller, who was absolutely wonderful. She was sort of short, and plump, and pink complected, and she always looked so clean and starchy in her white uniform, and she was always smiling and she had this sweet, soft voice. She was always so nice, and she used to make a fuss over me, I guess, and I wanted to be her.

I remember the Christmas I wanted a nurse's kit. I wanted it more than I'd ever wanted anything, and I talked about it and I told the Santa Claus in Langer's about it and I dreamed about it. Then on Christmas morning, when I came downstairs and Mother—Santa Claus, of course—had the packages all spread out underneath the tree, I remember looking from one to another, trying to find one that was just the right shape and size and being so afraid that it wasn't there.

Oh, yes, it was there all right. It had a nurse's uniform and cap and surgical mask and stethoscope and thermometer and tongue depressors and bandages and I forget what else. Then Mother had this sewing machine on which she used to make a lot of her clothes and most of mine, and there was this box of accessories—you know, chrome-plated attachments for ruffling and buttonholing and hemming and zigzagging and that sort of thing—and, naturally, they became surgical instruments. I had this small child's ironing board which became the examining and O.R. table, and my dolls were the patients.

As I got several years older, then, I think the fascination continued because maybe I had this idea that doctors and nurses don't get sick. It was always the patients who were sick, but Dr. Victor and Mrs. Waller always seemed to be fine. You know? Years later, when I was in high school I sort of rationalized, I think, that as long as I had this dread of illness and fear of doctors I might defeat it by joining them, and I think it worked. I mean I'm not avid to be whisked into the O.R. and go under the knife, but I've seen enough of it after all these years so that I can face it better than most. At least I should be able to, don't you think?

Oh, I don't know. I think those scenes in booth 7 have a lot to do with it. In the panic, you might almost call it, people who are usually polite and considerate and even most friendly, suddenly start screaming at one another and at us, and when you lose the patient anyway it leaves you sort of empty. Then, when you have a day like this on top of it, you end up glassy-eyed and not even seeing people.

I've spoken to my girls about that. I've told them that every now and then I see one or another of them with that waitress look on her face or in her eyes. You know what I mean, when you're trying to get a waiter or a waitress to replenish the butter or bring you the coffee and they see you and know what you want but they look right through you? I don't mean here. I like this place, and they're fine here, but I see my girls do that to members of a family, say, who are waiting outside a booth, and I tell them: "Look. This is an emergency room, and people come here because in their minds, at least, it's an emergency. They're frightened, and some of them behave badly, but they're not sticks of furniture. They're people."

Behave badly? I'll say. You have no idea. Oh, occasionally we'll get a VIP who wants everything right away, and it galls me right to my roots to have to accommodate them. You know who make most of the trouble, though? The welfare cases. They're getting everything for free and they demand the most and, I hate to say this, but it's especially the blacks. I understand it. I think I'm more liberal than most, and I know what they've gone through for centuries, but *my* people didn't bring them over here and *we* didn't own slaves. We weren't even in this country then, and I don't see why *I* have to take the abuse. Abuse? Why, I've been punched and I've had my uniform ripped and I've had my watch torn right off my wrist.

And complain? All the time. They go right over your head to the administration and beyond that to the mayor or the governor or the newspapers or anybody they can think of. We had one the other day—this female—and, sure enough, the next day down came Administration. It's not their fault, because they have to answer these things before they get blown up all out of proportion, and he had it all itemized and he was reading this tale of woe off to Dr. Hunter. Dr. Hunter was just listening and nodding his head through this whole thing, and when it was over, he just looked him in the eyes and said, very slowly: "I couldn't disagree with you more. This woman has been in here two and three times a week for the last month and they tell me it's been going on for almost a year. We've spent hours and hours on her already, and there's nothing wrong with her. She's just a chronic complainant, and I absolutely refuse to permit anyone on my staff to spend any more time examining her and listening to her and filling out her chart while she occupies them and a booth and we have patients who are really ill sitting and standing outside and waiting."

With that he turned and walked away. Usually Dr. Hunter is very calm, and he was calm through this, too, but you could see he was seething, and it was great.

You have no idea, really how many times I'd just like to blow my top. We had a drunk this morning who was screaming for God and hollering for help, and I let him have a few choice words, polite but positive, but most of the time you just have to suffer in silence.

We had this boy, five years old, brought in by his mother.

He'd fallen at play and landed on a broken bottle and had this nasty gash on his arm. The mother had alcohol on her breath, and she gave us the name and the address and then, when we turned around to get her permission to clean and suture the wound, she was gone. We looked all over the E.R. and had her paged on the P.A., but nothing. With the boy sitting there in Minor Ops and screaming we waited a half hour, and then I called the home. A child's voice answered and said, "Hello." I said, "Is your mother there?" The child said, "No," and hung up. So I called back. The same voice answered. I could hear noise of kids in the background and it sounded like a madhouse, and I told the child who I was and I said, "Is your father there?" I could hear some conversation and then this man's voice saying, "Tell them I'm not here." Then the child came back on and said, "He's not here," and hung up again. So I called back again—this is the third attempt—and I said, "Look. Tell your father that this is the hospital, and your brother is here." There was another pause, and more voices in the background, and then the child said, "He doesn't want to talk to you," and hung up again. Meanwhile, mind you, the poor boy is terrified and screaming, so we finally treated him—put eight stitches in—and about an hour and a half later the mother showed up and we got the belated permission.

People. Honestly, you've no idea of some of the people who have children. They're on the phone all day: "Every time my baby has a bowel movement there's blood in it. Is that normal?" Or: "My baby has a fever of 103 for two days, and it's crying all the time. What should I do?" "Have you had the baby to a doctor?" "We don't have a doctor." "Then you should bring the baby in here." "I don't know. I'm awfully busy, so can't you tell me what to do on the phone?"

On the telephone, mind you. I sometimes wish that Alexander Graham Bell, or whoever it was, hadn't invented the thing, and it's not just parents it's everyone. One of the phones will ring, and it's someone who thinks he has the flu and he wants a diagnosis over the phone. Then there's Charles Barger. Charles Barger is in his sixties now and he's got a half-dozen things wrong with him, and he's got a chart at the M.C. that goes back forty years. I mean it. If you ever had to send upstairs for it, by now it's so heavy that it would take a hand truck to move it down. Anyway, when we're really jammed up and the line at the desk is getting so out of hand that we're thinking of calling Security, it's almost inevitable that the phone will ring and it will be Charles Barger with his *latest* symptoms.

So, I just got off the phone, talking with the police sergeant about sending someone to inform this Bobby Carlton's mother, and at the desk there are two patrolmen with this college girl with an overdose. She's a nice-looking girl, but she doesn't know where she is and she's half out and she's saying: "Where am I? Where are you taking me?"

We took her into booth 5, and Stu Wyman, the other intern, was trying to find out what she'd taken. He didn't have much success, but finally he came out and he said, "She says she took Strawberry Fields. What the hell is that?" Nobody knew, so Dr. Hunter said: "Look. Try to find out where she's been recently."

Wyman went back, and he came out again and said: "She says she's been out in California for ten days, and she just got back to school today." So Dr. Hunter told me: "Call the Los Angeles County Hospital and get a psychiatric resident and ask him if he's ever heard of Strawberry Fields." I did, and got the psych resident, and he said: "Sure. The guys around here say it's acid."

This was our day for fouled up females, too, I guess. After the Strawberry Fields we had a woman, perfectly respectable, from Ohio, who'd run out of her pills and left the prescription at home. That was bright of her, of course, and I don't know whether she couldn't reach her doctor, or what, but she wanted them renewed. All she could remember was that the name started with NAT and ended in IN. With everything else going on, we had to get out the *Physician's Desk Reference to Pharmaceutical Specialties and Biologicals* and we had to pore through that until we came up with Naturin and showed her the color picture of it.

"Oh yes," she said. "That's it. It's one a day, and I'm going to be here thirty days."

Then we had the queen of them all. I shouldn't say that, because it's sad, really. She's in her early forties, and you'd know the name if I told you because it's one of the so-called best families in town. She's an alcoholic, which is just a symptom of whatever the problem is, of course, and when she goes off on one of these dedicated drinking bouts I think she starts boozing mornings as soon as her husband leaves the house. You'd know his name, because he's one of the Mister Bigs around here, but he's really a nice person. He's been in on a lot of fund drives—I mean he has a social conscience—and his picture and name are in the paper a good deal, but that doesn't matter.

Anyway, about a year and a half ago or more, they brought her in from some cocktail lounge or bar or somewhere, and we had her in the Psych Room which is at the far end, and soundproofed, thank heaven. We called Psychiatry, and Dr. Stillman came down and then he called the husband, and when he arrived I took him down to the room.

I'll never forget it. When we walked in, there she was, with this frenzied look on her face, delivering this tirade to Dr. Stillman and I've never heard more foul language in my life. I looked from her to her husband, and he just stood there aghast and he said: "My God! This is *my wife!*" Then he turned away and walked to face the wall and he put his head in his hands and he just sobbed.

I felt so sorry for him and I just couldn't understand it. I mean, I suppose you can acquire that language and those ideas anywhere today, but here was a middle-aged woman from one of the most socially prominent families. She'd had private schooling, and the coming-out party and the debutante cotillions and she was married to a totally respectable man and, well, they took her to a private institution but, obviously, whatever the cure was it didn't work, because here she was again today.

The first I knew about it was when we all heard this commotion in the hall, this woman's voice screaming, and this foul language. Three of the security men had her, trying to carry her bodily by the arms and legs while she was thrashing, and as they got her through the door Harvey Mosler and Wyman ran over and helped. We rushed her down to the Psych Room again, but you can imagine that scene, with all the patients and their families, including children, witnessing this wide-eyed, and listening to that language.

It was something. When she saw me she started on nurses, how we're all whores for the doctors, and then she started screaming how she'd take any doctor on who had $100 but how we all give it away to them free, and I don't know what else. We got Dr. Stillman again right away, and he gave her 100 milligrams of thorazine in the buttock, which sedated her, and then I heard him on the phone to her husband.

"Yes," he was saying, "we've got her here, so at least you know where she is, and that she's not in the river. I know, and I think the State Hospital has got to be the answer. Fine. And how are your daughters? Good. I'm glad to hear that, and I want to say again how much I admire how you've been handling it all. That's right. I'll be here."

Oh, at first they thought that a brain tumor might be involved, but they ruled that out. I really don't know. Stillman has said something about sexual anxieties and a reversal of the usual life style, or something, but psychiatry is one thing I don't know *anything* about.

So, that's the way it went, and by the time Inez came down I was exhausted and, as I've said, I've had it right up to my hair roots. I don't know what I'm going to do, and I certainly don't want to go back up on the floors.

I know, but a day like today, and we have many of them, certainly doesn't encourage marriage or parenthood, either. I realize that. We see all the mistakes, but do you want to know something? The girls who go into nursing to marry a doctor are never the ones who find them, and doctors lose their appeal after a while. Oh, I was involved once, but Mother was still alive then, of course. Now I'm too late for doctors, and do you know what I'd get? I'd probably get a chronic invalid who wants a full-time, live-in private duty nurse. That's right.

XIV

JOSEPH A. GARRETT

They don't make them like George O'Donnell any more. As a matter of fact, they never did, and we think so much of each other that you should hear our wives on the subject. The four of us will go out to dinner, and after listening to us for a while, the one or the other will shake her head and say: "Look. As we've said before, why don't you two just get married and be done with it?"

"We would," George said one night, "except for the fact that they won't let Joe take the vows with a cigar in his mouth."

It's not hard to understand, though, when you figure that in this business your partner is your life. I don't mean that once every week you have a shoot-out, like they do on TV, but it can happen any time, like today. Then you know the truth, that your partner is the most important person in your life, and he'd better be some kind of a man.

It's like in the Army, where you wanted to know who the guy next to you was. You're going to take some donkey of a town that you never heard of before and you'll never hear of again, and the lieutenant would lay it all out. He'd explain how the major said division artillery had promised to put it on the town for eight minutes and, as soon as it lifted, we'd make the rush over the open ground so everybody have his objective very clear in his mind.

Then the artillery would lay it on, and when it lifted you'd make your run. You'd get no return fire, and you'd flop down out of breath behind a stone wall about a hundred feet from the first house, which is your objective. You'd look through a crack in the wall at that house, or what's left of it, and you'd figure that maybe, with the artillery, the Krauts took off. Then you'd figure that maybe they didn't, because you've seen them take worse than this and still come up fighting, and they make damn good soldiers who might have had a chance of winning if they had just had one more general. Like somebody said, I mean General Motors, because when we got into their country over there they were plowing with oxen.

Anyway, you squint at that house through that crack in the wall. You don't see a sign of life. Nothing moves, but you don't know. How do you know what may be looking back at you? So you say to the guy next to you: "Cover me, pal. I'm gonna go."

That's what I mean. You'd better know this guy, and he'd better know you, because before you go there's a thought that crosses your mind. This guy is more important to you now than anybody else in this world. When you go he's going to have to raise up to cover you, and when he does he's going to have to expose himself. Will he do it? This is a frightening situation, and it's no place for strangers.

You want to know a funny thing about O'Donnell? After we were partners the first couple of weeks I thought I'd rolled a deuce. That first couple of weeks it's like two guys sparring in round one—where you grew up, how you happened to come on the force, how many kids you've got, what you hope to do on your vacation. You don't really know each other yet, and George has never been big at self-advertising anyway.

So we're partners about two weeks now, and we're on the 8 to 4 this day, and we're on our way to check out an overnight burglary in a dry goods store on Central, when what comes in but a holdup in a jewelry store just two blocks away on East Fourth. I'm at the wheel and I turn the corner and start up the block. As I do there's a uniformed man with his gun out running toward the scene on the sidewalk on our right and, with that, the holdup man comes out of the store, turns toward the cop, sees him, drops down to one knee and starts to fire.

I'm still bringing the car in, but even before it stops, O'Donnell is out. Luckily the sidewalk emptied when the fireworks started, and by the time I jam on the brake and jump out,

O'Donnell is in a firefight with this gunman. O'Donnell is behind this parked Buick, with his gun hand resting on the back right fender, and as I come up, the gunman lets one more go at him and then turns to run and O'Donnell squeezes one more out, and that was all for the matador.

It turned out that the uniformed man was winged in the right shoulder and there were a couple of holes that the owner didn't like in his Buick. The attaché case, with the jewelry in it, was lying next to the gunman, who was sprawled face down with his gun still in his hand. George had put two bullets in him, the last one in his back when he turned to run.

I got busy then for a few minutes, but all of a sudden I miss O'Donnell. I can't find him, and do you know where he is? I finally see him between a couple of parked cars, and he's just been sick to his stomach.

"You all right?" I say.

"I don't know," he said. "I guess so."

"What's the matter?" I said.

"What's the matter?" he said. "I just killed a man."

"I know," I said, "and I think you should get a citation."

"I never killed a man before," he said. "In eight years I had in the uniform I never even fired the gun, except on the range. Don't you see what I mean?"

"I'm not sure I see what *you* mean," I said, "but I'll tell you what *I* mean. There's a wounded cop and a dead thug. Would you like it the other way around?"

"I know," he said, "but I should have brought him down at the knees. I'm not a judge or a jury, but I sent a man to his death. Just because I had a gun in my hand I played God."

"C'mon," I said. "You'll get over it in a day or two."

He might have at that, for all I know, but after we finished up at the scene and saw the body off to the morgue we had the wallet of the recently deceased with his address in it. We went over there, and it was a furnished room and the landlady let us in. Among his belongings there was this package addressed to a Mrs. somebody in Ohio. We opened it, because it could be stolen goods, but it was coming up Mother's Day, and inside was a box of candy and a card signed: *To my Mother, from her loving Son.*

That did it. When we went off duty O'Donnell went on ten days sick leave, and I thought he might very well turn in his potsy. I know our chaplain talked to him, and I guess his parish priest did, too, and I'll tell you the truth. When he came back we never mentioned it again, but I wasn't exactly Joe Happy.

It's what I said about your partner in this business, and that you'd better know that he's a man. Just think of some of the sterling citizens you have to deal with. Even if they're not armed, half of them are half your age and some of them are twice as strong. If they're carrying a knife, they'd just as soon stick it in your belly or, if you're that stupid, into your back. If they've got the gun, they're not carrying it just for show, and do you know where you get your courage? From your potsy and from your gun, yours and your partner's, and if you're not sure that he's going to squeeze it when he should it doesn't exactly help your peace of mind. Somehow or other you don't feel quite like Dauntless Dan.

So, I don't know, it must have been three-four weeks after O'Donnell came back that we get this call right around the corner from the precinct. It was a domestic argument, if you want to call it that, on the third floor of this tenement. When we get to the scene there's the uniformed man from the beat and two more, and they don't know what to do next. Two of them, with their guns drawn, have the perpetrator cornered in the kitchen, and it's a shambles. There are broken dishes and pots and pans all over the floor. There's a busted chair, and the kitchen table is turned over, and behind it is standing this big gossoon. He's in this dirty T-shirt and undershorts, and he's about twenty-six years of age, over six feet tall and over 200 pounds. He's been drinking, and he's got this crazed look in his eyes, and he's got a busted kitchen stool in one hand and a bread knife in the other. The two cops, one of them looking the worse for wear, are just holding the guns on him from across the room and not saying a word, and it's a complete stand-off.

"What's going on here?" I said to the third man, who's standing in the doorway.

"He's a maniac!" he said. "He's got to be a psycho! He was trying to throw Kerrigan out the window when we got here. He had him halfway out when we arrived, and the fall would have killed him."

"Not the fall," I said. "The landing."

"What started this?" George said.

"God knows," the cop said, shaking his head. "You can ask the wife. She took an awful beating, and she's in the bedroom here."

She was sitting on the bed, with a bloody handkerchief to her face, and sobbing. I don't think she was much more than five feet tall, and she couldn't have weighed more than 100 pounds.

"Ma'am," George said to her, "what's your husband's first name?"

"Harry," she said. "It's Harry, but please don't hurt him. Please?"

"We won't, ma'am," George said.

"Please don't hurt him," she said. "He didn't mean it. He really didn't mean it."

He didn't *mean* it? When she took the handkerchief away you should have seen her face. One eye was closing, her nose was bleeding, her lower lip was cut. She looked like she'd lost a tough fifteen-rounder for the world title, and he didn't *mean* it?

"Joe," O'Donnell said to me when we were out in the hall again, "let me give this a try."

"What do you have in mind?" I said.

"I'm not sure," he said, and with that he turns and he walks into the kitchen. He walks right across the floor to where this maniac is standing holding the broken stool and the knife, and he sticks out his hand.

"All right, Harry," he says. "It's over now, so let's put down the stool and let me have the knife."

Well, you can hear the silence in the room. That maniac is

looking right at George and George is looking right at him, and then it happened.

"Yes, sir," this nut says, just as nice as you please. Then with one hand he puts down the stool and with the other he hands O'Donnell the knife.

I wish you could have seen the looks on the faces of the uniformed men, especially the one who almost went out the window for the fall and crash landing. I'd like to have seen the look on my own face, as a matter of fact.

"You want to know something?" I said, walking back. "If you want to make a living like that, I understand those fellas who go into the animal cages in the circuses make better pay than we do."

"I know," he said, "but this big goon is sick."

"So was Hitler," I said, "so let me ask you something else. If you want to think and act like a priest, how come you never tried for the cloth?"

"I thought about it for a while," he said, "but I found out I'm not built for it."

So for a while there I thought I might have a priest in mufti. I wasn't worried about his moxie, just about his sympathies. I wanted to be sure they were on our side. You understand?

George is different from the rest of us, though, and it took me a while to get this news. In the first place, I don't think anybody in the department works harder than George, as many years as he's been at it and as tired of it as you get. Like recently they've been dumping all the hit-and-runs on us. Now that's really uniformed work, not detective work, because either you've got a reliable witness or you haven't, and if you haven't, forget it. So the blacks have been threatening to storm City Hall, because they want more crossing guards for the school kids, especially since one little girl got hit bad there recently. As far as I know, they're still trying to save that girl's life here, but the point I'm making is that O'Donnell knows that without a witness your chances of getting the perpetrator are nothing, and still, I can't tell you the time he's put in on just that one.

You see, O'Donnell is really for law and order, and too many in the department today are just for putting in their eight hours. Then, when you're out after them with O'Donnell—pushers, pimps, picks, thieves, hit-and-run drivers, muggers, whatever they are—they're all maggots. He hates them for what they do, which I understood right from the beginning, but the minute we make the collar he understands them for what they are, which took, on my part, a little getting used to. Now, that's not me, mind you. That's him, but it makes for a good team. He's George Nice and I'm Joe Nasty, and there's nobody on the squad who can get a confession like he can. Half the time it seems like they stuck up the gas station or lifted the car just so they could tell O'Donnell, and when we get a tough one we can't crack we go into the act.

"Why, you crud," I'll say to one of them. "You know what I'm gonna do?"

"Wait a minute, Joe," O'Donnell will say.

"Wait, hell," I'll say. "Why this bum . . ."

"Now, hold it, Joe," O'Donnell will say. "In your mind Frankie here may be a bum, but that's only in *your* mind. Did it ever occur to you that maybe if you grew up the way he did, if you had to live like he's had to live, you might be what you call a bum, too? Now, Frankie knows his rights, but he's also got more on his mind than you have any idea of, so . . ."

"All right," I'll say. "All right. I don't have to listen to your violin music, either. When you're done with this bum I'll be back, and we'll get down to business."

I leave then, and I don't know what kind of a picture O'Donnell paints of me or how he does it, but whatever he tells them, you'd be surprised how often it works. After a while out will come O'Donnell, winking at me and asking for the stenographer to take it all down.

Now I don't mean to make him out any saint in street clothes. He's got the Irish in him, too, and he'll lean hard if he thinks he has to. As I said, half of them are half your age and some of them twice as strong, and you've got to make up your mind right away. I mean, what's he packing, and do you hit him, and how hard? If you don't hit him hard enough he might kill you, and if you hit him too hard are you brutal? I mean, it's a decision you have to make in a second, and if you make a mistake it should be understandable, shouldn't it?

I'll answer that. It should be understandable, but it isn't any more, and O'Donnell gets just as fed up as I do with the way it's going today. As O'Donnell says, to begin with you come on the force because you want to suppress crime—at least you did in our day—but you stamp on it here and it pops up in two other places. It's like trying to put out a forest fire with your feet, and you're not getting much help from upstairs. With the judicial decisions you get today and all this personal rights and civil rights it's like they're throwing wood on the fire and fanning it instead of helping.

Anyway, that was twenty-five years ago that we first hooked up—our silver anniversary our wives call it—and we've had our excitement. We've had the guns out on a few occasions, but as I said, it's not like the TV, and this was the first shoot we've had since that first one and the odd thing is that it starts over on East Fourth again, just four or five stores away.

That's right. Yesterday morning. We come on at 8, and about 9:32 we get a call on this DOA in the back of a store on East Fourth. We go over there and it's in Sol's Surplus, one of those places that after the war used to sell government surplus but now it's all new stuff, like tents and camping equipment and work clothes and that sort of thing. The owner, sixty-four years of age, white, male and named Solomon Hirschon, is lying face down near the back of the store, as they said, and there are a couple of uniformed men there.

"What does it look like?" I asked.

"Natural causes, I guess," one of them said. "There are no signs of violence. The only thing is, the cash register is open."

"Well, that could be," I said. "Some times these owners will leave them open after they empty them at night, so that they don't get broken into."

"And he's not far from the toilet here," O'Donnell said. "Very often people who are dying from natural causes feel the urge to move their bowels."

"Is that right, Doctor?" I said.

"That's right," George said. He was kneeling next to the

body now, and he had started to turn him over when he reached under and came out with the wallet, open and empty.

"How about that, Doctor?" I said.

"Now I don't know," he said. "We'd better take a closer look for a hit."

I don't blame the uniformed men for missing it. There was just this small hole, from a .32 it turned out, hidden in the hair about two inches above the right ear.

Then we put in some day. The two men from the lab processed the whole area, dusting for prints, the front of the store, back of the store, cash register, counters, doors, windows, everything. They got a lot of nothing, and so did we. We found no shell or anything else we could tie in, but that's only important, anyway, in questioning, or maybe as evidence, after you get the perpetrator, if you do. Then the photo unit took their pictures, and I called for the ambulance and O'Donnell called the family and got the son-in-law who decided he'd better come down because his wife, the victim's daughter, would be too broken up about it.

When the son-in-law arrived he was pretty busted up, too. It turned out the old man's wife had died about five years ago, and he lived with the daughter and this son-in-law. As far as he knew, the old man had no enemies. There hadn't been any problems at the store, or in the victim's past, that would motivate such violence, and then we came up with something.

The old man always wore a gold wrist watch and also a ruby ring, that the family had given him on some occasion about ten years before, and both were missing. The watch didn't mean anything. It was a Bulova, but had no inscription. The ring, though, had the old man's initials inscribed on the inside, so we jumped on that. I phoned in the description, to get them checking pawnshops, and I got Barnhart, who took over when the boss retired last week after thirty years, to take Locatelli, who grew up in the neighborhood, and Mason off the chart to help us.

Then we put in the rest of the day, working the street and the neighborhood. We talked with everybody. Did they see anybody go into the store? Did they see anybody who looked suspicious? We checked the license plates on cars. We talked to the bus driver and the mailman. Locatelli shook down everybody with an arrest record that he knew. We stayed on till midnight, and the score for the day, nothing.

We came in again at 8, but Barnhart, playing boss, didn't come in until 10. Meanwhile we sent Locatelli and Mason out again to try to find anybody they didn't wring out yesterday. At about 10:20 the call came in. The Equality Pawn Shop, over on East Seventh, had the ring. The proprietor's assistant was off yesterday, so he didn't get the message until the proprietor recognized the ring when he came in at 10, so naturally he let the perpetrator get away.

"Of course," Barnhart said. "They don't stall him and give us a call, and they let him go. I knew this would happen."

Barnhart always knows what was going to happen, but only after it's over. He's one of the new aces, college-educated and with a year of law studies. He's great on the exams, on the paper work and going by the book. He's also great at making friends on high, except the other night at the boss's retirement affair at the Wayside when he got loaded and started abusing everybody, including the comedian who shut him up pretty good. Incidentally, I saw in the paper where that comedian died here the next day of a heart attack, and young at that. I don't know.

So now O'Donnell and I are figuring that anybody who would drop that ring around here had got to be high, or an idiot, so we high-tail it over to Equality Pawn. It's the ring all right, initials in it and all, and the guy has signed the ticket with the name Arthur Womack, and he gives an address in Hoboken, New Jersey. As the clerk remembers him he's a white male, about twenty-five or twenty-six years of age, long blond hair but not over his ears, wearing a gray and black checked sports jacket and dark trousers, dark glasses but no identifying marks that he noticed.

Back at the squad room we get in touch with Hoboken, but they've got nothing on him and, in fact, there's no such address. Now we figure the name can be fiction, too, but on the supposition that he's still from out of town, we start checking motels and hotels with the name and the description.

"He's miles from here by now," Barnhart says. "Who would be stupid enough, with getaway money from the ring, to hang around?"

"I don't know," O'Donnell said, "but it might be anybody who's stupid enough, and sick enough, to commit Murder One or Murder Two."

In twenty minutes we've got the answer. You know who's stupid enough and sick enough? Arthur Womack, if that's his name. He's registered with a dame, as man and wife, in the old Hotel Brook, and as far as the manager knows, the two of them are in the room. At least he saw Womack go up in the elevator less than an hour before, so we tell Karasek and Allard who are there to cover the lobby and the back, but don't make a move until we get there, unless this Womack shows. Then we pull everybody who's on, and we all have a quick ten minute meet in the squad office with Captain Warneke of the uniformed force.

"Now we don't want any dead heroes," Barnhart says. "Is that clear?"

It's clear enough with me. As I look around the room now I can see and feel the nervousness. Most of them are up pretty tight, so what we ought to do is lay a plan out and cool everybody down, because my personal fear is not so much being shot by the gunman as by one of our own because of nerves.

"So what do you think?" Barnhart says, laying back to second guess.

"Well," I said, "let's be clear in our minds what we're doing before we leave here, because we don't want any conferences in the vicinity."

We decided we wouldn't go over in a group, but in pairs and from different directions. With Karasek and Allard there already, that would make eight in the raiding party, with Warneke's men backing us up but around the corners, and we'd freeze the elevators and cover all exits and put somebody on the switchboard.

"Like who?" Barnhart says.

"Karasek," George said. "He worked the board here for a year or more when he was still in uniform."

247

So, as we left, O'Donnell and I got our old service revolvers out of our lockers, and put them in our topcoat pockets. We've also got the small guns in the holsters, and we went over in a couple of cars and left them a block from the hotel.

Now I'm walking about ten paces behind O'Donnell, and I see a couple of uniformed men, one in one doorway and another in another, so I know Warneke's people are on the job. Then, all of a sudden, I see O'Donnell duck to his left, and now he's looking in this store window. With that I get the message, and I make a quick turn to the curb, like I'm going to cross the street, because who's ambling down the sidewalk toward us but this dame we call Fat Bessie. I forget her last name, but she's got this problem in that she thinks she's being vibrated, either by the FBI or somebody who wants to kidnap her for some sultan's harem, or something. As my wife says, I have trouble figuring out how to replace a light bulb, but this Bessie thinks I'm an electronics expert, and if she starts on me now I'll never make the scene. As luck will have it, though, she misses me and when I look for O'Donnell he's standing by that store window and shaking his head and laughing. Then he crosses the street at the corner and, when I get there, I just glance up at the hotel and I have to wonder what window is the window, and is the guy still in there.

When we get into the lobby I see Allard with his eye on the bank of three elevators, and when I look over to the desk I see Karasek at the switchboard and he gives me a wink. Barnhart isn't here yet, so I go over to the desk while O'Donnell is checking with Allard. The manager is behind the desk, answering some woman's question, but his eyes are moving back and forth, and there's a clerk there too, who's got his head down, but he's looking over the top of his glasses.

"This Arthur Womack," I say to the manager, after the woman leaves and I've identified myself. "What room is he in?"

"He's in 404," he says, swallowing.

"Just relax," I say, as Barnhart comes up. "It's going to be all right, and we'd like to see your floor plan."

He brings it out, and the room is across from the elevators, three doors down to the right. The stairways are at the end of the hall.

"So what's the layout of the room?" Barnhart says.

"The room?" the manager says. "Well, as you enter, the closet is on the left and the bathroom on the right, and then you're in the room."

"And no fire escape outside the window?" I said.

"No, sir," he said.

"So we're going to have to cut off your elevators," Barnhart says. "You just tell your guests that there's an emergency upstairs, and the service should be restored in a few minutes. We'll also have a man at the elevators to tell them the same thing."

"Yes, sir," the manager says.

"And one more thing," I said. "How long has this Womack been here?"

"They checked in the day before yesterday," the manager said. "He doesn't seem like a bad type, but nobody will tell me what he did and why you want him."

"For questioning," Barnhart said.

"And have you noticed if he's friendly with any other guests?" I said. "For example, have you any knowledge, by chance, of him ever being in another guest's room?"

"No, sir," the manager said, and then he looked over at the clerk, who shook his head.

"Then can we have a pass key?" I said.

He gave it to me, and Barnhart and I walked over to where Captain Warneke was talking with O'Donnell and Locatelli and Mason. The way we worked it out was that Barnhart, George and me, Locatelli and Mason would go up to the room. We'd listen for sounds of occupancy, and if we heard them in there, we'd give the word to Allard on the elevator to tell Karasek on the switchboard to call the room. Whoever answered, either Womack or the dame, Karasek would engage the party in conversation—something about how long they intended to hold the room—and meanwhile we'd have knocked on the door.

"The way I'd bet it," I said, "is that he'll answer the phone, and she'll come to the door, but at least we'll disconcert them."

"But what about the pass key?" Barnhart says.

"I've got it just in case," I said, "but I don't figure we should use it. If we open the door, but they've got the chain on it, we're stopped and they're alerted. Now, if he answers the phone and she comes to the door, even if the chain is on she may slip it."

"It may work," Barnhart says, "but I doubt it."

"You have any other suggestions?" I say.

"We haven't got the time," he says.

"We've got plenty of time," I said. "If we have to, we can cut off his water and his food and just starve him out."

"It might take a week," Barnhart says. "You tie up a whole hotel. Then he might decide to use the dame as a hostage, and then where are we? Let's get moving."

So Captain Warneke goes over to fill in Karasek about the call to the room, if we need it, and how to keep him engaged on the phone, and the six of us go up, with Allard, to wait in the elevator. Also, Warneke gives us two uniformed men, one for each end of the hallway to keep any guests, who may want to come out, in their rooms.

On the way up we get out of our topcoats and leave them in the elevator. We've got our guns out now, and when we get to the floor Barnhart says that he and George will go to the door, and he'll listen. The rest of us wait, then, while the two of them tiptoe down the hall and Barnhart bends down and puts his ear to the door. Then he straightens up, and nods to us and the two of them come walking back.

"They're in there," Barnhart says. "At least I can hear the TV going. On the other hand, they may have left it on and gone out."

Everything is always two-handed with Barnhart, and what difference does it make right now? We've still got to go through with our plan.

"So what we'll do," I said, "is this. Once that door opens, if it does, George and I will take Womack wherever he is, at the door or at the phone. Locatelli and Mason will take the dame. All right?"

Barnhart bought it, as I figured he would, because I didn't think he wanted a real piece of it, and I'm relieved. When it happens, if it does, we're going to have like one second to see who's where and make our moves, and I don't want Barnhart running the penal code through his mind or wondering what else we might be doing on the other hand. I want George.

"So, okay," Barnhart says to Allard. "When we get placed, and I give you the signal, you go down and get the word to Karasek to call the room. You got that?"

"Of course," Allard says.

Down the hall to the room we go then. Barnhart places the two uniformed men, and meanwhile, O'Donnell and I have our ears to the door, and we can hear the TV still playing. I'm telling you, waiting for that phone to ring, my heart is pounding so I'm afraid they might hear it through the door.

That's the way it is, and I don't care how many years you've got on the force, and I've got twenty-seven. It was the same in the war, too. Our outfit had two hundred and ten days in the front line, and we got all the dirty jobs, and every time we had to go I was as scared as the first time.

Anyway, I thought that phone would never ring. I'm looking at George and George is looking at me, and he shrugs his shoulders, and with that we hear the phone. It rings once, and it rings twice and then it stops. When it does, I knock on the door, three good loud raps to be heard over the TV, I hope.

This last wait, I don't know whether it was ten seconds, or what, but George is on my left and Locatelli and Mason are right behind us, and then it opens. There's no chain, and I just make out that it's the dame who opened it when O'Donnell gives me this shove with his shoulder, and in he goes with me after him.

The guy is still on the phone, back and to the left, and I couldn't see his right hand because of George, but he had the gun. All I know is, it sounds like the room is blowing apart. I don't know how many he got off, and whether George got one into him, but I know I squeezed off three and he just backed up, with his mouth open, and went down in the angle of the desk and the wall. I took one look to see that he was done, and then I looked for George.

He was face down on the floor, and I turned him over. He caught it right in the chest, but he was still conscious then.

"Damn it, Joe," he said. "Get me out of here."

"Right away," I said.

"And call Helen," he said.

"Of course," I said. "Don't worry about it, and we'll have you right out."

How do you think I feel? If he doesn't shove me out of the way and bust through first I get it, and I'm telling you, if he doesn't make it I may go into that morgue down the hall here and put two more into that scum. And you know what that Barnhart says to me while we're waiting forever for that ambulance? He says: "We shouldn't have done it this way." If he'd said he knew this would happen I would have belted him.

Anyway, I tried to get Helen on the phone from the hotel and then from here. She's not in, but in a way maybe it's just as well. What would she do, just sit here and wait and keep talking like I am just to keep my mind off it? Tom Hunter said he'd be out as soon as he knows anything, and Mary, Mother of God, this is him coming now.

XV

THOMAS R. HUNTER, M.D.

I was having a sandwich and coffee when I heard myself paged, and I called down and got Verna Palmer.

"We've got a cop shot," she said. "They should have him in here in five minutes or so."

"Critical?" I said.

"As far as I know, yes," she said.

"Head, chest or where?" I said.

"I was afraid you'd ask that," she said. "Gloria took the call, and they didn't say and she didn't ask."

"That's just fine," I said.

"I know," she said. "I've been over it with Gloria already, but she says whoever called was all excited and hung up. She's on the phone to the Police Department now trying to find out."

"All right," I said. "I'll be right down. We've got Mosler on in case it's abdominal, but meanwhile alert Neuro and Thoracic to have somebody ready, and we'll let them know just as soon as we know if we want one or the other."

I gulped down my coffee and left the rest of the sandwich, but by the time I got there they were already wheeling him in. They were making the turn into Minor Ops, and I didn't have a good look at the patient, but Stern was at the head with Harvey Mosler, the surgical resident.

"Why, you know who this is?" Stern was saying. "He's one of the two who were in here last week."

It half registered with me. I heard what Stern was saying, but at a time like this identity is not a primary concern.

"Where was he hit?" I said.

They had swung the stretcher around and rolled it in. They had the blanket off, and were transferring him now to the cot.

"The left chest," Harvey Mosler said.

"Then somebody call Thoracic," I said, "and get them down here right away."

"I think he's DOA," Stern was saying, trying to find a pulse in the left wrist.

"Let me in there," I said.

Mosler had pulled a gauze pad off the wound and was up on a stool at the patient's left, starting external cardiac massage, so I pushed past somebody and moved in on the other side. I took my first look at the patient, blue and unconscious, and when I did I had that sickening, sinking feeling in the stomach.

"Good God!" I said. "This is George O'Donnell!"

"Oh, no!" I heard Verna Palmer say. "No."

"What do you think, Doc?" I heard somebody else say, and out of the corner of my eye I saw it was Garrett, his partner.

"I'll let you know," I said.

The jacket was off, the shirt open and the undershirt pulled up, and I took a glancing look at the wound, just below and outside the left nipple, a small round hole ringed by dried blood and seeping slightly. I was reaching now to get a carotid pulse, but with the distension of the neck veins I could get nothing, so I unbuckled his belt, ripped his fly open and yanked his pants down. With my right hand I groped for the femoral artery in the right groin, while with the other I was still feeling for the carotid in the neck. Then there were those three or four seconds before I could feel anything, and when I did, at the femoral, I realized that it was the pulse in my own finger pad, that I was pressing—trying—too hard, and I backed my pressure off slightly.

"I can feel an occasional weak beat, but it's deteriorating rapidly," I said. "Let's get these pants off. Cut his shirt and undershirt off. Let's intubate him and start a couple of IVs of Plasymalyte 56, and somebody see if he's got his blood group in his wallet or somewhere."

"It's here, Doctor," Gloria Miller said. "He's O-positive."

"All right," I said. "Tell the lab it's unmatched O-positive and quick. I want four units in a chest."

"Look at the distended neck veins," Mosler was saying. "It's probably cardiac tamponade and tension pneumothorax."

What he was saying was that there was probably blood in the pericardium surrounding the heart. This would inhibit the expansion of the heart, and create a backup and account for the neck vein distension. The pneumothorax—air from the bullet wound in the left lung leaking into the chest cavity and destroying the vacuum—would have collapsed and impaired the respiration.

"So let's get a chest tube in," I said, "and let's also intubate him quick. Where's Anesthesia?"

"They're on their way," somebody said.

"Let's have a closed thoracotomy kit," Mosler said.

We moved him up on the cot and got his head back, and I got the endotracheal tube in and we were putting him on the bag to assist the breathing and oxygenate him when the two nurse anesthetists moved in. Meanwhile Mosler had made the skin incision over the third rib to go into the chest with the trocar catheter, and Ian Johnson arrived from Thoracic.

"I'll take it," he said to Mosler.

He pushed the trocar catheter in and then pulled the trocar out of the catheter. As he did there was the swish of air followed by the blood, and when he connected the catheter to the underwater seal and the bubbling had started, red now with the blood, in the drainage bottle on the floor, we knew we were getting expansion of the lung.

"It looks like cardiac tamponade, too," Mosler said.

"So let me have a 14-gauge," Johnson said.

He went in with the needle just below the ribs in the front and then up. As he penetrated the heart sac the blood started coming, spurting out of the open end of the needle in a stream and falling over the crotch before we got an emesis basin to catch it. Then the flow lessened, becoming pulsatile, so we knew the pressure confining the heart had been relieved, and the rhythmic leakage now was reflecting the transmitted pulses of the heart reviving.

"His color's getting better," Mosler was saying, "and the neck vein distension is receding."

"We may make it at that," Johnson was saying. "Call the O.R. and tell the heart lung machine crew to be set for a cardiopulmonary bypass, and let me know how long before they'll be ready."

"Here's the new blood now," somebody else said.

Arnold, our day orderly, had the four units in one of those styrofoam chests. I took one of the plastic sacks and handed it to Stern on the one IV and Johnson passed the second to Mosler on the other.

"And put the blood pumps on those bags," Johnson said. "If we can just stay ahead of this blood loss and get him upstairs where we can open him up . . ."

"How's he look?" I said to the nurse anesthetist at his head, while they were hooking up the new blood and starting it.

"I think he's coming back," she said. "His corneal reflex has returned, and I think I feel a temporal artery pulse."

"I thought I saw him swallow," the other one, who had the blood-pressure cuff on him, said, "and his muscle tone seems to be returning."

"Good," I said. "You getting a reading?"

"I see oscillation of mercury at 50," she said, "but I hear nothing."

"If we can just stay ahead . . ." Johnson was starting to say again, and then he said: "But, Jesus, look at this. It's not letting up and it's bright red. It must be the left ventricle, and . . ."

Right then he went. There was that agonal, transient seizure, and then there was the blood coming, spurting again from the needle in the pericardium and into the emesis basin, and pouring out of the chest tube again and into the drainage bottle on the floor.

"Goddammit!" Johnson was saying, and I was aware now of the odor of feces. "Goddammit! Damn it to hell!"

"Doctor?" somebody said, and it was Gloria Miller. "The cardiopulmonary crew are ready when you are, but all the O.R.s are occupied and it's going to be forty more minutes."

"Tell them the hell with it," Johnson said. "Tell them to forget the whole goddam thing."

"Excuse me," someone else was saying, and it was Father Tim Shea. "May I?"

"I'm sorry, Father," Johnson said. "I apologize."

"That's all right," Father Tim said.

We walked away then, and left Father Tim alone with him. I was only half listening to what Ian Johnson was saying.

"Will you tell me why this has to be?" he was saying. "Why can't we have the facilities of the O.R. in the E.R.? Why do we have to bring the E.R. to the O.R. instead of the other way around? You called me as soon as you knew. I got down here as fast as I could. Maybe, if we could have just put him on the bypass we might have been able to suture those holes. Maybe not, but why?"

"I don't know why," I said.

"Anyway," Johnson was saying, "my guess is that it must have hit the left ventricle, and any holes were temporarily closed by clots. With the improved heart action, though, they were knocked off. What could we do? We were hand-cuffed, unless we could get him upstairs."

"I know," I said.

"This is wrong," he was saying. "With all the money that's being spent today . . ."

"I know," I said.

I kept saying that I knew, but what did I know? All I knew was that I was experiencing again that sensation of emptiness, that helpless, hollow feeling of frustration and nothingness that comes with that most total of all defeats, the sudden and intimate death.

"I think I've seen him around here," Ian Johnson was saying. "Did you happen to know him?"

"Very well," I said. "For many years he was one of my patients."

"I'm sorry," Johnson said.

"But how did it happen?" Stern was saying. "Has anybody heard?"

"Excuse me," Verna Palmer said, and she was standing there

with Arnold. "When Father Shea is finished do you want the body to go right to the morgue?"

"What about the Holding Room?" I said.

"It's vacant," she said.

"Good," I said, "because his wife may want to see him here."

"Is she here?" Verna said. "Has she even been notified?"

"I don't know," I said, "but that reminds me that I've got to tell his partner."

He was sitting out in the waiting room with Jack Clarity, our public relations director. When he saw me come down the hall he got up and walked over to meet me and, fortunately for me, he could see it on my face.

"He didn't make it?" he said.

"I'm sorry," I said. "We did all we could do."

"I knew it," he said. "I knew it when we came in. I've been sitting here and running off at the mouth just to keep from thinking about it."

"We really didn't have a chance," I said.

"I knew it," he said, "and it's my fault, too. I don't know. I was the one . . ."

"Look," Clarity was saying to him. "Stop thinking that way. It's not your fault."

"What about Mrs. O'Donnell?" I said. "Is she on her way here?"

"No," he said, "and I have to find her. We've got somebody staking out the house, and I'd better get over there before she tries to reach me here. It's going to be an awful shock. I don't want to think what it's going to be like."

"Of course," I said, "and when you get a chance will you let me know if she's coming over? Just in case she is, we'll keep him in our Holding Room, but if we get crowded we may have to move him."

"Thanks," he said, and he left.

"Now about the press," Clarity said. "Beryl Williams is entertaining three of them in the Coffee Shop to keep them off our necks, so I've got to run up there. What happened?"

"We just couldn't keep ahead of the blood loss," I said. "We were hoping to get him upstairs so they could open him up."

"How many entry wounds?" Clarity said.

"Just one," I said. "It entered just below and outside the left nipple and collapsed the left lung. We were able to restore that function, but it must also have at least nicked a ventricle."

"Damn," Clarity said.

"Do you think that all that should go into the newspapers, though?" I said.

"No," he said. "In every group there's always one ghoul, but I'll shut him off. He simply expired of internal bleeding at whatever time it was."

"It'll be on the chart," I said.

"And I've got another problem," Clarity said. "If his wife doesn't know yet, we don't want it going out over the radio. She might hear it driving home."

"I hadn't thought of that," I said.

"They're very good about that, though," Clarity said. "Now I want to check the chart."

"Before you do that," I said, "can you tell me how this happened?"

"It's a damn shame," Clarity said. "Yesterday some punk—an acid head or whatever he was—shot and killed a storeowner, and they found him today in a room at the Brook. I guess four of them went in, and O'Donnell shoved Garrett out of the way to go first and took the bullet Garrett figures he'd have stopped instead. He ended up a real hero cop."

"And dead," Stern said.

"And the gunman?" I said, ignoring Stern. I was starting to feel the initial numbness subsiding now, and anger beginning to occupy the emptiness.

"The gunman?" Clarity said. "He's in the morgue."

But anger against whom or what? A dead thug? A Providence I am forced in desperation to accept but cannot understand or reach?

"It's ridiculous," I heard Stern say.

"What is?" Clarity said.

"The whole thing," Stern said. "This isn't the 1880s, and this isn't Dodge City. If they've got him in a room why don't they just surround it and wait him out? If they're going in, why

259

don't they use tear gas, or wear bulletproof vests? It's stupid."

"Okay, Commissioner," Clarity said to him. "You run the Police Department. I've got other things to do."

"I still say it's stupid," Stern said, as Clarity left to get the time off the chart.

"Doctor," I said, "are you busy with a patient?"

"No," he said. "Why?"

"Let's find an empty booth, if we can," I said, "and take a few minutes out. I just want to check at the desk first."

He followed me over and waited while I checked our traffic. Booth 6 was open, and we walked over there.

"Have a seat," I said.

"I'd just as soon stand," he said. "What's wrong?"

"Let's begin with this shooting," I said.

"You don't agree with me?" he said. "It was stupid, and it happens all the time. Every few weeks or so you read a story in the papers from someplace where this same kind of thing has happened. What is it with these cops? You want to know what I think it is? I think that once you give a man a gun he has a subconscious urge to use it. For all I know, maybe they've got a death wish. Maybe they all want to end up dead heroes. It's like I said. Why don't they just wait it out? Why don't they use tear gas? Why don't they wear bulletproof vests?"

"I don't know the answers," I said. "My knowledge of police procedures, and the reasons for them, is almost nil, but what you say makes sense."

"Of course," he said. "Then you have to agree that what happened today was stupid. So?"

"So let me explain something," I said. "George O'Donnell was a patient of mine for about twenty years, and beyond that we had a special relationship. Eight years ago it was his extremely difficult duty to have to come and tell me that our seventeen-year-old son, our only child, had just been killed in an auto accident. What I want to explain is that today, just moments after I stood helpless here and watched him expire, I did not appreciate listening to you describe George O'Donnell as stupid."

260

"I'm sorry," he said. "I didn't know."

"I realize that," I said, "and I realize something else. If I had to arrive at one word to describe you as both a doctor and a person do you know what that word would be?"

"I haven't any idea," he said.

"Ruthless," I said.

"Ruthless?" he said. "What do you mean by that?"

"By that," I said, "I mean what happened here today to my feelings. I mean . . ."

"I've already apologized for that," he said. "I told you I didn't know."

"Of course," I said, "and I don't suggest that, had you known, you would have behaved as you did. I haven't called you cruel. I have no reason to believe that you willfully set out to hurt others, but the characteristic of the ruthless person in the intense pursuit of his own objectives, is his disregard for others, and the damage and hurt that result can be just as severe as if they were intended."

"Well," he said, "I don't think that an isolated incident such as today's, for which I've already apologized, is . . ."

"I've already dismissed what happened today," I said, "but when you call it 'an isolated incident' it's obvious that you're completely unaware of the constant pattern of your behavior and the damage it does. Just yesterday I had a serious complaint about you by Miss Palmer on behalf of her nurses."

"They're complaining about *me?*" he said. "Believe me, if I wanted to file complaints about some of them I'd have plenty of cause."

"I believe it," I said, "but that just confirms what I'm saying about you. All of us who work with these girls realize that they're not perfect, but we also realize that we're not, either. They're good nurses and, more important, they're the best we can get. They work hard—in fact, they're overworked . . ."

"And so am I," he said. "I work harder than anybody. I'll bet I see thirty percent more cases than Wyman . . ."

"I know," I said. "I check the charts every day, and I admire your appetite for work and your zeal."

261

"Well, thank you for that," he said. "So what's Palmer complaining about?"

"Your attitude toward her girls," I said. "As she put it, you look and talk down your nose at them and order them around like they're domestic help. You have driven at least one of them to tears, and she asked me how much longer you're going to be on here."

"Six more days," he said.

"I know," I said. "We looked it up, because she said if you were coming back for another month there were a couple of her girls who were going to put in for transfer."

"I can't believe that," he said.

"Just believe it," I said. "You could go and ask her, but you'd just find it's true."

"I didn't think it was that bad," he said. "I really didn't."

"Well, it is," I said, "and that same attitude—that lack of concern for others—is reflected in your handling of patients. From my observation I would say that you are interested in them as technical problems, but not as human beings."

"If you mean," he said, "that I don't want to stand around and listen to a lot of personal history that's not pertinent to the problem, I agree. I haven't got the time."

"I know," I said. "That's a reaction that we all have, but it goes beyond that."

"In what way?" he said.

"You recall," I said, "that elderly patient we had in here— that Mr. Kobak?"

"The one who killed himself?" he said. "So I admit I left him unattended. With all we've got to do here, I just . . ."

"That's not what I mean," I said.

"You know," he said, "I was thinking about that a few minutes ago. Who would have thought, when those two detectives were in here interrogating everyone about that, that one of them would die right here within a matter of days?"

"Certainly not I," I said. "Now I'd like you to recall a scene. The old man had been X-rayed, and Ian Johnson, you and I were looking at the pictures. The one lung had collapsed, and the other . . ."

"Was invaded by a mass," he said, "that Johnson said he'd guarantee was CA. I remember."

"And do you remember," I said, "what you said?"

"I haven't any idea," he said.

"Your remark," I said, "was: 'I recommend that we give him back the electric cord.' "

"Well, after all," he said. "He was eighty years old. We could relieve the pneumothorax, but he had cancer of the other lung. He'd already tried to hang himself. He didn't want to live. Besides, it was just a remark."

"It wasn't just a remark," I said. "It stayed with me, and I'm sure it stayed with Ian Johnson, too, because it was reflective of this callous, insensitive attitude of yours. After the old man, through your negligence, finally succeeded in taking his own life, were you contrite? No. Your reaction then was what it is today, that he was old and incurable and wanted to die anyway, although it should go without saying that we're not here to dispense lethal weapons or overdoses of barbituates, or whatever, to the suicidal.

"You see, Doctor," I said, "Mr. Koback was a human being, old and incurable and possessed by a desire to die, but a human being. When a man, who has lived for eighty years and fathered children and inevitably touched other lives, reaches that point where the burden of living finally becomes too much and he takes his own life, there is a sadness involved that, to some degree, touches all of us who are aware of it. For the most part, because our emotions are not limitless and our objectivity must be retained, we in this profession turn our backs to it, but at least we are not disrespectful of it, and that's what you were.

"You're racing down a highway to somewhere, Doctor," I said. "I don't know where it is, but as far as you're concerned there's no one on the road but you. You're highly intelligent —maybe even brilliant—and you work hard, but I don't understand someone like you. I don't understand what you're doing in this profession."

While I had been talking he had sat down, and he was fingering a ball-point pen, clicking it. I had nothing else to say, and then he looked up at me.

"You want to know something?" he said.

"Yes," I said.

"I know what you say is true," he said, "I've known it since I was a kid. I'm a jerk, really."

"Well," I said, because I could think of nothing else to say.

"Look," he said. "You agree. That's what you think of me, and that's what just about everybody thinks of me, but I don't really care. Oh, I have periods when I decide to try to be different, but it doesn't really work because I'm a perfectionist and I can't stand stupidity and incompetence around me. I'm impatient with people who just can't cut it."

"But that doesn't give you the right to hurt them," I said.

"I know that," he said. "You're correct. I don't want to hurt them, really, but I just can't afford to be too concerned about that. You see, I just don't believe that I'm all that different from most people either, because I just don't believe that most people are as genuinely concerned with others as they appear to be. Their behavior isn't really being controlled by what they honestly think of others but, instead, by what they want others to think of them. I think that's phony, and as far as I'm concerned, I don't really care what other people think about me. All I want is to live my own life and do what I want to do."

"And what's that?" I said.

"Right now I'm not sure," he said.

"You're rotating right now," I said. "What do you go on next?"

"After this week?" he said. "General Surgery. Actually I'd like to be going on Neuro because, broadly speaking, they haven't made any major advances in years, and the department here is good, and it might help me come to a decision."

"You'd still be dealing with patients," I said, "when you're really more interested in the illness than in the ill."

"Correct," he said.

"What about research?" I said.

"Right," he said. "The more I'm around people the more I tend toward it. I've considered pathology."

And that would be ironic, I was thinking, if you, so short of empathy, should end up here under Jack Davis, who is so overburdened with it that he turned from clinical medicine because he could not stand what was for him the daily heartaches of treating the severely ill.

"But I'm thinking more about toxicology," he was saying. "I mean the new toxicology—the effects of drugs, of food additives, of cyclamates on livers, or whatever."

"Or whatever," I said. "You'll find your way, but meanwhile I want to ask a favor."

"I'm listening," he said.

"For the next six days," I said, "how about going into one of those periods when, as you've described it, you try to be different?"

"I'm off tomorrow," he said, "so it'll only be five days."

"Good," I said, and when he said nothing else we shook hands and we left the booth.

"Oh, there you are," Verna Palmer said, walking up to me. "We just had a call from someone in the Police Department and Mrs. O'Donnell won't be coming over here. I've called the morgue."

"All right," I said. "I've just had a talk with Dr. Stern about your complaint. Things may be a little better the rest of the week, although I can't guarantee it."

"Stern?" she said. "I need him right now like I need a strep throat. Why did it have to be George O'Donnell? It's such a shame."

"I know," I said.

I went to a phone, then, and I found the slip of paper in a jacket pocket and I called Sumner Rowell, who is Radiologist-in-Chief and whom I have never met. I told him of the complaint that had come down to me from our 11 P.M. to 7:30 A.M. shift, that after midnight our people are having to take the X-ray films to the House Officers' Quarters so that his people can look at them lying on their backs and holding them up to the light of the bed lamps.

"That's absurd," I said. "That's inexcusable."

"I agree completely," he said, "and without even checking I can tell you who it is. I apologize, and that's over as of now."

When I put down the phone Bob Mabry, the senior Neuro resident, walked over.

"I just heard what happened here," he said, "and I'm sorry to learn he was a friend of yours."

"That's right," I said.

"The other night," he said, "I had Nick Braff, the jockey, here after he ventilated his attic with a .22."

"I saw the chart," I said, "and then the story in the paper. How is he doing?"

"Good," he said. "Survived the expected relapse, but I'm just reminded that O'Donnell and his partner were here on that, and if I remember right O'Donnell was also here on our little hit-and-run up in Space Control."

"You remember right," I said.

And I remember, too. I remember the parents, decent, timid people, and how my pity went out to them, and the father in his innocence explaining the girl's innocence.

"But she was just on her way to school," he kept saying. "She was just going to school."

And I remember George O'Donnell coming in to pick up the clothing for the police lab, and the two of us, without mentioning it, sharing again that other, most awful moment of my life, and George angry again then in his frustration.

"And another maggot will get away," he said.

"And what's happening with the child?" I said to Mabry now, because I have been checking daily with the Trauma Unit, and the last I had heard they had about decided that, unless what remains of the life force within her somehow began to take over, it would be pointless to continue to sustain her artificially.

"Who knows?" he said. "The other day we were about ready to hang it up, but the numbers on the tote board are changing."

"For the better?" I said.

"Somewhat," he said. "If I were making book on her, I'd say she went to 100 to 1 the other night, but she's dropped back down to 50 to 1 now. It's all in the hands of the Big Handicapper, and I'm just praying that he doesn't send us another customer for the unit. I wouldn't want to be the one to have to make a choice, unless it's some kamikaze off an Emperor's Revenge."

"A what?" I said.

"Motorbike," he said. "We just shipped another one upstairs for Ortho. Eighteen years old. Commuted fracture of the femur. Compound fracture of the tibia. Compound fracture of the radius and ulnar. He was a human missile. You know what the curse of modern civilization really is? It's not coronary disease. It's not cancer. It's the internal combustion engine, and when my kids get too big for roller skates I don't know what I'm going to do."

"I know," I said again, and that I do know. Since moments after that first shock of George O'Donnell's passing and the ensuing emptiness, I had been aware of that vacuum filling once more with the memory of our Tommy and with the accompanying bitterness. It has lessened, but it has never left me, really, in eight years, and that is why I took that moment to assault Stern, however justly, and jump on Radiology and why, now again, I needed to find the only salve available in work.

"What's the problem here?" I said to Verna Palmer.

A woman, I would guess in her early thirties, her hair done up in pink curlers, was standing at the desk with a boy who, it turned out, is eleven years of age. The boy, it was obvious, had been crying and he was now attempting to hold back more tears.

"Abdominal pains," Vera said, "and vomiting."

I introduced myself to the woman, and led them over to booth 5. While I was helping the boy out of his jacket and shirt and trousers, and then taking his pulse and temperature, I was questioning the mother.

"And what time did the pains start?" I said.

"I think it was around two o'clock," she said.

"This morning?" I said.

"I think that's right," she said, and then she turned to the boy. "What time was it?"

"I don't know," he said, still struggling against the tears.

"It was around two o'clock," she said. "He woke up crying."

267

"And then he vomited?"

"That's right."

"More than once?"

"Twice."

"And he's had these pains ever since?" I said. "And you waited twelve hours to bring him in here?"

"I thought it was something he ate," she said. "He was at a birthday party yesterday and, besides, I had a lot of things to do this morning."

Like shampooing and putting up your hair? I was thinking. For what royal receptions do you women prepare, that you parade around in super markets and public places like this where dozens, or even hundreds, see you looking like Medusa? And why don't the manufacturers at least turn these repugnant rolls out in hair colors?

"And he's had no pains like this in the recent past?" I said. "Last week, or last month?"

"No," she said. "Never."

"Diarrhea?"

"No."

The temperature was 99, and the pulse up to 100. I helped him then onto the cot. I wanted to get him relaxed and unguarded.

"So tell me, Peter," I said. "Do you know what you want to be when you grow up?"

"Nope," he said.

"He wants to be a football player," his mother said. "That's all he's interested in."

"That's fine," I said to him. "And who's your favorite football player?"

"Joe Namath," he said.

"I guess he's the best," I said, probing now. "Do you practice passing a lot?"

"Oooh!" he said, starting to cry now.

"Now you stop that!" his mother said.

"That's all right," I said. "Everybody cries when it hurts enough. I'll bet Joe Namath used to cry when he was eleven."

I had found the more than normal rigidity of muscle in the

right lower quadrant that, of course, signals appendicitis. Acute throat infection or an early pneumonia may develop pain there, but there was no throat inflammation and the lungs were clear.

"Is it appendicitis?" the mother said.

"I don't know yet," I said. "Tell me, Peter. Do you practice throwing at an old tire?"

"Don't mention it," his mother said. "He's been pestering his father for one for a year."

Like our Tommy at that age, I was thinking. We hung it from that old wild cherry in the side yard, and when the other kids weren't around and I was too busy, his mother became his retriever.

"I just want to make a couple of tests now," I said.

I took the blood sample and got some urine, and when the lab results came back I called Surgery and got Otto Franz. The urine showed no sign of infection, but on the blood count the white was up to 13,800. On the differential count the segmented cells were 66 with bands of 16, lymphocytes of 12, monocytes of 6. It could still be mesenteric adenitis or an inflamed Meckel's diverticulum, but as we explained to the mother when Otto came down, the danger of appendectomy is minimal compared to the danger of it rupturing.

"I don't know," she said. "I was just hoping it was something he ate."

"But it isn't, madam," Otto said.

"I don't know," she said. "I'll just have to call my husband."

"Of course," Otto said, "and will you do it right away?"

I filled out the chart then, and left it and them with Otto. When I got back to the nursing station Stern and Stu Wyman were talking, and Wyman was shaking his head.

"I don't think so," he was saying.

"You have a problem?" I said.

"A girl of five," he said. "She's been running a fever for four days, and it's now 103.5. Eyes are red and runny, and she's got a cough. Her doctor saw her two days ago and prescribed aspirin, and then he went off on a three- or four-day vacation."

"Pneumonia?" I said.

"That's what I said," Stern said.

"No," Wyman said. "The lung fields are clear."

"And you put the scope on both axillae for upper lobe?" Stern said, and then he looked at me and nodded, because we had been through that just days ago.

"And got nothing," Wyman said.

"Did you call Pediatrics?" I said.

"I did," he said, "but they're jammed up for the next hour."

We walked down to booth 9, and Wyman introduced me to the mother. I put my stethoscope on the child, and Wyman was right. I got clear sounding fields, and then I checked her ears, her throat and, finally, her mouth—the mucous membranes opposite the molar sites.

"Take another look here," I said to Wyman. "The small red spots with white centers."

"Of course," Wyman said, after he had looked. "Koplik's spots. I missed it."

"That's easy to do," I said. "I've been looking at it for a quarter of a century."

"I'm sorry," Wyman said.

"Tell me," I said to the mother. "Has your daughter had measles vaccine?"

"When she was very small," she said. "I think when she was about nine months."

"Has she been exposed to measles in the last ten days?" I said.

"Well," she said, "my sister and her little boy were visiting us last week. After they got home my sister wrote that he was sick, but I haven't heard since."

"Your daughter has measles," I said.

"Can you imagine that?" the mother said. "That's just like my sister. You'd think she'd let me know."

"Elixir of phenobarbitol," I said to Wyman. "One teaspoonful every four hours, and an aspirin."

"And the darkened room," he said. "I'm sorry I blew it, and thanks."

I went from the child to a severe asthmatic, a thirty-two-year-old male, sweating, working for each breath, his pulse pounding at 120, and I finally got relief for him, after the warm saline mist with oxygen, and the aminophylline, adrenalin and intravenous steroids had failed, with 40 milligrams of Solu-Medrol intravenously. When 4:30 came I stayed on, and when I drove home at 5:45 and turned on the car radio, I realized that the news would be coming on shortly, and I shut off the radio even as, almost as mechanically, I have had to shut off so much of my own life.

There had still been two patients waiting that evening when George O'Donnell had come in. When I had seen his face I had known something was wrong, and I had motioned to him that I could see him right then.

"It's all right, Doc," he had said. "I'll wait."

XVI

TIMOTHY J. SHEA, S.J.

What's it like? I'll tell you, Eddie, you're like a fireman. You remember when we used to walk a mile to the Third Street firehouse and we'd hang around outside there for hours, waiting and hoping for an alarm to ring in so we could see them go out? Well, it's like that. The bells are ringing. People are in trouble. You go. For example, today. Normally by early afternoon I'm back at the hospital, and I've picked up my new intake cards at the chaplain's office and I'm making my rounds. They're little printed cards that the nurses collect, and the patient would like to talk to the chaplain, seek confession or receive Holy Communion. Generally, Holy Communion is offered first thing in the morning, so for two and a half or three hours in the afternoon you may be hearing a few confessions but mostly you're just talking with patients and their families.

Now that's normal, making rounds in the afternoon, but what's normal? After lunch today, for example, I couldn't get back to the hospital and start my rounds because I had this counseling session at the rectory with a young couple. Actually, they're not part of the hospital family, but this happens quite a bit. You're counseling a nurse or a medical student, say, and she or he has a friend who needs help and it's always nice to be recommended.

So after lunch today I was seeing this young working couple who are friends of a hospital lab technician. It was the wife's day off and the husband was taking a late lunch hour, which was the best way we could arrange it for the three of us. We were about three-quarters of the way through the hour, and into an in-laws problem, when the phone rings for me and it's the calling service.

You see, if I'm going to be around a phone for an hour or more I'll give them that number, but otherwise they'll reach me on the beeper which carries for twenty miles. It beeps once and then twice, and I peel it off my pocket like this, push down the button and listen. The girl's voice will say: "Father Shea, the hospital says there's a DOA in the morgue." Or she may say: "The hospital says there's an accident patient critical in the E.R." Or sometimes they'll give you the ward or the floor or room number.

Today I took it on the phone. She said: "Father Shea, the hospital has a critical gunshot wound that's just come into the E.R." Now, if I'd have been on my rounds I'd have been there sooner, but as it was I got there at the end. In fact one of the doctors—you know, frustrated—was using a few mild profanities, so when he saw me he apologized, although the truth is that I'm more embarrassed by the apology than I am by the profanities. After all, as you know, the Navy got me before the Church did, and when you put on the collar you don't just automatically stop thinking occasionally in profanities yourself. In fact, in trying to establish rapport you might employ a few yourself, because in this calling it's not how you say something that's important, and as you've probably figured out, that's undoubtedly one of the reasons I took to the collar in the first place.

In the E.R., though, when the heat is on you get very few apologies and very little deference, and I like that. I mean the prestige of the collar and cloth is fine, especially in the beginning, and you use it all the time, but sometimes you get so much of the "Father" . . . "Father" . . . "Father" that you wish they'd remember that you're a human being. That's why it's a pleasure to get out in mufti like this occasionally. Anyway, as I say, you come into one of those booths in the E.R., or into what they call Minor Ops, to anoint, and they're starting IVs or trying to zap somebody's heart back and they're all crowded around the patient and you're just another guy. In fact, in the minds of some of them you're just engaging in a superstitious practice anyway.

Of course, this was a tough one for me today because it was

George O'Donnell, the detective. It's on the front page of the paper tonight, and I don't think you knew him because as a uniformed cop he wasn't around our neighborhood, but when I was in the other parish here I used to see him occasionally and his wife and their two daughters were regulars. Long before that, though, when we were still growing up, I remember about him because of Frankie. You remember my youngest brother, Frankie. That's right, with the red hair. Well, he's Frank now and married and has three kids of his own, but he was just starting in DeWitt Clinton Elementary then, and George O'Donnell was his hero. I guess George O'Donnell was new on the force then, because he was in uniform and had the crossing guard duty, and Frankie would come home every day and tell us what Officer O'Donnell had said to him that day and how some day he was going to be a cop just like George O'Donnell. Instead he's in charge of the housewares department at Langer's, but he married a fine girl and they've got a fine family. I know.

So there was that personal involvement today. When I got there in Minor Ops, George O'Donnell, in the view of the doctors, had just passed on, but this would not necessarily be true in the view of the Church. You see, the Church's position is that the principal life force is the spirit, or the soul, and no one can be exactly certain when this life force leaves and death actually occurs.

Medically, for example, we see people shocked back. Occasionally, every now and then, you'll read a newspaper item about a patient, pronounced dead, who suddenly stirs—begins to revive—in the morgue. This is rare, sure, but it would seem to reaffirm the Church's position that it's impossible to know the exact moment of the departure of the spirit, or soul, and death is acknowledged only when the bodily injury is so gross that it's obvious, or when the signs, such as change in coloration and rigor mortis, set in.

That's right, and there's a lot of misunderstanding about this, about what one of the doctors—Dr. Bob Mabry, who's the chief neurosurgical resident at the M.C.—calls, when he kids around with me, my "Last Rites Concession." You see, the sacraments are for the living only. What it is, then, is the

Conditional Sacrament of the Sick and, as today, you grant the Apostolic Blessing: "By the power of the Apostolic See I grant you a plenary indulgence, in the name of the Father, Son and Holy Spirit." This is preceded by laying on of hands followed by the anointing, with the Holy Oil of the Sick, in the sign of the cross, on the forehead when possible and, if not, on the shoulders, and by the Anointing Prayer: "May our Lord Jesus Christ, by this Holy Anointing, forgive you whatever sins you may have committed."

Now, that's the short form, which you use in emergencies, and the longer form, which you use when the patient is fully awake, takes about twenty minutes. It's not magic, but a series of prayers, and the oil is employed because historically it has been used as an agent and a sign of healing. There must always be the faith response on the part of the recipient, and it's often made, hopefully, before they lapse into unconsciousness.

The oil? The oil is a mixture of olive oil and balsam, and on the Thursday before Easter it's blessed by the Bishop at the cathedral church. Then one priest is assigned to go and pick it up for the parish, and you keep replenishing your supply from what we call "the bird house" at the right of the altar. You anoint with your right thumb, and you also carry a supply of cotton with you to wipe the forehead and wipe your thumb. The oil has been consecrated by the Bishop, so you're supposed to burn the cotton. What I did when I first signed on for this duty was get a Maxwell House coffee can, and I'd go out in the back yard at the rectory and burn it there, but a lot of the time it's hectic duty and, as in everything else, it's first things first and you don't always get around to it. I mean you have to learn to adapt, to adjust.

And I mean you have to learn to adjust to people, too, although in my case I think I learned more about that in the war in Korea than I did in the seminary. Still, especially in the beginning when you're constantly doubting your fitness—your ability to fill the collar—you're nervous about, say, how you're going to handle the Sacrament of the Sick or what you're going to say to a bereaved family. I remember one of the first calls I had from the hospital, and this was on my first tour and about five years ago now, was for an old Italian. He reminded me of old man Locatelli. You remember old man Locatelli, who had the garden, and the night he caught us trying to get away with a few of his tomatoes? Anyway, you don't hear it much any more, but some of those old-country people used to call the priest "the black thumb man." You know: "Here comes the black thumb of death." So I went in and, of course, you ask first. I said: "I'm here as your priest and friend, and I would like to help you spiritually and physically by offering you the Sacrament of the Sick." He looked right at me, and then he spit right in my face.

That was a shocker, sure, but only for the moment because, as I say, the war was a great opener for me. As you know, I was only eighteen, and we were flying reconnaissance over the China Straits. We were based at Naha, near the southern tip of Okinawa, and it was a pretty good-sized city that had been leveled in World War II, and they were putting it back together again. Now, growing up the way we did in that mixed neighborhood, you know we didn't exactly lead sheltered lives, but I was really rocked by the behavior of the Americans. I really was. Some lived like monks, sure, but a lot of them lived like animals—drunk, arrogant, buying girls with no regard for them as human beings—and I haven't been really shocked since by anything I've heard or seen in the inner city parish or in counseling or whatever.

So I had the old Italian who spit in my face, and then I had the other extreme. Do you remember Marty O'Brien? Sure you do. A real heller, and I don't know whether you remember it or not but I ran with him for a while, kind of like a tail on his kite. Then he went his way, as you did and I did, and when I came back here he was in the parish, but we hadn't seen each other for years. Anyway, cancer hit him. That's right, and when the doctors decided it was terminal they sent him home, and one day he asked the family to call for me. I went over, and when I walked into that bedroom, Eddie, it was pathetic. He was wasting away, and he knew it was the end, and you could see the fear—the terror—in his eyes.

"Tim," he said, "for God's sake, please help me. I'm scared."

Now you have the prayers and the sacraments. You get all

that in the seminary, but nobody can teach you, or tell you, what else to say. So what did I say? I don't know exactly, any more, but I said something about how we'd been the best of friends and we still were and we'd been through a lot together and we'd be together on this, too. I started the prayers—"Peace to this house and to all who dwell here . . ."—and he had this tight, terrified grasp on my left wrist. I heard his confession. "May I offer you the Sacrament of Penance? . . . Are you sorry for all your sins in life? . . . May our Lord Jesus Christ absolve you, and by His authority I absolve you, from all sins in the name of the Father, the Son and the Holy Spirit." Then I started the anointing, and as I went through the prayers, I felt that grasp on my wrist soften, I saw the fear leave his eyes and face and, as I continued, I felt the most gentle pressure still on my wrist, and then the hand dropped away and he had died.

In this business you learn by doing. You could call it on-the-job-training, but you find your own way. In the seminary we were taught, by what we used to call in the war the Regular Navy types, that we had all the answers. You have Sacramental Theology, and a professional cleric, who's never really been out among the customers, comes in and the course takes a year. There are the Seven Sacraments, a rite for everything, such as Penance, the Sacrament of the Sick, Baptism, Marriage and the rest, but we were taught only how to administer the sacraments with very little attention to psychology or the behavioral sciences.

Then I got out—inexperienced and nervous—and I tried to rip off the clichés. You know: "It's God's will." "He's in Heaven." "Everything's all right now." Come on, Eddie! At that moment how many can buy that?

I remember one of the first cases I had in the E.R. A twenty-one-year-old had been killed—a car accident—and his wife was nineteen and eight months pregnant. So I started out about God's will, and I'll tell you now that often you run into anger and she just lit into me.

"God's will?" she screamed. "If it's God's will, the hell with God! If God's all good why did He do this? Why did He kill a good man who never hurt a soul in his life? Why? Why?"

You don't have the answers for them right then, so why try to sell them a line? These are struggling human beings, so what you try to do is help them to get their guts back in order. You do it—at least you try to—by your presence as a man of God and as another struggling human being. You hold their hands, you let them cry on you, and like today when I went to see George O'Donnell's wife, Helen, you reflect back their own feelings and, most important, you share their grief. He was a fine cop, and a fine human being, and the Department will miss him and the city will miss him. We were all fortunate in having had him among us as long as we did, but we'll all miss him.

Doctors, of course, have the same problem. Many of them just can't face the death of patients, so when they can avoid the families they often do. They leave it to the nurses, and for some nurses this becomes too much, and afterwards I see some of those nurses crying out their insides in the chart room.

I remember one Jewish doctor who had to inform the parents that their fourteen-year-old son was dead of drowning. When I got in there he was just standing in front of them and crying, and I have never forgotten his compassion, and my admiration of his humanity.

Doctors have to save the living, though, so in their minds they have to sort of abandon the lost. Right now in the hospital they have a little black girl who was hit by a car, and for a week or two she's been in what they call the Trauma Unit. They've been keeping her alive artificially, by intravenous feeding and forced breathing and I don't know what else. I don't know the child or her parents, but I know their minister, the Reverend Floyd R. Thomas of the Mount Hebron Baptist Church, because some time ago he and I worked together on sort of an ecumenical youth project in the inner city. He's been at the hospital every day now, as long as the girl has been there, and a day or so ago he was telling me that the doctors were considering taking her off the equipment, of abandoning her as lost. She was not responding to anything. She was being maintained mechanically, and there was the question of how long one could, or should, continue this. Fortunately the unit wasn't needed by anyone else, and, more fortunately, at the moment of decision, her vital signs began to show some slight response. She's not out of danger yet, by any means, but doctors have to grow calluses over their hearts, you might say, and to a degree a priest finds those calluses growing, too. You're only human.

Take your DOAs. The first one I ever had they called me on at 3 A.M. When I got over there the coroner said: "He's in the morgue." It turned out that he was a migrant farm worker, and I guess he'd been drinking because he'd jumped or fallen out of the back of a pickup truck and into the path of two cars that had hit him. In the morgue he was face down, open down his left side from his armpit to his thigh with his insides hanging out. I started my prayers, but I had to rush out of there and throw up.

Shortly after that I caught another one, a five-day-old corpse in the heat of summer. He was an old man who'd died at home in one of our better neighborhoods without anybody knowing it, and Baker, who runs Baker Ambulance here, and his assistant were there, and he said to me: "Father, before you go in there you'd better take a deep breath." I had all I could do to keep from being sick again, and so I had those doubts. You know, that maybe I don't deserve this office.

You see, we catch a lot of the DOAs and accident cases because they'll call for a priest not only when the person is a Catholic but also when the religion isn't known. The other day, for example, they called me for a young man—a nightclub comic, in fact—who was expiring in the E.R. from a heart attack, and it later turned out he was Jewish. No harm done.

Now, one of the things you notice is that, aside from accident cases, more people seem to pass on around 11 o'clock at night and 5 A.M. than at any other times. Therefore, when you have the duty, which is every other day, you don't go to bed until midnight. Then they call you at 3 A.M. It's 20 below. You've got to get up, dressed, try to start the car, and your reaction isn't: "Oh, soul! Oh, God!" It's more like: "Oh, damn!"

You get over to the hospital and you have your prayers—the hope that they're at home with the risen Christ—but now you've been doing this for a while, and it's 3:30 in the morning and you've got to be up again at 6. So your attitude is really one of zap-and-get-out, until you stop and realize that a callus has grown, and you've lost respect for the person.

What it comes down to, Eddie, is that routine is the killer of all human delights. When that call comes at 3 o'clock in the morning and you're thinking that "Oh, damn!" what you've got to say to yourself is: "Look, boy, you signed up for it. Get moving."

This is going to be my sixth year of the chaplaincy, though, and it's going to be my last, because it's really for when you're younger. You've got a partner, so you're only on every other day, but let's say it's your day on. You're up at 6. You shower, shave, dash to the church, grab your pyx—the Communion container—and you load up with seventy pieces of bread. You get in your car, and you're at the hospital by 6:30. You've got your list, from the previous day's cards, but you check the mailbox for any additions. Then you start on the eighth floor, and you work down.

It's only the bread, no wine, because of the possibility of the spread of disease from a common vessel. If they're awake fine, and if they're not, you awaken them. You've got to keep moving, and if you stopped before each one and said, "Behold the Lamb . . ." You'd never get done. So you say: "The Body of Christ." They say: "Amen." You place it on the tongue, trying not to touch them because you can't wash after every one, like a nurse or a doctor, and you move on. If all goes well you're finished by 7:45.

Now you're back in the car, and you dash back to the church. You say the 8:15 Mass, and then you have breakfast. After that you go to your room, and right then I like to start my Breviary, the daily offices and prayers, because if you leave it for the last thing in the day you're liable to fall asleep. It takes from forty-five minutes to an hour, and you can do it in parts, but you like to get it done and out of the way because some days you just become too pressed, and then you never get it finished. In the old days, if you skipped it, it used to bind you in sin, because you were taught that if you weren't praying you weren't communicating with God, and you'd lost your taste for spiritual things. It's still obligatory, but now it's more of an individual conscience thing, although there are still many priests who, if they missed it, would go out and dig up Central Avenue. I try to do it because I want to, but here again you're faced with that routine and, as I say, you're often forced to adjust.

Let's say, anyway, that it's 11 o'clock now, and you've got an hour of counseling. It may be a young couple, it may be a parish kid or it may be a nurse. Maybe she's a student nurse who just slashed her wrist, because it's getting toward the end of the year and she's been through a lot—seen things she never had any concept of before—and the old head nurse, power-hungry and frustrated, has decided, for some reason, to take it out on this girl and has put too much pressure on. Maybe it's a nurse in the E.R. who's been accused by an intern there of being responsible for the death of an old man who was left alone in one of the booths, and who stabbed himself with a scalpel. Actually she's innocent. Two detectives have questioned her and, in fact, it was the intern who left the old man unattended, but that's not her real difficulty. The incident just brought her basic problem to a head.

The basic problem that so many of these young nurses, like this one, have is that they're women meeting tragedy daily, and where they'd like to cry they have to stuff their feelings. They're having a hard time with the professional role. It tears them up, even as it does priests, and so, instead of finding other outlets, they get to drinking a lot, smoking pot and engaging in promiscuous sex.

Now you finish this counseling session, and sometimes it runs into your lunch hour, and it takes a lot out of a man. After lunch you go over to the hospital again, as I said, and you pick up your intake cards and you start at the top floor and you work down.

Let's say you've got fifty intake cards that day, and you'd like to get through all of them in the afternoon, so here again it's first things first. You'd like to give all of them all the time they want, but you've got to keep pushing on. With long-term patients you get to know the family. You meet the boy friend, and sometimes you end up doing marriages, which is all pleasant and rewarding, but your place is where the deepest pain is.

The deepest pain, of course, is with the terminally ill. As the psychologists say, we deny death in our culture—look at your wakes—so when faced with death the patient, as they put it, goes through the five phases of dying—denial, anger, bargaining, depression and, finally, acceptance. It's the priest's job, my job, to try to help get the patient from anger to acceptance, and it's heartbreaking.

There's this internationally known doctor—Dr. Elisabeth Kubler Ross—and she's done a real study on these phases of dying, and the more I see of it the more I agree with her. Take the first phase, denial. People know that everyone has to die some day, but they keep clinging to this hope that it's not going to happen to them. A couple of years ago a university—I forget which one—put in a course on the acceptance of dying. After all the intellectual exercising during the course, someone asked the 'professor—the psychologist—what defense he himself employed against the inevitability of his own death and he said: "The same defense as everyone else. It's not going to happen to me."

So there's the denial phase—"not me"—and although the family knows, the patient is denying it, so there's no comfort for anyone there. Then comes the anger phase—"Why me?" The patient is angry at God, at the hospital, at the nurses, at everyone. In the old days the patient used to die at home, with his loved ones around him, but now he's dying in this strange place, surrounded by strangers. Out in the hall he hears visitors, and even hospital personnel, laughing. If he's watching television he sees some woman, on a commercial, bragging about how healthy she and her family are because they take some patent medicine.

Cruel? Exactly, and just because it's unintentional doesn't make it any less cruel, so while they're in that anger phase what you do—at least, what I do—is go along with it. I tell them I would be angry, too, and that their anger is human and natural, and let's get it all out.

Next comes that bargaining phase. Maybe if they're nice to everyone—nurses, orderlies, the family, everyone—and if they genuinely regret their sins and become better Catholics they might live longer. Then comes the stage when they realize that this isn't going to work, that they're going to die anyway, and that's when the stage of depression sets in. That's the toughest phase, because now they know, and you don't try to cheer them up. What are you going to do? When they cry you let them cry, because they have to go through this before they come to the last phase of acceptance.

So, as I said, you've got your fifty intake cards that day, and while you're with one patient who needs you, you know that in the next room, or down the hall or on the next floor, there's another who needs you just as much. With that you get a call from the E.R. that a badly injured accident victim has just been brought in, or if it's a multiple car accident, there may be several victims.

I remember the war again now, and what it did for me. We were flying these long twelve-hour patrols over the China Straits in those single-tail B-24s—Privateers—and I was a reconnaissance man and turret gunner and part-time cook. We had this two-burner electric stove, and we used to cook steaks and French fries and make coffee. We had this one officer who kept complaining that his steaks were too tough, and finally he sent the order back: "I want them tenderized." Now, in the after part of the plane there was this corrugated deck, so we put the steaks on the deck and we jumped up and down on them with our GI boots, and the word came back: "Delicious."

Anyway, about 10 o'clock one morning I'd jumped up and down on the steaks, and I had them on the burner when all of a sudden we're getting fired on. We had come down out of the overcast to 500 feet to look over something, and three enemy landing craft turned their 50s right on us. I remember thinking to yank those steaks off that burner, before I jumped into the side turret and got my twin-50s going until, thank God, we were able to get back into the overcast.

So I learned to scramble, and it comes in handy. If you've got fifty intake cards you hope to finish them, if there are no emergencies, in two-and-a-half or three hours, because you've also got the chaplaincy of the School of Nursing and the School of Medicine, and at 4 o'clock you have conferences at one place or the other. By 5:30 you should be back at the rectory, so that you can eat and jaw for an hour, and then it's back to the hospital to finish the cards you didn't get to and pick up the new ones. Today I managed to finish them all, except a new one I picked up tonight, and I didn't feel I should see him immediately anyway. He's made two attempts to take his own life—he's a jockey, incidentally, whose name I remember from reading the sports pages—and I want to talk to Dr. Stillman, the psychiatrist who's on the case, before I see him.

Now, what makes or breaks this job is your partner, because this can be a goof-off job if you want to make it that, and in all honesty there are some priests I just wouldn't want to work with. With a good partner you can swap. Say you're running a dance in the parish, or he's got a youth meeting, so the one or the other can take the hospital duty that night. Right now I've been on five days straight, taking his two days so he can get away, and when the weather gets nice in the spring he'll do the same for me.

Out of the three partners I've had on two tours, two have been great and one was a real donkey. He was one of what we call the FBI—the Foreign Born Irish. That's right. They come out of the farm country of Ireland, where there's a surplus of priests, so they decide to "come to the colonies" to help us out.

This was a handsome dude, about thirty-two, with a little touch of gray in his hair, beautiful teeth and a very charming manner. He was also a good golfer—he shot in the 70s—and he hadn't been over here long before he became an avid skier, too. Now, I like to play a little golf myself, when I can find the time, but he made the time. I'd come on for my day, and I'd inherit half, or more, of his intake cards that he hadn't covered, and I'd have to add those to mine.

One afternoon, for example, he was out on the golf course, and he happened to be playing with some people from the parish, so I heard about it later. He's out there, and his beeper starts sounding. It beeps, and it beeps and it beeps, but he doesn't pay any attention to it. What had happened was, a DOA had come in—a young man killed in an auto crash. The family was devout Catholic, and they wanted a priest, and when they couldn't get one they called the rectory. I was exhausted from the night before—I'd had three calls to the E.R.—and I'd fallen asleep in my chair reading the Breviary, so I went.

Then, one night, he had the duty, and he and I were sitting in the rectory and watching a football game—it was Pittsburgh versus somebody—when the phone rang for him. It was a nurse calling from the gynecology wing. There was this Catholic woman who already had six children, and the problem was that they wanted to tie off her tubes—do a tubal ligation. She wanted to follow the advice of the doctors, but as a Catholic she was very troubled over the moral problem.

I heard him say: "Is she dying?" Later I found out that the nurse explained that she wasn't dying, but that she was very disturbed about this moral question. Then I heard him say: "It'll keep until morning."

So I went over instead, and as the nurse had said, the woman was in great distress. The Church's position is that you must not knowingly mutilate a healthy organ, and we discussed the alternatives—birth control pills, the diaphragm, etc. I left her to discuss it with her husband and to pray over it—as it turned out she had the tubes tied, anyway—and I went back to the rectory.

There was the good Father, with his feet up, the game almost over now, and when he didn't even look up and ask me what had happened I blew. Now, you're taught to be charitable, and priests find it hard to confront each other, but I just let it all out. I said: "I've had it. I'm sick of it. I've been taking the duty day after day, and if you're not out on the golf course or sliding down some mountain in the winter you're just sitting here on your prat. One of us has to go, so if you don't do it, I'm going to the Personnel Board or to the Bishop, if I have to, and apply for transfer."

He just said: "I'll do it." That was all, and as it turned out he wasn't long for the collar anyway. He married a rich gal he'd met at the golf club, and since then they've been divorced and the last I heard he's a car salesman.

There's some good in everything, though, and a clown like that makes you feel better about yourself by comparison. If you're honest you're doubting yourself—a lot at first, as I said —and you ask yourself if you're really in this to serve God, or only to serve yourself. What difference does it make? You shouldn't be in it if serving God doesn't serve you, too.

With me it came on during the war, and right after it, but not as any big revelation. Not being Catholic you wouldn't know it, but we weren't any more than a reasonably religious family and nobody suspected that one of us would go into the priesthood. Certainly the folks didn't push me into it, and the night I told them, after I came back from the war, that I was thinking about the seminary Mom looked at me and said: "I don't believe it. You?"

My mom? She's been gone now five years, and my dad went a year after her. He drove that bakery truck, and he never owned more than one suit of clothes at a time in his life. As you know, we never owned a car, and do you remember Dr. Tom Hunter, who had his office for a while down at the end of our street? Well, he's running the E.R. now—that's right—and he didn't have big cars, but I guess he put a lot of miles on them, because every year or so he'd have a new Ford, and I'd envy that. Whatever the family had, though, we shared. All four of us kids shared everything equally, including the altar boy duty when you turned twelve. You didn't question it, because you didn't have any choice. Besides, you wanted to do it because everybody else was doing it at that age, and it was like making the team and getting the uniform and it was an honor to serve Mass. That's the way it is the first year or so, and then you have to get up at 6 A.M. for 7 o'clock Mass, and it's freezing out and you have to walk over a mile, and meanwhile you've just got your letter in baseball, with a different uniform, and you start thinking of this as kid's stuff. By now you're fifteen, though, and there's a new kid ready to move in, so you're out.

So, I never gave much thought about the priesthood. As you know, I'd always had this speech impediment, anyway, which used to bother me when I was nervous or excited, and that still comes on a little when I'm very tired or, on occasion, like the night I let the good Father have it. Actually, it didn't seem like too much of a handicap while I was growing up, because all you kids in the neighborhood and in school knew me and sort of took it for granted. I don't think it was all that bad, either, until I got in the Navy, where I was away from home for the first time and with a lot of strangers and nervous. Then it became worse, and they used to call me "Machine Gun" Shea and "Ack-Ack." So I used to laugh, but it hurt, and it gave me this feeling of real inferiority.

At the same time, we had this great Navy chaplain at Naha. You probably wouldn't remember this, but one summer, when I was sixteen, I was a junior counsellor at the diocesan boys' camp, and it was staffed by seminarians. They were real good guys—the kind we don't seem to be getting enough of any more because we're getting too many of the arty types and the ones with sexual fears and the ones whose mothers are pushing them in. Anyway, I might have considered the seminary while I was in that camp, but it really hit me while I was having that adjustment problem in the Navy and we had this hero chaplain. He was a great big, six-foot-three, good-looking but tough Irishman, who'd played tackle for Georgetown on a football scholarship, and he was a legitimate hero. In World War II he'd been cited for heroism on the beach at Guadalcanal during the landings. During the shelling of a medical evacuation station, while a lot of the other personnel had run for cover, he'd thrown himself on top of a badly wounded GI, and he'd been wounded himself in the back.

The truth is, I didn't know him too well, because he was very popular and I was so shy that I didn't want to push myself on him, but he became for me the image of what a priest should be. Of course, I could never be like him, but the seminary, and the priesthood if I made it, could be a place where I could find understanding and, if I found it myself, bring it to others.

You see, we're brought up in our culture to idolize the champions—the champion athlete, the champion business executive, the champion scientist, or astronaut, or whatever. As a result, our culture leads most of us to have a poor image of ourselves. The Church is no different, because you're brought up in it to ascribe to a holiness that's beyond the human person, and so you have your doubts about your worthiness. In fact, that's the way they plot it. In the seminary, for example, they stretch the six-year course to eight years. Do you know why? To give you the chance to quit.

I remember we had this Irish priest from Brooklyn, who taught canon law and who talked out of the side of his mouth just like Jim Braddock, the former heavyweight champion. One night I happened to see Jim Braddock interviewed on television, and all I could think of was Father Mahaffey. Anyway, one day several of us brought up the subject of fitness, or worthiness, and I'll never forget Father Mahaffey. "Why, for chrissake!" he said. "You've got St. Rocco. You've got St. Philomena. You've got St. Anthony. Let's be honest. You know damn well that the average Irish peasant is better than any of them. Give it a shot for a year. At least it will teach you how to save your own souls."

Then I had this older scripture scholar. I had actually put off my orders, and I was about to leave the seminary when I went to see him.

"Sit down," he said. "I've been expecting you, and I know why you're here."

He handed me the Bible, and he told me to open it to Jeremiah. Jeremiah had a speech impediment, and he told the Lord he was unable to speak and the Lord put His words in his mouth.

"Give it a chance," Father Hess said to me. "You're like so many. You're on the edge of the cliff, and you're afraid to jump. Christ is at the bottom with his arms open. Take the risk."

So I jumped. I also took speech therapy, five days a week for three months, learning to breathe properly, practicing the sounds, reading poetry out loud, and that and the security I get from the collar did it.

What have I got to be insecure about? I'm working with two of the greatest priests in the world. They'd give their pay away, and nobody's trying to be champion. We don't sweat the power—the Bishop or anybody—because we're the poorest parish in the diocese, so who can hurt us? We'll never wear the red anyway, and if you don't aspire to rank, the priesthood can be the greatest job in the world. As I say, what have you got to worry about?

XVII

ARNOLD HENKEN

Of all the days I've had here by now today was the weirdest one. You know? I mean when I came on at 7 o'clock it was actually 6:53, because when I got up I was still like so tired that I forgot to put on my watch and some guy on the bus said the bus was late so I like half ran two blocks when I didn't have to. That was stupid—I mean starting with the guy on the bus—but, anyway, when I came in, the E.R. was like empty. All the booths down both sides of the room were empty, except booth 2, and in the nursing station the three nurses were just sitting there with their sweaters on already and their handbags in their laps. Only Dr. Walter Ralls—he's this black surgical resident—was writing on a chart, and it was so quiet that I thought maybe I should whisper.

"Good morning," I said.

"Hello," one of the nurses said.

"What's happening?" I said.

"Nothing," she said.

"Oh," I said.

With that Miss Palmer and Kay Conley came in, carrying their sweaters and handbags, so I thought I would check to see what stretchers might have to be made up clean in what booths. First, though, I thought I would just see who was in booth 2, and when I walked over there I was really surprised. There was this male patient lying there with a sheet over him, and his bare feet were sticking out of the bottom of the sheet and twitching like crazy, and he had a wrapped tongue depressor in his mouth and he was groaning. What really surprised me, though, was that there were two State troopers sitting there in the booth with him, these two great big guys with their gunbelts on and their big hats.

"Good morning," I said.

"Right," one of them said.

"Is this patient under arrest?" I said.

"Right," the same one said.

"But why is he under arrest?" I said.

"Because," the same one said, "we've got a paper duly signed and authorizing us to arrest him."

"Oh," I said.

"Right," he said.

So I walked out of there then, and I had to make up the stretchers in booth 5 and booth 9. When I finished that I went back to the nursing station, and Dr. Ralls was just sitting there and not doing anything so I thought I would ask him about the patient in booth 2.

"He had a seizure while they were transporting him," he said. "I'm waiting for the tests."

"But why did they arrest him?" I said. "What did he do?"

"I don't know," Dr. Ralls said. "He probably double-parked."

"Well, if he double-parked," I said, "why don't they have him in handcuffs?"

"You're absolutely right, Arnold," Dr. Ralls said. "He should undoubtedly be in handcuffs."

"Look over there now," I said.

You can look right across from the nursing station into booth 2, and the two State troopers were standing up now. One of them—the same one—had taken off his hat, and he had put it on the bare feet of the patient. Now, while the patient's bare feet were shaking under the big hat, the big hat was shaking, too, and the two State troopers were just standing there and watching it. I mean *that* was weird.

"Boys and their toys," Dr. Ralls said. "Boys and their toys."

So I was just going to check Minor Ops then when these two black guys, like about thirty years of age, came in. The first one, who was kind of stocky, was sort of leading the second one. The second one, who was kind of tall and thin, was holding this bloody handkerchief on his forehead over his left eye, and there was like old blood down the front of his T-shirt.

"May I help you?" Miss Palmer said.

"Not me," the first one said. "Him."

"What happened, sir?" Miss Palmer said, walking around the counter so she could look at him.

"I don't know," the thin one with the cut said. "I just got cut."

"So let me take a look," Miss Palmer said, but when she reached up to lift the bloody handkerchief this thin one pulled his head back.

"Don't touch that," he said. "It's stuck."

"Come on, Harland," the other one said to him. "Let the nurse look at the cut."

"What do you mean, let the nurse look at the cut?" this Harland said. "It ain't your cut. It's my cut."

"Come on now," Miss Palmer said. "I just want to look at it so I can inform the doctor."

"So let the doctor look at it," this Harland said, holding his head back. "Then the doctor can inform himself."

"Dr. Ralls?" Miss Palmer said.

"Right," Doctor Ralls said, walking up. "Let me see this."

"Wait a minute," this Harland said, looking at Dr. Ralls. "You a doctor?"

"That's right," Dr. Ralls said.

"You sure?" this Harland said.

"I'm sure," Dr. Ralls said. "Come on now."

"Wait a minute," this Harland said. "How long you been a doctor?"

"A long time," Dr. Ralls said, although of course he's only been a doctor for less than two years. "Let me look at this now."

"Well, all right," this Harland said, "as long as you been a doctor a long time."

"Now," Dr. Ralls said, and when he lifted one corner of the handkerchief this Harland let out this yelp like, and he pulled back again.

"Man," he said, "don't do that! That hurt!"

"Let's take him into Minor Ops," Dr. Ralls said to Miss

Palmer, "and clean him up. I'll be there in a couple of minutes."

"Take me into where?" this Harland said.

"Just into this next room here," Miss Palmer said. "Kay? And Arnold, will you go along, too?"

"Wait a minute," this Harland said. "What kinda room is that room?"

"It's just another room," Miss Palmer said, "where the doctor can fix your cut."

"It's just another room?" this Harland said. "What's the name of this other room? I heard that doctor give a name to that room."

"It's Minor Ops," Miss Palmer said. "Come on now . . ."

"Oh, no," this Harland said. "I ain't goin' in no room named Minor Ops. I ain't . . ."

"All right, now," Dr. Ralls said, and he'd walked back. "You're either going to that room and do what we say so that we can fix that cut, or you're going home where that cut will become infected and you'll be a very sick man. Now cut this out."

"Yeah, Harland," his friend said. "You do what the doctor says."

"Yeah," this Harland said, looking at his friend. "Don't you tell me what to do, too. It ain't your cut. It's my cut."

So, anyway, Kay Conley and I took this Harland into Minor Ops, and I guess Miss Palmer told his friend to wait outside. Anne Doucette, who's another nurse, had the duty in Minor Ops, so while Kay Conley was getting the handkerchief off this Harland and cleaning up around the cut and Anne Doucette was taking his personal history, I saw I should make up the other two stretchers. While I was doing that, though, I could hear all of it.

"Were you in the service?" Anne Doucette was saying.

"Who, me?" this Harland said.

"Yes," Anne Doucette said. "You."

"What service?" this Harland said.

"How do I know what service?" Doucette said. "Army? Navy? Marines? Air Force?"

"Nope," this Harland said, and then he started to holler: "What's that? What's that? What you doin'?"

"It's nothing," Kay Conley said. "It's just soap and water, because I have to clean up around the cut."

"It's just soap and water?" this Harlan said. "Then how come it burn?"

"Because you've got a cut," Conley said, "and it's my job to clean it up."

"I know I got a cut," this Harland said. "It's my cut."

"Who's your nearest relative?" Doucette said.

"I ain't got no nearest relative," this Harland said.

"A sister? A brother? A cousin? An aunt?" Doucette said.

"I told you I ain't got no nearest relative," this Harland said. "They all far away."

"I don't care how far away they are," Doucette said.

"They in South Carolina," this Harland said.

"Have you got a mother?" Doucette said.

"She ain't near, either," this Harland said. "She in South Carolina, too."

By then I was finished making up the other two stretchers, and I figured that I didn't want to hear any more of this so I thought I would just leave. Just as I was walking out of Minor Ops, though, Dr. Ralls came in.

"Wait a minute, Arnold," he said. "Unless you've got something else that's important we may need your help here. Okay?"

"Sure," I said. "Okay."

So I followed Dr. Ralls back in. When we got over to the stretcher this Harland was lying there, but he and Kay Conley were having a kind of a hassle.

"But I told you not to put your hand up there," Conley was saying. "I just cleaned it."

"But I did it," this Harland was saying. "I just put my dirty finger up there, so you all better clean it again."

"I did clean it," Conley was saying.

"So you all better clean it again," this Harland said. "It's your job. You said that."

"I'll take that," Dr. Ralls said.

"Yeah," this Harland said. "Let the doctor take that."

293

"So tell me something," Dr. Ralls said to this Harland. "How'd you get this cut?"

"I don't know," this Harland said.

"Of course you know," Dr. Ralls said, swabbing around the cut again. "When did this happen?"

"Last night," this Harland said. "I don't remember. Maybe this mornin'."

"And what happened?" Dr. Ralls said.

"Nothin'," this Harland said. "I was just walkin' by this alley, and somethin' came out of there—a brick or bottle or birdshot or somethin'."

"Boys and their toys," Dr. Ralls said. "Boys and their toys."

"What?" this Harland said.

"No birdshot," Dr. Ralls said. "He needs a tetanus shot."

"A what?" this Harland said, starting to sit up. "I don't want no shot."

"Now lie down," Dr. Ralls said. "You're a man, aren't you? Are you a man?"

"Yeah," this Harland said. "I'm a man."

"Then act like a man," Dr. Ralls said. "Do you hear me?"

"Yeah, Doc," this Harland said, lying down again. "That's right. I'll act like a man, Doc."

"Good," Dr. Ralls said, "and we're going to take your shoes off. Okay?"

"Yeah," this Harland said. "I'm actin' like a man, but don't throw them shoes away, because when you're all done fixin' me I'm gonna walk right outa here, right?"

"Right," Dr. Ralls said, "like a man."

"Then what's she stickin' me for now?" this Harland said. "What's she stickin' in my arm?"

"She's not sticking anything in your arm," Dr. Ralls said. "The nurse is just taking your blood pressure."

"Good," this Harland said. "What that pressure say?"

"It's good," Doucette said.

"You see that?" this Harland said. "I got good pressure."

"Excuse me, Doctor," Gloria Miller said, and she's the clerk. "I notified the police, and they want to know how many stitches you're going to put in."

"I have no idea," Dr. Ralls said.

"How many what?" this Harland said, and this time he sat right up. "I don't want no stitches. I don't like them needles. Ain't nobody sewin' me."

When he sat up, of course, the towels that Conley had draped around the cut fell off. I could see that there was this big cut over the eye and another one, but not big, under the eye like on the cheekbone.

"Now you lie down!" Dr. Ralls said to him, getting mad.

"I don't want no stitches," this Harland said. "I want my shoes back."

"You listen to me!" Dr. Ralls said, and I went around and helped him put this Harland down again. "You're acting like a child. I thought you told me you're a man!"

"Yeah, I'm a man," this Harland said. "I'm a man."

"Then I thought you told me you'd act like a man," Dr. Ralls said.

"Yeah, that's right, Doc," this Harland said. "I told you I'd act like a man, so I'll act like a man."

"Good," Dr. Ralls said, "so I'm just going to put a little dressing on here for the moment."

"Right, Doc," this Harland said. "You just put a little dressing on there for the moment. That's good, Doc."

So Dr. Ralls put this light dressing on the cut over the eye, and then he put another one on the small cut under the eye. Then he motioned to Kay Conley and me, and he walked over to the sink to wash his hands.

"We'd better X-ray him first," he said. "The brick, or whatever it was, may have done some bone damage. I'm going up to get a cup of coffee."

Dr. Ralls left then, so Conley and I went over to the patient. I went around to the head of the stretcher, and I started to push it out.

"Wait a minute!" this Harland said, sitting up again. "Where you takin' me?"

"Now you relax," Conley said. "You just lie down, because all we're going to do is take you to have some pictures taken."

"Some pictures taken?" this Harland said. "I don't want no

pictures taken. What do you want to take pictures for anyway?"

"So the doctor can assess the damage," Conley said.

"So the doctor can assess the damage?" this Harland said. "The doctor can look at the damage. He don't have to assess the damage. I don't want no pictures taken."

"Now, stop this," Conley said. "It doesn't hurt. You won't feel a thing. Haven't you ever had your picture taken?"

"Yeah," this Harland said. "I had my picture taken. You sure that's all you're gonna do, just have my picture taken?"

"That's all," Conley said.

This Harland lay back down then, and I wheeled him out with Conley like walking ahead of us. When we got to X ray, though, and Conley pushed the door open, this Harland sat up again, and when he saw the X-ray table and that equipment he not only sat up but he got right off the stretcher before I could grab him.

"Oh, no!" he said. "I ain't goin' in any room like that! I'm goin' home! I want my shoes back!"

"Now, you look," Conley was saying. "You . . ."

"I already looked," this Harland said. "I'm goin' home. I'm gonna leave this hospital. I want my shoes back."

It was some weird scene. I mean there were like three or four other patients and their families around then, and they were like all staring while this Harland was hollering about his shoes and going home. Then Miss Palmer came over, but she couldn't quiet him down, either.

"All right, Arnold," she said finally. "Go get his shoes."

"Yeah," this Harland said. "Go get my shoes."

So I went to get his shoes, and at first I couldn't find them where I put them when I took them off, and then I found them over in a corner. By the time I got back, Miss Palmer had brought one of those release forms that a patient or his family have to sign if he's leaving against the advice of a doctor.

"Now you'll have to read that carefully," she was saying.

"Yeah, I'm readin' it," this Harland was saying. "Certify . . . advice . . . I'm readin' it . . . and there it is: Re-lease! Right there: Release! It says it right there, and now I sign it."

296

Conley gave this Harland a pen, then, and he signed the release. Then he wanted his shoes, so I gave them to him, and we got him to sit on the stretcher and I helped him put them on. Meanwhile Dr. Hunter had come over, and he'd just come on duty and didn't know what was going on, so Miss Palmer was explaining it to him.

"Now just a minute," Dr. Hunter said then to this Harland. "You don't want to do anything foolish like this."

"Yes, I do," this Harland said. "Ain't nobody gonna sew me up in no room like that. It says right on that paper: re-lease! I got my re-lease."

I didn't know it, but I guess Miss Palmer must have called upstairs to the coffee shop for Dr. Ralls, or had him paged, because right then he came walking up.

"What's going on here?" he said to this Harland. "What do you think you're doing?"

"What do I think I'm doin'?" this Harland said. "I'm doin' my re-lease. That's what I'm doin'."

"What are you talking about?" Dr. Ralls said.

"My re-lease," this Harland said. "It's right there on that piece of paper that that nurse got and that I signed. I got my re-lease, and I'm goin' home."

"Hold it," Dr. Ralls said. "Just hold it now. You're a man, right? And I'm a man, right? So you and I are just going to rap a little, man to man, right?"

"I don't wanta rap," this Harland said.

"Now, listen," Dr. Ralls said. "Nobody is going to touch you. We're just going to talk, and after we talk if you still want to go home you can go home. Right?"

"I don't know," this Harland said.

"Of course you do," Dr. Ralls said. "You're a man who knows what's right and what's wrong, so we're just going to have a little talk."

With that everybody else just sort of like drifted away, like they were figuring that Dr. Ralls being black and this Harland being black they would let them have their own thing. I don't know that they were actually figuring that, but it reminded me of the other day when this little guy from the business office who wears the garters and that Dr. Mabry calls "Money Hooks" was trying to get some information from this patient who was lying on a stretcher outside the X-ray room. This patient was a young sort of colored guy from Puerto Rico, or maybe from some South American country, and I didn't hear what was going on, but when I came up Dr. Ralls was walking by and this Money Hooks called him over.

"Excuse me, Doctor," he said, "but can you tell me what he's saying?"

"What he's saying?" Dr. Ralls said, and then he turned to the patient and he said: "What are you saying?"

With that this patient let out this long string of Spanish. I mean he really let it out, and Dr. Ralls listened to it for about five seconds, and then he turned back to this Money Hooks and he said: "How the hell would I know what he's saying? I don't speak Spanish."

"Oh," this Money Hooks said.

Then Dr. Ralls turned away from this Money Hooks and started to walk away, and he saw me.

"He thinks we have our own tribal language," he said, shaking his head. "It's ridiculous."

Anyway, when everybody else sort of left Dr. Ralls and this Harland alone now, I sort of moved away, too. I just moved a few feet away, though, and turned sort of sideways like I wasn't paying attention, but so that I could still hear what Dr. Ralls might tell this Harland to try to convince him. I mean I was really interested.

Actually I couldn't hear all of it, but I could hear Dr. Ralls explaining again that it was a deep cut and that it would become infected and that then this Harland would become very ill. I could hear this Harland saying that he wasn't sure he'd become ill, and then Dr. Ralls argued with him some more.

"Look," Dr. Ralls said, finally. "You haven't even seen the cut. Let's go over here and find a mirror so you can see it. Right?"

"I don't know," this Harland said. "I don't know that I wanta see it."

"Sure you do," Dr. Ralls said. "If you go home you're going to have to see it, and you're a man, right?"

"Yeah, I'm a man," this Harland said.

"So let's just walk over here then, and look at that cut," Dr. Ralls said. "Like a man, right?"

"Yeah," this Harland said. "Like a man, right."

There are these two johns between booth 6 and the Poison Control Room, and the door to the ladies' john was open so Dr. Ralls took this Harland in there. When I got there they were standing in front of the washbasin, and this Harland was looking at himself in the mirror.

"Man," he said.

"Now I'm just going to take this bandage off the big cut," Dr. Ralls said. "All right?"

"Yeah," this Harland said. "Go ahead. Snatch it off."

"And you take a good look," Dr. Ralls said. "Okay?"

"Okay," this Harland said. "You just snatch that bandage off."

Dr. Ralls didn't actually snatch it off. He just sort of quickly peeled it back, and when he did this Harland let out this noise.

"Woo-ee!" he said. "Man! Look at that cut! Look at that big cut! It's bleedin' man! What you gonna do about that big cut? You gotta do somethin' about that big cut!"

"I know," Dr. Ralls said, putting the bandage back. "We're going to close it."

"You gotta close that cut, man," this Harland said.

"Right," Dr. Ralls said, "so let's just go back and we'll do it."

"Wait a minute," this Harland said. "Go back where? I ain't goin' back to that other room."

"What other room?" Dr. Ralls said.

"That picture-takin' room," this Harland said. "Where they take the pictures. I don't want no pictures."

"Okay," Dr. Ralls said. "No pictures. We'll just go back and close the cut. Right?"

"Right," this Harland said.

So Dr. Ralls took this Harland back to Minor Ops. At first this Harland didn't want to lie down again, but finally Dr. Ralls got him to lie down, and I took off his shoes again.

"Now, wait a minute," this Harland said, all of a sudden sitting up again. "What you puttin' on those gloves for?"

"Because I've got to clean the wound again, and then close it," Dr. Ralls said. "Now listen. Are you going to act like a man?"

"Yeah, I'm actin' like a man," this Harland said, lying down again. "Go ahead. You said you're gonna clean it up, so clean it up. Get it over with."

So Dr. Ralls finished cleaning up around the two cuts, and then he started to put some sterile towels above the eye and below it.

"Wait a minute," this Harland said. "What you doin' now?"

"I'm draping the area with towels," Dr. Ralls said, "to keep it clean."

"That's good," this Harland said. "Then what you gonna do?"

"Then I'm gonna give you a shot," Dr. Ralls said.

"Oh, no!" this Harland said, and he sat up again, and naturally the sterile towels fell off again. "I don't want no shot. I'm scared of them needles, so I don't want no shot."

"Listen to me!" Dr. Ralls was sort of hollering now, and he was mad. "You lie right down! Do you hear me?"

"Yeah. Yeah," this Harland said. "I hear you, but wait a minute. Just wait a minute, and just let me explain somethin'. I just want to explain. Okay, if I just explain?"

"All right," Dr. Ralls said. "Hurry up and explain."

"You see, Doc," this Harland said, "I'm scared of them needles. Right? Okay. Then if I'm scared of them needles, and you stick me with one of them needles, I might just jump right up. Right? So what I think is, that instead of lyin' down, I should just sit up, and then when you stick me with one of them needles I wouldn't have to jump right up. Right?"

"Wrong," Dr. Ralls said, "and you listen to me for the last time. You lie down, and if you don't stay down we're going to strap you down and . . ."

"I don't want no straps," this Harland said, lying down. "Don't strap me down. I'll stay down."

"You'd better," Dr. Ralls said, "and that was the last warning. Do you understand?"

"Yeah. I understand," this Harland said, "but if that was the last warning, then maybe you'd better give me some of that stuff."

"Some of that what?" Dr. Ralls said.

"To put me to sleep," this Harland said. "I wake up, and it be all over."

"Let's have some more clean towels," Dr. Ralls said to Anne Doucette.

"What's that?" this Harland said.

"We can't put you to sleep for a little thing like this," Dr. Ralls said. "I'm just going to give you a shot, that you'll hardly feel, to anesthetize the area, and after that it won't hurt at all. That's the way it's got to be done, so unless you want to be strapped down, you'd better make up your mind to take it like a man."

"Yeah," this Harland said. "I make up my mind to take it like a man. Go ahead, Doc."

"Now you'll feel this just a little," Dr. Ralls said, putting the hypodermic needle in. "Right now you can feel it. Right now, and now."

"Yeah, I feel it," this Harland said. "I feel that, but I'm takin' it like a man. Right, Doc?"

"Right," Dr. Ralls said, and then he said to Doucette: "Let me have some catgut, 4-o plain, please, and I'll need some 6-o silk, too."

"What?" this Harland said. "What you say you need?"

"Nothing," Dr. Ralls said. "I was just talking to the nurse."

"The nurse?" this Harland said. "What's this nurse's name?"

"Anne," Dr. Ralls said.

"Anne?" this Harland said. "That your name, nurse?"

"That's right," Doucette said.

"Good," this Harland said.

While they were talking like that I put the side rails up on the stretcher, and this Harland was holding on now with both his hands on the left rail.

"Now we'll just take your right hand off here," Doucette said to him, "and put it over on this other rail. Then you can hold onto both sides. Okay?"

"Yeah," this Harland said, "'cause I can't see nothin' lyin' here, but I gotta act like a man."

"That's right," Dr. Ralls said.

When this Harland had hold of the other rail now, Doucette took some of this like cloth strapping that we have and she wrapped it around his right wrist. Then she left some like slack in it, and she started to wrap it around the rail on that side.

"Wait a minute," this Harland said. "What you doin' with my wrist?"

"I'm just wrapping it," Doucette said, "so you won't bruise it against the rail."

"Oh," this Harland said. "That's good, so I don't bruise it. I already got a cut."

I thought that was sort of cool—you know?—Doucette telling him that when she was really tying his wrist to the rail in case he should try to reach up while Dr. Ralls would be sewing him. Then Doucette passed the cloth strapping to me under the stretcher, and I wrapped the other wrist and tied it to that side with some slack.

"That you, Anne?" this Harland said, while I was doing that. "That you wrappin' that other wrist over there?"

"That's right," Doucette said.

"I can't see nothin', lyin' here," this Harland said. "With these towels on I can't hardly hear nothin', either, and it sound like you over here when you over there."

"I'm right here," Doucette said, and she was standing like behind me now.

"Good," this Harland said.

"Now, listen," Dr. Ralls said. "You're not going to feel anything, but if you do I want you to let me know. Okay?"

"Wait a minute," this Harland said. "You gonna start sewin' me now, Doc?"

"That's right," Dr. Ralls said, "and you're going to take it like a man, right?"

"Yeah, but wait a minute," this Harland said, and then he said: "Anne?"

"What?" Doucette said.

"I wanna hold your hand," this Harland said. "I wanna hold your little old hand."

"In a minute," Dr. Ralls said.

With that Dr. Ralls shook his head at Doucette, and he motioned to me. What he meant with this motion was that I should take this Harland's hand, so I did.

"Anne?" this Harland said, feeling my hand. "Is that your hand?"

"That's right," Doucette said. "That's my hand."

"Good," this Harland said. "I just gonna hold your little sweet hand."

I mean I was like really embarrassed. I mean it was like when somebody is going to play what they call like a practical joke on some person, and if I know about it I always feel embarrassed for that person even before they do it and I don't like to watch it. You know? Anyway, I was thinking that what if this Harland should sit up again and see that it was *my* hand he was holding.

"Just your little sweet hand," this Harland was saying, all the time like feeling my hand. "I just want to hold your little sweet hand."

When this Harland said that, Doucette started to giggle.

"Who's that?" this Harland said. "Who's making that laughin'?"

"It's me," Doucette said.

"It's you?" this Harland said. "That you, Anne? Why you makin' that laughin'?"

"I don't know," Doucette said.

"Because you're holding her hand," Dr. Ralls said.

"Your little sweet hand," this Harland said.

"Good morning, Sidney," I heard somebody else say then.

It was Dr. Mabry, who's the senior neurosurgical resident. He always calls Dr. Ralls "Sidney" for Sidney Poitier.

"Hello, Champ," Dr. Ralls said to him.

"What's going on here?" Dr. Mabry said. "You getting ready to do a transplant?"

"What?" this Harland said, and I was afraid he'd sit up again, but he didn't. "What that man say?"

"Nothing," Dr. Ralls said to this Harland, and then he said to Dr. Mabry: "Take a walk, Champ. Will you?"

"Sure," Dr. Mabry said. "Then you take two, and hit to left."

"Who's that man?" this Harland said, while Dr. Mabry was walking out.

"He's just a comedian," Dr. Ralls said. "Now you let me know if you feel anything."

"He's just a comedian," this Harland said. "What's this comedian doin' in this hospital?"

"I wonder," Dr. Ralls said. "Now, you don't feel that, do you?"

"Yeah, I feel somethin'," this Harland said, "but what's that I smell?"

"It's the fluid the suture material comes in," Dr. Ralls said. "It smells nice, doesn't it?"

"Yeah, it smell nice," this Harland said, "and just holdin' this little sweet hand I'm takin' it like a man, right?"

"Right," Dr. Ralls said. "You're doing fine."

So I just stood there then, holding this Harland's hand for the longest time, and still feeling like embarrassed. Then, to kind of close my mind to it, I decided to sort of study how Dr. Ralls was doing the sewing, because once I asked Dr. Hunter how you sew and he explained it. He explained how you hold the needle, which is curved like, with the needle holder, and how, after you stick the tip of the needle in, you turn your wrist to like follow the curve of the needle until you pull it through. Then he explained how you line up the edges of the wound, and how you don't want to tie the sutures so tight that they would like strangle the tissue. Anyway, I was really interested, and so I was watching Dr. Ralls now, and I was thinking that he was doing a real good job when this Harland started to sort of like act up again.

"That's enough!" he said. "That's enough stitches! I don't want no more stitches!"

"Now you cut that out!" Dr. Ralls said. "And you keep your head still! Don't you dare move your head while I'm stitching you!"

"Then I move my legs," this Harland said.

When he said that he started to like bicycle with his legs. All of a sudden, just lying there, he was making his feet and his legs go round and round.

"Stop it!" Dr. Ralls hollered at him. "You stop that right now!"

"I can't stop it," this Harland said, still keeping his legs going. "It's not me that's doin' it. It's my legs that's doin' it, 'cause they're nervous and they wanta go home."

"All right!" Dr. Ralls said. "We're going to strap your legs down then."

"No!" this Harland said, and he put his legs down. "Don't do that! I don't want no straps, and somebody already strapped this other wrist. Who strapped this other wrist?"

"We did," Dr. Ralls said.

"Then you unstrap it," this Harland said. "Then you all stop stickin' me with that needle, and you all let me go home."

"When I finish," Dr. Ralls said, sewing again.

"When you finish?" this Harland said. "How many more stitches you gonna put in there?"

"Four or five," Dr. Ralls said. "Just act like a man."

"Four or five?" this Harland said. "Four or five *more*?"

"Four," Dr. Ralls said. "Just four."

"Well, do it," this Harland said. "Why don't you do it?"

"I am," Dr. Ralls said.

"Now what's makin' that pressure?" this Harland said. "What's makin' that pressure on my head?"

"It's still bleeding a little," Dr. Ralls said. "I have to put some pressure on."

"Well, do it," this Harland said.

"Okay," Dr. Ralls said, and when I saw he was finished putting the bandage over it and over the other cut, I let go of this Harland's hand before he could see it was me.

"You all done?" this Harland said.

"Yes," Dr. Ralls said, helping this Harland sit up. "Now just sit here, and let me know if you feel dizzy."

"I don't feel dizzy," this Harland said. "Where are my shoes? Somebody give me my shoes."

"If the cops call again," Dr. Ralls said to Doucette, "tell them it was thirty stitches."

"Thirty stitches?" this Harland said. "You all put thirty stitches in me?"

"That's right," Dr. Ralls said. "Do you feel dizzy?"

"Thirty stitches?" this Harland said. "Just from an old rock that come out of an alley? Thirty stitches?"

"That's right," Dr. Ralls said. "Now listen to me. In five days —next Monday—you have to come in here and have the stitches removed. Do you understand that?"

"Yeah," this Harland said. "Thirty stitches."

"Now remember that," Dr. Ralls said. "Next Monday come in here again, so we can take out the stitches."

"Yeah," this Harland said. "I got thirty stitches."

Doucette asked me, then, if I would check this Harland out. She gave me the copies from the chart and I went around the stretcher and I helped this Harland finish putting on his shoes. Then I took this Harland by the elbow, and I walked him out the side door into the hall. When we got out into the hall I started to lead him to the business office that they have there, but he pulled his elbow away.

"Wait a minute," he said. "Where you takin' me?"

"To the business office," I said.

"To the business office?" this Harland said. "What for?"

"So you can check out," I said. "You have to go to the business office before you can check out."

"I have to find my friend first," this Harland said.

"You have to go to the business office first," I said. "Then you can find your friend."

"Okay," this Harland said. "Then take me to this business office."

When we got to the business office I could see through the glass over the counter that this Money Hooks was in there. He was like checking over some papers, and so we just sort of stood there waiting for him to look up.

"Tell me somethin'," this Harland said to me. "You ain't no doctor."

"No, sir," I said.

"If you ain't no doctor," he said, "what's your job here?"

"I'm an orderly," I said.

"You an orderly?" this Harland said. "Good. You got a real orderly hospital here."

"Thank you," I said.

"You're welcome," he said.

Then this Money Hooks looked up over his glasses, and he came to the counter. When he did I passed this Harland's papers through the opening, and this Money Hooks looked at them.

"Let's see now," he said, looking out over his glasses at this Harland. "You're Harland Otis?"

"That's right," this Harland said, "and I got thirty stitches."

"I see that," this Money Hooks said. "Now let's see. You've got no Blue Cross-Blue Shield?"

"I got thirty stitches," this Harland said.

"I know that," this Money Hooks said, "but you've got no Blue Cross or Blue Shield?"

"Blue what?" this Harland said.

Right then I decided I wasn't going to hang around for that. I just decided that I would leave that to Money Hooks, because I didn't particularly want to listen to it, so I went back to Minor Ops and made up the stretcher with clean sheets, and then I went out to check at the nursing station.

When I got out to the nursing station there was this kind of young woman there, this mother, with this small boy like about four years of age. This mother had handed Dr. Hunter this pill bottle, and Dr. Hunter was looking at the label.

"The problem is," this mother was saying, "that he's hyperactive and I can't watch him every minute. He should probably have his stomach pumped."

"I don't think that will be necessary," Dr. Hunter said. "We'll just give him some ipecac, and that'll make him throw it up."

"You think so?" this mother said, and then the little kid said something to her and she said to him: "What are they going to make you throw up? What you took from that bottle. What's the name of it? What difference does it make what the name of it is? Honestly, you're just too much. What do I mean, you're just too much? Honestly."

307

Just then these two other guys came up to the counter. They were workmen, and the one guy was really weird. He had on blue jeans and this blue work shirt with the sleeves off at the shoulders, and the whole front of this guy—his clothes and his bare arms and his face—were splashed with this black stuff that right away I figured out was tar and it was in his hair, too.

"Good grief!" I heard this mother of the little kid say.

"What happened here?" Dr. Hunter said.

"It's tar, roofing compound," the other guy said. "They were raisin' a bucket to a roof when it dropped."

"How long ago was this?" Dr. Hunter said.

"About ten minutes ago," the guy said. "I got him here as fast as I could."

"Let's take him into Minor Ops," Dr. Hunter said to Miss Palmer and to me.

So, anyway, I took this guy into Minor Ops, and then Kay Conley came in and then Dr. Hunter and Dr. Martin Cohen, who's an intern who replaced the intern who replaced Stern, which I was glad to have happen. Dr. Cohen is sort of a with it guy and really okay, and Dr. Mabry calls him "Quinn."

"Are you experiencing pain?" Dr. Hunter said to this guy, who was just sitting there on the stool with this tar splashed all over him. There was like one blob that was holding his right eye shut, and when he opened his mouth to answer there was even some tar on his teeth.

"Not much," he said. "I feel it burn a little in places, and I kinda feel like I might be sick to my stomach."

"Let's get him up on the stretcher," Dr. Hunter said to Dr. Cohen and me, so we got the patient up there.

"Now what do you think?" Dr. Hunter said to Dr. Cohen.

"I don't know," Dr. Cohen said, and he was kind of like picking a small piece of this tar off this guy's right arm. "Maybe with a razor blade we can scrape some of it."

So Dr. Hunter told me to get a razor blade, and I went over to the cabinet where they keep the razors and new blades and I got a new blade. Dr. Cohen took it and he started to scrape a bigger piece of tar off the same arm, but when he did it this guy sort of winced and made a sound and Dr. Cohen stopped.

"I don't know," he said. "It might take forever."

"Let's try some ether," Dr. Hunter said. "That should dissolve it, and we'll need some gauze pads, too."

I got a can of ether and the gauze pads, and Dr. Hunter and Dr. Cohen started putting some ether on the pads and then dissolving the tar that way. It was working pretty good, so Dr. Hunter told Kay Conley, who was finishing up taking the patient's personal history, to take over for him.

"Now about this blob on your eyelid," Dr. Hunter said to the patient. "I think I can just pluck that. I don't think it will hurt too much. Okay?"

"Okay," the guy said. "What else can I say?"

"Good," Dr. Hunter said, and with that he just pulled that blob of tar right off. When he did the patient winced and pulled his head back, and when Dr. Hunter held out the blob of tar for us to see there was this row of eyelashes stuck in it that had come right out of the eyelid.

"I got some eyelashes with it," Dr. Hunter said to the patient, "but they'll grow back. Do you feel all right?"

"It felt like you were pullin' my eyelid right off," this patient said.

"That was the worst one," Dr. Hunter said. "The rest will take a little time to clean up, but they won't be bad."

"I hope," the guy said.

When Dr. Hunter walked out, then, I got Dr. Cohen and Conley some more gauze pads, and then I left, too. I checked down along the booths, and when I saw I had to make up the stretcher in booth 4 I went to the linen closet. On the way I stopped by the Poison Control Room, though, and looked in there because I heard the mother talking to the kid who swallowed the pills.

"C'mon," she was saying. "You've got to drink the rest of this, and then you'll throw up and throw up, and maybe that'll teach you not to take medicine."

I didn't particularly want to watch the kid throw up, so I got the clean sheets and pillow case out of the linen closet and I made up the stretcher in booth 4. Then I heard some talking in booth 3, so I looked in there, and here was another kid, about like eight years old, and they had his shirt and his undershirt off and he was scratching his stomach with both hands, and then he was rubbing his back against the stretcher and crying at the same time.

"I can't watch this," the woman who was standing there was saying. "What's the matter with him anyway?"

Dr. Hunter was there, and so was Arlene Woods, who's the pediatric nurse. Arlene Woods was trying to get the kid to stop scratching and stand still, and Dr. Hunter was trying to get a good look at his skin which had all these kind of like goose pimples all over it.

"All right now, Edward," Arlene Woods was saying. "The doctor is going to help you."

"And what did he have for breakfast?" Dr. Hunter was asking the woman.

"Just orange juice," the woman said, "and some cereal with milk. He has it every morning."

"And he's never had an attack like this before?" Dr. Hunter was saying.

"Never," the woman said. "What is it?"

"I don't know," Dr. Hunter said, "but I've put in a call for Dr. Banks, our pediatric resident, and she should be down here any minute. I'm sure she'll give him something that'll relieve him, and then very possibly a prescription that he should take for two or three days."

"Oh!" the woman said, and the kid was still scratching and twisting around and crying, "I just don't want to watch this."

I didn't particularly want to watch it, either, with the kid itching and scratching and screaming, and I certainly didn't want to be around when Banks came down, because there's no way I'm ever going to do what my mother calls seeking out the goodness in her any more than I would ever try to seek it out in Margaret Wittenauer either. In fact, just the other day my mother showed me this like one paragraph story in the *News-Argus* from some place in the Midwest where Margaret Wittenauer goes to college, and it said that Margaret Wittenauer, the daughter of Mr. and Mrs. Theobald W. Wittenauer, and it gave their address, was on the dean's list, or whatever they call it, at this college. My mother asked me what I thought of that, and I said that I'd rather have Weissbaum's disease. She asked me what that is, and I told her it's too complicated to go into, but actually I just made it up because I couldn't think of anything else to say. Then she said that wasn't a very nice remark to make about Margaret Wittenauer getting on the dean's list, or whatever it is, and then she wanted to know if the doctors have a cure for this Weissbaum's disease. I told her no, but that they're working on it.

Anyway, after I decided to not be around booth 3, I went over to the nursing station, and in a couple of minutes Carol Whitaker, who's another nurse, came out of the Poison Control Room, and when she got to the nursing station she was still smiling and sort of laughing.

"What's tickling you?" Miss Palmer said to her.

"The ipecac kid," Whitaker said. "He just vomited, and you should have seen his mother. She just loved it."

After that it was kind of a drag, and then I went up to lunch. When I went up to lunch I was really surprised at what a nice like spring day it was, with the leaves on the trees and the sunshine and everything, because when you're in the E.R. all the time you never know what the weather is like outside except when people come in with umbrellas or with their raincoats all wet or complaining that it's too cold or too windy or something.

So after lunch, just when I got back to the E.R., Baker Ambulance was coming in with this sort of old man, and with this woman like about sixty-five years of age walking behind the stretcher. The old man was very pale, and his mouth was open and he was having trouble breathing.

"It looks like a stroke," Baker said to Dr. Hunter and to Dr. Cohen, when they came around the counter to see what it was.

"Is seven open?" Dr. Hunter said to Miss Palmer.

"That's right," she said.

"Then take him in there," Dr. Hunter said.

After Baker and that sort of a nerd who works for him got the patient off their stretcher and onto the one in booth 7, I helped Carol Whitaker get him out of his shirt and shoes and socks and pants while Dr. Hunter and Dr. Cohen were starting to check him over. Miss Palmer had started to take his blood pressure, and then Whitaker took that over, while Dr. Hunter was trying to find out if the patient could hear him.

"Mr. Woods?" he was saying. "Can you hear me? I want you to straighten out this arm. Can you hear me, Mr. Woods?"

"He's trying to say something," Dr. Cohen said.

"He's saying 'Help!'" I said, because I could tell from the way the patient's mouth was moving that he was saying, "Help! Help! Help!"

"That's all right, Mr. Woods," Dr. Hunter said. "We're going to help you. You're all right now. We're going to help."

"Can you hear us, sir?" Dr. Cohen said.

"Let me have your tomahawk," Dr. Hunter said to Dr. Cohen, and Dr. Cohen gave him his reflex hammer. Then Dr. Hunter tapped the patient with it on the right knee and then on the left knee, and then he took the handle of the hammer and he scraped the sole of the patient's right foot and then the sole of his left foot.

"Mr. Woods?" he said, sort of half shouting like so the patient could hear him. "Can you hear me, Mr. Woods? I want you to move your right leg. Can you move your right leg? Good. Can you move the right arm? How about the other arm?"

"There's some facial asymmetry, too," Dr. Cohen said.

"I see it," Dr. Hunter said, and then he said to me: "Arnold, tell Miss Palmer or Gloria Miller to call Neurology and get somebody down here."

When I got to the nursing station Miss Palmer was talking with the woman who came in with the patient, and it turned out she was the patient's wife. Miss Palmer was getting the patient's history for the chart, but when I told her about calling Neurology she went to the phone and then she came back.

"So you don't know?" the patient's wife said to Miss Palmer then, and she was a nicely dressed woman and I remembered, too, that when I took the patient's shoes off they were like expensive shoes. "You have no idea how long he's going to be down here?"

"No," Miss Palmer said. "We don't know yet. You see, I've

just called upstairs for a neurologist. He'll be right down, but it will still take some time."

"An hour or more?" this patient's wife said.

"Perhaps," Miss Palmer said. "I can't say."

"You see," this patient's wife said, "there's a TV program that I watch every day, so I'd like to get home by two o'clock, and then I'd come back later."

"Oh," Miss Palmer said, and then she said: "Well, I think you might just wait for a while, don't you?"

I mean I thought that was weird, and I think Miss Palmer thought so, too, but right then Dr. Ralls came up with some X rays he wanted me to take down to Radiology. They were X rays of somebody's spinal column, and the radiologist stuck them up on the lighted wall over his desk and looked at them, and then he phoned Dr. Ralls and then I took them back. When I got back to the nursing station I found a *News-Argus* that somebody had been reading, and I looked up what TV programs are on at 2 o'clock.

"Isn't that something?" I heard Miss Palmer saying to Kay Conley, and it was what you might call like a coincidence. "What do you suppose she had to watch on TV at two o'clock?"

"*The Newlywed Game,*" I said, "or *Days of Our Lives* or *Love Is a Many-Splendored Thing.*"

"He's right," Conley said. "I know those shows are on, but I wouldn't be able to think of them."

"Tell me something, Arnold," Miss Palmer said. "How would you know what programs are on at two o'clock?"

"I have a photographic memory," I said. "Once, in the Sunday paper, I read all the programs that are on every station every hour, and all I have to do now is close my eyes and I can see any hour I want. It's really very easy."

"Stop it, Arnold," Miss Palmer said.

"Of course," I said, "they may have changed some programs since I took my mental photographs."

"Honestly, Arnold," Miss Palmer said.

"She probably wants to watch *Days of Our Lives,*" I said. "There's a woman on there whose husband is very sick, and

313

this lady probably wants to get home to see if this other woman's husband will live or not."

"While her own husband may be dying of a stroke right here," Conley said.

"Please, you two," Miss Palmer said. "That's enough."

Of course, I really don't know if there's any woman on *Days of Our Lives* whose husband is very sick, but my mother would know. She watches it every day, and almost every night she tells me about somebody's problems or somebody else's. I don't even listen, but she keeps telling me about them like they're real people, because I think my mother believes everything she hears or sees on TV. For example, she will say to me: "I'd like to know something, Arnold. They say on the television that most doctors recommend Milk of Magnesia? Do most of the doctors you know recommend Milk of Magnesia?" Or she'll say: "Tell me, Arnold. Do the doctors say Tums are more effective than Rolaids, or that Rolaids are more effective than Tums?" I usually tell her that they're still debating it, but the next time she asks me something like that I think I'll tell her that they all recommend ipecac.

"So, anyway," I said to Miss Palmer now. "How's that lady's husband, Mr. Woods?"

"They're probably about ready to take him upstairs," Miss Palmer said. "In fact, they may want you to take him if you think that, with that photographic memory of yours, you can remember how to find the elevators."

"Let me see now," I said, and I closed my eyes. "I'm concentrating, and yes, yes, I can see them just as clear as anything. They're down the hall to the right, and I see three of them—no it's four—and the door of the second one—no, it's the third one—is opening, and . . ."

"Okay, okay," Miss Palmer said. "That's enough. I don't need any more of that today."

I went over to booth 7 then, and the neurologist was just finishing up checking over Mr. Woods. Then he and Dr. Hunter had sort of what they call a consultation, and while they were doing that I got the patient's clothes together from where we had put them on the chair when we took them off.

Then I went and got one of those big brown paper bags, and I put them in that to go along with the patient.

"Okay," I heard Dr. Hunter say to the neurologist, and then he said to me: "Arnold, will you take the patient up to I.C.U. with Dr. Warren?"

I.C.U. is what they call the Intensive Care Unit, so I did that. On the way down the hall to the elevators I asked this Dr. Warren in sort of a low voice, so this Mr. Woods wouldn't hear me, how the patient was doing.

"Not too good," he said. "It doesn't look good at all."

After we moved the patient off the stretcher and onto the bed in I.C.U. I brought the stretcher back. When you get off the elevator in the basement you have to turn right, and then you pass this like narrow hallway that goes down to the morgue, and when I got there I saw Wallace Carter and Preston Jones in their green O.R. pajamas sitting on one of the stretchers without any bedding on them that they sometimes have like parked against the wall. Wallace Carter and Preston Jones are dieners, and there's a third one whose first name or last name is Gormley, but I don't know which, and they're like assistants to the Pathology doctors who do autopsies in the morgue. They're all black guys, and once I asked Wallace Carter if like all dieners are always black guys and he said no, that when he first got the job, there were two white guys, but one of them moved to Florida and the other one retired, and then Preston Jones and this Gormley just happened to come along and want the jobs.

"It's a good job," Wallace said to me that time. "It's very interesting work, and all the doctors in this department are nice and they're sympathetic people and they teach you. It's very educational, and you might like it, Arnold."

"No," I said. "I don't think so."

Then I told him about the first time I had to go into the morgue. That was when I was still working up on the fourth floor, before Miss Dimick and I got into the hassle about my hair, and serving food, and I had to bring down this patient—this man who died from I forget what—and I wheeled him into the first room where they have all these refrigerated like compartments in the wall with stainless steel doors on them. There wasn't anybody in that room right then, and I had to get somebody to sign the form, like a receipt, so I opened the door to the next room and I mean it really grossed me out. Right there in front of me, lying on this table, was this like naked patient—except he was dead, of course—and the top of his head—you know, his skull—was off, and his whole chest was cut open so you could see right inside where they'd taken most of him out.

What I did was I started to close the door. I mean I thought I might be sick, or something, but then I heard somebody say something, and I opened the door again and looked around to the side, and Wallace Carter was there with Dr. Davis, who is one of the pathologists, and they were washing some things at a sink.

"You looking for us?" Wallace Carter said then. When he came out I turned over the body to him, and this other time, when he was sort of suggesting that I might like to be a diener, I reminded him of that, and told him how I felt when I opened the door and saw that.

"That's nothing," he said. "The first time I ever came in here I saw this man on the table and this doctor and I thought: 'Man, he's crazy cuttin' that man apart like that.' I almost lost my cookies, too, but you get used to it. You just close your mind to the idea that it's a person, and then it becomes just a body. You could do it."

"I don't know," I said. "I might be able to, but then I might not. Suppose they brought in somebody that I knew?"

"That happened to me once," Wallace said. "There was this gal that I knew married this friend of mine. Then she was in this automobile accident, and the first three minutes with her I had butterflies, but after that it was all right."

He told me to think about it then, because with all the work they were getting they might be adding another diener, and I told him I would. Of course, I didn't think about it at all—I just told him I would to sort of get out of it—but, anyway, today when I was bringing the stretcher back, Wallace Carter and

Preston Jones were sitting there and just sort of watching the sort of like traffic in the hall.

"Hey, Arnold!" Wallace said to me when I came up to them. "What's happening?"

"Not much," I said. "What's happening with you?"

"Not much either," Preston Jones said. "Slow. Slow."

"That's good," I said.

"Yeah," Preston said, "but I get bored. I like to be busy."

"Where you been?" Wallace said.

"I.C.U." I said.

"Bad?" Preston said.

"I don't know," I said, because I really didn't. Sometimes, when I hear the doctors saying in the E.R. that some patient isn't going to make it, or when I can see it for myself, and if I'm going by the morgue or I see Wallace or Preston or that Gormley, I'll tell them about it to kind of alert them. Today, though, I just told them it was a stroke and that I didn't know.

"Listen, Arnold," Wallace said to me then. "I just thought of something. You still live where you told me?"

"That's right," I said.

"How do you get home?" Wallace said. "You got a car?"

"I take the bus," I said. "Why?"

"What time you get off?" Wallace said.

"Three-thirty," I said.

"Good," Wallace said. "Maybe you and I can deal. You want to deal?"

"Maybe," I said.

"I'll give you the deal," Wallace said. "I gotta take some cartons to the warehouse on East Second. If you help me load these cartons and deliver them we'll drop you off right at your house on the way home. Okay?"

"How many cartons?" I said.

"Oh, twenty-five or thirty," Wallace said.

"Heavy?" I said.

"Nope," he said. "Light. Okay?"

"Okay," I said, because I get tired of riding on that bus anyway, and then having to walk four blocks, too.

"Good," Wallace said. "I'll lay on the truck for three thirty-five. Right?"

"Okay," I said.

There was this black girl from Housekeeping who came along then, and Preston started to rap with her. At the same time Wallace got down off the stretcher to go back into the morgue, so after he told me not to forget our deal and I told him I wouldn't, I left. When I got back to the E.R. they had a woman emphysema patient I had to take up to C-3, and after that it was a drag until 3:30 when I went in to find Wallace.

Wallace was in that first room in the morgue. When I came in he and Preston Jones, who was still wearing his green O.R. pajamas, were just lifting this deceased person, this like middle-aged man, off a stretcher and onto the scale. This scale has like a platform on it that's the same height as a stretcher, and it has this big dial, and they had opened the sheet to maybe check the tag on the wrist or to be sure they wouldn't be weighing any clothing or anything else, too.

"One eighty-five," Preston Jones said after they had lifted this person onto the platform, and the like arrow on the dial was still moving back and forth.

"One seventy-eight," Wallace said, and then when the arrow stopped at 180, he said: "How much is that you owe me now?"

"I don't know," Preston Jones said.

"He likes to forget," Wallace said to me. "We bet quarters, and he must owe me two-three dollars by now."

"Not that much," Preston Jones said. "This makes it a dollar seventy-five."

"I know," Wallace said, and then he said to me: "They couldn't lay on the truck until 3:45, but we can move the cartons out to the platform. Okay?"

"Sure," I said. "That's okay."

Wallace and Preston Jones lifted this body back onto the stretcher then, and they wheeled it into the other room. There are two what they call like stainless steel autopsy tables in there, and they put this body onto one of them. I just waited, and then Wallace motioned to me to follow him and I did, and we went into this sort of supply room where there were all these light brown cardboard cartons stacked up. The cartons were like about a foot-and-a-half long and a foot wide and about six or eight inches high.

"What's in them?" I said, when I saw all these cartons.

"What's the matter, man?" Wallace said. "Can't you read?"

I guess I'd seen this like printing that somebody had done on the ends of these cartons with a black marker pen, but when I'd asked Wallace what was in these cartons I hadn't like, you know, paid any attention to what this printing said. Then when Wallace asked if I couldn't read I looked again.

"Hearts?" I said, and I mean I was like almost freaked out, but that's what it said. On every one of those cartons it said: HEARTS. Then under it, it said: 1973. Then on every carton there was like a code number like A-73-236-250, or something.

"Human hearts?" I said. "You mean, in every one of these boxes there are human hearts?"

"That's right," Wallace said. "We save 'em, and we got to take them to the warehouse. Okay?"

"Yeah," I said. "Okay, but why do you have to save them?"

"We don't have to save 'em," Wallace said. "We just do. The doctors here have one of the greatest collections of human hearts maybe anywhere in the world. We got maybe six thousand."

"Six thousand hearts?" I said. "But why do they save them?"

"For research," Wallace said. "For research into heart disease and its causes. Maybe right here in this hospital, with all these hearts we got saved, and with all the knowledge that they get from every place else, they might someday come across right here what it is that causes heart disease. You see?"

"Yeah, I see," I said, "but I don't see why they need so many, like six thousand hearts."

"Like I said, for research," Wallace said. "Let's say the doctors want thirty hearts from men of the same age who never smoked and thirty hearts from men of that exact age who smoked a pack or more a day. Let's say they want thirty hearts of people who had the same childhood diseases. If they had to wait for that many hearts of that kind to show up here it might take years, but we got 'em, and we got 'em all indexed."

319

"That's what those numbers are?" I said. "I mean on the ends of the cartons?"

"That's right," Wallace said. "The '73' is the year, and the numbers like 223 to 235 are the autopsy numbers of the hearts in that box. When some doctor calls down he has all the histories of the patients whose hearts he wants, and he has the numbers. Then we check his numbers against our index to be sure, and then we go get the hearts."

"So you can tell whose hearts are in that box right there?" I said.

"That's right," Wallace said. "We got 'em on cards."

"Who's 235?" I said, because I was really interested. I mean I never even thought about anything like this before in my whole life.

"What do you care who's 235?" Wallace said. "Besides, we got to get these cartons out because, any minute now, that truck'll be here."

"Just look up that one," I said, "so I can see how you do it."

"Okay," Wallace said, and he went to these card files like they have in a library except, of course, he didn't have so many. Then he started looking through those, and then he said: "Let's see. It's 73 and 235 and it's Carlton. Robert. Then it says 'Bobby.' Pretty young, too. Only thirty-one. Date and time of death is . . ."

"I know," I said.

"You know?" Wallace said. "You know him?"

"No," I said, "but I remember about it in the E.R. I was upstairs, then, or someplace, and when I got back they were talking about it, about him being a nightclub comedian, and I remember Preston came for him."

"Yeah," Wallace said. "I remember it, too, because Preston and I were trying to figure out what he did for a living. We do that. We try to figure out from the clothes somebody wears, or the way their hands look or maybe just generally the way they look, what a person did for a living. I remember this Carlton's hands were manicured, and from that and his general appearance I said I thought he was a hairdresser. Preston said he thought he maybe worked in a men's store, like an expensive one. Then, of course, later we found out."

"That's interesting," I said.

"Yeah," Wallace said, "but let's get goin' now. Otherwise that truck might leave again if we're not out there."

So we started loading these cartons, stacking them, on two stretchers, one for Wallace to wheel out and one for me. There were like about thirty of these cartons, and while we were doing this I kept asking Wallace more about the hearts. He explained that they keep them in some solution, like formaldehyde, until they get enough of them to take to warehouse, and then they put each heart in a plastic bag that they seal with a sealing machine. Then they put them in the cartons, and because some hearts are bigger than others there might be like twelve or maybe thirteen hearts in a carton.

"So they'll set here for months," Wallace said, "and the minute you bag one and box it away some doctor will come down and want it. You just watch. Tomorrow, sure enough, somebody will send down for one or more of these hearts."

When we wheeled the hearts out to the loading platform the truck wasn't there yet. There were a couple of workmen—like carpenters—building a sort of a roof out over the platform, and Wallace and I unloaded the boxes from the stretchers and stacked them at the edge of the platform. Then we took the stretchers back and left them outside the morgue, and when we got back one of the carpenters up on this ladder hollered down to us.

"Hey, you guys!" he said. "You two!"

"What?" Wallace said.

"While you were gone," he said, "one of those boxes moved."

Wallace didn't say anything, and I thought that was sort of stupid, too, so I didn't say anything either. Meanwhile there was this sort of traffic jam at the loading platform. There was this open truck backed up there, and two guys were unloading oxygen tanks, and then there was this green florist's truck waiting to get in and then there was our truck.

Finally our truck backed in. It was sort of a medium-sized closed truck, painted like aluminum, and when it stopped against the platform Wallace opened the back doors and he got into the truck and I passed the boxes to him and he stacked them. Then he closed the doors and we got into the front seat with the driver, with Wallace sitting in the middle.

"Joe," Wallace said to the driver, who was kind of like sixty years of age. "This is Arnold. Arnold this is Joe."

"Hello," I said.

"Yeah," this Joe said. "We'll probably catch it today."

"What's that?" Wallace said.

"The goddam traffic," this Joe said. "The first of it will just be lettin' out."

When we got to North Jefferson Avenue this Joe was right. I mean we got into this real traffic jam where there's that light at East Seventh. It was one of those traffic jams where even when the light changes nobody can move, and now we were just sitting there and then everybody behind us started to blow their horns.

"Yeah, you goddam fools," this Joe said. "That'll help. Keep blowin' your goddam horns, you goddam fools."

There was this one guy right behind us that I couldn't see, of course, who was really blowing his horn, so I had the idea that maybe I would get out of the truck and tell him that what he was blowing his horn at was like three hundred human hearts. I would have liked to have done that just to see his face, but I didn't do it and I just sat there and I started thinking about this Bobby Carlton.

I was thinking that, when I got back to the E.R. that day, he had just died, and when I went into booth 7 Father Shea, who's the Catholic chaplain, was in there. I didn't stay then, but while I was like turning around again to leave I saw him take something out of his pocket and take the top off, and then he sort of rubbed it with his thumb and touched the patient on the forehead and he started to make the Sign of the Cross. Later, like the next day, I asked Kay Conley about that, because she's a Catholic, and she said it's some kind of holy oil he puts on his thumb.

Anyway, after Father Shea left I helped Carol Whitaker prepare the body where you clean it up if you have to and like diaper it, and then the way you fold the sheet over it but not too tight over the face and feet. That's so that when the body is wheeled down the halls, people who are like visiting patients won't know that it's a body, but I remember that once I was wheeling this body from E-3, and there was this like young couple that passed me, and then they stopped and this young guy called to me.

"Hey!" he said, and then came up to me and he said: "Is that a body you got under there?"

"That's right," I said.

"You see?" he said to this girl. "What did I tell you? You see?"

So while we were in this traffic jam now, and everybody was blowing their horns, I was thinking about this Bobby Carlton. I was remembering that after Preston Jones came and got the body Dr. Harvey Mosler, who's a surgical resident, was saying that he had seen this Bobby Carlton at wherever this Bobby Carlton was like appearing. He said this Bobby Carlton was pretty funny, and then he told this story that Bobby Carlton told about some guy and his wife who smoked cigarettes just for the coupons or something.

"You know what I'm just thinking?" I said to Wallace now, and we were starting to move along, like creeping. "I'm just thinking that like maybe two people, who knew each other while they were alive but hadn't seen each other for years, might end up together in the same carton."

"It's possible," Wallace said, "but it ain't likely."

"Or maybe they didn't like each other," I said. "Maybe they actually hated each other. Or maybe this man and this woman secretly loved each other all their lives, but they could never marry, and now *they* end up together."

"You got some imagination, Arnold," Wallace said, like other people are always telling me, "but it ain't likely."

"And it ain't goddam likely that we're gonna get outa this goddam mess right away either," this Joe said, because we were still like just creeping along. "The goddam politicians are to blame. You know that, don't you?"

"That's what they say," Wallace said.

"You're goddam right," this Joe said.

After a while, though, we got moving better and then, when we got like a mile down Jefferson, Wallace pointed out the warehouse to me. It's that kind of big concrete like building on the corner of Terrace Street, and in the show windows there are these like rooms set up but with kind of old furniture.

"I know that building," I said to Wallace. "I've walked by there lots of times, but I never knew they stored hearts in there."

"They don't," Wallace said. "We store them. They store furniture and things, and we just rent the space in the basement."

This Joe turned to the right down Terrace Street then, and then he turned into this sort of beat up driveway behind this building. Then he backed the truck up to this like metal door, and I got out and Wallace got out and Wallace went to the door and he banged on it with his fist.

"He don't hear too good," Wallace said, and then he banged on the door some more. Finally, like in about a minute, the door opened and there was this old guy standing there and leaning on a cane.

"Hi," Wallace said.

The old guy didn't say anything. He just nodded, and then Wallace went back to the truck and he opened the doors.

"I gotta go get the dolly," Wallace said to me, "so why don't you hop up there, and then pass them down to me."

I climbed up into the truck, then, and when Wallace came back with this like wooden platform on wheels I passed the cartons down to him. While I was doing this I was thinking that this Joe wasn't helping us, but I figured it must be that his union doesn't allow it or something. Finally, though, we had all the cartons on this dolly, and Wallace pushed it into this warehouse, and I jumped down and I went in, too.

Inside this warehouse Wallace pushed this dolly with the cartons onto this elevator that was just an old wooden platform with no sides, so I got on, too. Then the old guy started the elevator down, and we went down like one floor, and then this old guy opened this like heavy wire screen door that

324

had this chain with a lock on the chain, and I followed Wallace into this big cellar room.

In this big cellar room there were just these sort of dim light bulbs hanging down from the ceiling every here and there, and there were sort of like aisles. The sides of the aisles were all these steel shelves, and on all these shelves there were these cartons like we had with HEARTS written on them and then the dates, like 1965 and 1966 and 1967, and the index numbers.

"Down here," Wallace said.

He was way down this one aisle, so I went down there, and then I passed the cartons to Wallace and he lined them all up on some empty shelves. After that we just went out and Wallace thanked the old guy and the old guy nodded, and then we got back into the truck and Wallace told this Joe that they were going to drop me off at my house.

"Just at the corner," I said. "You don't have to drive me down the street."

"Whatever you say," Wallace said.

"That'll be fine," I said, because I figured that if they drove me right up to the house my mother would probably see it, because she usually watches for me to come home, and then she'd ask me about what I was doing getting a ride in that truck. Then she'd want to know what that truck was for, and I didn't think I'd tell her all about the hearts, although I might.

Anyway, I just didn't want to think about that right then, so after I told them to let me off at the corner, Wallace got to asking me again what I think I might do when I get tired of being an orderly which, in fact, could be like any time now. I told him that I didn't know, and then he started talking again about his job and how the dieners and the doctors are like a team, and how he and Preston Jones and Gormley take pride in their work.

"Preston came up from Florida with his grandmother to pick crops," Wallace said, "and he never finished the ninth grade. Gormley practically educated himself, readin' at night, and after I got out of high school what could I do? I worked on the tracks for the railroad. I worked for the packing company on the line. Then I got the job as a porter at the M.C. and I worked my way up from the broom and mop, and now my boy says to me: 'I want to be a doctor like you some day.' He thinks I'm a doctor, and he's still so young I don't tell him different. I just tell him: 'You have to study.' "

"That's cool," I said, after Wallace finished telling me this, because I really think it is. "That's real cool."

"Yeah," Wallace said. "Like I told you once, you ought to think about it. Have you thought about it?"

"I did," I said, "but I think I'll go into physical therapy instead."

"Is that right?" Wallace said. "That's good, but that surprises me, because I didn't know you were thinkin' about that."

Actually, it kind of surprised me, too, because even I didn't know I was thinking about it, but I must have been. I mean the way it just sort of came right out I must have been thinking about it like without even knowing it, and then after Wallace and this Joe left me off at the corner and I was walking down the block, I kind of figured it out.

You see, like the few times I've been in the Physical Therapy Department I was like pretty impressed. I mean they have all this equipment there, like special bathtubs and whirlpool baths in one room, and then in another room they've got this half a bicycle that's fastened down and they've got ladders and like wrestling mats. It's sort of a gym, and I don't really care for the jock scene, but this is different because there aren't any jocks around. There'll be this little kid, with his legs sort of thin and weak, holding onto these like parallel bars and moving slowly along, and the physical therapist will be encouraging this kid to keep trying. Then the kid, with his face like all twisted, because that's how hard he's trying, will finally reach the end where the physical therapist is waiting, and when he does the physical therapist will throw his arms around this kid and hug him and laugh and tell the kid what a great thing he did. I mean that's why I was like really impressed.

Anyway, I figured out that another reason it just sort of came right out that I might go into physical therapy is that, when I delivered that woman emphysema patient up to C-3, and before I took the stretcher back, I stopped in to sort of check on Anita Wade. Anita Wade is that little black girl who was hit by some hit-and-run driver like a couple of months ago now. As I guess I said, for a while there, while they had her up in what they call the Trauma Unit, they didn't think she was going to live, and then she just started to get better. Like a month ago they moved her to C-3, to this semiprivate room, and every once in a while when I'm on C-3 I stop by there.

Actually, I don't really know Anita Wade, and she doesn't know me. When I stop there I just walk over to her, and if she's awake I sort of say hello. When I do she just looks at me, and then she doesn't say anything and she turns away, but I keep doing that because I'm sort of interested in her, you know?

I mean, Anita Wade is very thin and she still has casts on both her legs, and today when I went in to sort of check on her, there wasn't anybody in the other bed in the room. There was this physical therapist there—this Miss Sarkanian, who I kind of know—and she was sort of talking to Anita Wade and Anita Wade was just sort of crying a little and sobbing like.

"Now, that's all right," this Miss Sarkanian was saying. "Your mother will be back in a few minutes. You'll see. She'll be back any minute now."

I waited for Miss Sarkanian to come out of the room then, and when she did I asked her how Anita Wade is doing.

"Quite well, considering everything," this Miss Sarkanian said. "They'll be removing the casts before long, and I'm just trying to get acquainted with her. It's been a very traumatic experience for her, of course, so it will take a while before she learns to trust again."

"I guess so," I said.

When Miss Sarkanian left I went in then, and I went over to Anita Wade. When she saw me coming she turned her head, like she always does, and she was still sort of crying, so I thought I would try something. I thought I would make one of my hand noises that I make by squeezing the palms of my hands together and like pulling them apart, and that I hadn't made since that time, like months ago, when that Dr. Emily Banks, that pediatric resident, asked me if I thought I was some kind of a comedian or something. The hand noise I decided to make was not the one my mother calls my obnoxious noise, but the one that makes this sort of high squeaking sound, and that I call my mouse noise.

"Listen, Anita," I said, and I made my mouse noise, and then I said: "What's that? Did you hear that? It sounded like a mouse. I think there's a mouse in my hands. Can you hear it?"

Then I made the noise again. When I did Anita Wade sort of stopped crying, and then I made the noise another time.

"Do you hear him? He's in my hands," I said, and then I opened my hands and Anita Wade was watching my hands now, and I said: "Oh! He's gone! I guess he jumped away."

Then I made like I was catching this mouse in the sheet at the foot of Anita Wade's bed, and then I showed Anita Wade my hands again, and I made my mouse noise another time.

"There he is again!" I said. "I caught him. Can you hear him?"

When I said that I made my mouse noise once more, and when I did Anita Wade looked from my hands very slowly up to me, and then she didn't say anything, but just with her mouth she made a kind of a little smile.

"Yes," I heard somebody saying in the doorway, and it was one of the nurses talking to Anita Wade's mother. "I'm sure that'll be all right."

I left then. I just told Anita Wade I was taking the mouse with me back to where he lives, and then I just smiled at Anita Wade's mother and the nurse. Then, when I was walking down the block today after Wallace and that Joe left me off, I figured that maybe that's why it just sort of came out, talking with Wallace, that I might go into physical therapy. Of course I don't know. It just sort of came to me, so maybe I will, and then maybe I won't.